1140 Rue Royale

BADGER BLISS BOOKS

DEDICATION

I dedicate this book to more than 500,000 people of color who, during the infancy of this country, were taken forcefully from their homes and made to toil on the plantations of wealthy land owners, or who, like the brave souls who are the focus of this story, were forced into servitude as house servants for the elite.

These people were often subjected to starvation, hard labor, brutal violence, degradation, unspeakable acts of cruelty and torture, separation from family, and loss of dignity, simply because they were a darker shade of human.

If ever there was a good reason for war, slavery was.

From the first African American indentured servants arriving in the English colony of Jamestown, Virginia, in 1619 and the many slaves who followed, to the American Civil War, to the Emancipation Proclamation signed on January 1, 1863, to the final ratification of the Thirteenth Amendment in December, 1865, to the race riots in the twentieth century, to the Voting Rights Act signed on August 6, 1965, to the racial profiling and inequality of today that this country still struggles with. The fight goes on.

The struggle for freedom and equal rights is never-ending, whether it concerns people of color, women, religious intolerance, gender bias, discrimination based on sexual orientation, physical disabilities, social and economic disparities. The list is painfully long.

The very fact that there is a list, makes my heart hurt.

It's time we learn from history instead of repeating it.

ALSO WRITTEN BY KAREN D. BADGER AND
AVAILABLE FROM BADGER BLISS BOOKS:

ON A WING AND A PRAYER
YESTERDAY ONCE MORE
THE BLUE FEATHER
ALL MY TOMORROWS
1140 RUE ROYALE

The Billie/Cat Commitment Series:
  IN A FAMILY WAY
  UNCHAINED MEMORIES
  HAPPY CAMPERS
  COLLECTIVE IDENTITY
  SWEET ANGEL
  RELATIVE-LY SPEAKING

www.badgerblissbooks.com

1140 Rue Royale

B

A BADGER BLISS BOOK

By

Karen D. Badger

This is a work of fiction. All characters, locales, and events are either products of the author's imagination or are used fictitiously.

1140 RUE ROYALE

Cover design by Karen D. Badger
All photographs embedded in the book taken by Karen D. Badger, 2015

A Badger Bliss Book
Published by Badger Bliss Books
Georgia, VT 05468

www.badgerblissbooks.com

ISBN 13: 978-1-945761-00-3
ISBN 10: 1-945761-00-8

First Edition, September, 2016

Printed in the United States of America and in the United Kingdom

ACKNOWLEDGMENTS

I have the most amazing group of beta readers. Each and every one of them, in their own way, has contributed toward making this book as good as it can be. I'd like to acknowledge them for their specific contributions.

Darci Deo and Pennie Hancock – These two ladies took a day out of their GCLS convention schedule in New Orleans to visit the NOLA Chamber of Commerce in 98-degree heat and wilting humidity, where they did extensive research on the house at 1140 Royal Street. They came back with a whole handfull of photocopied material.

Carol Poynor (aka, Chief Master Sergeant Eagle Eye) – Once again, my friend, you are the master. I bow humbly to you. Thank you for all your hard work.

My mom, Ellie Atherton – What can I say, except I love you. You are my mother, my mentor, my friend, and my hero. Thank you for loving me just the way I am, and thank you for all you've done to make this a better book.

Chris Parsons – Our friend from across the pond. You did an amazing job and provided a very touching review. I choked up when reading it to Barb. Thank you for your efforts.

Donna Brown – As always, Donna, your willingness to beta read and provide feedback is appreciated beyond words.

Mercedes Lewis and Pennie Hancock – Special thanks to both of you for keeping me honest and for helping me to retain the dignity of the victims in this story. You ladies rock. I appreciate your help more than words can say.

To my wife, Barb Sawyer – Once again, you were a writer's widow while I toiled away at this book. Your imagination never ceases to amaze me as you help me over the rough spots and offer suggestions to improve the plot. I thank the gods for bringing you into my life. I love you, sweetie.

Finally, to my editor, Nann Dunne - You, my friend, are a treasure. Thank you for your superb editing skills, for making time for this book in your busy schedule, and most of all, for being our friend.

Monsters are real, and ghosts are real too. They live inside us, and sometimes, they win.

— Stephen King

1140 Royal Street, New Orleans, LA

CHAPTER 1

Elliot Walker tried to be quiet as she stepped into the darkened loft and set her briefcase by the front door. She pressed the Indiglo button on her watch. 11:45 p.m.

No wonder I'm tired, she thought as she entered the kitchen and opened the refrigerator to look for a bite to eat.

"You're late again," a voice said from across the room.

Elliot jumped.

"Jesus Christ, you scared me," Elliot said. "I thought you were in bed."

"You mean you hoped I was in bed."

Elliot squinted to make out the silhouette of her wife. Lia was sitting in a chair by the window, subtly backlit by the glow of the streetlight.

"Lia, I'm really in no mood to fight with you tonight."

"That's the third time this week, and it's only Thursday."

"I'm sorry. The experiments have a way of making one lose track of time, and you know the subway's always running late."

"I gave up making excuses for you around nine o'clock."

"Shit! I forgot about the dinner party with your Board of Directors. I'm so sorry."

She closed the refrigerator door, and faced Lia. She put her hands on her hips and listened to the deafening silence.

"Lia?"

Lia leaned forward in her seat.

"Elliot, do you love me? I mean—do you *really* love me?"

"How can you even ask me that?"

Lia rose and walked toward Elliot.

Not for the first time, Lia's distinct African features, dark brown eyes and mocha skin sent waves of warmth spreading

1

through Elliot. She loved everything about Lia Purvis. Everything, that is, except for the icy stare that was capable of stopping her cold. The icy stare that was being directed at her at that very moment.

Elliot reached to touch the side of Lia's face.

"No. Don't." Lia pushed Elliot's hand away. "I asked you a question."

"Lia, we've been together for what, twenty-two years? Would I still be here if I didn't love you?"

"I don't know. Sometimes I wonder about that. We hardly talk to one another anymore. Hell, it's been so long since we made love, I don't even remember. You're so wrapped up in your job that you can't even make it to a dinner date, after you swore you would be there."

"I said I was sorry."

"That dinner party meant a lot to me. It was my chance to impress the chairman, and to convince him to fund the new genome project."

"And you needed me there to do that?" Elliot asked sarcastically.

"I needed you there for moral support. You're my wife. Or have you forgotten that little tidbit as well?"

"How could I possibly forget that?"

Lia walked directly up to Elliot and stopped within a hair's breadth of her.

"Who are you, Elliot? There are times I see glimpses of the woman I fell in love with twenty-two years ago, but they are brief and fleeting. I don't even know you anymore."

"I'm not the only one wrapped up in her job. At least I don't bring my work home with me."

"People's lives depend on my research. I will never turn my back on that aspect of my career. I'll most certainly take a call at home if it means saving a life. The fact is, Elliot, I'm taking that call from home, and not from the office or the lab. I make a point of being home for you. I purposely make time for you in my life. Can you say the same for me?"

Elliot ran a hand through her boy-cut blonde hair. "I don't know what you want me to say. You're right. I'm a horrible person." She held her arms out to the sides for emphasis.

Lia shook her head. "That doesn't even warrant a response."

Lia walked back into the shadows and turned to Elliot, who waited, hands on her hips, staring at the floor.

"Elliot, something has got to change. I can't go on living like this. You've become a stranger to me. You couldn't even answer the simple question, do you love me?"

Elliot remained silent as Lia walked toward the bedroom. She stopped before entering, her back still to Elliot.

"Just so you know," she said, "I have no problem answering that question for myself, because I still love the Elliot you used to be. I love her more than life itself."

She slipped into the bedroom and closed the door.

What the hell? Elliot walked through the dark loft toward the window that overlooked the busy street below. She rested her forehead on the cool window pane and stared into the night.

Is Lia right? Have I changed that much?

Elliot thought back to when she had first met Lia twenty-two years ago. She was twenty-five and just out of grad school with dual degrees in Kinesiology and Computer Science. Lia was twenty-eight with a Master's degree in Chemistry and she was already three years into her employment with Lode-Star Pharmaceuticals. Elliot saw her for the first time at a local Starbucks.

For Elliot, it was love at first sight. She remembered the encounter like it was yesterday. *Tuesday, May twenty-ninth, nineteen-ninety, at seven-forty-five a.m.* Elliot had just ordered a cinnamon dolce latte and was waiting at the pick-up counter when Lia walked into the store.

Elliot literally struggled to catch her breath. There before her was this vision. Tall and slim, she wore a calf-length peasant skirt with a fringed scarf draped over one hip, knee-high suede boots, and a cream-colored blouse that highlighted her mocha skin and dark brown eyes. A wild mane of black curly hair fell to the middle of her back. The entire package reminded her of an exotic gypsy. Elliot couldn't take her eyes off her as this beautiful woman ordered her coffee.

The cashier rang up her order, and the woman reached for the purse she apparently thought was hanging on her shoulder.

"Damn. I left my purse in the car. I'll just run out to get it."

"No! No—let me," Elliot said, reaching for her wallet as she approached the woman. She felt like Sir Lancelot coming to the rescue of the beautiful damsel.

"That's all right. It'll only take me a minute to get my purse," the woman said.

"I insist. Please."

The woman tilted her head to one side and smiled. "Okay. Thank you."

Elliot nearly melted on the spot as she paid the clerk. "My pleasure," she replied. She extended her hand. "Elliot Walker."

"Elliot? That's an unusual name for a woman."

"I'm afraid my father wanted a boy. I guess with me, he got the best of both worlds." Elliot held the woman's hand firmly in her own.

"It's nice to meet you, Elliot Walker. I'm Lia Purvis."

"Lia. Beautiful name for a beautiful woman." Elliot suddenly blushed. "Sheesh! That was corny. Good one, Walker," she said out loud. "I'm sorry for being so forward."

"Oh, don't apologize. That was very sweet." Lia collected her coffee waiting at the end of the counter.

They stood facing each other as an awkward pause ensued.

"Do you have a minute or two to sit and enjoy your coffee?" Elliot asked.

Lia looked around the coffee shop, then back at Elliot. She smiled. "Actually, I do."

Elliot directed Lia to the closest table and held her chair as she sat.

Two hours later, they parted company after exchanging phone numbers.

That was the first day of a relationship that would last twenty-two years and counting.

Elliot sighed as she basked in the memory.

Lia is right. I have changed. In those early days, we shared a passion that couldn't be quenched. Even as the years went by, she was the most important thing in my life. I couldn't wait to get home to her in the evenings. We would talk for hours about work and life in general. I couldn't wait to lie with her in my arms at night.

And now?

Now, our paths barely cross and few words pass between us.

What does this mean, Lia?

You asked if I still love you.

Yes. I do. So why is it so hard for me to express that love to you? I suppose I've taken you for granted, expecting you to always love me regardless of my apparent indifference.

You're still an amazingly beautiful woman, in some ways more beautiful at fifty than when we met. I would love to see me through your eyes. To see how much I've changed compared to that fateful day in Starbucks when you forgot your purse in the car.

You said you can't go on living like this.

Does that mean you're leaving me?

CHAPTER 2

"Lia, may I see you in my office, please?"

Lia looked up from the article she was reading and placed it on the table in front of her. "Of course, Dr. Ovitt." She rose to her feet and followed the Director into his office.

"Have a seat," Dr. Ovitt said as he closed the door.

Lia's heart pounded in her chest as she struggled to recall any wrongdoing that may have caused her to be called on the carpet. Surely, her distraction caused by Elliot's absence at the dinner party the night before had nothing to do with this early morning summons.

Dr. Ovitt sat behind his desk, propped his elbows on the surface and made a teepee with his fingertips. "Lia, how long have you been with the agency? Specifically, how long have you been here at the New York City division?"

Lia suddenly became flushed as she waited for the hammer to drop. Her gaze darted around the room, frantically avoiding her boss' eyes. What she *did* see in her desperate attempt to avoid eye contact was a manila folder on his desk with her name on the tab.

I'm going to be sick, she thought. "Here at the NYC site? Twenty-five years, Dr. Ovitt. I've been here for twenty-five years."

"Twenty-five years," he repeated. "That's a long time. Have you ever thought of going anywhere else?"

Lia's hand shook as she pushed an errant tendril of hair back under the headscarf she was wearing. "I, ah, I've never given it any thought. I guess I always assumed I would retire from here in another ten years or so."

Dr. Ovitt sat back in his chair and crossed his arms. "Is there anything holding you here?"

"Holding me here? I don't understand what you're asking me."

"You have a partner, right?"

"Actually, Elliot is my wife. Why do you ask?"

"Your wife. Yes, of course. What does Elliot do for a living?"

"She is a research scientist in the field of prosthetic kinesiology."

"Prosthetic kinesiology?"

"She develops the interface between prosthetic limbs and the human body to better simulate normal muscular movement. She is specifically working on ways to promote improved muscle tone and balance by creating an electrical bridge between the stump and the artificial limb. It's really quite fascinating," Lia rambled nervously.

"I see. What did you say Elliot's last name was?"

"It's Walker."

"Walker." He scribbled Elliot's name on the note pad in front of him.

Lia's fear of being fired was suddenly overcome by her irritation at his personal intrusion. "Why the sudden interest in my wife?" she asked.

"My interest is not so much in your wife as it is in you. I just want to make sure she isn't an obstacle in the way of what I'm about to propose to you."

* * *

Lia returned to her office and sat at her desk, stunned. *I'm not sure Elliot is going to like this. It just might be the straw that breaks the camel's back.*

She thought back to the very first time she'd laid eyes on Elliot. She stopped at the local Starbucks on her way to work one morning, intent on getting an early start on the pharmacological project she was working on before the rest of the troops arrived at the lab.

She pulled her car into the parking space, threw it into park and rushed inside. Luckily, the coffee shop was nearly empty and she was second in line to place her order. As she waited she could feel someone watching her. She looked up and saw this white girl waiting at the pick-up end of the counter, periodically stealing glances at her. Not that she minded. The girl was rather cute with her with short, boy-cut blonde hair and blue eyes.

She distinctly remembered what the girl was wearing: blue jeans with rolled up cuffs and Converse sneakers; an Aerosmith T-shirt, tucked in; and a short tweed jacket. A backpack was slung over her left shoulder.

The flattery she felt under the girl's scrutiny quickly turned to embarrassment when she realized she'd left her purse in the car. She stammered something about going to fetch it, when Ms. Blue Eyes came to her rescue and paid for her coffee, despite her protests.

Before she knew it, they were sitting at a table and talking like they were old friends. All thoughts of getting to the lab early evaporated. Two hours later, after exchanging phone numbers, they parted company.

That was the first day of a relationship that began twenty-two years ago.

The question was, how much longer would it last after Elliot heard her news?

* * *

The aroma of freshly baked bread greeted Lia as she opened the door to the loft. When she walked in, Elliot was just removing dinner rolls from the oven.

Lia stopped short—not believing her eyes. "Who are you, and what have you done with my wife?"

Elliot wiped her hands on the frilly apron she was wearing, took Lia's face between her hands, and kissed her soundly.

"Here, let me take that." Elliot took Lia's briefcase and placed it on the counter. She led Lia toward the balcony. "Come, sit down. Dinner is just about ready."

Elliot seated Lia at the patio table where a fresh salad and glass of wine were waiting. She kissed her on the temple. "I'll be right back."

She returned a few moments later with a casserole dish of lasagna and the rolls which she placed in the middle of the table. She took the apron off and sat in the chair opposite her. Raising her wineglass in Lia's direction, she said, "Welcome home."

Lia frowned and sat back with her arms crossed in front of her. "Elliot, what's going on here?"

Elliot put her glass back on the table. "What do you mean?"

"This is totally unlike you. I can count on one hand the number of times you've cooked dinner for me in the past twenty-two years. Now, I'll ask you again. What's going on?"

Elliot stared at her wineglass for several seconds before looking Lia straight in the eye. "What you said last night hit a nerve. You're right. I've been disrespectful and indifferent to you for quite some time. You don't deserve that."

"Elliot—"

"No, let me finish. After you went to bed, I sat up for several hours thinking about the life we've built together and I realized that over the years, you've given so much more to me than I've given in return, and never once did you complain—that is, until last night. I've been selfish and ungrateful."

Elliot delivered the last sentence through a voice choked with emotion. She struggled to regain control before speaking again. Once more, her tear-filled gaze found Lia's eyes.

"You asked me if I still love you. Lia, you are my heart. I not only love you, I need you. The thought of you leaving me is more than my heart can bear. Yes, I still love you and there's nothing in this world I wouldn't do to prove it to you."

Lia reached across the table and took Elliot's hand in her own. Try as she might, she was unable to stem the flow of tears down her own face at Elliot's declaration. She brought Elliot's hand to her lips, kissed the palm, and held it close to her heart.

9

"Do you really mean that?" she asked.

"I mean it. I'll do anything to prove my love for you. Just name it, and it's yours."

Lia closed her eyes and inhaled deeply. When she opened them again, Elliot was staring directly at her. Her eyes clearly mirrored the love Lia felt for her.

"Anything," Elliot said again.

"Move to New Orleans with me."

Elliot sat back abruptly in her chair.

"New Orleans? Did you just ask me to move with you to New Orleans?"

"I did," Lia said, tentatively.

"Where the hell did that come from? Why New Orleans?"

"My boss called me into his office this morning. He offered me a position at the Louisiana Cancer Research Center in New Orleans."

"Just like that, he offers you a position in New Orleans?" Elliot asked incredulously.

"It turns out the grant money my colleagues and I were vying for was for the development of a new cancer-fighting drug at the research center in New Orleans. That tidbit of information wasn't shared with us until the Institute decided who to award the money to."

"And you were the lucky winner."

Lia nodded. "Winning the grant is dependent on my willingness to carry out the research in New Orleans."

"How long is this assignment?"

"I would be starting the project on the ground floor. All of the scientists involved in the development project would be."

"How long, Lia?"

"At least five years, and possibly up to ten."

Elliot leaned forward and took Lia's hands in her own. "What about my job, Lia?"

Lia squeezed Elliot's hands and smiled. "Funny, those exact words came out of my mouth when Dr. Ovitt offered me the position."

"And what was his response?"

"He apparently anticipated that my relationship with you might stand in the way of me accepting the position. He implied as much during our meeting this morning. Later in the day, he called me back into his office and informed me that he had arranged for a teaching and research position for you at Tulane University if you were interested in accepting it."

Looking stunned, Elliot dropped Lia's hands. "Teaching and research? Teaching what?" Elliot asked.

"Kinesiology, of course. Dr. Ovitt asked me what you do for a living and when I explained what you do and who you work for, he apparently did some research of his own and was quite impressed with what he found. At least he implied as much when we met again in the afternoon."

"Tulane University?"

"Yes, Tulane."

"Tulane is one of the most respected universities in the country, not to mention it's one of only four private research institutions in the South that's a member of the Association of American Universities. Your Dr. Ovitt must have some pull to secure that kind of offer for someone he hasn't even met."

Lia cupped the side of Elliot's face. "Sweetie, he couldn't have done it without your experience and reputation. You're good at what you do. You've written papers on your research and you've been published in some of the most prestigious medical journals in the country. You deserve this. We both do."

Elliot sat back in her chair and ran a hand through her hair. "What about the loft? We can't just leave it vacant for the next ten years."

"We'd have to sell it. We've done quite a bit of work on it over the past twenty years. It should sell pretty fast."

"Wow. I don't know what to say."

"Say we're moving to New Orleans."

Elliot hesitated only a moment, then she grinned. "I guess we're moving to New Orleans."

CHAPTER 3

"Lia, what time will Marissa and Julie be here?" Elliot called from the bathroom.

"I told them dinner was at six, but left the door open about when they should arrive. I expect it'll be soon."

Elliot combed the last tendril of hair into place then washed her hands and joined Lia in the kitchen. "Hmmm, that smells good." She reached over Lia's shoulder for a chocolate chip cookie from the still-hot cookie sheet.

Lia swatted her hand away. "Shoo! You'll ruin your dinner. Besides, these are to put into the hot fudge sundaes we're having for dessert."

Elliot took a bite of the cookie and scooted beyond Lia's swat. "I hope Marissa will be able to come up with some good real estate options for us."

"I'm sure she can tap into national real estate channels. I'm more concerned about depending on other realtors in the New Orleans area for showings," Lia replied.

"If she can at least point us in the right direction and line up a few nice places for us to see, that will be a bonus."

"I'm glad she's agreed to take the loft on. She said it should sell relatively quickly."

"It should. Like you said, we've done a ton of work on it."

"True. Sweetie, could you give me a hand and set the table?"

"I will on one condition."

"And that is?"

"I want another cookie."

"What are you—seven or forty-seven?"

"When it comes to your chocolate chip cookies, I will forever be a kid."

Lia shoved a cookie into Elliot's mouth. "You, my love, are exasperating. Now, please set the table."

Unable to speak around a mouthful of cookie, Elliot just saluted and collected the plates and utensils.

* * *

"What type of house are you looking for?" Marissa asked after dinner.

"After living in this loft for so many years, I'd like something relatively large and open," Elliot said.

"I second that," Lia added.

"I am so jealous that y'all are moving to New Orleans. I miss that area so much," Julie said.

"You're from there, aren't you, Julie?" Elliot asked.

"Yes. My family has owned property in the Garden District for near-on a century."

"How did your family fare with Katrina?" Lia asked.

"Luckily only about ten percent of the French Quarter was flooded by Katrina and the storm had only a minor impact on the Garden District compared to the rest of the 9th Ward. Some parts of the area still haven't recovered."

"It must have been fun growing up there," Elliot remarked.

"It is a far cry from New York City," Julie replied. "You two are in for a huge culture shock."

"I'm actually looking forward to the change," Lia said. "Elliot and I have fallen into a rut in so many ways. This will be good for us, and good for our careers."

"What do you say I help you clear away these dessert dishes, and then we get started looking at properties for sale?" Marissa suggested.

When they were ready, Marissa poised her hands over the keyboard of her laptop. "Okay, what area of New Orleans are you most interested in?"

"I wouldn't mind the Garden District, but I'm afraid the properties there would be cost prohibitive," Lia said.

"You got that right, darlin'," Julie said. "My family owns property there but if they were in the market today, there'd be no way any of us could afford it."

"I'd like to be within five miles or so of Tulane," Elliot offered.

"It would be great if we were close enough for me to walk to work as well," Lia added.

"And a small yard would be nice if that's possible," Elliot said. "Lia has always wanted a garden, which was next to impossible in New York City."

"Speaking of cost…what's our budget?" Marissa asked.

"I'd like to keep the financing under a million, so I guess it depends on what we get for the loft," Elliot replied.

"I'm pretty sure I can get you at least a million for your loft, if not a little more. Property in New York City is in high demand, and you two have done a great job upgrading your home. I shouldn't have any issues selling it for a decent price."

"That's good news. I agree with Elliot—let's try to keep the amount we have to finance under a million," Lia said.

"Okay. Let's see, the Louisiana Cancer Research Center is on Tulane Avenue. Walking distance is what—a mile? Maybe two?"

Lia nodded. "That sounds reasonable, except maybe when the heat and humidity are unbearable."

Marissa pulled up a map on her computer of the immediate area around Tulane Avenue. "Have you got a pen and paper I can use?" she asked.

"I'll get it." Elliot returned a moment later with the implements in hand.

"Thanks." Marissa held the paper up to the distance marker on the map and estimated the length of two miles by marking it on the edge of the paper. "Okay then. Let's say this is two miles. If I hold the left marker at where the Cancer Center is, and rotate the other end around it, we'll have our search area."

Four sets of eyes watched as the imaginary circle was drawn around the focal point.

"Okay," Marissa said, "from the Cancer Center, we should be looking east as far as Governor Nicholls, north as far as Broad, west as far as Euphrosine, and south as far as Felicity. If we can't find anything acceptable within that radius, we'll expand our area.

"Let me type in our search criteria, and we'll be good to go. Larger home, preferably stately in nature. Three or more bedrooms, two or more baths, off-street parking and optional green space."

Moments later, a list of properties for sale appeared on the computer screen.

"Bingo!" Marissa maneuvered the pointer to the link provided by the search engine. "Six listings within that two-mile radius. One on Erato Street, not far from Home Depot..."

"Elliot would like that one," Lia joked.

"Very funny," Elliot replied.

"One on Barone Street in the business district. Another on Magnolia Street, directly across from the Superdome, one on Royal Street in the French Quarter, and two to the north...one on Canal and the other on Conti." Marissa looked at her hosts. "Are there any here you'd like to eliminate right up front?"

Lia looked to Julie. "You're the native. Any advice?"

"I don't think you would want to live in the business district, and the Superdome area during football season is impossible to navigate, so I'd cross those two off the list. Canal Street's reputation leaves much to be desired, so I'd put that one at the bottom of the list. I am not that familiar with the area around Erato Street, so I don't have much to say about that one, however, Conti is a nice neighborhood."

"And the one on Royal Street?" Elliot asked.

"Royal is in the French Quarter. That part of New Orleans is unique. Opulent mansions stand side by side with residences that are quite run down. The eclectic nature of the French Quarter is very appealing to some. And Bourbon Street is just a stone's throw away, as is Jackson Square."

"I hear a 'but' in your voice," Lia said.

"But it depends where on Royal Street the property is," Julie replied.

"Let's take a closer look." Marissa clicked on the link for the property and began to read, "Large properly on the corner of Royal and Governor Nicholls. A three-story building that sits flush with the sidewalk. The house has been through many restorations, but has retained its original architectural details including elaborate ceiling medallions, carved doors, tiled entryways, Greek columns and a frieze of winged angels in the dining room."

"It sounds remarkable," Elliot said.

"There's more. Listen to this," Marissa added. "The 10,000 square foot mansion and its former slave quarters have been divided up and pieced back together several times over the years."

"Slave quarters?" Lia exclaimed. "I'm not sure I want to own a home that held slaves."

Elliot rubbed Lia's back. "That was years ago. There are obviously no slaves there now."

"I know that, but just knowing slaves lived there makes me cringe."

"I totally understand how you feel, love, but please have an open mind until after we look at it."

"I agree with Elliot," Julie said. "You'll be hard-pressed to find any stately home in New Orleans that doesn't have a history of slavery associated with it."

Marissa looked up. "Should I go on reading?"

"Yes, please," Elliot said.

"Over the decades, the house has been a private residence, girls' school, furniture store, rental apartments, homeless shelter, and again, back to a private residence.

"The kitchen sports a marble island and a round kitchen table made of marble and surrounded by Louis XVI chairs. The kitchen flows into the dining room where the angel frieze overlooks the dining room table.

"The house also offers a formal parlor and spiral staircase leading all the way to the third floor where four of the six bedrooms are. There are multiple living rooms, bathrooms, and sitting rooms as well as an enclosed court yard." Marissa sat back in her chair. "This place appears to meet all your requirements and more."

"It sounds amazing, but I don't know if we need 10,000 square feet, or six bedrooms," Elliot said.

"Maybe not, but we could use the extra rooms for offices. And I've always wanted a room for crafts," Lia replied. "Heaven knows, there was never enough room in this loft for one."

Elliot smiled indulgently. "Okay, let's definitely take a look at that one."

"Hold on a minute. There are pictures here to look at."

Marissa clicked on a slideshow of pictures and they all looked on in awe as the opulent décor of the mansion paraded by.

"Wow. This house is beautiful," Lia said. "I agree with Elliot—this one is definitely on the list of must-see homes."

"Okay. I'll call our branch in New Orleans and set up a showing for when you're out there next week. Let's go look at the house on Conti next."

Before Marissa could click on the link, Julie interrupted her.

"Marissa, click on the satellite-view link. I'd like to see the area around the house."

"Okay." Marissa navigated the mouse around a three-hundred-and-sixty-degree view of the property.

"Wait. Stop." Julie said. "Go back a bit to the front entry of the house. A little bit more. Right there. Oh, my."

Julie stepped back and covered her mouth with her hands.

"Jules—what is it?" Marissa asked. Lia and Elliot stood there, intently staring at their friend.

"Look at the address. Eleven-forty."

"And that's important—why?" Marissa asked.

"The house is haunted."

"What do you mean, the house is haunted? You can't be serious," Elliot said.

"I'm *very* serious, Elliot. Eleven-forty Royal Street. It's considered the most haunted house in New Orleans."

"That's rubbish, Julie," Lia said. "Ghosts? Really?"

"Look, I know you two are scientists and all, but not everything can be explained away with science."

"I disagree," Elliot said. "There's a logical explanation for just about anything."

"Key words—'just about,'" Julie said defensively.

Marissa's words defused the situation. "Why don't we set up the showing, then you can decide whether to pursue it further. In the meantime, let's take a look at the properties on Erato and Conti. Okay?"

CHAPTER 4

"Where are you going?" the cabby asked over his shoulder.

"Hilton Riverside," Elliot replied.

"Are you ladies here on vacation?"

"Actually, we're moving here," Lia said. "We're on a house-hunting trip and staying at the Hilton until we find something…then it's back to New York to pack up and move."

"New York, huh? I've spent a fair amount of time there. New Orleans is a very different place. I hope you'll enjoy living here."

"We're moving here for our jobs, so we don't really have a choice," Elliot said. "But I have to say, I'm excited about the change."

"What type of work do you do?"

"We're scientists," Lia replied. "Elliot is a Kinesiology expert and I'm a research scientist, currently working on a pharmaceutical treatment for cancer."

"Wow. Let me be the first to wish you good luck in your new jobs."

"Thanks," Elliot said. "We're actually looking at homes on Erato, Conti and Royal on this trip. Any thoughts on those areas?"

"They're all nice areas. Good luck with your search."

* * *

At the Hilton Riverside, Lia placed the last of the clothing in the dresser and then sat on the bed. She looked toward the bathroom where Elliot was setting up the toiletries on the sink. "The cabby who picked us up at the airport was really nice. I hope everyone in New Orleans is just as pleasant."

"Yes, he was. I found myself fascinated by his accent. You'd think after knowing Julie for more than twenty years, I'd be used to it by now," Elliot replied.

"It'll only be a matter of time before both of us pick up a Southern twang."

"Maybe it will help us to get over the New Yawk accents we've developed."

Lia walked to the bathroom door and leaned against the door jamb.

"Elliot, I'm nervous about seeing the Royal Street house tomorrow. What happened there was horrible. It makes me sick to think about it. I'm not sure I could ever live in a house where such atrocities were committed against anyone, never mind against my own people."

Elliot turned off the light in the bathroom and approached Lia. She took her face between her palms.

"Sweetheart, I totally understand how you feel. When we read about the place on the Internet, I too was shocked at what happened there, but if we like the Royal Street house best and decide to buy it, we'll have the opportunity to honor the slaves that suffered there."

Tears ran down Lia's face. "My heart breaks every time I think about it. And those monsters got away with it. My ancestors suffered so much at the hands of the white aristocracy. It was such an injustice. I have a hard time wrapping my mind around how they must have felt, being treated like property."

Elliot drew her close. "I know, love. I know. I struggle with that too. At least, according to the research, the people of New Orleans didn't turn a blind eye to it. They stormed into the house and ransacked it after they learned what had happened there. Those assholes might have quite literally gotten away with murder, but they were driven out of town in the process. That has to give you some measure of satisfaction."

"Elliot, in the 1800's the general public turned a blind eye to most abuse of slaves. It took something as heinous as what that family did to those poor slaves before the townsfolk said enough is enough. Think of all the years slaves suffered at the hands of slave owners in this town—and in this country—while nothing was done about it."

"That's all in the past now, Lia. All we can do is our part to make sure it never happens again."

"It's in the past, but I feel an intense sense of indignity at the treatment of those people. *My* people, Elliot. They were human beings who could feel love, sorrow, humility, and pain. It makes me sick to think about this. I hope to God history never repeats itself. I think I'd take my own life before I'd allow that level of abuse to be inflicted on me."

"I would die before I let anyone do anything like that to you," Elliot said.

Lia raised her head and looked at Elliot directly. "What do you see when you look at me, Elliot? Do you see my brown skin? Do you see my African heritage?"

Elliot smiled. "I see the most beautiful and most amazing woman I have ever laid eyes on. Do I see brown? No. I see your soul and I see our hearts entwined. I do not see the color of your skin or the shape of your nose or the texture of your hair. My love for you is colorblind, Lia. I'm proud to be your wife and I'm proud to share that fact with the world."

Lia laid her head against Elliot's chest and hugged her tight. "Thank you, my love."

"No reason to thank me. I'm helpless about the way I feel. You captured my heart and soul that day in Starbucks. I know this move to New Orleans is scary, but I'll do my best to make this as seamless as possible for both of us."

"I'm nervous about house hunting tomorrow."

"I am too."

Elliot took a step back and knelt before Lia, who was still sitting on the bed.

"Lia, I want you to be happy and comfortable in this new environment. If you truly have reservations about the Royal

Street house after we've looked at it, then I won't push it—no matter how fantastic the house may be. Okay?"

Lia touched the side of Elliot's face. "Thank you."

* * *

"This is Conti Street," Bob, the realtor, said as he pulled up to the curb in front of a bungalow.

Elliot opened the back door, climbed out, and helped Lia out of the front seat. She looked up and down the street. "This seems like a nice quiet neighborhood."

"I like the trees lining both sides." Lia gazed toward the pink house they were parked in front of. "Is this the home we're looking at?"

"Yes. Yes it is," Bob replied.

"It's smaller than I thought it would be," Lia said.

"And much thinner. And pink." Elliot examined the long, narrow, single-level home nestled between others of nearly identical design. "It reminds me of development housing. What does a house like this go for?"

"The median sale price for houses in this area is around one hundred and seventy-five thousand."

"Whoa," Elliot replied. "That seems like a lot of cash for so little house."

"I'll ask that you keep an open mind until you've seen the inside," Bob said.

"Okay, lead the way." Elliot took Lia's hand and ascended the front steps.

"As you can see," Bob said, "we walk directly into the living room. Beyond that is the dining room, with the bathroom located to your right, and finally, in the back of the house, is the kitchen."

Lia and Elliot walked through the house and admired the tiny, but well-maintained dwelling.

"It's very cozy, and nicely kept, but where are the bedrooms?" Lia asked.

"They are downstairs, but before we go down there, let's take a look at the backyard."

Bob led them to the back porch where they spent a few minutes looking at the back yard, which was neatly trimmed and surrounded by a chain-link fence. A large dog in the neighbor's yard directly behind them stood close to the fence and barked the entire time they were on the back deck.

"Don't worry about the dog. Once you've moved in and he's used to you, the barking should stop," Bob said.

Lia raised her eyebrows to Elliot as soon as the realtor turned his back to them to lead them into the basement.

In the basement, they found three small bedrooms and a water closet containing a sink and a toilet.

After the basement tour, Bob led them back upstairs to the sidewalk in front of the house. "What do you think?" he asked.

"It's a very nice and well-maintained property," Elliot said, "but I don't think it's what we're looking for."

"Could I ask what you found lacking?" Bob asked.

Elliot turned to Lia. "I don't want to speak for you, love, but I found it to be a little claustrophobic. I was hoping for something much larger than this. It's really narrow and long and I don't like the fact that the bedrooms are in the basement, and they're really small and dark."

"And the lack of tub and shower in the basement bathroom is pretty much a non-starter," Lia added.

"My sentiments exactly," Elliot said.

"Okay then, would you like to see the property on Erato?" Bob asked.

"Yes, please," Lia answered.

Bob turned down a sparsely populated street with vacant lots on one side and a few large warehouse-type buildings dotting the other side of the road. "The homes in this area are roughly one hundred and thirty-five thousand dollars."

"This area looks pretty industrial," Lia remarked.

"Yes, there are relatively few single-family homes on this street." He pulled over to the curb in front of what appeared to be a tenement building.

23

"Are you sure you have this right? This looks like an apartment building," Elliot said.

"Actually, it was originally intended to be tenement housing for warehouse workers, but a few years back, after the warehouses fell vacant, developers converted them to condominiums."

Without getting out of the car, Lia said, "This is not at all what I picture us living in. If you don't mind, I'd like to pass on this one."

"I agree," Elliot said.

"Fair enough. So that leaves the Royal Street home, which I must say is significantly different than the other homes you've seen today."

Elliot reached into the front seat and placed her hand on Lia's shoulder. "Lia?"

Without turning around, Lia nodded. "Yes. Let's see the Royal Street property."

On the drive to Royal Street, Bob filled them in on what he knew of the house.

"This house is said to be a showplace in the heart of the French Quarter. I must admit I'd never been inside it until I prepped for your visit. This house has a bit of a history that has discouraged some buyers, although based on my walk-through yesterday, I can't imagine why.

"The house was built in the 1800's and the original owner spared no expense when it came to high-end finishes. It still has tons of ornate architectural features, original woodwork and carved doors, not to mention extensive marble throughout. It has three stories and a total of six bedrooms, several bathrooms and living areas, a study and library, a very large kitchen, and a spiral staircase that connects all three floors. The house is roughly ten thousand square feet. And it includes a carriage house and an enclosed courtyard. I've seen many stately homes in my day, but this one is at the top of my list. I'm looking forward to showing it to you."

"Six bedrooms? Isn't that excessive?" Lia asked.

"Normally, yes, but the original owners had several children, and of course, servants."

"Don't you mean slaves?" Lia challenged.

Bob looked uncomfortable. "Ah, yes."

"We're looking forward to seeing it," Elliot said quickly in an attempt to diffuse the situation.

"Bob," Lia said, "you mentioned other buyers shying away from this house due to its history. Would you care to elaborate?"

Elliot watched Bob's reflection in the mirror as he contemplated how to answer Lia's question.

"It's my understanding that one of the previous owners— someone who owned it in the eighteen thirties—mistreated her slaves. Some believe the property has bad juju, if you believe in that kind of thing."

"Do you mean it's haunted?" Elliot asked.

"I suppose that's what they mean, but personally, I believe it's just a bunch of mumbo-jumbo. I, for one, don't believe in ghosts. Heck, if ghosts actually inhabited all of the properties in NOLA that are rumored to be haunted, nothing would sell. Our realty firm is very successful at moving properties in this town, so I don't put a lot of credence in rumors like that."

Elliot and Lia fell silent as Bob turned onto Royal Street. Their gaze flitted back and forth across the narrow street, taking in the wide variety of architecture and wrought-iron railings overflowing with colorful flowers that graced the second story of most of the buildings along the street. Finally, near the end of the street, they came to eleven-forty and pulled to a stop out front.

They were unprepared for the size of the home. It covered an area forty-six by ninety feet on the ground floor alone. The front entrance literally opened onto the Royal Street sidewalk while the second story balconies, sporting ornate wrought-iron railings, shaded the sidewalks below. The stone building was painted the color of gray flannel. Ten-foot-tall windows, trimmed in white and framed by black shutters, graced the middle level. All the windows on the ground level were covered with dark sheets that prevented anyone from seeing within.

Lia and Elliot exited the car and stood staring up at the structure, awestruck at the sheer magnitude and presence of the building.

"Impressive, isn't it?" Bob asked as he stood beside them.

"I have no words to describe it," Lia said. They approached the front entrance.

Governor Nicholls Street (left), 1140 Royal Street (right)

The main entry door and the ceiling of the vestibule surrounding it were intricately carved and painted white, while the numbers, 1140, were mounted on the left wall. A black, wrought-iron gate blocked entry into the vestibule.

"As you can see," Bob said, "this side of the building houses the main entrance to the mansion. Before we go in, let's go around the corner to see the other side of the building."

1140 Royal Street Front Entrance

1140 Royal Street – Address mounted inside the vestibule

The trio walked toward the intersection of Royal Street and Governor Nicholls Street and made a right hand turn, revealing the other side of the building. As they walked, Bob explained what they were seeing.

"This side of the building holds the entrance to the carriage house, which is used today as a garage, as well as the entrance into the courtyard. If you cross the street with me for a moment, you'll have a clear view of the balcony overlooking the courtyard from one of the rooms on the second level."

Gov Nicholls side – Courtyard entrance and balcony

Balcony overlooking the courtyard

Once they were safely on the sidewalk on the opposite side of the street, Bob pointed to the gate of the courtyard.

"It is said that the former owners of this house eluded capture by the authorities when they escaped in a carriage from this very gate."

"Escaped the authorities for what reason?" Lia asked.

"That, Ms. Purvis, I will leave for you to discover. So, are you ready to see the inside?"

"Before we go inside, I'd like to know what this property is selling for," Elliot said.

"I'd rather share that information with you after you've seen the inside," Bob replied.

"No. I want to know before we go in." Elliot watched as a frown crossed his brow.

"Very well. The property was originally listed for two point three million dollars, but since it's been on the market for so long, the seller's willing to accept a price as low as one point seven-five million."

"Based on the outside," Lia said, "and the photographs we've already seen of the inside, I can't imagine why this property didn't sell quickly. Why has it been on the market for so long?" Lia asked.

"As I said, Ms. Purvis, I'll leave that for you to discover. I can assure you it's not because of the quality of this residence. Shall we go inside?"

"Yes, please," Lia said.

Bob led them back to the front entrance of the house and unlocked the wrought-iron gate. "After you, then."

As they stepped into the vestibule, Lia immediately felt chilled and shivered uncontrollably.

Elliot placed her arm around Lia's shoulder. "Are you okay, love?" she asked.

"I'm fine. Just a chill is all."

"Seriously? It's ninety-six degrees out here."

"I'm fine, Elliot, really."

Bob unlocked the heavy front door and pushed it open, revealing a spectacularly ornate entryway. "After you, ladies," he said.

Lia took three steps into the foyer, with Elliot right behind her. Suddenly, Lia fell back into Elliot, as though she had been pushed, and fainted away in Elliot's arms.

Elliot slowly lowered her to the marble floor.

"Lia, sweetheart, talk to me. Lia."

CHAPTER 5

"Well, don't just stand there. Help me get her up," Elliot yelled to Bob.

Just as they began to lift her from the floor, Lia's eyes flew open. "I didn't mean to pull yo hair, mistress. Please forgive me," she said in a strange voice.

Elliot cupped the side of Lia's face. "Sweetheart, are you okay?"

Lia looked around with confusion on her face and a hint of terror in her eyes.

"Lia?" Elliot said again.

Lia closed her eyes and when she opened them again, she looked at the realtor, then back at Elliot. "Elliot. What happened? Why am I on the floor?"

Elliot and Bob helped Lia to the settee by the entryway. "Sweetheart, sit." Elliot dropped to one knee in front of Lia and took her hands between her own. "Are you okay?"

"I'm fine. Really. I'll ask again—why was I on the floor just now?"

"You fainted. Thank God I was behind you. All of a sudden, you just fell backward into my arms, like you'd run into something."

"I fainted? I don't remember that."

"What *do* you remember?" Elliot asked.

"I remember walking into the room, then looking up at you and asking why I was on the floor."

"You don't remember saying anything to me?"

"I remember asking why I was on the floor, if that's what you mean."

Throughout this exchange, Bob paced uneasily back and forth in front of them. "Ladies, I don't want to rush you, but if you're still interested in seeing the house, we should begin our tour. I believe there's another client scheduled to look at it within the next hour."

Elliot looked at her wife. "Lia?"

"I'm fine. Yes, let's finish the tour."

Elliot helped her to her feet. "Are you sure you're all right?"

"I'm fine. Now stop yer fussin' darlin'. We have a lot of house to see in very little time."

Elliot frowned. "Since when do you have a southern accent?"

Lia grinned. "Sorry. That kind of slipped out. I guess it's from bein' 'round all these fine southern folk."

Elliot narrowed her eyes at her wife a few seconds longer before turning her attention to the realtor. "Okay, Bob, I guess we're good to go. Lead the way."

"All right then. Follow me. We're entering on the ground floor which, when the property was originally built, would have housed the laundry facilities, storage, tack house, stable, carriage house and living quarters for the stable hands. As you can see, these rooms have been remodeled and can be used for nearly anything you want. There are currently eight rooms on this level, as well as two baths, the garage and the courtyard. And let me point out the spiral staircase that connects all three levels of the house."

Lia and Elliot walked through each of the rooms on the ground floor, admiring the intricate woodwork and high-end furnishings. They completed their tour of the bottom floor in the courtyard.

"What do you think so far?" Bob asked.

"It's huge," Elliot exclaimed. "We're going to have to hire a full staff just to keep it clean."

"This floor alone," Lia said, "is larger than our loft in New York City. We're going to need a lot more furniture."

"Actually, the home comes furnished with everything you see," Bob replied.

"Seriously?" Elliot looked at him. "So, what's the catch? This is a lot of house and furnishings for the price."

"We have a motivated seller," Bob explained. He ushered the women back into the house. "Let's go see the second level."

As Lia and Elliot followed Bob into the vestibule from the courtyard, Elliot leaned in close to Lia's ear. "Motivated by what, is what I want to know," she whispered.

"Behave," Lia whispered back.

As they mounted the spiral staircase to the second floor. Bob said, "The main living area is up here, including two kitchens, a dining room, three living rooms, a bedroom, and a bonus room over the garage that's currently being used as a library."

Lia and Elliot inspected each room, expressing awe and admiration along the way.

"Do you ladies have any questions before we head to the third floor?"

"No, I think we'll save them for the end of the tour," Elliot said.

"Okay then, one more flight up the spiral staircase. Follow me, please." Bob waited for Elliot and Lia to ascend to the third level.

"Lots of stairs," Lia said. "At least we'll get our exercise."

"You got that right. There wouldn't happen to be an elevator in this place, would there?" Elliot asked.

"I'm afraid not, but I suppose you could add one," Bob replied. "As you'll see, this level contains the main sleeping quarters. There are two large and two small bedrooms, four more baths, and a beautiful porch, as well as the balcony I pointed out earlier that overlooks the courtyard."

After quickly touring each room, they regrouped on the porch.

"I have to agree with Elliot, Bob. This is a lot of house for the money. I would really be interested in why the seller was so quick to reduce the price of the house, and by so much," Lia said.

"Like, I said, the seller is motivated. The house is vacant, and empty houses cost money. The owner is indeed anxious to sell."

"Yes—but why?" Elliot asked again. "Could it possibly be the rumors we've heard about it being haunted?"

"Again, Ms. Walker, as a scientist, I'm sure you'll agree that the rumors are simply a bunch of hooey. I believe the seller is motivated because of delinquent taxes, but you can ask the owners yourself if you choose to put in a bid on this property. "

"Fair enough," Lia said. "Let's head downstairs and talk about what's next, if anything."

Bob reached into his pocket and handed Elliot a copy of his business card. "I'm afraid we won't be able to hang around much longer. That other client is due to arrive soon. Here's my card. Please call me to set up a follow-up appointment and I'll be happy to discuss how to move forward, if that's what you choose to do."

Elliot accepted his card and handed it over to Lia. "Maybe that's for the best. It'll give us time to discuss the pros and cons before meeting again."

"I agree. Now, if you'll follow me, I'll escort you back to the car."

* * *

"How hungry are you, love?" Lia perused the menu of the Crazy Lobster Bar and Grill.

"Not starving, but definitely peckish," Elliot replied.

"How about we share a few appetizers?"

"Sounds good to me."

"What strikes your fancy?"

"Besides you?" Elliot asked with a hint of mischief in her eyes. "Why don't you surprise me?"

Lia touched Elliot's arm. "We could skip appetizers altogether and enjoy the main course in our room, you know."

"Why don't we do appetizers here, and enjoy *dessert* in our room afterward?"

"It's a date. Here comes the waiter."

"What can I get for you ladies tonight?" the waiter asked, pen poised over his order pad.

Lia quickly scanned the list of appetizers. "Bring us an order of coconut shrimp, gator bites and hushpuppies. And two voodoo juices, please."

"Will that be it?" the waiter asked.

"Yes." Lia scanned the waiter's name tag. "Thank you, Jared."

"I'll get your drink order in first."

Elliot sat back in her chair. "What did you think about today's adventure?"

"The first two properties were definitely not for me. The Royal Street property was amazing, but that is a lot of house to keep clean."

"I'll say. Do you realize there are eleven toilets in that house?"

"It has its pros and cons. There's a ton of space. In addition to all the bathrooms, I think I counted twenty-two rooms, including at least four kitchens. There'd be plenty of room for each of us to have our own office, and maybe we could set up a rec room and a theater."

"I like where you're going with this," Elliot said.

"On the other hand, do we really need that much space? Our loft could fit completely into just one of the levels of that house. And we've been pretty comfortable in that amount of room for twenty-two years."

Just then, the waiter returned with two very tall, orange containers, which he set down, one in front of each of them. "Your drinks, ladies. And the glass is on the house."

"Holy moley." Elliot took a sip of the potent drink and whistled. "Drink this one slowly, love. It's pretty strong."

Lia took a sip of her own drink. "Yum, that is good. Now, where was I? Oh, yeah, the Royal Street house. It's much larger than we really need. I'll bet it costs an arm and a leg to heat."

Elliot reached forward and knocked on Lia's forehead. "Hello? Anybody home? Lia, we're in New Orleans. We are not going to be living through any Northeastern winters here."

"Oh, yeah, that's right. Habits die hard, I guess."

"It *is* a really good price for such a large property," Elliot said. "And Marissa thinks we should get at least a million for the loft, so that would offset the cost enough to keep us within budget."

"Yes it is a good price. Too good if you ask me. What did Bob say? It was originally listed for two point three million, and the owner suddenly drops it to one point seven five, just like that? Doesn't that seem odd to you? That's just over a half-million dollar reduction in the selling price. Who in their right mind does that? Maybe there's something wrong with it."

"I looked pretty carefully at everything that was visible on the tour, and I didn't see anything that might concern me. It's in really good shape."

"That's the problem, Elliot. We can only make a judgment on what we can see. I'm more concerned about what we can't see. And of course, there's the house's history. That still bothers me."

"I know. I just wish Bob hadn't ignored our subtle questions about what happened here all those years ago. You can't tell me we're the first ones to express concerns about the rumors."

"They're probably just that – rumors, although I have to admit, I did feel a presence in the house while we were there."

Elliot cocked an eyebrow at her wife. "A presence? What do you mean?"

"I don't know how to describe it. I could feel the history of the house. I'm not ready to admit it's haunted, but an unexpected feeling of excitement, and maybe a little heaviness, was pressing on my heart while we were there. When I thought about actually living there, the feeling became almost overwhelming."

Elliot took Lia's hand in hers. "Look, we don't need to make a decision tonight. Why don't we sleep on it and call

Marissa in the morning. Maybe she can line up a few more showings on short notice. Okay?"

Lia touched the side of Elliot's face. "You always know what to say, don't you? All right. Let's put this aside for tonight and enjoy our dinner."

"And dessert," Elliot added, her eyebrows dancing up and down on her forehead.

A throaty laugh escaped Lia's lips. "You, my love are incorrigible."

CHAPTER 6

Elliot exited the bathroom in their hotel room and immediately embraced Lia from behind. "I am so psyched that our room has a Jacuzzi. I'm filling the tub right now. Care to join me?"

"Try to keep me away. You know what a water ho I am. Did you add any bubble bath?"

"Does Dolly Parton sleep on her back? Hell, yeah."

Lia turned around in Elliot's embrace. She cupped Elliot's face between her palms and kissed her soundly. "You're such a big kid. Don't ever lose your sense of humor, okay?"

"The feeling is moo-chal dahling," Elliot replied in her best foreign accent. "Need some help getting undressed?"

"How can I turn down an offer like that?" Lia lifted her arms above her head for Elliot to remove her blouse.

Before long, there was a pile of clothing on the floor at their feet and both of them stood naked in each other's arms, hands roaming over smooth skin, groping and squeezing as their tongues danced with choreographed perfection in one another's mouths.

Finally, Lia broke the kiss and leaned her head back to allow Elliot access to her neck. "Hmmm, keep it up and we'll never get that bath."

"Oh, yes we will. Nothing says we can't continue this in the tub. And besides, if we don't shut the water off in there soon, it will spill over the top."

Lia chuckled. "Like I said, you always know what to say. Lead on, Ms. Casanova."

As they made their way to the bathroom, Lia suddenly stopped. "Wait, hold on a sec." Before they left the bedroom,

Lia grabbed a hair elastic from the dresser. "Gotta tie my hair up before I get into the tub."

Elliot turned the water off in the Jacuzzi, and watched as Lia pulled her hair back into a big fluffy plume on top of her head. She grinned broadly then reached once more for her wife. "You are so damned cute with your hair like that."

Lia batted her hands away. "In the tub with you, woman. I am so looking forward to this soak."

"I have so much more in mind than just a soak. Let me give you a hand getting in." Elliot helped Lia into the tub, and climbed in behind her.

Elliot settled gingerly into the hot water and leaned her back against the tub while pulling Lia back to sit between her legs, reclining her against Elliot's torso. She pressed the button to turn on the jets and sat back to watch the mountains of bubbles rise around them.

"Comfy?" Elliot asked.

"Oh, yeah."

Elliot scooped handfuls of bubbles from around their bodies and piled them on top of Lia's chest, building two rather large mounds over the area where Lia's breasts disappeared below the surface of the water.

"Elliot, you're such a goofball."

"You've hidden your beautiful breasts from me under the water, so I'm improvising."

Lia sat up and maneuvered herself to her knees, then she knelt between Elliot's legs and faced her. "They're not hidden now."

Elliot abdomen spasmed and her breath caught in her throat. She reached forward and fondled the nipples that were mere inches from her face. She slowly, methodically, suckled each one, causing Lia's back to arch and moans to escape her lips. "Do you have any idea what you're doing to me?" Elliot asked as she released one swollen bud.

"God, yes," Lia said. "I know exactly what I'm doing to you."

Elliot slipped one hand under the surface of the water and cupped Lia's womanhood. She squeezed gently, driving Lia to push herself down onto Elliot's hand.

"I need more," Lia whispered into Elliot's ear.

Elliot responded by biting harder on Lia's nipple at the same time, she slipped two fingers between her folds.

Lia cried out in a mixture of pain and pleasure as she once again pushed herself down onto Elliot's hand. "I need you inside me," she rasped.

Elliot obliged as she thrust three fingers deep within her lover.

Between the movement of the jetted water on Elliot's own heated core and the sensuality of her fingers sliding in and out of Lia, it wasn't long before they both climaxed, causing Lia to fall limply onto Elliot's chest. Elliot wrapped her free arm around her wife and held her close, while Lia's body rhythmically contracted around her fingers and ripples of spasms continued to run through her own body.

"I've got you, my love. I've got you," she cooed into Lia's ear. "I love you with everything I am. Don't ever doubt that."

* * *

I didn't means to pull yo hair, mistress. Please forgive me. Please, mistress. I didn't means to. Please don't be mad. I promise never to do it again. Mistress, no. Please, mistress, don't. I won't do it again. I promise. Mistress, no.

"No!" Lia suddenly bolted upright in bed. "Oh, my God."

"Lia, what is it? Are you okay?" Elliot grabbed for her.

Lia looked at Elliot. Her eyes were wild with fear. "El...Elliot..."

"Come here." Elliot pulled Lia into her arms. "I've got you, love. You're safe."

Lia shook uncontrollably as she wrapped her arms around Elliot.

Elliot pulled her down onto the bed and drew the covers over their naked bodies. She kissed Lia's forehead and held her as close as she could. "Shhh, it's okay. It's okay. You're safe. It was only a dream, love. It was only a dream."

After several long moments, the trembling began to subside and Elliot relaxed her hold on her wife. "Are you okay?" she whispered into the night.

Lia nodded.

"Do you want to talk about it?"

"I don't remember. It was more of a feeling than a dream."

"What do you mean? What feeling?"

"Fear, mostly. I kept hearing this small voice saying over and over, 'I didn't mean to pull your hair. Please forgive me. Please don't. Please, no.' Elliot, there was such fear in the voice, it was tangible."

Elliot propped herself up on one elbow so she could look into Lia's face. "Are you serious? Are you sure that's what the voice said?"

Lia rolled onto her back and looked into Elliot's face. "Yes. I know what I heard. The voice said it over and over."

"Lia, when we went to the Royal Street property and you fainted after walking inside, that was exactly what you said when you regained consciousness."

"I did? I don't remember that. You're scaring me."

Elliot reclined once more and took Lia into her arms. "There's got to be a logical explanation for this. I'm betting it's residual thoughts and emotions from the research we did on the property. What happened there was pretty awful. I can understand why it might still affect you days later."

"Do you think that's it? Could it be that simple?"

"What else could it be? You and I both toured that house, top to bottom. I didn't see anything out of the ordinary. Did you?"

"No, I didn't. You're probably right. Maybe we should just forget about buying that house."

"Maybe we should. We can talk about it in the morning. Right now, try to relax and sleep, okay? I'm sure we'll both have a fresh perspective on things tomorrow."

"Okay. Thank you for being there for me, Elliot."

"Always, my love. Always."

* * *

The next morning Elliot stood behind Lia as she sat at the vanity putting her makeup on. She watched Lia in the mirror as she slipped her arms into her shirt and secured the buttons. "You know, you're beautiful, even without makeup."

Lia smiled. "I'm glad you think so, love, but my fifty years are starting to show in the lines and wrinkles on my face."

Elliot kissed her on the cheek then proceeded to tuck her shirt into her trousers. "You will always be beautiful in my eyes. Even when your hair is snow white and you're walking all stooped over with a cane."

Lia raised her eyebrows and looked at Elliot in the mirror. "You are such a romantic."

"Just speaking the truth."

"What time is your appointment at the university?" Lia asked as she applied her eye shadow.

"Ten o'clock."

"Any idea how long you'll be?"

"Hard to say. I would plan on at least a couple of hours. Are you sure you don't want to come?" Elliot asked.

"No. Since I'm going to be tied up at the Cancer Institute for the rest of the week, I was hoping to get one more look at the house on Royal Street today before we make a final decision. But it can wait until you get back."

Elliot slipped her suit coat on and pulled her cuffs an inch below the ends of the sleeves. "How do I look?"

Lia rose to her feet and faced Elliot. She extracted Elliot's collar from inside the suit and arranged it outside, over the lapels. "Turn around," she instructed, and watched as Elliot turned around in a complete circle. "What are you wearing for shoes?" she asked.

"I thought I would wear my heeled boots."

"Good choice. Go put them on then let me do a final once-over."

Elliot retrieved her boots from the closet and sat on the bed. As she pulled them on, she glanced up at Lia. "You don't have to wait for me to go see the Royal Street house again. I completely trust your judgment."

"I just might do that."

Elliot rose to her feet and stood at attention. "Ready for inspection, Sir!"

Lia walked in circles around Elliot, brushing imaginary dust from her shoulder, straightening her collar, and at one point, pinching her behind. "Nice. Very nice, Private Walker" she said, stopping in front of Elliot.

"Is everything in order, sir?" Elliot tried hard not to smile.

"Congratulations, Walker. You have passed inspection. Now go knock 'em dead."

Elliot kissed her on the nose. "Thanks, love." She picked up her briefcase from the bed. "Give me a call later and let me know what you want to do about the house."

"I'm not making this decision by myself."

"No, I'll help you make it, but I want you to be happy with whatever we choose. If the Royal Street property isn't meant to be, we'll just keep looking."

"Okay. Good luck meeting the new boss today."

"Thanks. I'll see you this afternoon. Love you lots."

"Right back atcha. Now off with you."

Lia closed the door behind Elliot and fished the realtor's card from her purse. She sat on the bed and punched his number into her cell phone. "Hello, Bob? Lia Purvis."

"Good morning, Ms. Purvis."

"Good morning to you too. Bob, I'd like to see the Royal Street house once more before we make a final decision."

"That can certainly be arranged. What time are you available?"

"I'm available now if you are."

"I can pick you up in fifteen minutes. Is that okay?"

"Perfect. I'll be waiting in front of the hotel. See you then."

"Bob, what do you know about what happened in this house a hundred and eighty years ago?" Lia slowly made her way through the elaborately decorated living rooms on the second floor.

"Ms. Purvis, I know this house has somewhat of a tainted past, but one shouldn't dwell on such things. As you can see today, this is a beautiful home. I believe one should let history lie in the past where it belongs."

"If what I've read about this house is true, many slaves were tortured here, and many died. I'm sure you've noticed that I have a kinship of sorts with the victims of these atrocities. Part of me wants to flee this house and never return, yet another part of me wants so much to celebrate their lives and honor them by buying this home."

"There's been a lot of hearsay about what happened here, Ms. Purvis. Some of it may be true, but I'm sure some of it was greatly exaggerated as well. I do however, understand how you might feel."

"It certainly is beautiful, and pretty much move-in ready. I can't believe all of this period furniture comes with the sale. It's a pity this house has sat empty for so long. Could it be due to the rumors that it's haunted?"

Bob followed Lia into the kitchen. "Do you believe in such things?" he asked.

"Personally, no, but let's say for the moment that it is possible. That would certainly explain why it has changed hands so many times over the years."

"I'm with you on that one, Ms. Purvis. With all the ghost stories running around this town you'd think you might encounter a ghost or two over your lifetime. I for one, have not. A bunch of hogwash designed to draw tourists, if you ask me."

Bob's pocket suddenly began to ring.

"Please excuse me, while I take this call." Bob pulled his cell phone from his pocket and left her alone in the kitchen.

While Lia waited for Bob to return, she strolled around, opening cupboards and admiring the black-and-white marble floor. The kitchen was very modern, with stainless steel appliances and granite counter tops, but if she narrowed her eyes, Lia could imagine what this kitchen might have looked like in the eighteen thirties. She rested her backside against the granite-topped island and closed her eyes.

In her mind's eye, she pictured a double sink with a water pump and a gigantic cast iron cooking stove, fueled by wood. In the far corner, she imagined a larder, filled with home-canned vegetables, jellies, and jams, and shelves lined with home-baked goods. In the center of the room was a large wooden table, dusted with flour. She instinctively knew this was the room where family meals were prepared, but where the aristocracy seldom set foot.

Suddenly the aroma of freshly-baked apple pie invaded her senses, making her smile. She kept her eyes closed, lest the sensation cease. She could imagine the slaves sitting around the wooden table, talking all at once about the toils of their day as an elderly black woman served them dinner.

"Da mistress done whipped da stable boy agin t'day," one of the men said.

"Samuel, don't you be talkin' out of turn, or you get a whippin' too," the old woman replied.

"He didn't do nothin' to d'serve it, Gran," Samuel insisted.

"None of us ever does, child. None of us ever does. Now where's that granddaughter of mine gone off to? Nary a wonder the mistress be gettin' after her. She gotta be learnin' her place 'round here or she be endin' up dead. Or worse."

Lia could see the older woman walk to the back porch overlooking the courtyard. A chain on her ankle clanking as she moved.

"There you are child. Come up here and eat afore the mistress calls ye. You goin' to be the death of me yet, child."

Lia watched the older woman stand at the door for several long moments before her temper got the best of her. *"Lia, get yoself in here right now afore I whips ye myself!"*

Lia's eyes flew open, and she grasped the counter top for support. "Did she say, Lia?"

CHAPTER 7

Lia paced back and forth across the hotel room and waited for Elliot to return. Finally, she heard Elliot's key in the lock and rushed to open the door.

Elliot jumped. "Damn, woman! You scared me, flinging the door open like that."

Lia placed a quick kiss on Elliot's lips. "Sorry, love, it's just that I'm excited to tell you the news."

"News?" Elliot entered the room and closed the door.

"Yes. I've decided we should buy the Royal Street house."

"You have? Why the change of heart?"

Lia helped Elliot off with her jacket and hung it in the closet. "It's not really a change of heart. We were undecided as of this morning."

"So, what happened during your second tour to make up your mind?"

"I can't put my finger on any one thing. It's more of a feeling I have. A feeling that we belong there. That I belong there."

Elliot took Lia's hand and led her to the bed where they sat side by side. "So tell me about the visit."

"Bob took me through the entire house again, a little slower this time, and we ended up in the kitchen. I asked him about the haunted history of the house, and he pretty much pooh-poohed it as nothing more than sensationalism designed to bring tourists to the town."

"He's probably right. New Orleans is supposed to be one of the most haunted cities in the United States. If the number of hauntings was as bad as they say it is, no one would live here, especially if you believe in ghosts—which I don't."

"Anyway, his phone rang and he left me alone in the kitchen while he took his call. I spent my time imagining what it might have looked like in the early eighteen hundreds, when all of a sudden, I could smell the aroma of fresh-baked apple pie."

"Seriously?" Elliot asked, a hint of incredulity in her voice.

"Yes, seriously." Lia saw the doubt on Elliot's face. "Hear me out. I closed my eyes, and after a time, I swear I envisioned a group of slaves sitting around a large wooden table having dinner. And then an old woman, who I assume was the cook since she was chained to the stove, went to the back door to call a young girl into the house to eat."

Lia reached out to touch Elliot's arm. "Elliot, this is where it became really strange. The old woman called the little girl Lia. She called her Lia! Do you believe it?"

Elliot frowned. "The question is, do you believe it? Surely you just projected yourself into the middle of that daydream."

Lia looked at her hands clasped in her lap. "I suppose that's possible. You're probably right, but when I opened my eyes, this feeling of belonging swept over me, like I was home. I don't know how else to explain it. I felt like I belonged there."

"Lia, look at me." Elliot tilted Lia's face so she could see her eyes. "Are you sure about this? Putting aside that it's one hell of a lot of house and one hell of a lot of money, you need to feel comfortable living in a place where unspeakable cruelty was committed on slaves. Are you sure you want to do this?"

"I *have* to do this. I have to."

Elliot inhaled deeply. "Okay then. It looks like we're buying a mansion."

* * *

"Are you excited?" Elliot asked as she maneuvered the car slowly down Royal Street, weaving in and out to avoid pedestrians and parked cars.

"I am," Lia replied. "I hope there's a place to park out front."

"Bob said the keys to the carriage house are on the kitchen table. The next time, we'll be able to pull into the garage."

"After we install a garage door opener," Lia said. "I don't cherish getting out in the pouring rain to manually open the garage door."

"Yes, dear, we'll install a garage door opener. You've been spoiled all these years with the parking garage right under the building we lived in," Elliot teased.

Elliot continued toward 1140 Royal Street. "We're in luck," she said. "From here, it looks like the space right out front is open." She pulled into the parking space and turned off the ignition.

Lia looked wide-eyed at the building without getting out of the car. Suddenly, she gasped.

"What is it?" Elliot asked.

"I don't know. It's probably nothing more than the light playing tricks on me, but I thought I saw a curtain move on the third floor." Lia rolled down the window and was immediately hit by nearly overwhelming humidity that chased the coolness from the air-conditioned car. "Ugh! This is one thing I'm not going to like about living here."

Elliot leaned lower so she could see through Lia's window. "Where did you see the curtain move?"

Lia pointed. "Up there. The left-most window on the top floor."

"It might be just the wind. It's an old house, after all."

"With this humidity, there isn't enough wind to float a feather. In fact, judging by those dark clouds, this humidity will turn into a downpour soon." Lia looked upward again. "I'm sure it was just my imagination."

"I have to admit, I'm a little nervous about this whole thing," Elliot said.

Lia looked sharply at Elliot. "Seriously? We waited for two whole weeks for this closing to be scheduled, and you're admitting that now? We just put ourselves into nearly a million dollars of debt. Is that what you're worried about?"

"I'm not worried. I'm just a little apprehensive, considering what we know about this place. And I'm worried about you."

Lia placed her hand on Elliot's. "Sweetheart, please don't worry about me. I admit I'm more than a little bothered by what went on in this house, but don't you see what sweet revenge this is? I mean, nearly two hundred years ago when the atrocities happened, slaves were considered property, and now...well, now, here I am—a black woman—actually owning the very house those crimes were committed in. Bittersweet, for sure, but oh, what a statement about how far we've come."

"I'll do everything I can to make you happy here, Lia, but I didn't feel a lot of warm fuzzies at the closing."

"What do you mean?"

"For starters, the owner didn't even show up. With that amount of money on the table, I found that kind of odd. Then, when we started questioning a few items from the inspection that needed fixed, the owner's lawyer didn't hesitate one second to cut another two hundred thousand off the price to cover the cost of repairs. I got the distinct feeling the lawyer was given a lot of leeway to get rid of the property. But what topped it off for me, was his comments after we signed the papers. Good luck with that monstrosity. What the hell did he mean by that?"

"I'm sure he was just referring to the size. Ten thousand square feet is a lot of house. Look, love. I know I made the decision on my own to buy it, but I really think living here will be very interesting."

"I sure hope so, for both our sakes. And just for the record, I would have supported your choice even if you decided we were going to live in a cardboard box. As long as I'm with you, I know we'll be happy."

Lia kissed Elliot tenderly on the cheek. "I love you too, sweetheart. Now what do you say we get out of this oppressive humidity and into our new home?"

"Can I carry you across the threshold?" Elliot asked, a

grin spreading across her face.

"Not on your life!"

Lia and Elliot climbed out of the car and met on the sidewalk under the overhead balcony. Lia attempted to look into one of the heavily draped windows on the ground level.

"One of the first things I want to do is throw these drapes back and let some sunlight into this house," Lia said. "It was so dark inside when we toured the place, it felt like a tomb."

"You'll get no argument from me." Elliot unlocked the iron gate blocking the front entrance. "I'm sure it could use some airing out as well, considering it's been awhile since anyone has lived here." Elliot held her hand out to Lia. "Are you ready?"

"More than ready. Lead the way."

Elliot and Lia stopped in front of the main entrance door and admired the intricate carving of Phoebus in his chariot as well as wreaths of flowers and garlands in bas-relief. "Beautiful," Elliot whispered as she unlocked the door and pushed it open. A rush of cool air met them head-on.

"Thank God we asked Bob to leave the central air on," Lia said.

Just before she could step into the foyer, Elliot grabbed Lia by the waist and threw her over her shoulder.

"Elliot, put me down. What do you think you're doing?"

"I'm carrying you over the threshold."

"Like this?" She strained to look at Elliot.

"What do you expect me to do? You're taller than me and I'm not strong enough to carry you in my arms." Elliot stepped into the house and set Lia on her feet inside the foyer.

"Well, wasn't that romantic," Lia quipped.

Elliot shoved her hands deep into her trouser pockets and shrugged her shoulders. "Hey, you gotta give me credit for trying."

Lia realized she had hurt Elliot's feelings, and she grinned sheepishly at her. "It was kind of sweet. Come here."

Elliot walked into the circle of open arms and allowed herself to be wrapped in the cocoon of Lia's love. Lia kissed her on the head. "Welcome home, sweetie."

"I was home the moment I walked into your arms," Elliot said. "But these digs are pretty awesome too, if I should say so myself."

"Yes, they are. What do you say we go exploring before we drag our suitcases in from the car?"

"Not before I give you a welcome-home kiss." Elliot took Lia's face between her palms and kissed her, gently at first, followed by a kiss of searing passion.

"Welcome home, indeed," Lia whispered.

Suddenly a loud thump was heard above their heads, and they both jumped.

"What in God's name was that?" Lia asked.

Elliot looked at the ceiling, and maneuvered Lia behind her in an unconscious attempt to shield her from harm. "I don't know, but I plan to find out." She made a bee-line to the spiral staircase at the far end of the foyer.

"You're not going anywhere without me," Lia said as she followed close behind.

Elliot stopped when she reached the bottom of the stairs and looked up. "Damn, I had forgotten how beautiful this is. I can see clear to the third floor from here."

"What level do you think the noise came from?" Lia asked.

"I don't know, but it was pretty loud, so I assume it was right above our heads. We'll start with the second floor."

"Do you think we need something to protect ourselves?"

"Good point." Elliot looked around the foyer. "There's an umbrella stand by the front door. Stay right here." Elliot scurried to the entryway and grabbed the only umbrella that occupied the stand. When she returned to Lia, she said, "It's not much, but it's better than nothing. Stay behind me."

Elliot ascended the spiral staircase slowly, looking intently at her surroundings as they made their way to the second story. She could feel Lia's hand on her back as she followed. When they reached the second story landing, they paused and listened.

"Do you hear anything?" Elliot asked in a loud whisper.

Lia shook her head.

"Okay, let's start over there." Elliot pointed to the room directly in front and slightly to the right of them. "That one is pretty much above where we were standing in the foyer."

Lia followed as they crossed the hall and pushed the door open to the room in question. Elliot held the closed umbrella above her head, ready to strike their unseen assailant if necessary. When it became apparent the room was empty, she lowered the umbrella.

"It's the dining room," Lia said as she took in the long, dark maple, antique dining table, surrounded by five chairs on each side and one on each end. An arrangement of dried, cut flowers and two ornate candlesticks graced the center of the table, and an embroidered placemat rested at each setting. Beautiful tapestries, displaying Italian vineyard scenes lined the light-gray walls and medallions decorated the ornate ceilings. An angel frieze, painted bright white, framed the far wall. In addition to the antique table, in the corner sat an 18th century Italian tabernacle. "This is beautiful."

Elliot looked around the undisturbed room. "Well, beautiful or not, the sound obviously didn't come from here. I'm going up to the third floor. I assume you're coming with me?"

"Of course."

Lia followed Elliot into the hallway and up the spiral staircase to the third level. At the top of the stairs, Elliot once again pointed to the room on the right and held the umbrella high. They approached the door and pushed it open into an opulently decorated bedroom. Wall-papered in a royal blue Harlequin pattern, it contained a queen-size Victorian four-poster bed. The first thing Elliot noticed when they looked into the room was an open window.

"How the hell did that window get opened? This is the Royal Street side of the house. I don't remember noticing any open windows when we pulled up out front."

"And look—the lamp from the bedside table is on the floor. That must have caused the noise we heard," Lia said.

She made a move to enter the room, but Elliot held her

back. "Wait. Let me check it out first."

No sooner had Elliot walked two steps into the room, than a streak of black shot out from the long ornate dresser that was hidden behind the open door. It dashed to the center of the bed.

Lia screamed.

Elliot raised the umbrella, ready to strike.

"Elliot. Wait. It's a cat."

"Well, I'll be." Elliot lowered her weapon. "I wonder how it got in. This bedroom door was closed before we got here."

Lia walked to the open window and looked out. "There's a ledge right below these windows that runs all around the building on this level. I'm sure that's how it got in."

Elliot picked the animal up and scratched behind its ears as it purred loudly. The cat was totally black except for a white patch on its neck, just below its chin. Elliot dipped the cat back to determine its gender. "Well, Miss Thing, I hate to break it to you, but you don't live here."

Lia sat with her backside against the window pane. "I wonder who she belongs to."

"She certainly belongs to someone. Judging by her girth, she's been well fed."

A distant rumble of thunder drew their attention to the open window.

"The tour will have to wait until we get our things in from the car, or we'll get caught in the downpour." Elliot scratched the cat once more. "Sorry, princess, but you need to go outside."

"You're not going to put her on the ledge outside the window are you?" Lia asked as Elliot walked toward the window.

"Don't be silly. I'm just closing the window before the rain begins. I'll let her out into the courtyard. I'm sure she'll find her way home from there."

They went downstairs, put the cat outside, and began unloading the car.

Lia handed Elliot another suitcase. "Is that the last of it?" Elliot asked.

"Yes, which is good because here comes the rain."

A bolt of lightning lit up the sky, and both women instinctively looked up.

"Holy cow," Elliot said.

"What?"

"Look. Third story. Left-most window. It's open."

"Isn't that the window you closed not ten minutes ago?"

"You're damned right it is. Come on. I want to get to the bottom of this."

CHAPTER 8

Elliot grabbed the umbrella again and took the stairs two at a time, totally ignoring the pile of luggage in the middle of the foyer. She was out of breath by the time she reached the third story and had to pause before entering the bedroom to allow her heart rate to normalize. By the time she recovered, Lia had joined her in the third-story hallway.

"Elliot, be careful," Lia whispered as they crept toward the room.

To maintain an element of surprise, Elliot quickly pushed the door open and ran in, stopping dead when she got to the center of the room. There, before her, in the middle of the bed, was the cat.

"How in God's name did you get in here?" Elliot asked loudly while Lia once again closed the window.

"Obviously through the window," Lia said from across the room.

Elliot threw the umbrella on the bed and joined Lia at the window. "But how did the window open? Don't tell me the cat did it." Elliot tested the window by opening and closing it a few times. "It's not on a spring mechanism," she pointed out. She opened and closed the window one more time then engaged the locking mechanism. "That ought to do it. Now, to take care of Miss Thing, here. Come on, princess." Elliot collected the cat from the bed. "You need to go home."

"I think while you're doing that, I'll drag the luggage up to the master suite," Lia said.

"Why don't you come with me to let the cat into the courtyard through the ground-level floor, then we can explore down there and work our way back up here with the luggage? I've only seen it once during our rushed tour with Bob."

"Okay, let's go."

As Lia and Elliot walked together down the two flights of stairs leading to the ground floor, they admired the mahogany banisters and white marble steps that adorned their path.

"I still can't believe this is ours," Lia said. "It's so grand. I feel like a queen."

Elliot stopped mid-step, while Lia stepped down one more and turned to look up at her. With her free hand, she cupped Lia's chin and placed a feather-light kiss on her lips. "Sweetheart, you *are* a queen. You have always been royalty in my book. I feel good about this move. It's a new beginning for us, and an opportunity I don't plan to waste."

Lia smiled through misty eyes. "I love you, Elliot Walker."

"I love you too, Lia Purvis, with all my heart."

When the ladies reached the foyer at the bottom of the stairs, Lia looked around and narrowed her eyes.

"Okay, what's that look for? Something is brewing in that beautiful brain of yours. Spill it," Elliot said.

"I was just thinking that this area is so clinical looking. It reminds me of a hotel lobby. It even smells like a hotel lobby."

Elliot nodded. "I would have to agree with you. With the black and white tile floor and the marble staircase, it does kind of look more like a business than a home. What did you have in mind?"

"I don't know. Maybe an area rug. Maybe a nice framed picture above the settee by the door. I'll think about it."

"Well, you did a wonderful job decorating the loft in New York City, so I'm sure this place will look even more beautiful when you're finished with it."

Ground Floor Layout – Street Level Entry

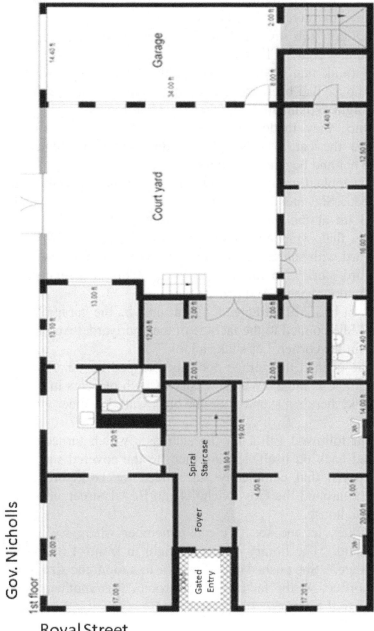

"To be truthful, there's not much to do on the upper two floors. Down here though, is another story. It's pretty sparse compared to the rest of the house."

"Didn't Bob say this level was used as servant quarters and laundry area?" Elliot asked.

"I think that's what he said, although he also said the entire house had been broken up into apartments at one time. That might explain all the kitchens and bathrooms."

Once they made their way into the courtyard, Elliot released the cat, who simply sat down quite contentedly beside her and began to clean herself.

Lia looked around the courtyard. "I'm glad the rain has stopped." She stood in the middle of the open space and looked up at the building. There were outdoor patios and porches that wrapped around the inside perimeter of the courtyard with staircases that led down from both the second and third stories, to the ground level. "This is a relatively large outdoor space. And private too."

"Not bad," Elliot agreed. "That must be the garage over there." She pointed to the far side of the courtyard. "And I see a door in the corner. Let's take a look."

She opened the garage door and stepped inside. "Wow. This garage is huge. We can easily fit both our cars in here. Oh, look, there's a stairway on the back wall. I wonder where it leads."

Lia followed Elliot up the staircase, which turned and doubled back on itself, leading them to the covered second-story porch that completely surrounded the courtyard and wrapped around the Gov. Nicholls and Royal Street sides of the main house.

"Okay, let me see if I can remember where we are," Elliot said. "The library should be right in front of us, over the garage." She pushed open the door to a room the size of a small office. At the far end of that room, was another door that led to the library.

2nd Floor Layout – Main Living Area

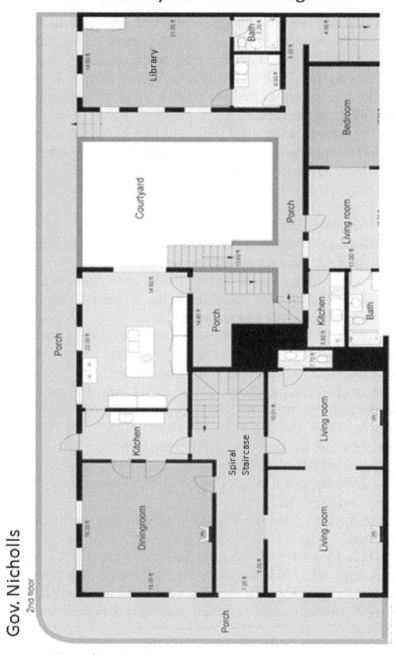

Gov. Nicholls
2nd floor

Royal Street

They entered the library to see hundreds, if not thousands of books lining the walls. "I am so going to enjoy this room," Lia said. "I know where I'll be spending most of my time. And look, there's even a powder room in the corner."

"Moving on..." Elliot led Lia back onto the porch and around the courtyard to find yet another small apartment that overlooked the courtyard.

"I'm amazed with all of the small living quarters we've seen so far throughout the house," Lia said. "There's room for maybe three apartments on the first level, plus this one."

"They were probably servant quarters at one time," Elliot said.

"That makes sense."

Elliot took Lia's hand. "Let's go see what's through that door," she said, pointing toward the far end of the porch.

It turned out to lead them directly into the kitchen. Beyond the kitchen, they found the butler's pantry which led to the dining room they had visited earlier.

Across the hall from the dining room was a large living room and parlor, both decorated in dark, texture-rich, masculine colors. The living room contained cream-colored cashmere chairs and a scarlet-colored velvet sofa. The mantel over the fireplace was a thick slab of black, polished marble. A powder room was also found at one end of the room. They ended their tour of the second level in the hallway.

"I just love how this house has a sexy French feel to it," Lia said. "I suppose that's not an accident, considering we're in the French Quarter."

"Okay, let's fetch the luggage and head upstairs," Elliot suggested."

Three trips later, all the luggage was on the floor of the master bedroom. Elliot threw herself on the huge four-poster bed. She looked around at the claret-colored lacquered walls and the Victorian furniture and felt like she had died and gone to heaven. "I'm beat."

Lia put her last bag on the floor. "Really? Are you that out of shape? You're younger than me, and I'm not tired at all."

Elliot sat up quickly and grabbed Lia's arm, pulling her onto the bed beside her. "Come here, woman."

Lia laughed and rolled over to lie directly on top of Elliot. "Before you get any big ideas, I want to see the rest of the house, and then we need to get ready for dinner."

"Geez, Louise!" Elliot complained. "All right, I'm up." She climbed off the bed. "Where do you want to start?"

"How about in the hall?"

"Okay, come with me." Elliot took Lia's hand and led her into the hall. "As you know, that bedroom over there belongs to the cat, although, I suppose Marissa and Julie can use it when they visit. As you also already know, there's an adjoining bathroom off that bedroom."

Lia kissed Elliot on the nose. "You're such a cute tour guide."

"Keep that up and this tour will be a lot shorter than you think."

"Sorry. Lead on."

Elliot led Lia through a doorway in the corner of the hall and down another short hallway to a much smaller guest bedroom, painted in cream and white, which also had an en-suite bathroom. That bedroom led to a porch with a balcony that overlooked the courtyard. The balcony connected to another covered porch that ran down the entire length of the master bedroom suite and to the same stairway in the far corner of the building that led from the garage to the second level.

After inspecting the stairway, Lia and Elliot turned to walk back down the porch, but stopped abruptly when they encountered a door with a padlock on it, right across from the stairway. The room was located directly atop the library.

"I wonder what's in there," Lia said.

Elliot lifted the lock and inspected it. "Good question. I'll have to see if one of the keys Bob left fits this lock. I guess we'll come back to see this room later."

3rd Floor Layout – Bedroom Area

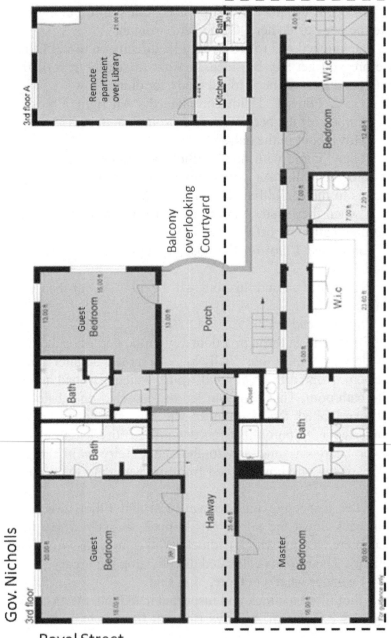

A short way farther down the porch, Lia and Elliot reentered the master suite and strolled into a small bedroom with a walk-in closet.

"I wonder what this bedroom is for. It's kind of odd to have a second bedroom in the master suite," Elliot said.

"I assume it would have been a nursery, but I think it's the perfect place for you to sleep when you're in the dog house," Lia joked.

"Ha-ha, very funny. Seriously, what would we use this room for?"

"We *could* use it as a yoga room, or maybe an office. It has its own bathroom too, so it could even be used for a guest room. Surely, we'll think of *some* use for it," Lia replied.

"I guess. If I remember right, this hallway leads past a walk-in closet and into our bathroom, which in turn, leads back into our bedroom," Elliot said.

"I believe it does. Let's check it out."

* * *

Elliot lay on her back on their bed, with Lia tucked firmly into her side. "That was a nice tour. Thanks for taking the time to go through it with me. When we saw it for the first time, we were so rushed to get out of here before the next client came that I really didn't have time to inspect everything as thoroughly as I wanted to. Overall, I'm pretty impressed with how well maintained this place was—especially considering it had been empty for so long."

"We still need to get into that locked room," Lia reminded her.

Elliot sat up. "That's right. I almost forgot about that. I'm going to run down to the kitchen and grab the keys Bob left. Hopefully, there's one there that will unlock that door. I'll be right back."

Lia stood over Elliot's shoulder, patiently watching as Elliot tried multiple keys in the lock. None of them worked.

"What the hell?" Elliot exclaimed. "Now, why wouldn't we be given the key to this lock?"

"Maybe we should call Bob," Lia suggested.

"Good idea. Do you still have his card?"

"It's in my purse. I'll get it."

Moments later, Lia returned with card in hand. She pulled her cell phone out of her pocket and dialed Bob's number. "Bob, this is Lia Purvis."

"Ms. Purvis. Is everything all right?"

"I hope so. Bob, we discovered a room that's padlocked, and we don't seem to have a key for it. We were hoping you might have it."

"I'm sorry, Ms. Purvis, but I left all the keys I had for the property on the kitchen table."

"That's too bad. I was hoping maybe your firm was using this room for storage while showing the house and that you had the key."

"No, ma'am. I'd recommend cutting the bolt."

"All right then. Thank you for your time." Lia disconnected the call and looked at Elliot.

"No luck, huh?" Elliot said. "I guess we need to find a bolt cutter. I'm going to take a look in the garage. Hopefully, they left tools behind as well as all the other stuff in the house."

"I'll wait for you right here," Lia said.

Lia sat down on the floor and leaned her back against the wall opposite the locked door. Before long, the cat joined her, climbing into her lap and purring loudly.

"Hey there, Miss Thing." Lia scratched under the cat's chin. "What 'cha doing, huh? Have you come for a visit?"

Before long, Elliot returned with a large bolt cutter. "We're in luck. "I found a toolbox full of tools in the cabinet beside the stairs. I don't know about you, but I feel like someone left here in a hurry, not caring that they left valuable stuff behind."

Lia pushed the cat off her lap and stood. "Will that cut the padlock?" she asked.

"It should. Here goes nothing." Elliot cleanly ripped through the padlock with only minor effort. "Bingo."

Lia looked at Elliot with excitement in her eyes. "I feel like we're opening a present."

"Me too." Elliot reached for the door knob.

Suddenly, the cat, who had been weaving in and out around their legs, began to growl.

Lia frowned. "I wonder what's wrong with her."

"Beats the hell out of me." Elliot opened the door a crack.

The cat began to hiss loudly.

Elliot gently nudged the cat with her foot. "What's up with you? Scat. Get out of here if you can't be civil. Sheesh." She looked at Lia. "Are you ready?"

Lia nodded.

Elliot pushed the door full open.

The cat hissed once more and ran away.

The room was dark. Elliot flipped the light switch just inside the door, illuminating a small kitchen. They exchanged expectant looks, and walked into the room.

"We've got our work cut out for us in here." Lia ran her finger across the counter top, leaving a distinct path in the dust. "I don't remember seeing this on the floor plan, do you?"

"No I don't. I wonder why the door was locked." Elliot. opened and closed several of the cupboard doors, revealing dishes and old canned goods.

"Look," Lia said, "there's even dirty dishes in the sink. You're right it feels as though someone left in a hurry. This is just plain creepy."

"I would have to agree with you on that one, my love. I assume that door leads into the living area." Elliot indicated a door to the left of the refrigerator. She opened the door and was immediately hit by an overpowering odor of decay.

"Oh, my God. What is that smell?" Lia exclaimed.

"You stay here. I'm going to take a look."

While Elliot inspected the other room, Lia waited impatiently in the kitchen, pacing back and forth. Finally, she decided to brave the situation and have a look for herself. She threw the door open, marched directly into the room, and stopped dead three feet inside the door.

Suddenly and completely incapacitated, she was glued to the spot and unable to turn, run, walk away or even scream. Her eyes darted back and forth. Her vision blurred and dizziness overtook her. She began to hyperventilate and gasp for breath.

"Lia, are you okay?" Elliot came out of the small bathroom and grabbed her arms. "Lia, talk to me."

Lia's gaze met Elliot's. "Elliot," she whispered before losing consciousness.

CHAPTER 9

"Lia? Come on, baby, open your eyes." Elliot repositioned the cold cloth on Lia's forehead.

Lia's eyes fluttered. "What happened?"

"You fainted. How do you feel?"

"I fainted? Why don't I remember that?"

"What do you remember, Lia?"

"I...I remember being impatient while I waited for you in the apartment kitchen. What took you so long?"

"I found the source of the smell and I was trying to put it into a plastic bag I found in the bathroom."

"The smell. I forgot about that. What was it?"

"A dead rat. It apparently got trapped in there. I looked all around for a place it could have gotten into the apartment, but I couldn't find any."

Elliot helped Lia sit up. She looked around and realized they were on the porch.

Elliot noticed her confusion. "I had to drag you out of there. I didn't want to be in the middle of that stench for any longer than we had to be."

Lia reached her arm forward. "Help me stand."

"Of course." Elliot helped her to her feet. "Are you okay?"

"I think so."

"Lia, I want you to see a doctor and get this fainting issue checked out. Maybe you're having problems with your blood pressure or something."

"I'm fine."

"No, you're not fine. Someone doesn't pass out for no good reason. I want you to see a doctor. You're due soon for a checkup anyway, aren't you?"

"Okay. I'll go while you're in New York. All right?"

"Promise?"

"Yes, I promise."

"Thank you." Elliot took Lia into her arms and held her close. "I don't know what I would do if I lost you."

Lia placed her palm on the side of Elliot's face. "You're not going to lose me. You're stuck with me till the end of time. But thank you for being concerned about me, love."

"Always."

* * *

"We're going to have to buy more hangers." Elliot grabbed the last two from the clothes bar in the closet.

"We have tons of hangers in New York," Lia replied.

"Yes we do, but they're not doing us much good here. I think there's a convenience store on Bourbon Street. I'll run over and pick up a few so we can get the rest of our luggage unpacked. Do you want to come with me?"

"No, you go ahead. I'll put the rest of the folded clothes away while you're gone."

Elliot pulled Lia into her arms. "Will you be okay while I'm gone?"

"No need to worry about me. I think I was just overpowered by that smell in the apartment. Go. I'll be fine."

"Okay. I'll be back soon." Elliot kissed her and then left her to her task.

Lia watched Elliot go and turned her attention back to the clothes. After several trips between the luggage on the bed and the two bureaus in the room, she finally had all the folded clothing stowed away. As she organized the remaining shirts, slacks and dresses that needed to be hung, she glanced into the mirror and saw a movement in the hallway outside their bedroom.

After recovering from momentary, startled inaction, Lia went into the hallway and cautiously looked around. As expected, she didn't see anything or anyone. As she turned to walk back toward the bedroom, she heard a scurry of footfalls coming from the spiral staircase, followed by what she was sure, was the sound of a child giggling.

She moved rapidly toward the stairs and peered down all three stories. "Who's there?" she called. She listened intently for the response that didn't come. "Hello?" Again, there was no response. *Must have been my imagination.* When she started back to her bedroom, she caught a movement out of the corner of her eye. She looked over the railing once more and saw the cat running down the stairs. "No way. How did she get in here again?" Lia whispered aloud.

She returned to the bedroom and searched through the dresser drawers until she found clean sheets for the queen-sized four-poster bed. By the time she finished making the bed, Elliot returned.

"Lia, are you still up there?" Elliot called from the first-floor landing.

Lia walked to the spiral staircase and looked over the railing. She could see Elliot on the landing below. "Yes, I am. We need to freshen up before dinner. Are you coming up?"

"Actually, if you don't mind coming down here, there's someone I'd like you to meet."

Lia descended the staircase and joined Elliot on the first floor. There in the foyer was an elderly black gentleman.

"Lia, this is Samuel McGinty. Samuel says his great-grandmother..." She looked toward him.

"Great-great-great-great-grandmother, ma'am," Samuel said.

Elliot turned back to Lia. "Yes, of course. His great-great-great-great-grandmother was the cook in this house in the eighteen thirties."

Lia's eyes grew wide. "Seriously? She was the cook here when...when..."

"Yes, ma'am. When that she-devil was the mistress here."

"Oh, my." Lia's body trembled and she reached out to Elliot for support.

Elliot's arm immediately went around Lia's waist. "Are you okay?"

Lia's eyes teared as she stared at Samuel. "I'm so sorry."

Samuel had yet to break eye contact with Lia. "No need to be sorry, ma'am," he said. "You ain't done nothin' wrong."

"I know, but…but…"

Samuel took Lia's hand between his calloused ones. "But nothing. This old soul know a pure heart when he see one. No need to apologize for a past you be no part of. I just wanted to let you know Lia be a good girl. She a bit of a mischief maker, but she don't mean no harm."

Elliot frowned. "What do you mean by that?"

Samuel nodded in Lia's direction. "Miss Lia know what I mean." Samuel put his hat on and reached once more for Lia's hand. He kissed the back of it and looked her directly in the eyes. Lia's heart caught in her throat when she saw the depth of emotion and meaning in his eyes.

"Good day to you both." Samuel turned toward the door.

"Wait," Elliot said. "You can't just walk away. I want to know what you meant by that."

Lia grabbed Elliot's arm. "Let him go, love."

* * *

After the door close behind Samuel, Elliot turned sharply toward Lia. "What the hell was that all about?"

"We need to get ready for dinner," Lia said.

"I'm not going anywhere until you tell me what happened just now."

"I'm not sure I understand it myself. How did you happen upon him anyway?"

"He was waiting outside the door when I got back from the store. He apparently found out this house had new owners and wanted to let me know he had blood ties to this place."

"Had or has?"

"What the hell does that mean?"

"The ties are still here."

"What? I'm in no mood for fun and games."

"Oh, this is far from fun and games."

Elliot ran a hand through her hair and walked a few feet away. Then she turned and faced Lia. "Whatever he meant, I hope we've seen the last of him. He's a little creepy if you ask me."

Lia seemed deep in thought as she stared at the door.

"Lia?"

She snapped out of her reverie. "Huh?"

"How about we blow this joint and get some dinner?" Elliot suggested.

Lia smiled broadly. "That sounds like a wonderful plan, love. Let me change my clothes and we can head out."

"I'll join you. I've got to hang the rest of the clothes anyway, since I went to the trouble of going after these hangers." Elliot picked up the bag of hangers from the settee where she had put them when she arrived home.

As they climbed the stairs to the third floor, Lia placed her hand on Elliot's arm and said, "By the way, Miss Thing has found her way into the house again."

* * *

"Elliot, what do you think about Samuel?" Lia asked over dinner.

"I don't know what to make of him. A lot of people who have lived their whole lives in New Orleans have very strong convictions and they form spiritual connections to things and places for generations. I'm sure some pretty horrid stories were passed down through the years from his ancestors."

"If only a fraction of what we've read about the house is true, horrid is hardly an adequate word," Lia said.

"We knew that going into this, Lia. And like Julie said, any stately house in New Orleans is bound to have a connection to slavery. Unfortunately, brutality by slave owners was pretty commonplace."

Lia contemplated her napkin for a moment or two before turning her attention back to Elliot. "Do you think it's possible for spirits or souls, to linger behind after death?"

Elliot sat back in her seat. "Are you serious? You're a scientist. You know ninety-nine percent of all paranormal events have some kind of scientific explanation behind them."

"It's the one percent I'm concerned about."

Elliot narrowed her eyes. "Want to tell me what's behind your question? Did something happen in the house to make you wonder about these things?"

Again, Lia toyed with her napkin without making eye contact with Elliot.

"Lia?"

"I was making our bed while you were gone to the store, and in the mirror, I saw a movement behind me. Then I heard the sound of footfalls like bare feet on the marble stairs, and I heard faint giggling. I ran to the railing to see who it was, and all I saw was Miss Thing running down the stairs. I'm sure it was just the cat I saw in the mirror, or just my imagination."

"It's an old house, Lia, and one we're unfamiliar with. I'm sure we'll hear all kinds of creaks and groans over the next several months."

"You're probably right."

Elliot reached across the table to take Lia's hand. "I'm concerned about you."

"How so?"

"Like I said earlier, you've passed out inside that house twice, and we don't know why. That concerns me. A lot."

"Please don't worry about me, El. I said I'd see a doctor about it. I'm sure the first time was caused by excitement over seeing the house, and today's event…well, the smell in that apartment was enough to 'gag a maggot,' as my mother would say. I'm sure it's nothing to be concerned about."

"That reminds me, I still need to call someone about cleaning that apartment," Elliot said.

CHAPTER 10

One week later—Friday

Lia supervised as the contractor put the finishing touches on the sheetrock work in the master bathroom, after running supply and drain lines for the new washing machine and dryer that were scheduled to be installed the next day. Elliot had yet to return home from work.

"Okay, Ms. Purvis. It's ready for paint. Are you sure you don't want my guys to do that for you?" the contractor said.

"No, Jim, that's okay. I'm kind of looking forward to doing it myself."

"All right. I'll tell the office they can submit the invoice right away then."

"Sounds like a plan. Thank you for doing such a wonderful job."

"You're welcome, ma'am."

"Let me walk you to the door."

Lia led Jim through the master bedroom, into the hallway, and down both flights of stairs to the ground level.

"That's quite a hike. I can see why you wanted to move the laundry upstairs from this level."

Lia and Jim stood in the front foyer. An awkward silence fell between them.

"Is there anything else?" Lia asked.

"I was just wondering if you've seen or heard anything odd in this place since you moved in."

"Odd? What do you mean?"

"You gotta know it's haunted. I mean, everyone knows it."

"How so? Has there been any proof?"

"There's all kinds of reports of ghosts and voices. Heck, when I was a kid, it was a rite of passage to spend the night in this place. It was empty then, and my friends and I dared each other to stick it out for one night. If you didn't, you were considered a candy-ass."

Lia crossed her arms and grinned. "Really? And did you make it through the entire night?"

Jim stood up tall. "Yes, ma'am, I did."

"And did you hear or see anything odd that night?"

Jim chuckled. "Can't say as I did, ma'am. I was only thirteen and scared out of my wits, but I gained some creds with my peeps for doing it."

"Well, Jim, I'm a scientist, and there's very little I attribute to the supernatural, and very little about the noises old houses make that scares me. So far we're enjoying our new home, quirks and all."

"If you don't mind me asking, ma'am, how long have you been here?"

"One week today."

Jim tipped his cap back and extended his hand. "Well, I hope you continue to be happy in your new home. It was nice meeting you, ma'am."

"Likewise. I'll keep you in mind if we need additional work done."

"Thank, you, ma'am."

Lia let Jim out the main entrance, then reentered the foyer and closed the door. When she turned to face the staircase, she gasped. She could have sworn she saw a small child standing in the doorway to the room at her right. By the time she did a double-take, the child was gone.

"What the hell?"

Lia entered through the doorway the child was standing in and walked into the adjoining room. As suspected, there was no one there. Oddly, the curtains she had opened the day before were closed. "That's strange," she said and opened them again.

She moved farther through the ground floor and into the vestibule that led to the courtyard. She saw no one. Once in the courtyard, she looked up and scanned the second and third-story porches, ending with the balcony outside the master suite.

"Oh, my God." She gasped as the child appeared on the balcony.

"Lia, are you home?"

"I'm in the courtyard," she called out.

Elliot appeared on the second-story porch, just off the kitchen, and directly below the balcony outside the master suite. "Hey, you," she said. "Are you enjoying this beautiful weather?"

Lia continued to look at the balcony above Elliot's head. "Actually, this is the first time I've been out all day. The contractor just left."

Elliot leaned over the railing and peered above her head. "What are you looking it?"

"I thought I saw something on the balcony."

"Really? Let me change my clothes, and I'll go out and take a look."

"Give me a minute and I'll join you."

While Elliot changed her clothes, Lia walked to the far end of the courtyard and used the corner stairway to climb to the third floor. She exited onto the porch in front of the previously locked apartment over the library. As she passed by the door, a strange chill came over her, despite it being nearly ninety-four degrees. She paused and totally against her will, reached for the doorknob. That is, until she heard Elliot's voice from the balcony.

"You were right, Lia. There was something on the balcony. Miss Thing." Elliot held the cat up for her to see from across the courtyard.

"Miss Thing," Lia said under her breath. "Why is it, more often than not, you show up whenever there's something odd happening in the house?" Lia took one more look at the door leading into the apartment and then made her way around the porch toward Elliot.

* * *

"Sorry, fellas, but its two floors up, and no elevator," Elliot said as she directed the appliance movers into the foyer.

Elliot spent the next hour supervising the movers as they transported first the washing machine, then the dryer, into the master bathroom and hooked them up.

Just as they completed these tasks, Lia appeared with four tall glasses of iced tea. "Here you go, guys. Take a break. You've earned it."

Within minutes, the movers consumed their teas and wished them a good day as they moved on to their next delivery. Elliot saw them to the door and returned to the bathroom to admire their new purchases with Lia.

"You did a nice job painting that wall," Elliot said.

"It was no big deal. It's just paint."

Elliot took Lia into her arms. "Yes, it's just paint, but it looks great, and I appreciate your efforts. Now, how about a kiss on this fine Saturday morning?"

After a long, sensuous kiss, Lia nuzzled her face into Elliot's neck. "Hmmm, this feels good. I'm going to hate seeing you go back to New York on Monday."

"It'll only be for a couple of weeks. Someone's got to supervise the packing, and you start your new job in two days, so, tag, I'm it."

"Marissa said she's already shown the loft to four couples, and she expects to have an offer from one of them soon. It will be good to get that monkey off our backs. Leaving most of the furniture behind is a definite bonus for the buyer, and we certainly don't need it here."

"All the more reason for me to go there next week. It will have to be done sooner or later anyway. Besides, it will be nice to have our personal stuff around us again. It should make this place feel more like home," Elliot suggested.

"It's great that Marissa and Julie are going to follow you back in my car. I can't wait to see them again."

"It's only been two weeks since we left, Lia. It's not that long since you've seen them."

"True, but we've been used to seeing them whenever we want, and knowing we can't do that anymore makes me homesick for them."

"We'll have them here for about a week. We'll need to make sure we show them the town before they leave."

"Actually, I think we should ask Julie to show *us* the town, since she grew up here," Lia said. "Hopefully, she'll have time to visit with her family while she's here."

"You're right. I'd forgotten about that. What do you want to do for the rest of the afternoon?"

"Why don't we go to the aquarium? It's been awhile since we've had a play day. I understand there's an IMAX theater there as well."

Elliot stepped back and swept her arm forward. "Marvelous, idea. Lead the way, m'lady."

* * *

Elliot unlocked the door and pushed it open for Lia to enter. "I'll be in right after I lock the gate for the night," she said.

Lia entered the foyer and waited for Elliot, and they ascended the steps holding hands.

"I had a really nice afternoon, Elliot. Thank you."

"You're welcome. I'm glad you suggested the aquarium. It felt great just to relax and enjoy an afternoon unencumbered."

"Dinner was great too. I forgot how much I love Bubba Gump's."

They stopped at the landing on the second floor.

"How about I grab a bottle of wine and a couple of glasses, and we soak in the tub for a while?" Elliot suggested.

Lia smiled. "You read my mind."

"Go on ahead. I'll be right up."

"Run, Forrest, Run!" Lia quipped.

"Smart-ass," Elliot replied over her shoulder as she walked toward the kitchen.

* * *

"I can't believe we drank two whole bottles of wine." Lia chuckled as she flopped down, naked, onto the bed.

Elliot threw herself onto the bed beside Lia. "I can't believe I ran wet and naked through the house to fetch the second bottle."

"Run, Forrest, Run!" Lia teased for the second time that evening before bursting out in giggles.

"Keep that up and I'll give you a run for your money, sweetheart."

"Run, Forrest, R...ummm." Lia was silenced by Elliot's tongue invading the depths of her mouth.

Elliot lay completely on top of Lia, pinning her to the bed. The feel of skin on skin, as well as the probing kiss, stirred a need so great in the pit of Elliot's core that she pressed herself hard into Lia and deepened the kiss.

Suddenly, Elliot found herself on her back. The move was so forceful that she literally flew to the edge of the bed and nearly toppled over the side. The next she knew, she was dragged back to the center of the bed by her ankles and straddled by the dark-skinned beauty above her.

Elliot looked up at Lia and was immediately turned on by the intensity on Lia's face and how her curly, black mane of hair fell in total disarray around her head. Elliot allowed her hands to roam up Lia's legs, to her hips and buttocks.

Lia suddenly placed her hands on Elliot's shoulders and pushed them hard into the mattress beneath her. Lia's face was only a short few inches from her own.

"Ou vle mwen ta dwe fuck ou, fanm deyò?" (Do you want I should fuck you, mistress?) Lia asked in a strange language.

"I...I don't understand," Elliot said.

Lia grabbed Elliot by the chin. "Si se plezi ou, mwen gen aswè a jennès ou." (If it be your pleasure, I be your whore tonight.)

Elliot furrowed her brow and looked up helplessly at Lia. Elliot remembered from her research that many people in this area, especially the slaves, spoke Haitian Creole years ago, and some people still do, and she wondered if that was what Lia was speaking.

Lia shifted her weight to one side and moved her hand down between Elliot's legs. Her deft fingers slid into Elliot's wet folds.

Elliot's hips began to rise and fall in rhythm with Lia's fingers.

"Ou tankou sa yo, pa fè sa ou, fanm deyò?" (You like that, don't you, mistress?) "Celeste sa a konnen ki jan yo dwe fè yon fanm santi bon, repons lan se wi?" (Celeste knows how to be making a woman feel good, yes?)

Elliot grabbed Lia's wrist with one hand to still the motion while cupping her cheek with the palm of her other hand. "Lia, I can't understand what you're saying. Please speak in English."

Lia sat up and frowned at Elliot. In thick, accented English, she said, "Lia be dead. She be but a child, and she be dead. Do you fancy children, mistress?"

"Lia, this isn't funny anymore. Stop it right now."

"You want Lia? I be Lia for tonight. I be Lia for you, mistress. To be safe, Celeste do what mistress wants." Lia once again began to administer to Elliot, sliding her fingers between Elliot's folds and suckling on Elliot's breasts.

Elliot couldn't resist the tender way Lia was making love to her. *I see what you're doing, my love. It's been awhile since we've role-played. You want to play? Then we'll play.* Elliot stopped fighting the passion brewing in her core. She at first gave in to Lia's caresses, and then encouraged them. Soon, a powerful orgasm ripped through her abdomen and plunged her nearly into unconsciousness.

Sometime later, Elliot felt Lia draw circles around her left nipple, igniting the flames once more. She opened her eyes and looked directly at Lia, who was smiling down on her.

"De mistress be happy?" Lia asked.

"The mistress be very happy." Elliot gathered Lia into her arms and returned the favor twofold.

Before long, exhausted, but fully sated, they fell asleep in each other's arms.

* * *

The next morning, Lia awoke early and looked at the woman sleeping beside her. A powerful surge of love filled her heart as she thanked the gods above for that fateful day in Starbucks twenty-two years earlier.

Lia gently kissed Elliot on the cheek and climbed out of bed. *Damn, I'm sore this morning,* she thought as she stretched. *A nice hot shower will fix that.*

Moments later, she stepped into the shower and reveled in the feel of the hot water cascading over her. She methodically washed herself, beginning with her face and working downward. When she slipped the soapy cloth between her legs, she paused and wondered why she felt tender between her legs. *Did we make love last night?*

Lia finished her shower and stood in front of the mirror with her bathrobe on and her hair wrapped in a towel. She was applying moisturizing cream to her face when Elliot came in to use the facilities.

When Elliot was finished, she washed her hands and then kissed Lia on the cheek. "Good morning, love."

"Good morning to you."

"How does coffee sound?" Elliot asked.

"Wonderful."

"I'll be back in a jiff." Elliot moved toward the door, only to stop and look back at her wife. "Last night was amazing. I didn't know you could speak Creole."

Lia looked at her, confused. "I can't speak Creole. Where did you get that idea?"

Elliot placed her hands on her hips. "You can't speak Creole?"

"No. It's based on French, right? I was horrible at French in school."

"Are you sure?"

"Elliot. Listen to me. I. Cannot. Speak. Creole. How many times do I have to tell you?"

"Then who the hell did I make love to last night?"

"So we did make love?"

"Son of a bitch. You don't remember making love last night?"

"No, I don't. I kind of figured it out in the shower this morning, but I have no memory of it."

"Well, I'll be damned. What exactly do you remember about last night?"

"I remember soaking in the tub with you, and polishing off two bottles of wine. And I remember climbing into bed, but after that, my next memory is of waking up beside you this morning."

Lia watched Elliot pace awhile longer before she stepped into her path, and stopped her short. "Sweetheart, talk to me. What happened last night that I don't remember?"

Elliot sat on the bed, her hands shoved deep into the pockets of her robe. "Like you said, we climbed into bed after drinking two bottles of wine. You were tipsy. We both were, but I never would have guessed you were so drunk you wouldn't remember things the next day."

"So, what happened?" Lia asked.

"We began to make love. I was lying on top of you, kissing you, when all of a sudden, I was on my back and you had turned into a different person."

Lia's eyebrows took up residence high on her forehead. "What do you mean?"

"For starters, you were talking in Creole. At least I think that's what it was. I couldn't understand most of what you said, but I got the gist of it based on what you were doing to me. You completely took over the lovemaking. And you kept calling me, mistress."

Lia sat down next to Elliot. "Why can't I remember that?"

"Maybe it was the wine. We did go through two bottles."

"Maybe," Lia said, not truly convincing either one of them.

Elliot took Lia's hand in hers. "Maybe I should put off the trip to New York."

"There's no need to do that. Marissa and Julie have arranged time off from their jobs to help us. Not to mention the time the university is giving you to do this. We can't reschedule it at this late date. No. You will get on that plane to New York tomorrow morning as planned."

"Lia—"

"No. You're going to New York tomorrow. End of discussion."

CHAPTER 11

Monday

Lia dropped Elliot off at the airport at six-thirty the next morning, and headed to work after they promised each other they would stay in contact throughout the day.

Lia became engrossed in her research project nearly as soon as she arrived at the Cancer Institute. After meeting her new colleagues, she sat through a two-hour kickoff meeting and then immediately got to work on her portion of the genomic testing. At nearly noon, she emerged from the lab for the first time and went to her office. She checked her cell phone for incoming messages, and noticed Elliot had called four times. She keyed in Elliot's number and waited for her to answer. She didn't have to wait long.

"Jesus, Lia, I've been scared to death here," Elliot exclaimed.

"I'm sorry. I left my phone in my office. The lab has next to no signal." Lia listened to a prolonged silence on the other end of the line. "Elliot?"

Elliot cleared her throat. "I was worried about you. I've never not been able to reach you before. Considering the crap that's been going on in the house, I was afraid for you."

"Sweetie, I'm fine. As far as what's 'going on in the house,' I think we're both a little jittery about being in a new place and our imaginations are working overtime. You said so yourself yesterday."

"You're probably right. So, how's your first day on the job going?"

"Great so far. I met the team this morning in a two-hour meeting in which we were each assigned our piece of the project. I've been working on it ever since. It's only day one, but if things continue to go like today has, I think I'm really going to enjoy this job. How about you? How was your flight?"

"Right on time. Marissa collected me from the airport and brought me home. She should be here any minute to pick me up. We're meeting Julie for lunch."

"How's the loft?"

"A little dusty, but otherwise fine. I've been looking around and didn't realize just how much packing there is to do. You never really know how much stuff you have until you have to touch each piece. Thank God the movers will do most of the packing for us."

"So the plan is for the three of you to head south in about a week?"

"That's what I'm guessing at this point. The movers aren't even scheduled to show up for several days yet. In the meantime, I'll pack up our valuables so they ride home in the car with me. Once everything we're taking is in boxes and I've made sure it all gets into the moving van, we'll be on our way. The movers have a couple of other stops to make along the way, so they'll be a few days behind us. My best guess is that it will be early next week before we're on the road."

"Did you remember the list of things I want to make sure you grab?" Lia asked.

"Yes, I did. Essentially, it's everything except the larger pieces of furniture."

"That pretty much sums it up."

"Okay then, love. I'm glad things are going well for you today. I expect to hear all about it when I get home. Marissa should be waiting outside by now, so I'd better get going before the traffic cops ticket her for being double-parked."

"All right, love. Have a good lunch and hug the girls for me. Tell them I can't wait to see them next week."

"I will. Why don't you call me tonight when you get home?" Elliot said.

"Okay. I love you."

"I love you too. Bye."

* * *

"So how's Lia?" Marissa asked after they placed their drink orders.

"She seems to be fine. She started her new job today, and judging by her comments this morning, she's pretty excited about this new project," Elliot replied. "By the way, she sends her love to both of you and says she's looking forward to seeing you next week."

"And the new house?" Julie said. "How do you like it?"

"The house is amazing for the most part. You'll see for yourselves next week."

"For the most part?" Marissa asked. "What does that mean?"

Elliot kept her eyes trained on the menu as she replied. "It means that we're still getting used to its quirks."

"Quirks?" Julie said.

"Yeah, you know, the unfamiliar noises and things like that. It is an amazingly large house. Our whole loft could fit in just one of the three levels."

"Have you seen any ghosts yet?" Julie asked.

"Jules!" Marissa frowned at her. "You promised you wouldn't bring that up."

"I can't help it. We're about to live in this house for several days, Marissa. There are countless reports of ghost sightings there. How can I not ask about it?"

Marissa turned her attention to Elliot. "Have you?"

"Have I what?"

"You know damned well what I'm asking," Marissa said. "Have you seen any ghosts?"

"You know I don't believe in such things," Elliot said.

"So nothing odd has happened in the time you've been there?" Julie asked.

"I didn't say that."

Marissa closed her menu and put it on the table. Her eyes were wide with excitement. "Spill it."

"It's nothing, really. Just a few odd sounds. A window opening by itself. Drapes closing themselves. Nothing harmful."

"Did you actually see the windows and drapes moving on their own?" Julie asked.

"No. It was always after the fact. I'm sure there's a perfectly logical explanation for it," Elliot said.

"And none of that spooks you?" Marissa asked.

"Not really. I'm more spooked by Lia's fainting than I am about things that go bump in the night."

"Lia fainted? You never told us that," Marissa said.

"In the twenty-two years I've known her, she has never fainted, at least not in my presence. But since we've been here, she's fainted twice."

Julie sat back in her chair. "This is not good, Elliot."

"She's promised to go see a doctor about it while I'm here. I'm sure it's nothing but the excitement of buying the house. And maybe the heat and humidity. New Orleans is a far cry from New York City, after all."

"That's possible," Marissa said.

"It's more than possible. It's probable," Elliot said.

"Well, I don't like it. Has anything else happened?" Julie asked.

"Miss Thing."

"Miss Thing? Who the hell is Miss Thing?" Marissa asked.

"The cat."

"A little more detail would be good," Julie said.

"Miss Thing is a cat who has apparently adopted us, and by the looks of it, she's pretty much lived in the house for a while. We can't seem to get rid of her."

"Is she a nice cat?"

"Yes, she is. She's taken a shine to Lia."

"Maybe that's not a bad thing," Marissa said.

"Maybe," Elliot agreed. "She's a little stinker. There's been a few times when she's appeared out of nowhere and startled Lia. Lia even thought she heard footsteps on the staircase and when she went to investigate, all she saw was the cat."

Julie picked up her coffee and sipped it. "Outside of the fainting, it all sounds relatively harmless. As least no one is talking in tongues," she joked.

Elliot frowned at her.

"What's the frown for?" Marissa asked.

Elliot looked at her friend. "Marissa, you've known Lia for a long time, right?"

"Yes, ever since grade school. Why?"

"Do you know if she's bilingual? Does she speak any language beside English?"

"Not that I know of. Elliot, you've known her for more than two decades. Don't you think you would have heard her speak in a language other than English by now?" Marissa replied.

"One would think so, Marissa. One would think so."

"I sense a story behind that question. Wanna share?" Julie asked.

Elliot shrugged. "You'll think I'm nuts."

"Cross my heart and hope to die, I won't," Julie promised.

"Well, Lia and I had a little too much wine while soaking in the tub Saturday night and we were quite tipsy when we went to bed—"

"Wine and tub, huh? That sounds like a recipe for good sex," Marissa interjected.

"The sex was amazing," Elliot admitted, "but I'm not sure Lia was really present."

"What the hell does that mean?" Julie asked.

"She kind of turned into another person. She became really aggressive and started talking in Creole."

"Let me guess. She said she doesn't speak Creole," Marissa pointed out.

Elliot nodded. "That's what she said."

Julie stood and started to pace. "I don't like this one bit."

"What it is, Jules?" Marissa asked.

Julie stopped and put her hand on Elliot's shoulder. "Was her behavior like, totally different than normal?"

"Very different. She called herself Celeste. I convinced myself that she was role-playing so I played along. Like I said, the sex was great. It was pretty wild in fact, but the next morning, Lia didn't remember any of it."

"Are you serious?" Marissa asked.

"I'm dead serious."

"Don't' use the word dead, Elliot. It's in pretty poor taste here," Julie said.

"What are you implying, Julie?" Elliot asked.

"I'm implying there might have been something supernatural at work."

CHAPTER 12

Tuesday

Lia tucked the hospital gown under her legs and stared at her sock-clad feet while she waited for the doctor to enter a few notes into her computer.

"Your file says you're from New York," the doctor said.

Lia's gaze rose to meet the doctor's eyes. "New York City."

"And you've been here how long?"

"Three weeks."

"The temperature and humidity in New Orleans are at least ten points higher than in New York. The combination of higher temperatures and higher humidity can cause you to dehydrate. Have you been drinking more water since you've been here?"

"No more than usual."

"Ms. Purvis, your vital signs are good. Your heart and lungs sound fine, and you appear to be carrying around a healthy amount of weight. For all intents and purposes, you're the picture of health. We'll do some blood work in the event there's something going on behind the scenes, but I can see no clinical reason for you fainting other than the change in climate and lack of hydration."

The doctor typed a few more notes on her laptop, and stood. "Go ahead and get dressed. I've put an order in to the on-site lab for blood work. When you're finished dressing, open the door and the nurse will escort you to the lab. Do you have any more questions for me?"

Lia shook her head. "Not really. Like I said earlier, I feel fine."

"Okay then. We'll send the results to your home as soon as they come in. If the tests warrant it, we'll schedule a follow-up appointment. Otherwise, I want you to drink a minimum of eight glasses of water per day." The doctor looked at her laptop once more. "Just let me verify we have your address. 1140 Roy..." The doctor's voice faltered. "I'm sorry. 1140 Royal Street. Is that correct?"

"Yes, that's correct," Lia replied.

A deep scowl crossed the doctor's features. She closed the laptop, picked it up, and walked out the door.

* * *

Lia stopped by the grocery store on the way home, making it nearly dinnertime when she pulled the rental car into the open space in front of the mansion. She walked around the car, retrieved the two bags of groceries from the front passenger seat, and closed and locked the car door. As she faced the building, she immediately noticed that the drapes in the first-level room were closed again. "What the hell?" she murmured under her breath.

She put the grocery bags down on the sidewalk in front of the iron gate in order to fish the keys out of her purse to unlock the gate. She moved the bags to inside the entryway, relocked the gate, and picked the bags up again. As soon as turned toward the main door, she realized she had to unlock that door as well. Putting the bags down a third time, she unlocked the main door and once again collected the bags. *Elliot, we need that garage door opener sooner rather than later. This is a pain in the ass.*

Grasping both bags of groceries in one hand, she turned the handle and pushed the door, only to meet resistance.

Seriously?

She pushed harder, to no avail. "God damn it. Open up," she growled out loud.

Finally, she put the groceries down again and tried her key in the lock once more, turning it both ways to re-lock and then unlock it a second time. "You'd better work this time," she warned as she turned the handle with one hand and pushed with the other.

With a tremendous amount of effort, she managed to open the door about an inch before it slammed shut again. By this time, a bead of sweat had formed on her brow and a headache began to pound in her temples.

A sudden rage overtook her. She threw her weight against the door and screamed, "Bondye andige, manman mèrdik, pitit yon femèl chen—louvri!" (God damned, mother-fucking, son of a bitch—open!)

* * *

Lia bolted awake, disoriented and searched around for her phone. She found it inside her purse which was sitting on the table beside her bed. "Hello?" she said into the receiver.

"Lia? It's about damned time you answered your phone. Where were you? I've been out of my mind with worry!"

Lia looked around the darkened room, and then realized she was still completely dressed. "Elliot? What time is it?"

"Nearly ten o'clock."

Lia could hear Elliot sobbing on the other end of the phone. "Elliot, sweetie, why are you crying?"

"Why am I crying? I've been trying to call you for the past three hours. The last thing I knew, you were going to see the doctor after work. I've been calling and calling, and no answer. All kinds of things ran through my mind. I even called the hospital to see if you were admitted."

"You did? Elliot, I'm fine. The doctor thinks the fainting was due to dehydration."

"Where have you been? Why didn't you call me?"

"I don't know. I stopped at the grocery store, and when I got home, I had a hard time opening the front door. That's the last thing I remember before the phone woke me up."

"I wonder if you fainted again."

"I guess that's possible, but I don't remember it."

"Where are you now?"

"In bed. Fully clothed, mind you, but in bed."

"And you don't remember getting there?"

"No. I was trying to open the front door, but it must have been stuck. I remember becoming really angry about it and feeling hot and headachy. But it's a blank after that, until your call woke me up."

"I want you to go down to the kitchen right now and drink some water. Do you hear me? Do it now, and take me with you," Elliot insisted.

"Okay." Lia swung her legs over the side of the bed and stood. She sat right back down again as dizziness overtook her. She moaned slightly and held her head.

"Lia? Are you okay?" Elliot said through the phone.

"I'm a little dizzy, but okay."

"I'm catching the next plane home."

"Don't be foolish. I'm just dehydrated. You don't need to come home early just to see that I drink water. I'll be fine. I stood up too fast, that's all."

"What else did the doctor say?"

Lia slowly rose to her feet and shuffled across the room toward the bathroom, all the while holding the cell phone to her ear. "She said I was in good shape, that all my vital signs were good. She took some blood, but she's pretty sure it's just dehydration." She reached the bathroom sink and turned on the water.

"What's that noise?" Elliot asked.

"I'm in the bathroom, getting a drink of water, Ms. Worry-wart."

"Good. Sit on the toilet and drink several cups until the dizziness passes. God, Lia. I really want to come home."

"Don't you dare. By the time you get here, all of this will have passed and you'd just have to turn around and go back to New York. I'll be fine."

"Promise me you'll take better care of yourself."

"Believe me, I've learned my lesson. From this point on, I will drink so much water, I'll have to learn the location of every public bathroom in New Orleans."

Elliot blew her nose. "Damn, I hate crying. Nothing comes of it except a stuffy nose and red blotches all over my face."

"Everything will be okay. Thank you for loving me."

"You don't have to thank me. I can't help myself. Are you feeling better now that you've had some water?"

"Actually, I do."

"Okay, sleep will do you some good as well, so why don't you take me to bed with you so I can say goodnight."

* * *

Lia hung up the call and placed her phone on the bedside table. She lay on her back with her head nested in her downy pillow and smiled into the darkness. *You are such a worry-wart, my love. I'm so lucky to have someone who loves me like you do.*

As she lay there, she thought back to the struggle she had with the door. What was up with that? She didn't remember it ever opening that hard. It was almost as though someone was holding it closed from inside. Why didn't she remember getting into the house, or putting herself to bed?

Lia suddenly sat up. "The groceries!" she said out loud.

Swinging her legs over the side of the bed, she turned on her bedside lamp. She stood up and grabbed her robe off the hook in the bathroom. Hurrying down both flights of stairs to the foyer, she opened the front door, fully expecting to see her two bags of groceries still sitting inside the gated entryway. She was surprised to find it empty.

Where were they? she thought. She bet someone noticed them, fished them out of the entryway through the bars and was now enjoying her cheese and crackers, and her bottle of wine.

Lia closed and locked the door and climbed the first set of stairs to the main living area. When she reached the second floor landing, she glanced toward the kitchen and decided to grab a bottle of water to bring upstairs.

She made her way through the butler's pantry and into the kitchen. She flicked the light switch on as she entered the kitchen, and stopped dead in her tracks. There on the marble island was a small platter with the sliced and partially eaten cheese and crackers she had purchased earlier, as well as the half-empty bottle of wine and two stemmed wineglasses with small amounts of wine in the bottom of them.

Lia's hand immediately flew up to cover her mouth and the other hand held onto the door frame for support. After a moment or two, she regained her composure and rushed into the room. She checked the refrigerator and cupboards for the remaining grocery items she had purchased. All of the items were neatly stowed away as if she had put them there herself.

She closed the refrigerator, leaned her back against it, and looked again at the plate of food on the island. It was then she realized there were two wineglasses.

What was going on here? she thought. Lia picked up the wineglasses and examined them closely. There was red lipstick along the rim of one of the glasses.

Suddenly, a loud crash came from the porch outside the kitchen door. Startled, she nearly dropped the glasses. She placed the glasses carefully on the island, reached into the drawer in front of her, and pulled out a large butcher knife.

"Who's there?" She slowly approached the door and listened carefully for a response. "I said, who's there?"

Once in front of the door, she reached for the knob. The door was locked. Her normal routine was to make the rounds of the house before bed to lock the doors and windows, but having found herself in bed earlier, with no recollection of how she got there, she wasn't sure the house was secure. Finding the kitchen door locked was a relief. She stood next to the door and pushed the curtain aside to see who was on her porch. Unfortunately, she couldn't see anything in the dark.

As she reached for the switch to the porch light, a dark object jumped from the floor of the porch to the window sill she was standing in front of. The motion was so quick and unexpected, she screamed. It took her a few moments to realize her intruder was the cat.

Lia's hands shook as she put the knife down on the countertop and opened the door to let the cat in. The cat immediately began to do figure eights around and between her feet, rubbing against her shins, and purring loudly.

Lia closed and locked the door and scooped the cat into her arms. "Miss Thing, you scared the daylights out of me. Was that you making all that ruckus on the porch?" She scratched the cat under its chin for a few moments and put her on the floor. "You can come with me if you want, but I need to make sure the house is locked up before hitting the sheets."

Lia made her rounds of all three stories, beginning with the ground floor, turning lights on and off as she entered and left each room. She ended on the third story, walking down the hall beyond her bathroom to verify the door leading from the smaller bedroom onto the porch was also locked. As she locked that door, she looked out the window and gasped. A light shone from under the door of the previously locked room, diagonally across the porch.

"Oh, my God. Someone's in there," she whispered hoarsely.

She ran back through the hall, through her bathroom and into her bedroom, where she grabbed her phone and called 911.

* * *

Lia waited in the foyer on the first level for the police. She unlocked the iron gate after they arrived and climbed out of their cruiser. "Thank you for coming, officers," she said as she let them in.

"That's what we're here for, ma'am," one officer said. "So what seems to be the problem?"

"I think I might have an intruder in my house."

"An intruder? Ma'am, if you really believe you have an intruder, you should have gotten out of the house," the older officer said.

Lia looked at the name tag above his pocket. "I'm sorry, Officer Nash. What I meant to say, is that the intruder might be in a room on the other side of the porch. It can only be accessed by going outside the main house. I've locked all the windows and doors so he can't get in here."

"Ma'am, locks only keep honest people out," Officer Nash said sarcastically.

The younger officer stepped in. "Ma'am, I'm Officer Rocque. Could I have your name?"

"Lia. Lia Purvis."

"Are you here alone, Ms. Purvis?" Officer Rocque asked.

"Right now, I am. Normally, my wife is home, but she's on a trip to New York right now."

If Officer Rocque's interest was piqued by her relationship status, he didn't show it. "Okay, Ms. Purvis. Why don't you show us this room you're concerned about?"

"All right. Follow me."

Lia led the officers up both stories to the third floor, through her bedroom and bathroom and down the hall toward the smaller bedroom in the back of the house.

Lia held the curtain aside. "There. Across the porch. See the light coming from under the door?" she said.

"What's in that room?" Officer Nash asked.

"Nothing. It was an apartment at one time, but it's empty right now."

Officer Nash drew his weapon from the holster on his hip. "Let's go check it out."

Officers Nash and Rocque cautiously approached the room with weapons drawn, while Lia stood a safe distance away in the doorway of the bedroom. Officer Rocque stood on one side of the doorway while Officer Nash stood on the other and reached for the doorknob.

"On the count of three," Nash said. "One, two, three."

Both officers disappeared into the room. After several moments, Lia tentatively closed the distance between her and the open door. When she reached it, she stood outside. She could see through the kitchen and into the living room beyond. The lights were on in both rooms.

"Officer Rocque?" she called out.

"All clear," she heard Officer Nash say.

Moments later, both officers reentered the kitchen area.

"There's no one in there," Officer Rocque said.

"Nothing but a lot of stink," Officer Nash added. "It smells like something—or someone—died in there. Go see for yourself."

Lia backed away several feet, feeling terrified. "No. I don't think I will."

Officer Rocque stepped onto the porch and rubbed his hand on her upper arm. "Hey, are you all right? You're as white as a ghost."

"Um, I'm fine. There's no one in there?"

"No one. Whoever used that room last must have left the lights on," Officer Nash said.

"That's funny. We've been in this house for more than a week and haven't noticed it before. It's possible Elliot's been in there. I'll have to ask her. I'm sorry to have called you here for nothing, officers."

"Better to be safe than sorry," Officer Rocque said. "And besides, it broke up an otherwise dull evening."

"If you don't mind, could you close that door for me? I'd appreciate it."

Officer Rocque frowned. "Are you sure you're okay? What is it about that room you don't like?"

"Nothing, really. I'm fine. Really, I am."

"Well, if you see or hear anything else, don't hesitate to call us."

"I will, Officer Rocque. Thank you for your concern. Unless there's something else you need to do, I'll see you out."

CHAPTER 13

Wednesday

The next morning, Lia finished her coffee and bagel and carried her dish and cup to the sink to rinse them before putting them into the dishwasher. She noticed the two wineglasses still in the sink from the night before.

The cat rubbed up against her legs and meowed for attention.

"Why do you suppose there are two glasses, Miss Thing? I can understand there being one, even though I don't remember drinking from it last night. I really need to drink more water. These blackouts are beginning to concern me."

Lia rinsed her dishes and both wineglasses, and put them into the dishwasher, then she bent to lift the cat from the floor. "Sheesh, you weigh a ton. Someone's feeding you well." Lia opened the kitchen door and stepped onto the porch. "Sorry, little one, but you need to go outside while I'm at work."

Still holding the cat in her arms, she walked over to the railing and looked directly across the courtyard at the library. Above the library was the apartment. Her eyes were drawn to the windows of the apartment that faced the courtyard. She replayed the conversation with the police officers from the night before. She recalled Officer Nash saying, "It smells like something—or someone—died in there."

The cat began to fidget in her arms, a low growl emitting from deep within the animal.

"Hey, what's up with you?" Lia said.

The growl turned into a deep and menacing howl as the cat's hackles rose.

"If you're going to act like that, you can just get down."

Lia put the cat down on the porch and watched as it walked sideways, back hunched high, until it encountered the wall of the house. All through this, Lia noticed that the cat stared at the building across the courtyard. She looked at the cat and then at the library. "What is your problem?" she asked. "Look, there's nothing there."

Lia attempted to pick the cat up once more, but it hissed and ran down the staircase to the lower level.

"If you feel that way about it, you're on your own." Lia stood erect. "I wonder what spooked her?" she mumbled under her breath.

She looked again at the library and convinced herself there was nothing there to be afraid of. Unable to resist, her gaze was drawn once more to the apartment above.

Ice shot through her veins.

A figure stood in the window with its hands pressed against the pane and a blank expression on its face.

"Oh, my God." Lia ran into the kitchen and locked the door. She was shaking like a leaf as she pulled back the curtain to look once more. This time, there was nothing to be seen.

Was it her imagination? The words haunted her. *It smells like something—or—someone died in there.*

* * *

Immediately after work that day, Lia stopped at the hardware store and purchased a padlock. As soon as she arrived home, she went directly to the apartment and secured the padlock in place. Then, she called Elliot.

"Hey, love. How was your day?" Elliot said.

"It started out with a bang, but once I got to work, things were pretty busy."

"Started out with a bang? You didn't black out again, did you?"

Lia could hear the concern in Elliot's voice.

"No, I didn't, but I'm beginning to think there might be some truth to this ghost thing."

"You can't be serious. What happened?"

"After we hung up last night, I remembered that I had put two bags of groceries on the ground in the entryway when I was trying to open the door, and since I woke up in bed with no knowledge of how I got there, I assumed the groceries were still out there, but they weren't."

"They weren't?"

"No. During the blackout, I must have put them away without knowing it, because they were all in the cupboards where they belonged."

"That's odd," Elliot said.

"That's not even the half of it. When I went into the kitchen last night to grab a bottle of water before going back upstairs, I found partially eaten cheese and crackers on the island, along with a half empty bottle of wine and two wineglasses, one of which had red lipstick on it."

"You're creeping me out here, Lia."

"I have no explanation for it. I didn't even wear lipstick yesterday. I bought the wine, cheese, and crackers on my way home from work, so whoever put the groceries away helped themselves to them."

"All of this happened last night?"

"Yes."

"But you said your morning started off with a bang."

"I'll get to that. I'm not finished talking about last night yet."

"There's more?"

"Oh, yeah. I made the rounds to lock all the windows and doors, and when I got to the small bedroom at the end of our suite, I looked out the window and saw a light under the door of the apartment."

"Get the hell out of Dodge!"

"It scared the bejesus out of me, Elliot. I actually called the police, and they came by to check it out. Of course, there was no one in there. Could you have by chance, left the light on when we went in there last week?"

"I guess it's possible. Jesus, Lia. Are you all right?"

"After the police left, I felt a lot better, so I went to bed. When I got up this morning, I ate breakfast and put the cat out onto the porch before leaving for work. When I was on the porch, Miss Thing started spazzing out on me. She was all hunched up and hissing. I had no idea what caused that behavior until I looked up and thought I saw a figure in the window of the apartment."

"Damn it. I'm coming home. Today."

"Slow down, Elliot. The cat had me so spooked, I'm thinking it was only my imagination. After I saw it—or at least thought I saw it—I ran into the house and looked several more times and didn't see anything."

"Maybe it was a mistake buying that house."

"Odd thing is, the house doesn't scare me. I feel safe here, even after finding the wine and cheese last night. And the blackouts don't scare me. I'm pretty sure the doctor's right about the dehydration thing. The apartment, on the other hand, gives me the creeps. I stopped on the way home and bought another padlock. Needless to say, nothing will be going through that door for a while."

"None of this is making me feel good about being away from you."

"You need to take care of this move for us. Now that I've locked that room, I feel better about everything. I know there's probably a logical explanation for all of this and I'm just overreacting."

"You're probably right, but learning that you felt the need to lock that room makes me uncomfortable being away from you."

"So far, nothing bad has happened. Let's just say for a moment that this ghost thing is possible. We've been here for two weeks, and nothing bad has occurred. No one has been hurt. It's just odd things happening in a home we're unfamiliar with. I'm sure things will settle down."

"Lia, promise me, if one more thing scares you, you'll move back into the hotel until I get home."

"Really?"

"Yes, really. Promise me, or I'll be on the road toward home this afternoon."

"Okay, okay. I promise."

* * *

"Mama. Mama, reveye." (Mama. Mama, wake up.)

The woman rolled over in her sleep and brushed the annoyance away.

"Mama. Mama, tanpri reveye. Fanm deyò, li dwe reyèl fache." (Mama. Mama, please wake up. Mistress, she be real mad.)

She opened her eyes and looked directly at the light-skinned girl in front of her. "Ki sa ou t'fè kounye a fache li?" (What did you do now to upset her?)

"Mwen koule atè te li. Mwen pa t'vle di. Tanpri, pa kite l'voye m' anwo kay." (I spilled her tea. I didn't mean to. Please don't let her send me upstairs.)

The woman bolted upright in bed and grabbed the girl's shoulders, drawing her close so that their noses were but a mere inch apart. She shook her firmly.

"Kouman mwen ka kenbe metrès a kontan lè ou aji tankou sa a? Mwen pa ka kenbe ou san danje ak fason neglijans ou yo. Mwen prostitue tèt mwen kenbe ou nou tou de an sekirite nan baton yo. Ou pa konprann sa? Si konpòtman sa a ap kontinye, mwen gen dwa pa kapab yo sispann li." (How can I keep the mistress happy when you act like this? I cannot keep you safe with your careless ways. I prostitute myself to keep us both safe from the beatings. Do you not understand that? If this behavior continues, I may not be able to stop her.)

"Mwen regrèt sa, Mama. Mwen eseye yo dwe bon, depi koulye a. Mwen te pwomèt mwen pral." (I'm sorry, Mama. I try to be good from now on. I promise I will.)

A movement at the far end of the room drew her attention away from the little girl. Her eyes grew wide with fear.

"Fanm deyò. Li se men yon timoun. Tanpri padonnen li," (Mistress. She is but a child. Please forgive her.) she begged when she saw the whip in the woman's hand.

The mistress approached the bed, causing the child to scurry for cover in the corner nearest the bed. She raised her arm and hit the woman across the face with the backside of her hand. "How many times have I told you to speak English when you address me, Negress whore?"

The woman climbed to her knees and held her hands together as if in prayer, her chin tucked low against her chest, her breathing labored as she struggled not to cry. "I am sorry, mistress. I will try harder next time."

The mistress grabbed her by the chin and forced her to look at her. "What you need to try harder at, Celeste, is disciplining your bastard child. She is evil and wicked."

"She is but a child, mistress. She means no harm. Please allow me to punish her for you."

The mistress released Celeste's chin. "No. No, I think this calls for more drastic measures. I think you need to bear the burden of her insolence."

Celeste lowered her chin to her chest once more. "If you wish, mistress."

The mistress walked to the other side of the bed. She mercilessly lashed the whip across Celeste's back no fewer than ten times. The child curled into a fetal position in the corner and stifled her own cries behind her hands. When the mistress finished, fine dots of blood appeared through the thin muslin material of Celeste's nightdress.

"I hope you've learned a lesson, Celeste. That child of yours is a bastard, not worthy of breathing the air I so generously provide by allowing her to live here. She is the very bane of my existence. Learn to control her, or more of the same, or worse, will befall both of you."

The mistress reached for the door handle, her back to Celeste. "I expect to see you in my room in one hour, and you'd better pray to your heathen god that you don't disappoint me."

"Yes, mistress."

"No!" Lia sat up quickly, unable to catch her breath. She jumped out of bed, tore off her nightshirt, and ran to the bathroom. She turned the light on just inside the door, stood in front of the full-length mirror mounted on the wall, and looked over her shoulder at her back, only to find an expanse of unblemished, mocha-colored smoothness stretched over soft curves.

Shakily, she walked over to the toilet, sat on the cover, and rubbed her palms over her face. "It seemed so real," she mumbled softly. Her thoughts turned to the child cowering in the corner while her mother was being beaten. Tears ran down her cheeks as her heart broke for the little girl.

After her breathing returned to normal, she stood and faced the bathroom mirror. "You need to get a grip, Lia. It was only a dream," she said to her reflection. She picked up the cup on the side of the sink and drew herself a glass of water, which she drank thirstily. She then returned to the bedroom and picked up her nightshirt from the floor where she had dropped it.

As she slipped the nightshirt over her head, a soft sound came from somewhere within the room. She strained in vain to see through the darkness and reached for the pull-string on the bedside lamp. As soon as the light flooded the room, she saw the source of the noise. In the corner nearest the bed, curled up in a ball, was the cat.

CHAPTER 14

Thursday

The next morning, Lia stood at the railing on the porch outside the kitchen, sipping her coffee. The cat sat on the floor beside her. She scanned the windows of the buildings surrounding the courtyard and thought about what it might have been like one-hundred and eighty-four years earlier.

"If walls could talk, I'll bet this house could tell one hell of a story, Miss Thing," she said to the cat. "I'm sure that dream I had last night came purely from my imagination, but from what I've read about this place, it's probably not too far off the mark." She scanned the buildings once more. "I wonder where the torture took place."

The ringing of her phone abruptly interrupted Lia's thoughts. She fished it out of her pocket and looked at the screen. Elliot. "Good morning, my love," she said.

"Good morning to you too," Elliot replied. "Did you sleep well last night?"

"More or less."

"Care to elaborate?"

"I had a disturbing dream, but I was able to fall back to sleep afterwards. Other than that, I slept pretty well."

"What kind of dream?"

"It was about the little girl. You know, the one named Lia. She had apparently angered the mistress of the house and ran to her mother for protection. In the end, the mother was punished instead of the child."

"That was an odd dream."

"Yes, it was. It was so real. I could almost feel the whip on Celeste's back."

"Did you say, Celeste?" Elliot said, a serious tone tingeing her voice.

"Yes. That was the mother's name."

"Holy shit."

"What is it?"

"The other night, when we made love, when I thought you were role playing and talking Creole—"

"Elliot, I've already told you I don't speak Creole."

"I know. I know. But during our lovemaking, you referred to yourself as Celeste."

"No I didn't. I think I would have remembered if I had," Lia said defensively.

"I swear you did. This is really freaking me out. What did Celeste look like?"

"What do you mean?"

"What did she look like? It's an easy question, Lia."

"She was a black woman."

"A black woman? That's the only description you have?"

"Surely, after twenty-two years together, you know what a black woman looks like, Elliot."

"My point exactly. She looked like you—didn't she?"

Lia fell silent while she contemplated Elliot's comment. *She did look like me. I'll be damned.*

"Your silence says it all, Lia. I think it's time you move back into the hotel, at least until I get home."

"No, I don't think so. I said I would go if something scared me. I wasn't scared last night. It was a dream, that's all. It was disturbing. That much I'll admit, but I wasn't scared."

"Lia—"

"Look, Elliot, it's late and I need to get to work. We can discuss this further when I get home this evening, okay?"

* * *

Lia arrived at the lab early enough to go through her e-mail before the rest of her co-workers showed up. She was shutting down her computer when one such co-worker stopped by her office.

"We're heading into the lab. Are you coming?"

"Good morning, Claire. Give me a minute, and I'll be right behind you."

Claire sat in the chair beside Lia's desk. "I don't mind waiting," she said.

Lia felt Claire staring at her.

"Is there a problem?" Lia asked.

"No. I was just thinking you look tired today."

"Yes, I am tired. I had a very odd dream that woke me up in the middle of the night."

"Odd, in what way?"

"It was set in the eighteen-thirties, and it involved a slave woman."

Claire narrowed her eyes. "Slave woman? You didn't cast yourself in the leading role, did you?"

"As a matter of fact, I did. I guess I'm just too sensitive to the history of the house we just purchased. It has a connection to slavery."

"Most of the older houses in this town do. Where did you buy?"

"Royal Street."

"Seriously? It wouldn't happen to be on the corner of Royal and Governor Nicholls, would it?"

"Yes, it is. You know of it?"

"Who doesn't? Jesus. No wonder you're having nightmares."

"What exactly does that mean?"

"You've got to know it's the most haunted house in New Orleans."

"You don't really believe in ghosts, do you?"

Claire stood. "Let's just say I'm open-minded about it. What about you?"

"I tend to believe there's a logical explanation for almost anything."

"Almost?"

"Even I have to admit there are some things that are difficult to explain with science."

"Knowledge of the unknown chases away the fears. I recommend you visit the New Orleans Chamber of

Commerce on your way home and do some research on your home. I guarantee you'll find some clues there."

Lia closed the cover to her laptop and pushed her chair back. "I just might do that. Thanks, Claire."

"You're welcome. Now on your feet, woman. We have a job to do."

* * *

Lia spent two hours at the Chamber of Commerce after work. By the time she'd completed her research, she had several photocopies of stories and accounts of the people who had lived in her home throughout the eighteen-hundreds. When she left, it was late in the day, so she made additional stops for a small pizza and a bottle of dessert wine before heading home. She was met at the front gated entrance by the cat.

"Hey, little one," she said as she unlocked the gate. She slid her key into the lock of the entryway door and turned it. The door opened easily.

The cat followed her into the foyer where she put her handbag, computer bag, keys, and purchases on the table just inside the entrance. She relocked the door then picked the cat up and scratched her behind her ears.

"I wish I knew your real name, Miss Thing. You're so fat, you obviously belong to someone. I wonder if they miss you when you spend the nights here with me."

After a few more cuddles, Lia put the cat on the floor. "Time for dinner and homework." She picked up the pizza, wine, and reading material, and after making the rounds to assure all the doors and windows were locked, she headed to her bedroom on the third story. She sat on her bed and made herself comfortable, leaning against the headboard. The cat jumped onto the bed and curled up in a ball on Elliot's pillow.

"Make yourself at home, why don't you?" Lia chuckled.

She grabbed a slice of pizza and picked up the documents she had photocopied. "Okay, what do we have here?" she mused out loud as she sorted through the reference material. "This looks interesting, Miss Thing. According to a local radiologist who was often a guest at this house, there were strange events that happened regularly in this home. Things like footsteps on the stairway leading to the attic, voices in the guest bedrooms, and sounds of movement in attic spaces. It also says the attic stairs are located near one of the upstairs bathrooms. That's funny. I don't remember seeing stairs to the attic. And we certainly didn't tour the attic space when we came to look at the house. There are five bathrooms on this level. I wonder which one these alleged stairs are near? Maybe we should do some exploring this weekend."

Lia continued to read. "Jesus Christ, Miss Thing, listen to this. 'While taking a cigarette break on the balcony overlooking the courtyard, the owner and a guest heard children laughing, accompanied by the sound of feet running over the courtyard bricks. Rumor has it that what they heard was the sound of ghostly children who had died in the house.' I wonder if the footsteps I heard on the spiral staircase the other day are related."

The more Lia read, the more fascinated she became with her new home. At one point, she put the package of research material aside and climbed off the bed. The cat awoke abruptly from her nap and cried inquisitively.

"Don't worry, little girl. I'll be back. I need to get my computer from the foyer so I can take some notes. Wait right here."

Lia walked toward the door with the cat right behind her.

"Okay, so don't wait right here," Lia said as the cat followed her into the hall.

The first thing Lia noticed as she stepped into the hall was that it was already dark outside. She walked to the window at the end of the hall that faced Royal Street and looked out into the night. It seemed the city never slept. That much it had in common with her former hometown. She looked up and down the street from the third-story window and observed people sitting on stoops and visiting their neighbors. It brought a measure of comfort to her heart to see such normalcy in the neighborhood.

While she scanned the street, her gaze stopped at the corner, directly across the narrow street from her home. Startled, she saw Samuel standing under the streetlight and staring intensely at her as she stood in the window. When she made eye contact with him, he tipped his hat to her, and sauntered away.

Lia ran down both flights of stairs to the first-level foyer, where she flung open the door and threw herself against the bars in the gated entry. "Samuel!" she called.

Samuel, who had walked nearly a half-block by that point, stopped and turned to face her.

"Samuel, please come back. I need to talk to you," Lia said.

Samuel slowly made his way toward 1140 Royal Street and crossed the road to stand on the sidewalk directly in front of Lia. "Not much to talk about, Miss Lia."

Feeling safe and protected by the iron bars separating them, Lia confronted him. "Why were you staring at me, Samuel? Do you do this often?"

"Near every night, Miss Lia."

"Why?"

"Just lookin' in on you."

"I don't need looking in on. What you're doing borders on stalking."

"Don't mean no harm. Just makin' sure you be okay."

"Why wouldn't I be okay? I get the distinct feeling you know something you're not telling me."

"I just knows you was called home. I knows it and Lia knows it, and if you listens to your heart, you knows it too."

"What in God's name are you talking about?"

"They needs you, Miss Lia. They needs you to set them free."

"Who needs me? Samuel, you're not making any sense."

"Listen to Lia. She knows."

"Samuel, Lia was a child who died one hundred and eighty years ago."

"Lia knows. That's all I gots to say. Good night to you, Miss Lia." Samuel turned and walked away once more.

"Damn it, Samuel. Come back here," Lia demanded, but the old gentleman continued to walk down Royal Street and didn't look back.

Lia stomped back into the foyer, shut the door, and locked it. The cat was sitting in the same doorway she thought she'd seen the little girl in just before Elliot left for New York.

"Come on, Miss Thing. Let's head back upstairs," she said as she bent to scoop the cat up.

The cat had other intentions as she scurried into the darkened room. Lia followed her, turning on lights as she followed the cat deeper into the first level. Finally, the cat stopped at the door that exited into the courtyard and began to scratch at the doorframe.

"Stop that. You'll damage the woodwork, silly thing." Lia opened the door and let the cat out. She closed the door and flicked on the outside light, illuminating a large area of the courtyard. She watched through the window as the cat ran to the center of the courtyard and began furiously digging at the ground.

Lia threw the door open and stepped into the courtyard. "Hey! Stop that. What's wrong with you tonight?"

The cat looked up at her, hissed, and ran away just as the door slammed behind Lia.

Startled, Lia swung around. She saw nothing out of the ordinary, except the door that she had just swung open was now closed. She stepped tentatively forward and reached for the door handle. It opened easily. She quickly scurried inside and shut and locked the door. After giving it some thought, she decided she must have flung the door open harder than she intended and it bounced back and closed after hitting the wall.

Lia scanned the courtyard once more to see if the cat was still lingering. Satisfied that it had probably gone home to its owners, she shut the light off. The courtyard fell into darkness, save a beam of light coming from the locked, third-story apartment above the library.

"That light is on again! How can that be? I padlocked that door yesterday." Lia took a deep breath and consciously calmed herself. It must be faulty wiring. The room was locked. There's no other explanation for it. It was probably faulty wiring the first time too, she said to herself.

She returned to the foyer where she climbed both flights of stairs to the bedroom level. She then made her way through her bedroom and bathroom and down the long hallway to the small bedroom that was diagonally across the porch from the locked room. She pulled the curtain aside and looked out the window, fully expecting to see a light emitting from beneath the door of the locked apartment, but there was none.

Lia breathed a sigh of relief as the evidence further convinced her that it was either her imagination, or indeed faulty wiring. As she went back to her bedroom, she made a mental note to call an electrician the following day.

She collected a clean nightshirt from her dresser and took a quick shower before climbing in between the sheets. As she was turning down the bed, she noticed the cat on the ledge outside her bedroom window, which faced Royal Street. Lia walked to the window and opened it to admit her visitor.

"Hey, Miss Thing. Are you ready to be civil now?"

The cat entered through the window, jumped onto the bed, and curled up once more on Elliot's pillow.

Lia grinned at the feline and walked over to close and lock the window. When she did, her attention was drawn once more to the streetlight on the corner across the street. Samuel was again standing there intently staring at her.

CHAPTER 15

"Hey, love, how was your day?" Elliot asked.

"Busy at work. My co-worker Claire recommended I stop at the Chamber of Commerce on the way home today to research our house. I found some pretty interesting stuff." Feeling a sudden chill, Lia pulled the covers up to her chin. "How's the packing going?"

"Slow and boring. Thank God I have Marissa and Julie helping me. The movers are scheduled to arrive on Monday of next week, so if all goes well, the girls and I will be home no later than next Friday, and maybe even on Thursday. I can't wait to get home to you, Lia. I miss you like crazy."

"I miss you too, love. It's been kind of odd being here without you."

"I sense something subliminal in that comment. Has something new happened?"

"Yes, and no."

"Stop being so cryptic."

"I've been thinking about Samuel."

"Why? Did he stop by again today?"

"Yes, and no."

"Lia, please. You're pushing my panic buttons here. Spill it."

"He has apparently been watching the house every night since we moved in."

"Call the police. Call them now."

"I don't think he's dangerous. I actually talked to him tonight. He seems harmless enough, but he talks in riddles."

"He did that the first time we talked to him. What did he say?"

"He's appointed himself guardian over me. He said he watches the house to check on me to be sure I'm okay. He also said something about *they* needing me to set them free, whatever the hell that means. I asked him to explain, but all he said was that Lia knows."

"He sounds like a kook. I want you to report him to the police."

"I will if he becomes threatening."

"I'd rather not wait until he becomes threatening. It might be too late by then."

"Elliot, when have I not been a good judge of character? Please just let me handle it my way, okay? I promise if things get any stranger with him, I'll call the police."

"I'll hold you to that."

"I expect nothing less from you."

"Okay. I know it's getting late and you need to work tomorrow, so I'll say goodnight. I love you, Lia. Sweet dreams."

"Sweet dreams to you as well, Elliot. Love you too. Bye."

Lia hung up her cell phone and put it on the nightstand beside the bed. "Damn, why is it so cold in here all of a sudden?" she whispered out loud before turning out the lights and snuggling deep under the covers.

* * *

Celeste grabbed the arms of the elderly woman hovering over her. "Fè li sispann, Gran. Tanpri, fè li sispann!" (Make it stop, Gran. Please make it stop.)

Gran swabbed the sweat from Celeste's forehead. "Samyèl te ale nan jwenn mèt la. Li se yon doktè. Li pral sou byento, timoun. Li pral sou byento." (Samuel has gone to get the master. He is a doctor. It will be over soon, child. It will be over soon.)

"Ahhh!" Celeste doubled over in pain; her arms wrapped around her swollen abdomen.

Gran pulled Celeste's nightgown up around her waist. "Se konsa, anpil san." (So much blood.)

Celeste grabbed Gran's arm. "Gran, pa kite fanm deyò nan konnen." (Gran, don't let the mistress know.)

"Mwen gen krentif pou li deja konnen, timoun." (I fear she already knows, child.)

Just then, the door burst open, admitting a middle-aged white man, followed by Samuel, who stood against the back wall, a look of fear fixed firmly on his face.

The man set his bag on the end of the bed. "When did this begin?" he asked the elder woman.

"She be like dis for near on twelve hour," Gran replied.

The man swatted Gran across the face with the back of his hand. "Fool! You should have called me sooner. If this child dies, I will hold you personally responsible."

Gran wiped the blood from the corner of her mouth. "We didn't want the mistress should know."

The doctor examined Celeste without directly acknowledging her. "She has lost of a lot of blood. I will do what I can to save the child."

"Please, master. Please don't let Celeste die. The child be needing her."

"Surely one of you could wet-nurse. You breed like rabbits. If she lives through this, it will be a miracle."

Celeste looked back and forth in horror between her grandmother and the doctor as she listened to their exchange. She squeezed the old woman's arm as hard as she could. "Gran, mwen pa ka mouri. Fanm deyò nan ap touye ti bebe mwen an." (Gran, I cannot die. The mistress will kill my baby.)

"What did she say?" the doctor asked curtly.

"She say the mistress will not want the child here," Gran replied.

The doctor ignored her comment as he inserted both hands into Celeste's vagina to turn the child. Celeste screamed loudly as her hips came off the bed.

"Shut her up," the doctor shouted. "If she continues to scream like that, she won't have to worry about dying during childbirth. The mistress will make short work of her afterwards."

"You're hurting her," Gran said.

"The child is breech. If I don't turn it, they'll both die."

Gran turned her attention to Celeste. "Ami, ou dwe eseye yo dwe trankil. Li pral sou byento." (Sweetheart, you must try to be quiet. It will be over soon.)

A low growl began to emerge from deep within Celeste's throat. Gran turned sharply to Samuel who was still pressed against the back wall. "Samyèl, limyè bouji yo ak lansan. Souke cham yo. Ti bebe a ap vini." (Samuel, light the candles and incense. Shake the charms. The baby is coming.)

Samuel did as he was told and then began a low, soothing chant.

"Heathens," the doctor commented. "I'm afraid there's little your gods will be able to do to help."

The growl from Celeste's throat began to escalate.

"Cover her mouth," the doctor ordered.

Gran picked up a piece of rolled up leather from the table beside the bed and placed it between Celeste's teeth. "Celeste, mòde desann sou sa a. Li pral ede ak doulè a. Ou dwe kòm trankil ke posib, renmen m 'yo." (Celeste, bite down on this. It will help with the pain. You must be as quiet as possible, my love.)

"Push!" the doctor ordered.

With all her will, Celeste forced herself to expel the child from her womb before falling back onto the bed and losing consciousness.

A deathly silence fell over the room as the doctor lifted the pale-skinned child from the mounting puddle of blood on the bed between Celeste's legs.

"It's a girl." He cut the cord and handed the child to Gran.

"She be white," Gran whispered before turning to Samuel. "Samyèl, mwen bezwen yon sèvyèt ki pwòp. Byen vit." (Samuel, I need a clean towel. Quickly.)

"Her skin will darken." The doctor wiped the blood from his arms and hands while looking at the child over Gran's shoulder.

"She looks like—" Gran began to say.

"She looks like her mother," the doctor interrupted her. "And if I hear otherwise, there will be hell to pay. Do you understand?"

Gran looked into the doctor's eyes and saw something pitiful there. She saw the look of regret, and self-preservation. "I understand."

The doctor glanced at Celeste, still unconscious on the bed. "You'll have to deliver the placenta and clean her up."

"Will she live?"

"I don't know. She has lost a lot of blood. I suggest you pray to your gods for help. She will need it."

"Thank you, master," Gran said.

"How touching." The voice coming from the doorway drew everyone's attention.

"Mistress," Gran said softly.

Samuel cowered into the corner of the room.

The baby began to cry.

"My dear," the doctor said.

"Don't you dare *my dear* me." The mistress sauntered across the room and looked at the child in Gran's arms. She raised her eyebrows and looked at her husband. "How long did you think you could keep this from me?"

A low moan from the bed saved the doctor from answering the mistress's question.

"Celeste. She be awake," Gran said.

"Gran, ki kote se ti bebe mwen an?" (Gran, where is my baby?)

"Li se isit la, Celeste. Isit la se pitit fi ou yo." (She is here, Celeste. Here is your daughter.) Gran gently laid the child on the bed beside Celeste.

"Yon ti fi? Mwen gen yon pitit fi? Mwen pral non Leya li." (A girl? I have a daughter? I will name her Lia.)

The mistress shoved her husband aside and stepped toward the bed. "Your child is a bastard."

Celeste's eyes opened wide as a wail escaped her throat. "Nooo!"

* * *

Lia bolted upright in bed, clutching her abdomen. She was disoriented by the dream and the pain she was experiencing. She turned the bedside light on and threw back the covers. "God damn it!" she exclaimed as she saw the very large circle of blood she was laying in. "This is great. Just great."

She climbed out of bed and just made it to the bathroom before large clots fell from her body into the toilet. She carefully pulled her soiled nightshirt over her head and threw it in the sink. "This is all I need. Jesus, I hate perimenopause."

Lia sat there for several moments, recalling the dream she had had. She needed to get a grip. Her imagination was running wild. Christ! She was substituting menstrual cramps for childbirth. Maybe doing research on this place wasn't such a good idea. It was giving her nightmares.

After doing her best to clean herself up, Lia stepped into the shower. When she was finished, she put on clean panties, along with protection and a clean nightshirt. She ran cold water over the garment in the sink and returned to the bedroom to take care of the soiled bedding.

Lia stopped short when she entered the bedroom. She could smell incense. "What the hell?" she said out loud as she looked around the room. She stepped into the hall to see if she could detect the smell of something burning. Satisfied that everything was normal, she assumed the odor was coming from outside.

She returned to her bedroom and collected the soiled bedding, thanking the heavens above that she had a waterproof mattress pad on the bed. As she put the bedding into her new washing machine in the bathroom, she could have sworn she heard a baby crying from the small bedroom at the end of the master suite. When she went to investigate, she found the cat sitting by the door that led onto the porch.

"Miss Thing, you sounded just like a baby there for a minute. Do you want to go out?" Lia opened the door for the cat and watched as she ran diagonally across the porch and sat in front of the padlocked door.

"You're wasting your time, girl. There's no one in there," Lia said, just as the lights inside the room suddenly turned on. She could see it coming from under the door, as well as through the windows that overlooked the courtyard. She was frozen in place, unable to move until, just as suddenly, the lights turned off.

Lia let out a breath. "I really need to call an electrician today," she mumbled before closing and relocking the door.

CHAPTER 16

Friday

Lia met the electrician at her home after work and led him to the locked room. She handed him the key then backed away from the door. "Go on in. The light switch is just inside the door," she told him.

The electrician frowned. "You're not coming in with me?"

"No, I'll wait right here."

The electrician unlocked the door and stepped into the kitchen area. He turned on the light and looked around. "It looks like no one has lived in here for a while. Do you know where the breaker box is?"

"Breaker box?"

"Yeah. The main power box for this apartment. It is an apartment, right? Generally each unit has its own breaker panel and electrical meter."

"I'm sorry. I don't know. My wife and I just purchased this home almost three weeks ago, so I'm afraid we're not very familiar with it yet."

"Okay. I guess I'll look around then. Give me a minute." A few minutes later, the electrician exited the apartment. "I found it. It was inside one of the upper cabinets. You said the lights came on in both rooms?"

"Yes. The kitchen and the main living area have windows that overlook the courtyard. I could see light in both rooms from the porch outside the kitchen over there." Lia pointed across the courtyard to the kitchen. As she was explaining the phenomenon to the electrician, she noticed a small pile of dirt in the backyard where the cat had been digging the night before.

"Ma'am?"

"I'm sorry, what did you say?"

"I asked how long the lights were on."

"The first time I noticed them, they had been on for quite some time. Long enough for the New Orleans police to come to the house to investigate. The second time I'm unsure how long they were on before I noticed it. That was last night, actually. This last time, the lights were only on for a minute or so before they went off."

"And when did the last event happen?"

"Close to dawn this morning. I was up letting the cat out when they came on and then went off again all within a minute."

"Well, the switch was off when I came into the room. How about the other times?"

"To be truthful, the first time the lights were on could have been our fault. My wife might have left them on, and the police officers turned them off—that was Monday evening."

"And the next two times?"

"I padlocked the door on Tuesday, and to my knowledge, no one has been in that room since. What could be causing the lights to go on and off when the switch was obviously in the off position?"

"I'd say you have ghosts."

Lia turned ashen at the electrician's words and leaned against the wall for support.

"Whoa, hold on there. Just a little electrician humor. I actually don't believe in ghosts. It's probably a short or an unintended hot connection somewhere. I'll take a look at it and let you know."

"Okay. If you don't mind, I'll wait for you in the kitchen. You can join me there for lemonade when you're finished. Just take the stairway in the corner there, go down one flight, and follow the porch around to the kitchen. And if you don't mind, please padlock the door again when you leave."

"Will do. I'll see you in a few minutes."

Fifteen minutes later, the electrician met Lia in the kitchen. "It looks like I need to replace two breakers and two light switches. The light switches are pretty old and crackled a bit when I flipped them, so that could be the cause of the problem, but to be sure, I'll replace them both, as well as the breakers they're wired to."

"Will that take long?"

"Not really. I carry supplies in my truck, so I should have the parts with me. It will take about a half hour to do all of it."

"Okay. Well, if you have the time to do it today, I'd really appreciate it."

"No problem. Just so you know, it smells pretty bad in the main living area. Just a guess, but it smells like something died in there."

"Yes, I know. My wife found a dead rat in there the day we moved in. We have someone scheduled to come in and disinfect it next week."

"All right then. I'll be back in about a half an hour for that lemonade."

While Lia waited for the electrician to replace the fixtures, she descended the stairway between the second-story porch and the courtyard to inspect the pile of dirt dug up by the cat the night before. In the short amount of time the cat dug, she'd managed to excavate one whole cobblestone. "Now what possessed you to do this, Miss Thing?"

Not wanting to leave a hole in the middle of the courtyard, Lia went in search of a shovel, beginning with an enclosed area under the stairs to the second-level porch that appeared to be a shed. Her intuition was correct, and she found a spade, watering can, rake, shovel, and an array of flower pots, neatly arranged inside the shed. "I know what I'm doing this weekend. I'd say a trip to the local greenhouse is in order," she said as she grabbed the shovel and proceeded to fill in the hole the cat had dug. When she finished, she returned the shovel to the shed and closed the door, just as the electrician appeared on the porch outside the locked room.

"All finished Ms. Purvis," the electrician said as he looked at her over the railing.

"Wonderful. I'll be right up," Lia replied. She ascended the stairs and met him outside the kitchen. "Come in. I've got cold lemonade in the refrigerator."

"Don't mind if I do."

A short time later, Lia let the electrician out the front entrance and locked the iron gate behind him. She returned to the kitchen and put the two lemonade glasses into the dishwasher. "Now, what to have for dinner?" she wondered.

Settling for a small salad and bowl of soup, she quickly prepared her dinner fare, and while the soup warmed in the microwave, she ran up the stairs to her bedroom and retrieved the research material she had collected the day before. She returned to the kitchen, sat on a stool at the kitchen island, and enjoyed her dinner and a glass of wine as she read.

When she finished, she took care of her dishes then stood in the kitchen and stretched the kinks out of her back from sitting hunched over at the island. "I sure could use a more comfortable place to do this reading," she said under her breath. "Of course. Duh, Lia. You have a library, remember?"

She collected her reading material and cell phone, as well as her glass and the rest of her wine, and followed the porch around from the kitchen to the library. She pushed the library door open and immediately felt the welcoming warmth of the richly decorated room. As she stepped into the room, she felt a sense of protection and serenity. As an added measure of security, she locked the door after closing it and settled down into one of the overstuffed, wing-backed chairs positioned in front of the fireplace. She turned on the light that sat on the chair-side table and began to read.

She was about an hour into reading when the phone rang, startling her. "Jesus Christ," she exclaimed as she looked at the caller ID. "Elliot." She pressed the answer button. "Hey, baby."

"Hi, love. Just checking in. How was your day?"

"It started out in the early morning hours with a very unwelcome visitor—Aunt Flo."

"Ugh! Judging by the last few times, I'll bet it was a pretty nasty visit."

"Worse than nasty. Let's just say I had to completely strip the bed. With any luck, it will be like the past couple of times and last only a day or two. Perimenopause is not fun."

"Oh, love, I'm so sorry you have to go through that. I'm not looking forward to the day it happens to me."

"Hopefully it won't be as bad for you. Every woman is different."

"Well, we should be pretty experienced by then. You must have felt horrible at work all day."

"Crampy, to be sure, but I had a supply of painkillers on hand, so it was bearable. The worst part is running to the bathroom nearly every hour. Ugh! What amazes me most though, how my mind can take an event like a menstrual period and turn it into something totally different."

"What do you mean?"

"When I woke up and realized what had happened, I was in the middle of a dream about Celeste—and she had just given birth. She too was lying in a puddle of blood. Odd, don't you think?"

"I'm a little concerned about all these dreams you are having."

"They're just harmless dreams. Though I learned through this last dream is that the master of this house was the father."

"Are you listening to yourself, Lia? You don't know that for sure. Learning something through a dream is not exactly scientific fact checking."

"From what we've already read about this house, we know there was a young girl named Lia who jumped to her death from the roof to escape the mistress's whip. It would make sense that she would hate the little girl if the girl's mother was her husband's mistress, and if the girl was her husband's illegitimate daughter. Don't you think?"

"Yes, I have to admit that it would make sense, but you don't know for sure that this was the case."

"You're right. But it's helping me come to cope with what happened in this house nearly two hundred years ago. There is so much rich history here, Elliot. I can feel it, and the more I learn, the more I'm coming to terms with it."

"I'm just concerned about you, Lia. I don't want to see you hurt in any way. Physically or emotionally."

"I know, sweetie, but like I've already said, I feel safe here. I'm actually beginning to become accustomed to the odd noises, creaks, and groans in this house. The only part of the house that makes me uncomfortable is the locked apartment. Which reminds me, I had an electrician replace a couple of switches and breakers in there this afternoon. The lights went on and off again last night."

"Seriously? The switches were off, weren't they?"

"Yes, but he said they were really old and could have caused an unintended hot connection, whatever that means."

"That makes sense, I suppose. Thank you for taking care of it. That's something I should be doing. If I was home, that is."

"Elliot, you know I don't like falling into the helpless femme role. I can take care of things when I have to."

"I know you can, but it makes me feel good to take care of us. I guess it's the butch in me."

Lia chuckled. "Heaven forbid you lose your butch card!"

"Ditto on that one. So, what are you up to tonight?"

"I'm actually enjoying the library for the first time. This room is amazing. It's so warm and cozy in here. I'm sitting here with my research material and a bottle of wine while talking to my best girl. Doesn't get any better than that. Unless of course, you were here sharing the experience with me."

"I'll be home by this time next week. And I would love to spend time in the library with you. I'm actually excited about browsing that extraordinarily large collection we've inherited. I'll bet some of the books are as old as the house."

Suddenly, a crash came from overhead, causing Lia to jump and let out a scream.

"Lia! Are you okay?"

Lia recovered quickly from her unexpected scare. "I'm fine, Elliot."

"What the hell was that?" Elliot said. "It was loud enough for me to hear over the phone."

"I don't know. Something crashed above my head."

"The locked apartment is over your head."

"I know. Maybe I should go look."

"No. Call the police and ask them to investigate."

"The last time I called them, it was for nothing. I'm not going to do that again. I'm going to investigate. I'll call you back."

"Take me with you."

"Elliot—"

"Don't argue with me."

"All right, all right. I need to go to the kitchen first for the key to the padlock."

Lia made her way to the door of the library and opened it. It was now dark outside. She turned the porch light on outside the library before stepping onto the porch. The light cast just enough glow over the entire courtyard for her to make her way safely around the balcony to the kitchen. She spoke with Elliot along the way.

"Elliot, we need to install a floodlight or, at the very least, a chain of lights on each porch level that will turn on all at once on each of the internal switches. It's kind of inconvenient to have the library detached from the house with no way to light the path between it and the main house adequately."

"That's a great idea, Lia. Maybe you can hire the same guy that installed the switches in the apartment."

"Good suggestion. Okay, I've got the key. I'm going to go through the house so I can turn the porch light on outside the master suite."

A few moments later, Lia stood outside the locked room. "All right. I'm here. I just need to remove the padlock."

"I really wish you'd call the police to do this for you."

"You said you couldn't find any way for that rat to get into the apartment, so unless the electrician locked someone inside, the apartment should be totally empty. There—I've removed the lock. Here goes nothing." Lia pushed the door open and quickly reached inside to turn the light on.

"Lia? Talk to me," Elliot said.

"Humph. It appears the electrician left his step stool behind and it fell over. He also left the door open between the two rooms."

"Question is, who knocked it over?" Elliot asked.

"Ahhh. Oh, my God. You scared the shit out of me." Lia said.

"Lia! What happened?"

"It's the cat. She must have snuck in before the electrician locked the room."

"The cat is still hanging around?"

"I've come to accept that she's adopted us, Elliot. She's been here every day since you've been gone. Ewww, the electrician is right. This room still stinks to high heaven!"

"Close the door between the two rooms. That should minimize the smell in the kitchen area."

"That would require that I go into the apartment. I think I'll just shut off the light and relock this door."

"I scheduled the cleaning service to take care of that next week. Why are you still afraid of going into the apartment, Lia? I've been in there, and it appears the electrician has as well and we're fine."

"I don't know. It really gives me the creeps. I can't explain it."

"Well, at least we understand where the crash came from."

"That we do. Now I can go back to my reading in peace."

"Okay. The girls and I have just knocked off packing, and we're heading out for a late dinner, so I'll let you go. I hope you put in a better night's sleep."

"I do too, but I will have to remake the bed first. Kiss the girls for me and thank them again for all their help. I love you, sweetie, and I hope you have sweet dreams tonight."

"Good night, my love. And don't stay up to late."

"I won't. I love you. Good night."

Lia settled once again into the overstuffed chair in the library with the cat snuggled in beside her. "Okay, Miss Thing. I think we can relax now and enjoy this beautiful room for the next hour or so."

She picked up her reading material from the chair-side table and began to read while sipping her wine. Within a few moments, the cat jumped off the chair and began to pace in front of the fireplace.

"What's up with you, little one?"

The cat continued to pace, a low growl emitting from deep within her.

"You know, this is really getting old."

The cat suddenly stopped pacing and jumped onto the hearth.

"Miss Thing?" Lia said.

The cat hissed and ran to the door of the library just as very distinct footsteps could be heard overhead.

Lia froze. *Did I hear what I just thought I heard? Surely it's just my imagination. That's been happening a lot lately.*

Just as she convinced herself she was hearing things, the cat hissed once more and began clawing at the door.

"Really, Miss Thing?" Lia stood to let the cat out and froze once more as the footsteps returned. "Oh, my God," she whispered. She grabbed her reading material, turned off the light beside the chair, and quickly made her way to the door. The moment she opened it, the cat ran into the night.

She stepped onto the porch and pulled the door closed, then quickly traversed the length of the porch toward the kitchen. Once inside, she locked the door and looked out the window. Half-expecting to see the lights on once again in the apartment, she was surprised to find it totally dark. What the hell was happening here?

CHAPTER 17

Saturday

Lia arose the next morning feeling remarkably refreshed, despite the unexplained events of the night before. Prior to falling asleep, she had convinced herself that if there was indeed something paranormal behind the strange occurrences at the house, they had ample opportunity over the past week to do her harm—but they hadn't.

That morning, she decided to go to the local home-improvement store to purchase hanging baskets for the wrought iron balcony that surrounded the second floor of her home. While there, she talked to the construction specialists about the random noises the house was making. The scientific part of her mind just couldn't let go of a potential real-world explanation for what was happening.

"So the banging could be air in the pipes? Could it sound like footsteps?" she asked a gentleman named Alex.

"It could sound like hammering, banging, and yes, like footsteps if the air pressure came in spurts. Did it happen right after a toilet was flushed or a faucet was turned on?"

"Actually, no, and it was in a part of the house that is more or less isolated from the rest of the living space," Lia explained.

"Do you know if that part of the house shares the same water system as the rest of the house?"

"I would assume so, but I was the only one home and I know I didn't flush the toilet or run water before I heard the footsteps."

"Hmmm. How about the laundry?"

"I did put a load of laundry in the washing machine earlier that morning, but it was more than twelve hours later that I heard the footsteps."

"The part of the house in which you heard the noise is isolated?"

"Yes. It's a good thirty or forty feet from where the washer is, and it's on the next floor down."

"Where did the sound come from?"

"From the ceiling of the library—and before you ask, the rooms above the library are empty."

"And the library is on the floor below the washing machine?"

"Yes."

"Then considering the ceiling of the library is below the floor where the washing machine is, then the pipes are actually on the same level as the washer. I'm not saying air pressure in the pipes caused the footsteps, but there's a very good chance that it did. The fact that the noise happened so far away from the washer could explain the delay."

Lia felt a sense of relief wash over her. "That makes sense. So, how do I stop it from happening again?"

"Call your water service and ask them to shut off the main line going into the house and to drain all the lines. Be sure to open all the faucets in the house and flush all the toilets to allow them to drain before turning the main back on. If there's any trapped air in the lines that should get rid of it."

"I knew there had to be a logical explanation for all of this. Thank you so much, Alex."

When Lia arrived home, she decided to pull the car into the courtyard to unload the flowers rather than carry them through the house. To accomplish this, she parked the car on the Governor Nicholls side of the house but entered in through the front in order to unlock the courtyard from the inside.

She opened the ground-level door that led to the courtyard and stopped in her tracks when she saw a large hole dug in the same location she had caught the cat digging earlier in the week.

"What the hell? Miss Thing, where are you? I can't believe it. It's large enough to drop my front tire into. I'm going to have to bury it before I can pull the car inside. Goddamned cat!"

Twenty minutes later, Lia had filled the hole and set aside the loose cobblestones to be replaced professionally, allowing her to pull the car into the courtyard and close the gates. For the next several hours, she transported flower baskets from the trunk and backseat of the car to the wrap-around porch, arranging them equidistantly along the edges of the railings. It was early afternoon when she finished.

Wanting to see what it looked like from street level, she exited the front gate and stood on the corner diagonal to her home on the opposite side of the street. This afforded her a chance to see both the Governor Nicholls Street and Royal Street views of the house.

"They be even more beautiful when they mature," a voice said from over her shoulder.

Lia swung around and came face-to-face with Samuel.

"Samuel, you scared me!"

"Didn't mean no harm, Miss Lia."

"I really don't appreciate you hanging around my home all the time. I saw you staring at my bedroom window two nights ago."

"Free country, ma'am. Ain't doin' no harm. Just keepin' an eye on things. Has Lia showed you the way, yet?"

"I have no idea what you're talking about, but if you insist on stalking me, I'll have to call the police."

"No, ma'am. Samuel ain't stalking nobody. Ain't doing no harm."

Lia backed up a few feet. "I'm going now. I'd appreciate it if you went home, or where ever else it is you hang out." Lia took several more steps backward before turning and running across the street. When she reached her entryway, she saw Samuel still standing on the corner, staring at her. She quickly locked the iron gate, slipped inside the house, and fastened the foyer door.

* * *

Over a very late lunch, Lia decided to review once more some of the reference material she had already read. Specifically, she was looking for the article that talked about the random noises coming from the attic.

"Now where is that article? I'm really curious if there are any clues about where the attic stairs are," she mused out loud. "Ah, here it is. 'According to a local radiologist who was often a guest at this house, there were strange events that happened regularly in this home. Things like footsteps on the stairway leading to the attic, voices in the guest bedrooms, and sounds of movement in attic spaces. The attic stairs are located near one of the upstairs bathrooms.'"

Lia took a bite of her sandwich. "The trick is determining which of the bathrooms it's near. There are five of them if you count the one in the locked apartment. Heaven knows, if it's in there, I may never set foot in the attic. I don't remember ever seeing a stairway leading above the third floor."

With curiosity getting the better of her, Lia finished her sandwich, cleaned her dishes, and headed upstairs. Rationalizing that the staircase would most likely be against an outer wall, she began her search in the far left guestroom that opened directly onto the balcony overlooking the courtyard. The bathroom in that guestroom was relatively small and sported no clue as to a staircase or a door that might reveal a staircase behind it. The same was true of the front bedroom they had affectionately assigned to the cat the day they arrived. That left the two bathrooms in their master suite and the one inside the locked apartment.

Lia held out hope that the staircase would be near the bathrooms in their master suite. She dreaded the thought of entering the apartment over the library again.

She entered her bathroom and looked around. On her left was the tub. On the right-hand wall were a linen closet, a separate toilet stall and the laundry closet. Directly across from the laundry closet was a double sink with a small window that looked out onto the porch, but no staircase, and no door leading to one, could be seen. She sighed heavily while she stood in front of the sink and looked out the window. She could see clear to the end of the porch to the locked apartment. *I can't do it. I can't go in there. I guess I'll have to give up my search.*

Suddenly, she noticed something that wasn't obvious before. Right outside the bathroom window, the ceiling of the porch slanted down to meet the wall about three feet off the floor.

"Oh, my God. There it is." She gauged where the stairway access might be inside the house. Judging the access to be on the other side of the wall from the double bathroom sink, she ran back through her bedroom and into the hallway. At the end of the hall leading to the smaller guest bedroom was a closet.

For several minutes, Lia paced back and forth in front of the closet door, trying to drum up the courage to open it. Finally, she turned the doorknob and swung the door open.

The closet was empty. It was a space approximately three by five feet with four walls, a ceiling and floor, and multiple shelves that began approximately three feet off the floor and extended to the top of the door opening.

Lia stepped back and frowned. How could that be? There should be a stairway there. The architectural details on the outside of the building support that.

Another idea came to her as she took a shortcut through the smaller guest bedroom and onto the porch. She walked around the area where the ceiling slanted down and met the wall and further convinced herself that there had to be a staircase on the other side of the slant.

She reentered the house through the smaller guestroom and stood once again in front of the open closet. "I wonder if these shelves come out?" she asked out loud. She grabbed the lowest one and lifted. It moved easily. Before long, she had all the shelves out and standing against the open door.

She walked into the closet and looked around. Something didn't look right to her. The placement of the outside wall on the left wasn't congruent with the outside wall in the hallway.

She straddled the threshold of the closet. With her left hand, she knocked on the wall in the hallway. With her right hand, she knocked on the closet wall. The closet wall produced a markedly more hollow sound. "I knew it. It's a fake wall."

She ran through the guest bedroom one more time and onto the porch, leaving the doors open. She quickly traversed the length of the porch, past the locked apartment, and down two flights of stairs leading to the garage where she found a crowbar and hammer. When she retraced her steps and arrived back in front of the closet, she found the cat pacing back and forth nervously. She rubbed up against Lia's legs as soon as she saw her.

"So, there you are, Miss Thing. Want to tell me why you dug another hole in the courtyard? If you keep behaving like that, you won't be welcome here. Keep that in mind if you get the urge to dig another one. Now steer clear of my feet. I've got a wall to take down."

Lia nudged the cat away with her foot and began to pry the first shelf support off the wall. She quickly realized that what she thought was sheetrock, was actually a full piece of plywood. The entire wall moved slightly when she pulled at the shelf support.

"Hmmm, this might not be as hard as I thought, Miss Thing. All I need to do is pry out the nails holding it from top to bottom on both sides, and it should come out in one piece."

A half hour later, the last nail pried loose and the entire wall canted slightly forward. "Okay, let's see what we have here." Lia put her tools on the floor and maneuvered the plywood away from the end wall. She leaned it against the opposite inside wall of the closet.

When she faced her handiwork, she was sorely disappointed. There before her was a door with flat steel bars running across it in four places, each end of which was held in place by padlocks.

"Damn it," she said. "Think, Lia. Think. Of course. The bolt cutters. Elliot put them back into the tool box after she cut the padlock off the apartment. Wait here, Miss Thing."

Lia returned a few minutes later with the bolt cutters and made short work of the eight padlocks holding the door closed. When the last padlock fell, the cat hunched up and hissed.

"Hey! What's that all about? I just want a quick look. And besides, the sun is setting and I'm not sure there's much lighting up there. I'll be right back."

When Lia opened the door the cat hissed once more and ran off. A musty odor rushed out as she looked up the darkened stairway. To call it a stairway was a bit of an exaggeration. It more closely resembled a ladder, pitched at a much steeper angle than a stairway would be.

Much to Lia's surprise, she found a light switch just inside the door. She turned it on, and the dark shadows were chased away, revealing a low, flat ceiling. She slowly climbed the ladder until she reached the top and looked around while still standing on the stairs.

"Manman kay ki apa pou Bondye a," (Holy Mother of God.) she said before she lost consciousness and began to fall down the stairs.

"Mwen te resevwa ou. Pa enkyete, mwen te resevwa ou," (I gots you. Don't worry, I gots you.) a voice said from below.

* * *

Elliot paced back and forth across the loft while she held her cell phone to her ear. "Come on, answer your goddamned phone, Lia," she said impatiently. "Something's wrong. I just know it. It's ten o'clock. I've been calling her all day, but all I get is her voicemail."

Marissa stood in her path, mid-pace. "Look. The packing is finished. All we need to do is meet the moving van on Monday then drive the two cars down to New Orleans. I think Julie and I can handle that. Why don't you catch a red-eye home. You'll be by Lia's side by morning."

Elliot looked once more at her phone then alternately at her two friends. "Really? I hate to ask you to do that."

Julie joined her wife. "Really. Go home. We'll be there in a few days. Hell, we'll even drive you to the airport."

Marissa took her by the shoulders. "Look, Elliot, you're right to be worried. After what you told us about Lia speaking Creole, anything is possible."

"You aren't suggesting she was actually possessed, are you?" Elliot asked.

"I agree with Marissa," Julie added. "We can't rule anything out. You need to keep an open mind. It might go against your nature to consider this, but there are some things that just cannot be explained away by science. Just ask yourself if you're willing to risk Lia's life for your staunch beliefs."

CHAPTER 18

Sunday

Lia awoke to find herself chained to a wall in a dimly lit room with low ceilings. All around her, she could hear moans. The smell of decay was everywhere. *Am I in the apartment?* she thought. *The smell is overpowering.*

She blinked her eyes several times to focus her vision. Soon, the full extent of her situation was revealed to her. All around her were black men and women, some of them chained to the wall as she was. Some were strapped to tables, and still others locked in cages. Scattered about the floor were pools of blood and body parts. Human heads and organs were thrown into buckets, brains and hearts stacked on shelves.

Lia lost her voice to the terror around her. She tried calling out, but failed to make anything more than choking sounds.

A man chained to the wall beside her begged for mercy. "Please, kill me. Please. I want to die."

Lia lifted her head from the wall as far as her chains would allow and saw the man's stomach was sliced open and his intestines were pinned to the wall on both sides of him. He stood stooped over, suspended by the chain around his neck and the meager strength he still had in his legs, begging for it all to end.

The woman to her right was also chained by her neck and wrists to the wall. Her eyes and mouth had been sewn shut with thick rawhide stitches. Not able to see, the woman strained to hear the sound of movement beside her.

A man strapped to the table in front of her had no eyes and his fingernails had been pulled out by the roots. A large hole had been drilled into his skull from which a stick protruded. The man appeared to be dead.

A movement from across the room drew Lia's attention. There, also chained to the wall, was a man whose private parts had been sliced off and his hands sewn to his thighs. He too was begging to die.

A rattling noise from the far corner of the room startled her. From a distance, she could make out the form of a woman whose limbs had been broken and reset at odd angles to resemble a crab. She was confined to a cage meant for an animal.

Lia felt sick and began to vomit. As she watched the contents of her stomach spew onto the floor, she noticed a limbless woman snaking her way across the floor. Great widths of skin had been peeled from the woman's body in a corkscrew fashion around her torso.

It took only a few moments for Lia to see the horrors around her, but it felt like an eternity. A guttural, agonizing scream erupted from deep within her while she chanted over and over in her mind. "Papa ki gen tout pouvwa, pwoteje m 'anba mal, pwoteje m' anba move kote sa a, pwoteje m 'anba men dyab la a, kenbe m' soti nan mal." (Almighty Father, protect me from harm, protect me from this evil place, protect me from the devil's hand, protect me from harm.)

* * *

Elliot paid the cabby and climbed out of the taxi. The first things she noticed in the early morning light were the new flower baskets that graced the edges of the wrought iron railings on the second level. She made a mental note to compliment Lia on her handiwork as she unlocked the gate and let herself into the entryway. Moments later, she was inside the house and climbing the stairway to the next level. A deathly silence prevailed over the house.

She noted the time on the grandfather clock in the second-story hallway. Seven a.m. Lia was usually awake by now—even on weekends.

The silence concerned her. She picked up the pace and nearly ran up the stairway to the third level.

Not wanting to awaken Lia in the event she still was asleep, Elliot quietly opened the door to the bedroom and looked inside. The bed was still made, but rumpled, almost as though someone had been lying on top of the bedding. "Lia? Where are you?" she called out.

Elliot walked through the empty bathroom and down the long hallway toward the small bedroom at the end. Each room was empty. Determined to search the whole house, she walked back down the hall and into the bathroom where a whimpering sound stopped her in her tracks. "Lia, is that you? Where are you?" The whimpering came again. Elliot pulled open the door to the linen closet. "Lia?"

"Nooo!" came a scream from within the closet. "Papa ki gen tout pouvwa, pwoteje m' anba mal, pwoteje m' anba move kote sa a, pwoteje m' anba men dyab la a, kenbe m' soti nan mal." (Almighty Father, protect me from harm, protect me from this evil place, protect me from the devil's hand, protect me from harm.)

Elliot fell to her knees in front of Lia who sat as far back into the closet as possible, her knees drawn into her chest. Tears flowed freely from her terror-stricken eyes. "Lia! Oh, my God! Sweetheart, it's Elliot. I won't hurt you, love. I promise." Elliot reached into the closet to take Lia's hand.

Lia violently fought Elliot's hand away. "No! Papa ki gen tout pouvwa, pwoteje m' anba mal, pwoteje m' anba move kote sa a, pwoteje m' anba men dyab la a, kenbe m' soti nan mal." (Almighty Father, protect me from harm, protect me from this evil place, protect me from the devil's hand, protect me from harm.)

Elliot sat back on her heels and thought about what Julie had said to her before she left New York. *You need to keep an open mind, Elliot. Just ask yourself if you're willing to risk Lia's life for your staunch beliefs.*

Elliot took a deep breath and lunged forward to grab Lia's ankles. Lia fought with all she was worth as Elliot pulled her out of the linen closet. Elliot had to straddle Lia's body and pin her arms to the floor to control her.

"Pa gen fanm deyò, tanpri pa fè m 'anyen." (No, mistress, please don't hurt me.)

Elliot understood the fear more than the words as she leaned down close to Lia's face. "Celeste, I am not your mistress. I won't hurt you. I would never hurt you. You're safe. Please return Lia to me. I love her." Elliot's voice broke as she choked back tears. "Please, Celeste. Let her go. I need her more than you do."

Almost instantly, Lia stopped fighting. "Elliot?"

Elliot knelt on the floor beside Lia and gathered her into her arms. Lia trembled visibly as she clung tightly to Elliot. Elliot kissed her on the temple then buried her face in Lia's hair and cried uncontrollably for several long moments.

After a time, Elliot regained her composure and helped an obviously exhausted Lia to her feet. "Come with me. I need to hold you."

Elliot led Lia to the bedroom and helped her to remove her clothing. She turned down the bedding and held it up until Lia climbed into the bed. She removed her own clothing, walked around to the other side, and climbed in. Meeting in the middle, they melted into each other's arms and reconnected through the most basic need for human touch.

Elliot kissed her once more on the temple. "I'm so sorry, my love," she whispered.

"You've done nothing wrong," Lia whispered back.

"I did. I left you here to face the demons alone."

Lia began to cry. "There were so many of them. I was in the attic. I saw them. I saw what she did to them. My heart hurts so much. There was so much pain and so much suffering. How can anyone treat other human beings like that?"

Elliot tightened her arms around Lia. "I know, baby. I know. I'm here now. I'll protect you. Sleep, my love."

"I love you, Elliot."

"I love you more."

* * *

Elliot was awakened several hours later by the feeling of being watched. She opened her eyes and found Lia's face just a few inches away from her own. Lia was staring at her. Without a word passing between them, she rolled to her side and returned her gaze.

Elliot studied Lia for several moments, noticing the pained look in her eyes and the dark circles forming under her lids. Tears formed in her own eyes as her heart broke for the emotional pain Lia was in. She reached forward and cupped the side of Lia's face with her hand and felt Lia press her cheek into her palm as she closed her eyes. Elliot blinked rapidly as tears escaped and rolled across the bridge of her nose to the pillow.

Lia opened her eyes and attempted a weak smile.

Elliot smiled back. "Tell me what you're feeling," she gently coaxed.

Lia's eyes misted over. "There is so much pain in this house, El. All the things that have happened over the past week. All the signs. I tried to explain them away with logic, but what I'm feeling isn't logical."

"We need to leave this house, Lia."

"No. We're here for a reason. I don't know what it is yet, but I know it's essential we stay."

"But you've been through so much."

"I've been through nothing compared to those who died here."

"Tell me what happened yesterday."

Lia took Elliot's hand from her cheek and held it close to her heart as an unspoken message that she needed to feel connected. "I should probably start with the night before. After we talked, the cat and I went back to the library with my research material. We weren't in there but a few minutes when I heard footstep on the floor above me."

"In the apartment?"

"I assume so. Anyway, Miss Thing began to spaz out so I got up to let her out and before I even made it to the door, I heard the footsteps again. It really spooked me, so I decided to call it a night and went to bed."

"You know this house makes all kinds of odd noises."

"True, but it really sounded like footsteps. I actually described the noise to one of the guys at the home improvement store and he guessed it was air in the pipes that run through the floor of the apartment. It kind of made sense because I had washed the bedding earlier in the day. After I talked to him, I felt a lot better about it, so I put it out of my mind."

"He's probably right."

"I thought so at the time. Anyway, I bought several baskets of flowers..."

"Which are beautiful, by the way. I noticed them as soon as I got out of the cab this morning."

"Which reminds me, why are you home so early? I didn't expect you until Thursday or Friday."

"I spent all yesterday afternoon trying to reach you, but you didn't answer your phone. I was out of my mind with worry. Marissa and Julie convinced me to take a red-eye home. They insisted on meeting the mover tomorrow and then driving our cars down here without me."

Lia drew Elliot's hand to her mouth and kissed the knuckles. "They are good friends, El."

"The best."

"I'm so happy you're home."

"Me too. So, continue with your story."

"I bought all these flowers, and when I tried to pull the car into the courtyard to unload them, I saw that Miss Thing had dug a huge hole right where I needed to park the car."

"Why the hell would she do that?"

"I don't know. It was the second one she had dug. I actually caught her digging in the same spot the day the electrician came to replace the switches in the apartment."

"That's strange."

"I thought so too. Anyway, I filled the hole and took care of the flowers. By that time, it was around two in the afternoon, so I decided to have a quick lunch and go in search of the attic stairs I read about in the research material."

Elliot frowned. "Lia, isn't the attic where the slaves were tortured?"

"Yes. At least that's what the research says."

"Why would you do that? Why would you intentionally seek out something you knew would upset you?"

"I thought it would help me to understand what I was feeling."

"Did you find the stairs?"

"I did, but it wasn't easy. They were hidden behind a wall in the hallway closet. And the door was blocked by four bars and eight padlocks."

Elliot's frown deepened. "And that didn't tell you something? Like, do not enter?"

"By that point, I couldn't stop myself. It's almost like I was driven. I wasn't afraid, Elliot. I felt absolutely no fear."

"So you found the bolt cutters in the garage."

"Yes. Exactly."

"Holy Mother of God."

Lia squeezed Elliot's hand. "What did you just say?"

"I said, Holy Mother of God. I can't believe you did that."

"Holy Mother of God. I've heard that just recently, but I can't remember where."

"What happened next? Did you go into the attic?"

"I remember climbing the stairs, but everything is a blank after that."

"You blacked out again?"

Lia rolled onto her back and stared at the ceiling. "I must have. I don't remember."

"How did you get into the bathroom linen closet, Lia?"

"I was in the linen closet?"

"Yes. That's where I found you when I got home. Why were you in there?"

"I don't know."

"What is the first thing you remember after climbing the attic stairs?"

"I don't remember anything, Elliot. Everything is a blank between climbing the attic stairs and then suddenly realizing you were sitting on me and pinning me to the bathroom floor."

Elliot propped herself up on one arm. "But you said you saw them."

Lia looked directly at Elliot. Tears filled her eyes. "I did. It was horrible. So much pain. Elliot, there were so many of them there. Some were dead. Others were dying. Everything we read about what happened is true. The smell! Oh, my God, Elliot. There were limbs all over the floor. And there was so much blood." Lia began sob wildly.

Elliot climbed to her knees and lifted Lia into her arms. "I've got you, my love."

"Why, Elliot? Why did it happen? Why does it hurt so much?"

Elliot kissed the side of her head. "I don't know why it happened. Maybe it was about power. Maybe they got their rocks off sexually through torturing those people. I don't know why. I wish I did."

"My heart hurts. Such a senseless loss of life. It's so unjust. I will carry that image with me for the rest of my life."

Elliot pulled back a bit so she could see Lia's face. "Sweetheart, how do you remember seeing them when you blacked out climbing the attic stairs?"

"I don't know. The memory and images are burned on my mind, Elliot. I saw it—I know I did."

"Maybe they're not your memories."

CHAPTER 19

Lia sat up cross-legged in front of Elliot. "What do you mean they're not my memories? They're in my head. Whose memories would they be if not mine?"

Elliot climbed off the bed and started to pace.

Lia watched her for a few minutes before losing patience. "I asked you a question. You can't say something like that and then not respond."

Elliot returned to the bed and sat down. She took Lia's hand in her own. "Lia, when I found you in the linen closet, you were Celeste."

"The Creole chick?"

"Yes, that's the one. You were terrified of me. You wouldn't come out, but instead, fought me tooth and nail when I reached for you. You actually kicked me at one point."

"I did?"

"Yes, you kept babbling something over and over again in Creole. I'm guessing it was some sort of chant. Maybe a protection spell."

Lia turned Elliot's hand over and exposed a large bruise just inside Elliot's elbow that she had seen earlier. "Did I do this?"

"No, Celeste did."

"Elliot—"

"Hear me out. You wouldn't come out of the linen closet. I had to grab you and drag you out. It's a good thing the neighbors didn't hear us because surely someone would have called the police to report domestic violence."

"Why don't I remember this?"

"Because it wasn't you. It was Celeste. Sweetheart, remember the first time she appeared? No, strike that—of course you don't. The first time she appeared was that night you totally don't remember making love and then later denied that you could speak Creole."

"I can't speak Creole."

"I know. I believe you. What I'm trying to get at is that she called me mistress that night, and she said to be safe, she would do what the mistress wanted. I got the distinct impression she had sex with the mistress against her will, and she needed to do that to protect herself."

"Did you make love to her knowing she wasn't me?"

"Oh, for crying out loud, Lia. Yes we made love, but I totally thought you were role playing. Give me a break here. You know I'm as faithful as the day is long. Trust me, if she comes on to me again, nothing will happen. It will be hard to resist because, damn, you are really sexy as a Creole wench, but I can assure you, nothing will happen. Now where was I?"

"She called you mistress that night."

"Yes, she did. And she called me mistress when I pulled her out of the closet last night. That's how I knew it was her and not you in control. That, and the fluent Creole. My point is, Lia, she was terrified of me. The fear in her eyes when she saw me was palpable. I'm convinced that what you saw in that attic was actually witnessed through Celeste's eyes."

It was Lia's turn to pace as she climbed off the bed and walked a few feet away. "But if what you say is true, I don't remember anything when she takes over, so why is it, I remember what happened in the attic?"

"Maybe she wants you to remember."

* * *

"Are you sure you want to do this?" Elliot asked as she slipped a T-shirt over her head.

Lia sat on the bed, tying her shoes. "Elliot, if these truly are Celeste's memories that means she has the ability to take control of my consciousness whenever she feels like it. And she has the ability to do it to different degrees. That freaks me out on so many levels. I want you to be there the next time it happens, and if we can force the issue, then I'm all for doing that."

"Even if it means reliving those memories again?"

"I'm hoping it doesn't come to that." Lia finished tying her shoes. "The stairway is in the hallway closet. Are you ready?"

"The question is, are *you* ready?"

Elliot followed Lia through the hallway and stopped in front of the closet. Lia took a deep breath and opened the door. "What the hell?"

Elliot looked over her shoulder. "Looks like a closet to me."

"But I took all these shelves down. Someone put it all back together again. Who did this?"

Elliot stepped around Lia and reached for one of the shelves. It was nailed into place. "It looks like these shelves have been here for quite a while."

"No, Elliot. I took them all down yesterday. And I removed this wall, right here," she said as she pointed to the outside wall of the closet. "The door to the attic stairs is behind it."

Elliot inspected the wall. "Lia, there isn't enough room behind this wall for a stairway."

"There is if the stairway extends onto the porch. Come with me and I'll prove it to you." Lia took Elliot's hand and led her through their bedroom and into the bathroom. "Look out that small window near the sinks."

Elliot did as she was told. "I don't see anything. What am I looking for?"

"The slant of the stairway going from the middle of the wall to the ceiling—" Lia stopped mid-sentence as she pushed Elliot out of the way and looked for herself. There was no evidence of a stairway extending onto the porch. The ceiling and the porch met at a ninety-degree angle at the top of the outside wall.

Lia turned to Elliot. "It was there. I swear it was. Elliot, I didn't imagine all of that. I made the conscious decision to remove the shelves from the closet. I made two trips to the garage for tools, first for a crowbar and hammer, and then for the bolt cutters. It took me all afternoon, but I removed that wall in the closet and there was a door behind it." Lia grabbed her head at the temples. "I feel like I'm losing my mind. What's happening to me, Elliot?"

Elliot wrapped her arms around Lia and held her close. "You're not losing your mind, love. Something else is happening here. Maybe we should consider moving back to the hotel."

Lia pushed Elliot away from her. "No. Leaving is not the answer. I need to understand why all of this is happening. If you want to leave, then go. I'm staying here."

Elliot shoved her hands deep into the back pockets of her denim jeans. "I go where you go. You know that."

Lia leaned her backside against the sink and crossed her arms.

"Are you okay?" Elliot asked.

Lia shook her head and wiped the tears from her eyes with one hand balled into a fist.

"Come here." Elliot opened her arms for Lia. She held her close and rubbed her back while Lia wrapped her arms around Elliot's waist and rested her head on Elliot's shoulder.

After a few minutes of holding her, Elliot heard a loud rumbling coming from deep within Lia's stomach. She held Lia an arm's length away and looked questioningly at her. "When was the last time you ate?"

Lia gazed off in the distance as she thought about Elliot's question. "Hmmm. The last time I remember eating was lunch yesterday. Who knows what happened after Miss French Fry possessed me."

"You don't like her very much, do you?" Elliot said.

"I don't trust her very much. It isn't cool to take over someone's body and then seduce your wife with it."

"On my, the cat has claws, but once more for the record, I thought it was you doing the seducing—not her. Now, how about I take my best girl out for an early dinner?"

"I'd better be your only girl."

"Well, there is Miss French Fry…"

Elliot dodged Lia's swat as she ran through the bedroom toward the stairs, with Lia right on her heels.

* * *

Lia sipped her voodoo juice while they waited for their food to arrive. "This was a good choice. I really like that there are several nice restaurants within walking distance of the house. We'll have to bring Marissa and Julie here."

"It makes it feel like we're still in New York in some ways," Elliot said. "Everything is close by, although the atmosphere is definitely different from the City."

"I know what you mean. Everything is so hectic and fast-paced in New York. It's really laid back here, despite the fact that it's a good-sized city. I really like that there's Cajun and jazz music always playing somewhere. My co-worker, Claire recommended some farmers' markets nearby. Apparently they close off both ends of a city block and set their tables up right in the street. Now that you're home, maybe we can do that one night during the week."

"Or we can wait until the girls get here and we can all go. It might be nice to have a cookout this weekend."

"We'll have to buy a grill. I didn't see one in the courtyard or garage. They'll be here before the weekend, right?"

"As long as they don't run into any delays on the way, they should be here by Thursday."

"I'll need to prepare a room for them. I'm thinking the front guestroom across the hall from us."

"Good choice. You'll need to steel yourself for lots of questions—especially from Julie. She is totally into the paranormal thing, and she's very curious about what's been happening in the house."

"Well she's from New Orleans," Lia pointed out. "I'm willing to bet she grew up with all the folklore and superstitions that are so much a part of this city's culture."

Elliot fell silent for a long pause, as she studied Lia.

"What?" Lia asked. "Why are you staring at me?"

"I was just thinking about how much I missed you." Elliot reached across the table for her hand. "When I think of how close I came to losing you before we left New York, it makes me disgusted with myself. I was such an idiot."

Lia smiled. "You would have never lost me, Elliot. I would have willingly lived on the fringes of your life rather that live without you."

"Well, I'm glad you opened my eyes. I just hope we haven't stepped into bigger problems than we left behind, with this house of ours."

"I like the house. Despite everything that has happened, I feel safe there. I'm not afraid. I have been horrified and saddened by what I've seen, or at least think I've seen, but I've never been afraid. Not yet, anyway."

"You know, we're going to have to open that apartment up at some point," Elliot said. "Now that I'm home, I want to have a cleaning service come in and get rid of that smell."

Lia frowned.

"What's that look for? Did you suddenly remember something?" Elliot asked.

"That smell. It was the same odor I smelled in the attic. It was the smell of death and decay."

"Judging by the dead rat I found in the apartment, I'd say that is just what that odor was. By the way, have you seen the lights come on in the apartment since you had the electrician here?"

"No, I haven't. I totally expected I would, after hearing the footstep above the library, but surprisingly, no."

"That's good. I guess we can blame that one on faulty wiring. In fact, I'm willing to bet all the strange goings-on we're experiencing are due to the age of the house."

"You could be right, but that doesn't explain the dreams, or French Fry's visits."

"You got me on that one."

Lia squeezed Elliot's hands. "How did we go from being practical, fact-based scientists to superstitious believers in the paranormal?"

"The jury is still out on that for me, although I did promise Julie that I would have an open mind about all of this. I have to admit, Celeste has me questioning my beliefs."

Just then, their food arrived. Elliot raised her glass to Lia. "Bon Appétit."

CHAPTER 20

Lia and Elliot walked hand in hand back through the French Quarter on their way home, passing several establishments with New Orleans jazz music spilling out onto the street. Elliot stopped and bought a single, long-stemmed rose from a street vendor and handed it to Lia, who inhaled its scent and then kissed her tenderly for the gift.

Elliot glanced at Lia as they walked. "You look happy, my love."

"I am, now that you're home."

Elliot stopped and faced Lia. She took Lia's face between her palms and kissed her. "No more long separations, agreed?"

Lia couldn't look away. She placed her hands on Elliot's hips and drew her closer until they were standing nearly nose to nose. "Take me to bed," she whispered hoarsely. "I need to feel you."

"It will be my pleasure," Elliot replied as she kissed Lia once more and took her hand to walk the final block home.

The elderly gentleman stood on the street corner and watched as Lia and Elliot entered 1140 Royal Street. He could tell by the way they touched each other that they were deeply in love.

"Celeste," he whispered to himself. "Metrès la pa ta apwouve nan zafè ou a ak fanm blan sa a." (The mistress would not approve of your affair with this white woman.) "Li te move ase lè pitit mèt ou a te fè ou yo. Fanm sa a ap mennen ou tou dwat nan bra yo nan lanfè. Metrès la ap wè nan li." (It was bad enough when your bore your master's child. This woman will lead you straight into the arms of hell. The mistress will see to it.)

* * *

"Shower with me," Lia suggested as they stepped into their bedroom.

"Okay. I'll start the water."

Elliot opened the glass door to the shower and turned on the spray. She waited until the temperature was just right before closing the door. By that time, Lia had already removed all of her own clothing.

"Let me undress you." Lia pulled Elliot's T-shirt over her head and dropped it to the floor.

Elliot pulled off her own sports bra, took Lia's face between her palms, and kissed her passionately. Lia unbuttoned and unzipped Elliot's cargo shorts and slipped one hand inside the front of her panties. Her fingers deftly slipped between moist folds.

Elliot nearly doubled over and held on to Lia for support. She grabbed Lia's wrist and removed it from her shorts. "Much more of that, and it will be all over for me before it even begins."

Lia smiled. "Horny, are we?"

"Always, where you're concerned."

Lia slipped her hands into the back of Elliot's panties and guided the clothing downward until it was in a puddle around Elliot's feet. She knelt down to help Elliot step out of it and placed a gentle kiss just above the blonde triangle of hair between Elliot's legs.

Elliot's abdomen spasmed as her hands found support on Lia's shoulder. "We'd better get to into the shower. I don't know how much more of this I can take."

Once in the shower, Elliot made short work of bathing herself. Then she took the bar of soap away from Lia.

"Hey," Lia objected. "How am I supposed to bathe without soap?"

"Paybacks are a bitch, my love." Elliot created a large mound of lather between her hands. "Come here."

Lia grinned and stepped closer to Elliot.

"Look at me, Lia. Don't close your eyes, and don't look away," Elliot said as her soapy hands began an exploration of Lia's body.

Maintaining eye contact with Elliot was difficult, as Lia's eyes nearly rolled into the back of her head in reaction to what Elliot was doing to her.

Elliot's hands danced happily over Lia's breasts while deft fingers pinched her dark-brown nipples. Lia's eyes closed and she moaned in response. "Open your eyes, Lia," Elliot whispered. Her hands roamed to Lia's bottom where she squeezed and kneaded firm glutes. Finally, the soapy path continued to the space between Lia's legs.

Lia widened her stance slightly to allow Elliot access. "I need you, Elliot," she said without breaking eye contact.

Elliot slipped soapy fingers into Lia's folds while her other arm held Lia upright. "I've got you, love," Elliot said as Lia's eyes once again closed and her head rolled back.

"Elliot, I've missed you so much. I've missed your touch. I've missed your closeness."

Elliot knew Lia was referring to much more than their week apart. She pulled her closer and rained a barrage of kisses and bites along Lia's exposed jawline. "I've missed you too, sweetheart."

Lia opened her eyes and looked directly at Elliot. "I am so close," she said.

"Do you want me to stop?"

"Yes and no. We have the whole night ahead of us and I want to prolong this as much as possible."

Elliot removed her hand and kissed Lia tenderly. "Okay. Maybe we should rinse off and take this to the bedroom."

Elliot shut off the water and reached for their towels hanging on hooks beside the shower enclosure. Once dry, Elliot took Lia's hand and led her toward the bedroom. She turned down the bedding and invited Lia onto the bed's pillowy softness. Side by side, skin to skin, their hands explored each other's curves while their lips locked in a passionate, searing kiss.

Lia tilted her head back to allow Elliot access to her throat, which she took full advantage of. Moans of pleasure escaped Lia as Elliot sucked on the sensitive skin of Lia's neck while her fingers slid into the moist folds between her legs.

Lia dug her fingers into Elliot's back and pulled her closer. "My God. That feels so good."

Elliot struggled to contain her own passion as she withdrew her hand and shifted her weight to hover over Lia. "I want to taste you, love," she said as she slowly kissed her way down Lia's body while resisting the gentle pressure Lia was applying to her shoulders. Elliot looked into Lia's face and smiled. "Be patient, my love. All in good time."

Elliot took her time feasting on Lia's breasts then traced a line with her tongue from Lia's ribcage to her navel.

Lia raised her hips in a silent plea for fulfillment as Elliot placed kisses between Lia's navel and hip bone where once again she sucked on the tender skin.

"Elliot, please. I need you."

Elliot shifted her weight once more and lowered herself between Lia's legs. For the next several minutes, she feasted on the nectar of Lia's being, while Lia moaned and raised her hips to meet Elliot's mouth.

Before long, when Elliot felt Lia's need increase, she slipped three fingers inside her and massaged the sponge-like tissue on the front wall of her vagina. Lia arched her hips off the bed and stiffened. A low growl began to emerge from her throat. It soon turned into a full scream as waves of orgasmic intensity flowed over her.

"Come on, baby. Let it go," Elliot cooed. "I'll catch you. Let it go."

For what seemed like an eternity, ripples of orgasmic spasms ran through Lia until finally, she lay like a boneless rag doll on the bed. Elliot removed her fingers and crawled up to lay beside her. She gathered Lia into her arms and held her close. "I will love you forever," she said as Lia trembled in her arms.

Lia tilted her head back so she could see Elliot's face. "That was amazing," she said. "Thank you so much for loving me."

"You make that so easy to do."

"Give me a minute to recover and I'll return the favor."

"Trust me. It won't take long. Your passion was so intense, I nearly came along with you."

"Really? I'll be the judge of that," Lia said as she reached down and slid her fingers between Elliot's folds. "Oh, my. You're soaked."

Elliot's abdomen immediately spasmed. "I told you so," she said haltingly. "That feels so good. I need more, love."

Lia climbed to her knees. She slid her fingers deeper into Elliot as she suckled at Elliot's breasts. Without warning, she simultaneously bit down on Elliot's nipple while driving three fingers deep into her.

Elliot's reaction was immediate and intense. Her hips came off the bed and her head pressed into the pillow. "Oh, my God. Harder. Please, baby, harder. I'm coming."

Lia intensified her efforts as Elliot's hips bucked up and down. Lia could feel Elliot's muscles tightening in waves around her fingers as the orgasm ripped through her wife's body. She laid her cheek on Elliot's abdomen and continued to administer to her until the spasms subsided and Elliot asked her to stop. Finally, she removed her fingers and kissed her way up Elliot's torso until she was once again lying beside her.

Elliot turned to face her. "Thank you."

Lia kissed her gently. "I will love you forever," she said, mirroring what she heard just a few minutes earlier.

"What time is it?" Elliot asked.

Lia raised her head to look at the clock on the bedside table. "Ten p.m."

"You have to work tomorrow."

"Yes, I do. We should probably get to sleep."

"Right after I go to the bathroom." Elliot got up and walked around the bed.

When she returned a few minutes later, she looked out the window. "Well, I'll be. Samuel is standing on the street corner again."

"He does that every night," Lia said.

"Maybe I should go talk to him."

"I tried. I told him to go home and that we didn't need to be stalked. He insisted he was, in his words, watching over us."

"Is that all he said?

"He also asked me if Lia had shown me the way yet. I have no idea what he meant by that. Anyway, he won't leave, so I've chosen to just ignore him at night."

Elliot climbed into bed. "That's all fine and good, but if he tries anything, I'm calling the police." She lay down and opened her arms to Lia, who snuggled against her shoulder. "Good night, sweetie. I love you."

"Good night, Elliot. I love you too."

CHAPTER 21

Monday

The alarm woke Lia the next morning. She shut it off quickly then glanced at Elliot's side of the bed. It was empty. Lia sat up and looked around. "Elliot?"

After receiving no response, she climbed out of bed and walked into the hall, just in time to see the closet door open. A woman dressed in garb reminiscent of the eighteen hundreds stepped into the hallway and close the door. Lia was stunned into inaction. Apparently unaware of her presence, the woman walked toward the spiral staircase and disappeared.

Finding her bearings once more, Lia ran to the staircase and leaned over the railing. The woman was nowhere to be seen. "Elliot?" she called loudly.

"I'm in the kitchen," Elliot answered from the second story. A moment later, she appeared on the landing below.

"Good morning. I'll have breakfast ready for you by the time you finish your shower and get dressed," Elliot said.

"Did you see her?" Lia asked excitedly.

"Did I see who?"

"The woman. A woman just walked out of the hallway closet and down these stairs."

Elliot frowned. "There are the only two people in this house, and I'm looking at one of them. I didn't see, or hear anyone come down these stairs."

"I saw her as plain as day. She was dressed in a long, black gown. I'm going to take a look in that closet." Lia turned on her heel.

"Not without me, you aren't." Elliot ran up the stairs.

Lia waited for her, and together, they walked across the hall and opened the door. Nothing was amiss in the closet.

"I saw her, Elliot."

"I'm sure you saw something. Maybe it was the shadows. The sun is just rising and it shines directly into the front window."

"Sunshine wouldn't open and close the closet door."

"You've got a point there. Did the woman appear threatening in any way?"

"I assume she didn't see me. She went directly from the closet to the stairway, and then she was gone."

"Hmm. Well, we're not going to solve this right now and you need to get ready for work," Elliot pointed out.

"What are you doing up so early? You don't have to go back to work for another two weeks."

"I thought I would make my wife some breakfast to start her day. Got a problem with that, missy?"

Lia grinned and walked up to Elliot. "No problem at all. Thank you." She planted a quick kiss on Elliot's lips. "I'll be down in about twenty minutes."

* * *

"That smells yummy," Lia said as she entered the kitchen and walked directly to the coffeepot. She placed a pod in the machine and pressed start.

Elliot glanced up from her position at the stove. "Whoa! Are you really wearing that to work today?"

"What's wrong with it?" Lia looked down at herself.

She wore a long skirt and peasant blouse with the neckline pulled down beyond her shoulders. A contrasting scarf wrapped around her middle and fell across the front of her skirt like an apron. And she had on work boots.

Elliot placed a plate filled with scrambled eggs, turkey bacon, and English muffins in front of her. "For working around the house, its fine, but I'm not sure it's appropriate for a scientific lab setting. Besides, your hair is a mess and you're wearing bright red lip stick."

"Well I think I'm perfectly okay. This looks great. Thanks for cooking. What's on your agenda for the day?"

Elliot fixed a plate for herself and put it on the opposite side of the island from Lia. "The first thing I'll do is call the cleaning service to take care of the smell in the apartment. After that, I plan to do a thorough inspection of the apartment to see what might have caused the sound of footsteps you heard the other night. If I have time, I might even go to the land registrar's office to see if they have blueprints for this house. Your nightmare about the attic has made me very curious now as to where that stairway is."

"If you find it, don't go up there until I get home. I want to go with you. Oh, and the key to the padlock on the apartment is hanging over there on the hook by the kitchen door." Just then the clock on the wall struck seven a.m. "Looks like it's time for me to head out."

"Do you want a ride this morning?" Elliot asked.

"No, I have an entire hour to get there. I think the walk will do me good."

Elliot got up and cleared Lia's dishes as Lia finished her coffee. "Are you sure you want to wear that outfit to work?" Elliot asked.

"Positive." Lia kissed her and hugged her close. "I'll see you tonight."

"Why don't I pick you up from work and we can shop for a new grill on the way home," Elliot said.

Lia smiled. "That's a great idea. I'll see you around five then?"

"Five it is. Have a great day, love."

"You too."

* * *

Lia began walking down Royal Street toward Canal, totally oblivious to the odd stares she was receiving along the way. It wasn't until she was halfway down the street that she caught her reflection in a store-front window. She stopped dead. "Oh, my."

Ten minutes later, she reentered 1140 Royal Street and scurried up the stairs, passing Elliot who was exiting the kitchen on the second floor.

"What are you doing back here? I thought you were on your way to work?" Elliot said.

Lia stopped and put her hands on her hips. "I can't believe you let me walk out of here this morning looking like this."

"But...but..." Elliot stuttered.

"I'm dressed like a scullery maid for crying out loud. I need to change my clothes. And I guess I'll need that ride to work after all."

She returned to the kitchen a few minutes later wearing a tucked-in white blouse, a form-fitting, knee-length navy-blue skirt, and hose and heels. She had replaced the red lipstick with transparent lip gloss and tamed her hair with clips. "How do I look?" she asked.

"Good enough to eat," Elliot said. "And much more professional. Definitely better than the scullery maid costume."

"Okay. I'm ready. Thanks for the ride, love. That will still get me there on time. Don't let me walk out of the house like that again, okay?"

* * *

"The room in question is right over here." Elliot led the cleaning company's representative up two flights of stairs to the third-level porch. He stood at the railing and looked at the courtyard while Elliot unlocked the door. "Kind of a big hole out there in the yard."

"Hole?" Elliot removed the lock and stood beside the contractor to get a look. "Oh, man." In the middle of the courtyard, was a large hole, at least ten feet in diameter, with the cat still digging in the middle of it. "Damn it, Miss Thing." Elliot studied the hole for a minute then said to the contractor, "The room is open. Go on in while I chase that cat away."

Elliot returned ten minutes later after shooing the cat away with a broom. She stepped into the room and noticed the smell was no less offensive than it was when they bought the house a few weeks ago. "What do you think?"

"Something has definitely died in here. We'll have to find the source of the odor to permanently get rid of it. I can have a crew here tomorrow if that's soon enough for you."

"That's great. Anytime is fine. I should be home all day."

"Tomorrow it is, then."

After seeing the contractor to the door, Elliot realized that her inspection of the apartment would have to wait until the next day, or even the day after. She needed to refill that hole in the courtyard before she headed to the land registrar's office.

She found a shovel and rake in the shed under the stairs in the courtyard. For the next half hour, she shoved dirt back into the hole and did her best to rearrange the cobblestones over the top. "Humph, there are some cobblestones missing. I wonder where they are." She looked around and spotted a stack of cobblestones on the lower porch beside the shed. *These must have been from the first time that damned cat dug a hole.* She carried the stones to the newly-patched hole and arranged them as symmetrically as she could. When she stepped back, she realized the stones lay on top of the mound of dirt rather than embedded in it. With any luck, they will all settle down to the same level as the other stones after it rained.

* * *

Elliot sat in the records room at the land registrar's office, surrounded by several large, and very old ledger books. For the next three hours, she read. She learned that the elderly black cook who was chained to the stove, intentionally set fire to the kitchen during a dinner party because the mistress threatened to send her to the attic for making a stew too salty. Apparently, knowing the fate that awaited her in the attic, she chose to die by fire, chained to the stove.

She read about the horrifying scene found in the attic by the firefighters and policemen when they responded to the fire.

When the mistress and master of the house realized their torture chamber had been discovered, they fled the scene in a horse-drawn carriage. They were never seen again. Despite the apathetic attitude about slavery at the time, the townsfolk became incensed with the level of cruelty administered to the slaves and reacted by totally destroying the inside of the mansion and much of its contents.

Elliot read the history of the house with intense curiosity. The house was placed on the market in 1837, three years after the fire and the subsequent restoration. The new owner abandoned it three months later when he couldn't tolerate the strange noises, cries, and groans he heard on a regular basis. After the Civil War, the mansion was turned into a school for poor black children, but that venture lasted only a year and the place was once again abandoned.

Seven years later, the house was turned into a conservatory of music and dance for the finest families of New Orleans. The school operated out of the mansion for several years until one of the male teachers was accused of improper behavior with a female student and the school was promptly closed.

In 1892, someone discovered the body of a member of a wealthy New Orleans family in the house. Rumor had it that he secretly lived there from the late 1880s until his death. He was found on a filthy cot and evidently had lived in squalor, despite the thousands of dollars he had stuffed in his mattress.

Over the next several years, during the great immigration of Italians to America, the mansion was subdivided into apartments and rented out. During the time it served as tenement housing, there were several sightings of ghostly figures, including an encounter between one of the tenants and a large black man in chains who abruptly vanished after attacking him. Some of the tenants' children claimed to have been chased in the courtyard by a ghostly figure with a whip.

Other tenants claimed to see apparitions of slaves walking around the balconies at night, some of them screaming in agony. One young mother even claimed to see a woman dressed in elegant clothing bending over her child asleep in a crib. It wasn't long before the building was once again abandoned.

Elliot further read that the house later became a bar and then a furniture store—neither of which lasted—run out of business due to lack of patronage. Some assumed this was caused by the paranormal history of the house. In the more modern history of the house, it was owned by a famous actor but later foreclosed on for unpaid taxes.

"Damn," Elliot said out loud. "Every single owner and occupant of the house fell on hard times, or worse, while living there."

Elliot continued to search through the records until she finally came across what she had actually come for—drawings of the layout of the house at the time the slave torture had taken place. She studied them carefully and noted that, with a few exceptions—primarily for modernization—there were very few changes in the first and second-story room layouts. The third story, however, had significant changes.

For starters, the walk-in closet in the current master suite was a nursery, with the far bedroom designated for the nanny. There were also three toilet stalls instead of one in the master bathroom. The apartment above the library was identified as slave quarters, which by all indications, was one large room with a single bathroom for all slaves to share. The one piece of information Elliot was looking for was placed squarely in the middle of the third floor's primary living area—the stairs to the attic.

"Oh, my God. Lia was right," she whispered when she saw the placement of the stairway. "Access to the attic must have been completely eliminated after what was found up there. But if the stairs are no longer there, how did Lia get into the attic?"

CHAPTER 22

"Hey, love, how was your day?" Elliot asked when Lia got into the car.

Lia leaned over and kissed her. "It was a great day. We completed the first phase of the genome project early. Granted, it was the easy phase, but completing it early means we win bonus grant money that we can apply to anything we want. How cool is that?"

"Congratulations. I'm very proud of you. It feels good to be part of a winning team, huh?"

"It certainly does. How was your day?"

"Relatively productive. The cleaning crew is coming tomorrow to start on the apartment, and I found some very interesting information at the land registrar's office today. And that damned cat was at it again. She dug another huge hole in the courtyard. I fixed it as well as I could, but we may have to get a professional landscaper to come in to properly place the cobblestones."

"That little shit. That's the third time she's done it. I wonder why?"

"We might have to figure out how she's getting into the courtyard and take steps to stop her."

"I hate to do that. She's a very loving cat. She was my constant companion while you were gone."

"I totally get how cute she is, but we need to draw the line at damage, Lia. Sometimes she thinks she owns the place and has every right to be here. I'd like to know how she gets into the house. Despite the locked doors and windows, she still manages to get in."

"Well, that rat found its way into the apartment. I'm sure there are all kinds of small entryways into the house. It *is* almost two hundred years old, after all."

"I'm sure you're right, but it's still frustrating as all hell."

"Agreed. We're going after a grill tonight, right?"

"Yes. They're on sale at Home Depot this week."

"Do you mind stopping at the grocery store afterwards? I'll pick up some steaks and salad fixings so we can test-drive the grill for dinner."

"That sounds like a wonderful plan. Over dinner, I can show you what I discovered about the house at the records office today."

* * *

Lia stood at the kitchen island assembling two garden salads while Elliot grilled the steaks on the porch outside the kitchen door.

"Sweetie, could you please bring me the plates? These steaks are just about ready," Elliot called through the screen door.

"Sure." Lia grabbed the plates from the island and brought them outside.

Elliot moved the steaks from the grill to the plates. "One for you, and one for me. I'll be in as soon as I shut the gas off and clean the grill."

"Okay. It will take me a minute or two to finish the salads anyway."

Elliot entered the kitchen just as Lia was pouring the wine. "Dressing?" Lia asked as she recorked the wine.

"Raspberry vinaigrette, if you don't mind," Elliot replied.

"That sounds good to me too." Lia retrieved it from the refrigerator then sat on a barstool in front of the island. She picked up her wineglass and held it toward Elliot. "To bonus grant money."

"To new gas grills," Elliot returned.

Lia chuckled. "You are crazy, my love."

"Only for you, sweetheart. Only for you."

Lia sipped her drink, cut into her steak, and savored the first bite. "I'm in heaven. This steak is wonderful. Thank you for cooking. Do you want steak sauce?"

"You're welcome. And no, I don't want to ruin this fantastic piece of meat with sauce. It's not so bad, if I say so myself."

They finished their meal and Lia sat back. "What a good meal." She patted her stomach. "I want to thank you for driving me to work this morning. I never would have made it on time otherwise."

"What was up with your outfit this morning?"

"Quite honestly, I don't know. I don't remember choosing it. Thank God I saw a glimpse of myself in that store window or I would have been the laughingstock of the lab."

"Or maybe you would have started a new fashion trend."

"Very funny. Tell me what you found today."

"That's right. I left it in the backseat of the car. I'll get it."

Lia picked up her wineglass and stepped onto the back porch. She walked to the railing and held her glass up high. "Byento, nou pral dwe gratis." (Soon we will be free.)

"Lia?" Elliot called from the kitchen.

Lia closed her eyes and grasped the railing for support. She nearly dropped her wineglass into the courtyard before regaining her composure.

"There you are. Enjoying the nice breeze?"

Not wanting to alarm Elliot, she forced a smile to her face. "Absolutely," she said. "It's not often the wind blows around here. Got to take it when you can get it."

"You're right about that." Elliot held the door open. "Come in. I want to share what I found about the house today."

She laid the photocopied documents between them on the kitchen island. Lia refilled their wineglasses.

"These documents here chronicle the history of the house," Elliot said. "This place changed hands a couple dozen times or so over the last one hundred and fifty years. Most new owners only stuck around for a few years at a time."

"Why?" Lia asked.

"These documents make you believe it's the haunting that caused it. There are countless records of people hearing strange noises, disembodied voices, screaming, and in several cases, actual ghosts attacking people. Others left because of bad luck, which of course, they blame on the bad juju."

Lia frowned. "Do you think Celeste is a ghost?"

"That's a good question. The research suggests people have actually seen ghosts. I can't say that we've seen Celeste."

"Maybe she's a spirit."

"Is there a difference?"

"I don't know. Let me look it up." Lia retrieved her cell phone from the counter and called up the Internet. She typed her request into the search engine: "What is the difference between a ghost and a spirit?" A list of websites was immediately displayed. "This one says spirits are people who have died and have come back from the grave to visit loved ones. Ghosts, on the other hand, are people who have died but haven't yet crossed over after death."

"So ghosts have unfinished business."

"Or maybe there's something preventing them from crossing over," Lia suggested.

"We're no closer to knowing whether Celeste is a spirit or a ghost. Maybe I'll ask her the next time she shows her face," Elliot joked.

"Very funny. What else did you learn about the house?"

"I learned that you are absolutely right about where the attic stairway is."

Lia's eyes opened wide. "Really? But we've pretty much ruled out the closet in the hallway."

"Look at this." Elliot pushed the pre-fire map toward her.

Lia studied the blueprint. Her eyes were drawn to the slave quarters. "They lived above the library? No wonder I have such negative feelings about that space. There were dozens of slaves here when all of that horror happened. Do you really think they all had to live in that one room?"

"I think most of them lived there. Don't forget there were stable hands and maintenance guys here as well. I suspect the male slaves lived in the basement, probably in the rooms closest to the courtyard, while the female slaves most likely lived where the apartment is today."

"And Celeste? Where do you think she lived?"

"You probably won't want to hear this, but that first night, when I thought she was you, the things she said implied she serviced the mistress on a regular basis—I assume not by choice—so if she was one of the favored slaves, she might have had better living conditions."

"The mistress was a lesbian?"

"I suspect not. She was married three times, after all."

"The little girl, Lia, was Celeste's daughter, and the master was the girl's father," Lia said.

Elliot's head snapped up from looking down at the blueprint. "How the hell do you know that?"

Lia looked shocked that the statement had come out of her mouth. "I don't know. I just knew it. Maybe it was from the dream I had when the mistress whipped Celeste and called the little girl the 'bane of her existence.' Or maybe it was the childbirth dream."

"Another piece of information that she subliminally shared with you, most likely."

"Elliot, don't say that. I don't like the idea that she can get into my head and my body. I would prefer to think I absorbed that information from the research we've done on this place."

"If the master really fathered her child, I wonder why the mistress would force her into sexual servitude. I would have thought she'd become one of the victims in the attic."

"Maybe she was. If my memories of the attic truly come from her, she would have had to be there, either as a witness, or as a victim herself. As far as the sexual servitude is concerned, maybe it was a vindictive, revengeful payback against her husband."

"You have a good point there. What else do you see on the blueprint?"

Lia studied the layout once more. "Wait. There's a stairway in the hall upstairs that isn't there anymore."

"Exactly."

"I want to take this map upstairs and compare it for myself."

"Okay. Let's go."

3rd Floor Layout – Prior to 1834 fire

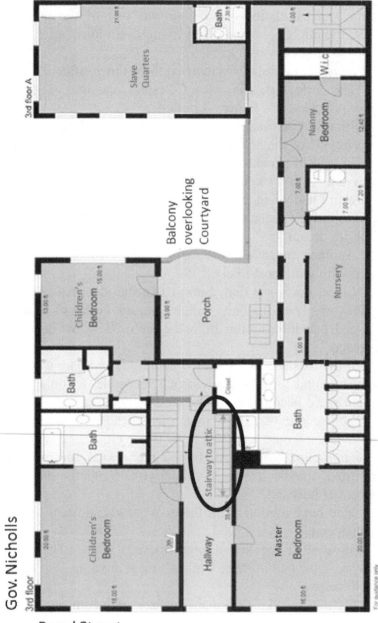

3rd floor A

Slave Quarters

Bath

W.i.c

Nanny Bedroom

Nursery

Balcony overlooking Courtyard

Children's Bedroom

Porch

Bath

Bath

Closet

Stairway to attic

Bath

Gov. Nicholls

3rd floor

Children's Bedroom

Hallway

Master Bedroom

Royal Street

For guidance only

Lia and Elliot stood at the top of the spiral staircase and looked at the opposite wall. Lia pointed straight ahead. "That's where the stairs were, right?"

"Stay here and I'll walk it out for you." Elliot strode directly to the closet in the corner. "From what I can make out on the blueprint, this closet extended maybe three or four more feet into the hall, and these two steps leading to the smaller guest room were three or four more feet to the left as well. That would allow the stairway to the attic to be built on the other side of the closet, where it extended into the hall. The first step would have been maybe five or six feet away from our bedroom door over there."

Lia walked to where she estimated five or six feet to be from the bedroom door and faced the end of the hall toward the closet. "So this would have been where the stairs began, and they would have ended at the ceiling just where the closet started."

"Yes, exactly. Wait a minute. I'm going to turn the ceiling light on." Elliot flicked the light switch on at the top of the spiral staircase while Lia was looking at the ceiling.

"Elliot, come look at this. I can see the outline of where someone closed the hole in the floor leading to the attic." Lia looked at Elliot with tears in her eyes. "We found it. We found it."

Elliot wiped the tears from Lia cheeks. "Why are you crying, sweetheart?"

"I don't know. I just feel this intense emotion in my chest. I can't explain it."

"You have the biggest heart of anyone I know. Do me a favor and don't ever change, okay? I love you just the way you are."

* * *

The belt struck Celeste across the face. The spiked collar she wore prevented her from turning her head away from the blows. She tried with all her might not to make a sound, but her traitorous body cried out.

"Stop whimpering, you Cajun whore, or there'll be more where that came from."

"Yes, master. Celeste be sorry, master."

"You told my wife about the child."

"No, master. Lia be white. Dat is how mistress know."

"Liar!" he screamed and the belt struck again—this time, across her naked breasts.

Celeste's lip bled from biting so hard to hold in her cries.

The master leaned in close to her face. "Look around you. What do you see?"

"Celeste see pain. Celeste see suffering."

"You're damned right, that's what you see. Do you want to be like them? Do you want to endure their pain?"

"No, master. Celeste not be wanting dat. Please, master, Celeste be good. Celeste give master what master wants."

"I will let you live this time, but if you cross me again..." The master walked over to a slave woman he had strapped to a table. She was on her back and awake, with her chest opened to expose her heart. "If you cross me again, this will be your fate." He picked up a large knife and plunged it directly into the woman's heart.

Celeste closed her eyes and tears cascaded down her cheeks.

The master approached her once more and released the chain holding her collar and wrists to the wall. He took the collar from around her neck and threw it to the floor. Then he reached forward and pinched her left nipple, which had been bruised by the belt. "Now get out of my sight. You make me sick. But before you go, remember this – you are to do as you are told, by myself, or by the mistress. You are to do it without question if you want to keep your bastard child safe. Do you understand?"

Celeste nodded quickly. She dared not open her mouth, lest she cry out over the pain in her nipple.

Finally, he released her. She ran out the attic door as fast as she could move.

"No!" Lia bolted awake and looked around desperately.

The sudden scream woke Elliot from a sound sleep. She turned the bedside light on. "Sweetheart, what's wrong?"

Lia looked at her, her expression frozen in a mask of terror.

Elliot climbed to her knees on the bed and took Lia by the shoulders. "Lia. Wake up. You're dreaming. Baby, wake up."

Lia's expression suddenly took on a seductive edge. "Mistress, you want Celeste should fuck you?"

"Oh, shit," Elliot said. "Celeste, I'm not your mistress, remember? I'm Elliot. I'm Lia's wife."

Celeste's brow knit together and she looked confused. "How you be her wife? You be a woman. You be white."

"Just trust me. She's my wife and I love her very much."

"Why your woman be called Lia? Lia be my daughter."

"I don't know why she has the same name as your daughter, but she does. Celeste, why are you here? Why would you want to be with the mistress when she causes you so much pain?"

"She know where da bones be."

"Bones?"

"If mistress finds pleasure wid Celeste, she tell Celeste where dey be."

"I don't understand why Lia—*my* Lia—is in the middle of all this."

"She must see. She must find da way."

"You're talking in riddles. I don't understand what you're saying."

"Celeste not say. She must see."

"What must she see?"

"Pray to the Holy Father dat she see what she must see. My Lia be knowing the way. Celeste go now."

"Celeste, no. Please stay."

"Elliot?"

"Lia? Honey, are you okay?"

Lia threw herself into Elliot's chest and wrapped her arms tightly around Elliot's waist. "I had the most horrific dream. It was both of them—the master and the mistress.

They both tortured. They both killed the slaves. They had Celeste in the attic." Lia began to cry.

"Lia, you're shaking like a leaf."

"He let her go after murdering another slave in front of her as a warning. I could feel her fear. I could feel her pain."

Elliot held her at arm's length. "Sweetheart, it was a dream. It was only a dream. You're safe."

"No, it wasn't a dream. It was Celeste's life. And the lives of all the other slaves who suffered and died at their hands. It wasn't just a dream."

Elliot nodded. "You're right of course, but as real as it felt, know that it happened almost two hundred years ago. Please try to sleep. It's almost midnight and you have to work tomorrow."

"I will. Will you hold me?"

"Of course I will."

Elliot reached for the light, illuminating parts of Lia that had fallen in her shadow. "Oh, my God. Lia, lay down for a minute."

As Lia did, a look of horror crossed Elliot's face. "Elliot, what is it?" She followed Elliot's gaze, directly to her breasts. On her left nipple was a very large and angry looking bruise.

CHAPTER 23

Tuesday

Elliot paced back and forth on the back porch with her cell phone pressed to her ear. "Yes, Julie, she had a bruise on her breast. A bruise she didn't have when we went to bed last night."

"Did she get out of bed in the middle of the night and hurt herself accidentally?" Julie suggested.

"I suppose that's possible. I tend to not wake up when she has to use the bathroom in the middle of the night, so I can't say for sure."

"Well, ask her. I'm sure she'd remember if she ran into something hard enough to cause that size bruise on her breast."

"I'm not so sure about that, Julie."

"What do you mean?"

"You're going to think I'm crazy."

"Look, Elliot. There's a reason you called me and not Marissa. You live in a haunted house for Christ's sake. I suspect it has something to do with that fact. Let me guess, the Creole chick came back. Am I right?"

"Yes."

"Did you talk to her?"

"I did, but she was talking in riddles."

"And I assume Lia doesn't remember the possession."

"No, she doesn't. At least not all of it."

"What do you mean, not all of it?"

"She remembers certain things. Things I'm convinced Celeste is allowing her to selectively remember."

"What kinds of things?"

"Like the torture that reportedly went on here."

"Jesus Christ, she couldn't pick something more pleasant for her to remember?"

"My point exactly. I'm hoping when you two get here we can have a serious talk about it and maybe come up with a plan of action on how to deal with it."

"I'm not a medium, Elliot, but I still have connections in the town. As soon as we arrive, I'll look a few of them up."

"I can't begin to tell you how much I appreciate it, Julie."

"Anything for family, love. We should be there in two days."

"Okay. Hug your lady for me and give her our love. And be careful on the road."

"Will do. See you in two days."

Elliot shut off her phone, reentered the kitchen, and found Lia making a cup of coffee.

"Phone call so early in the morning?" Lia asked.

"Julie. She was calling to check in and to let us know they're on schedule to arrive on Thursday."

"It'll be nice to see them."

Elliot wrapped her arms around Lia's waist and kissed her on the nose. "How are you feeling this morning?"

"I'm a little tired, but I guess that's understandable."

"How's the bruise look?"

"Purple, and my bra rubbing against it isn't helping with the discomfort."

"Can I see it?"

Lia lifted her loose-fitting top and carefully pulled down the front of her bra.

"Damn, baby. It's huge. Maybe you should have it looked at."

"It's just a bruise. I'll put some ice on it when I get home."

Elliot kissed the bruised and swollen area around the nipple before helping Lia tuck herself back in. "You look very nice today."

Lia smiled. "Thank you, love. I'm glad you approve."

"I do. Sit yourself down. I have bagels in the toaster, ready to go."

"Sounds great."

Elliot took the cream cheese and two small yogurts from the refrigerator and put them on the island, along with a butter knife and two teaspoons. "Why don't you get started on your yogurt while the bagels toast?"

Just then, both sides of the toaster popped and Elliot gathered their breakfast on plates and carried them to the table.

"Elliot, did you talk to Celeste last night?"

"I did, but she didn't make much sense. It almost seemed like she was talking in code."

"What did she say?"

"She said something about finding bones and that the mistress knew where they were."

"Maybe that's why she was having sex with her."

"Maybe, although I suspect it was also due in part to survival."

"Did she say anything else?"

"Only that you must see."

"You must see? As in you?"

"No, as in you. We were talking about you. She said you must see and you must find the way. She also said something about *her* Lia knowing the way. I have no clue what that means, do you?"

"Beats the hell out of me."

"When I pressed her to say more, she said she had to go, and then you resurfaced."

"Did she come on to you?"

"So that's what this is all about. When she first appeared, she thought I was the mistress again and kind of got seductive, but when I reminded her who I was, she recovered quickly and the conversation turned to you. I told her you were my wife, and she had a hard time wrapping her head around that since we're both women."

"Well I'm sure relationships like ours were frowned upon back then, although from the sounds of it, she had something going on with the mistress."

"I'm sure it wasn't her choice, love."

"You know, you don't have to defend her," Lia said.

"If I don't, who will? You've seen firsthand what she's lived through. I'm sure she did what she had to do in order to survive and to protect her kid."

Lia put her elbows on the island and lowered her face into her hands. She sighed deeply before looking at Elliot again. "I'm sorry, love. I don't mean to be testy. I'm just tired and more than a little on edge about all that's been going on. I really don't appreciate the possessions. It makes me feel out of control."

"I understand. Would you like a ride to work today?"

"Would you mind?"

"Not at all. Come on."

* * *

Elliot met the cleaning crew supervisor on the porch outside the apartment. "What do you think, Mike?" she asked.

"Well, it's certainly the smell of decay of some sort, Ms. Walker."

"Elliot. Please call me Elliot."

"Will do, ma'am. Like I was saying, it's definitely some kind of decay. Me and the boys have searched every crevice of the kitchen, bathroom, and living room, but we haven't come up with anything."

"I pulled a dead rat out of here a few weeks ago. God only knows how long it was in there. Could that be causing the stench even three weeks later?"

"Totally possible. I recommend letting us do a thorough cleaning of the walls, ceilings, floors, windows, cabinets, and utilities. We'll even clean the drains in the kitchen and bathroom. If it's on the surface, that should do it."

"What do you mean by 'on the surface'?"

"Well sometimes when a smell has been in a room for a long time, it permeates the walls and wood surfaces. When that happens, the only two ways to get rid of it are to either cover it up with paint and polyurethane, or to rip everything out and replace it. But we're getting ahead of ourselves. Let's see what a thorough cleaning will do before we talk about more-drastic measures."

"Okay then. Have at it." Elliot pointed to the kitchen door across the courtyard and down one level. "Just let yourself in the kitchen through that door over there and give a shout if you need me. I'll be somewhere in the house."

"Will do, Elliot."

* * *

"I can't believe an alternate entrance to the attic wasn't fabricated when the contractors removed the stairway," Elliot mumbled to herself as she walked through each room on the third floor looking for some type of trapdoor. "What if a leak had to be fixed or an electrical problem had to be dealt with?"

Her search began in the small guest bedroom that bordered the courtyard on the Governor Nicholls Street side of the house. She thoroughly inspected the bedroom as well as the closet and bathroom ceilings, to no avail. She then moved into the front bedroom, followed by every room in the master suite. After inspecting the walk-in closet off the small bedroom at the end of the suite, she peeked out the window and noted the activity going in and out of the apartment diagonally across the porch. Satisfied that things were progressing well on that front, she made her way back through the master suite and into the hall by the spiral staircase.

Elliot sat down on a settee strategically placed against a wall in the hallway. "Damn, there has to be an entrance. There just has to be." While she sat there, she envisioned what the hallway would have looked like before the fire in 1834. In her mind's eye, she saw an ornately carved stairway with rich mahogany railings and an oriental rug running up the center of the steps. She imagined a six-panel door at the top and a chandelier hanging overhead. All of that was gone. All that was left behind was the vague outline of the floor opening that could only be seen when the light hit it at a certain angle.

She looked next at the closet area beyond where the staircase would have been. The landing inside the attic—on the other side of the attic doorway—would have fallen directly on top of the closet. "I wonder..." Elliot stood and walked toward the closet. She opened the closet door and looked up. "That's odd." A false ceiling had been added to the closet, using the same wood as the shelves were made of, only it was mounted literally at the top of the door opening.

Elliot stepped back into the hallway and looked at the distance between the top of the closet door and the ceiling. There was at least a foot of space above the closet door. *There should be at least that much space between the real ceiling inside the closet and that shelf mounted up there. I wonder how hard it will be to get that shelf out of there.*

Elliot inspected the shelf a little closer. She needed the crowbar and hammer from the garage, so she went through the smaller guestroom to the porch and made her way toward the stairway in the corner by the apartment. Before she was halfway there, she heard a distinctively male scream coming from the apartment. A moment later, one of the workers ran out of the apartment, followed closely by Mike.

"I told you this fucking place was haunted," the worker yelled.

"That's bullshit, John. Now get back in there and do your job."

"No fucking way. She grabbed me, I tell you. I wasn't imagining it. I need a fucking drink."

"If you don't get back in there, you're fired," Mike said.

"Then fire me. No, better yet, I quit," the worker yelled. He stomped down the staircase to the courtyard level and let himself out through the courtyard gates.

Elliot looked at Mike. "What happened?"

"He claims he was on a ladder washing the wall in the far corner of the room and he felt a tug at his leg, and when he looked down, there was this lady standing there, dressed in a long black dress. He says she was trying to pull him off the ladder and when he kicked at her, she simply disappeared."

"Holy shit."

"Yes, indeed."

"Do you think he was telling the truth?"

"Hard to tell. I knew he was superstitious when I hired him. Unfortunately, he also has a bit of a drinking problem, so I'm not sure what came first, the pony or the cart."

"How are things going in there otherwise?"

"We're making progress. The bathroom and kitchen are totally clean, and it does smell better in those two rooms. We're tackling the big room now. We'll try to complete it today, but we might have to come back tomorrow—especially now that we're down a man."

"I'm totally okay with you working a second day if necessary, just as long as we get rid of the smell." Elliot headed toward the stairs. "If you or your guys would like something to drink, I have a large pitcher of lemonade in the refrigerator."

"Thanks for the kind offer, but the guys usually bring drinks with them." Mike looked at his watch. "In fact, it's just about lunchtime, so we'll be taking a break soon."

"Okay. Just know the offer stands."

"We appreciate it."

Elliot continued toward the garage and returned a few moments later carrying a hammer, crowbar, and stepladder, which she banged into the wall several times while she carried it up the stairs. As she passed the apartment, Mike stuck his head out.

"I was wondering what all that racket was. Do you need help with that?" Mike asked.

"If you don't mind, yes." Elliot allowed him to take the ladder.

"Where are we going with it?"

"Just follow me."

Elliot led Mike along the porch, across the balcony, and through the small bedroom to the closet in the hallway.

Mike put the ladder down and opened it up. "This is an amazing house. I'll bet it has lots of history."

"Yes it does, and not all of it good, I'm afraid," Elliot replied. "You can set the ladder up in front of the open closet door."

"What are you trying to do here?"

"I did some research on this place yesterday and learned there used to be a set of stairs against that wall, leading to the attic. I've been looking for the entrance to the attic all morning and so far, I haven't found it. It occurred to me that the stairs would have led to a landing directly above this closet, so I'm removing that false ceiling inside the closet to see if there's an attic access behind it."

"You looking for something in the attic?" Mike asked.

"I'm thinking there might be something loose banging around up there that might be causing some of the odd sounds we hear coming from overhead."

"It *is* an old house, and old houses sometimes make odd noises. It could be as simple as the shrinking or expanding of rafters or joists due to the weather."

"True, but I'll have better peace of mind if I can see for myself."

"Would you like me to remove that board for you?"

"If it's not too much trouble – I would appreciate it."

Elliot stood by as Mike removed the board in a matter of ten minutes. When he handed it down to her, she said, "Wow. That would have taken me an hour."

"Have you got a flashlight?" Mike asked.

"Sure. Give me a minute." Elliot went to her bedroom and grabbed the flashlight she kept in her bedside table in the event of a power outage in the middle of the night. "Here you go." She handed the flashlight up to him.

"You were right. This leads directly to the attic. I hate to tell you this, but it smells pretty bad up here as well, which is pretty normal for attics. All kinds of critters tend to find their way into them."

Mike descended the ladder and handed the flashlight back to Elliot. "Before going up there, I recommend getting an extension ladder. It will be a lot safer than standing on the top of this six-foot stepladder. And you might want to remove a couple more shelves to give yourself more room."

"Okay. Good advice. Thank you."

"I'd better get back to the guys. You know what they say about the mice when the cat's away."

Elliot chuckled. "I do indeed. You can go back out through the bedroom if you'd like. Thanks again."

"You're welcome."

Mike left and Elliot turned back to the closet. "Damn. Now I have to find a bigger ladder. Mike's right, this ladder's a bit too short."

Elliot folded the ladder, leaned it, against the wall next to the ceiling board Mike removed, and closed the closet door.

CHAPTER 24

Elliot's cell phone rang as she took the spiral staircase to the second level. She checked the caller ID before answering the phone. "Hey love."

"Hey, baby. Just calling to see how things are going with the apartment."

"I just spoke with the supervisor, Mike. The kitchen and bathroom are finished and they're now working on the main room. Things are going fine, although they didn't actually find what was causing the smell."

"That doesn't sound good. If they don't find the cause, won't it come back again?"

"Maybe. If it does, we're looking at new paint and urethane, or maybe a renovation."

"Ouch. Let's hope the cleaning does the job. But if not, we'll do what we need to in order to get rid of it."

"I almost forgot. One of the cleaning guys came screaming out of the apartment, claiming a ghostly woman tried to pull him off his ladder while he was washing walls in the main room."

"A ghostly woman? Did he describe her?"

"He said she wore a long black dress."

"Jesus, Elliot. That woman I saw walking out of the hall closet wore a long black dress. Do you think it could be the same one?"

"Perhaps. Wait. Stop right there. Do you realize how crazy this all sounds? Here we are, talking casually about a potential ghost like it's no big deal."

"After everything that's happened in the house, and after numerous possessions of my body by Miss French Fry, does it really sound that crazy, Elliot?"

"Well, when you put it that way..."

"Did the woman try to harm him?" Lia asked.

"Other than pulling on his leg while he was on the ladder? No, I don't think so. That didn't prevent him from quitting, anyway."

"I'm sorry to hear that."

"From what Mike said, this guy has other issues he's dealing with. He didn't seem too broken up about losing the guy. Oh, I have some news for you."

"Really? Spill it."

"I found the access to the attic."

"You didn't!"

"I did. You were very close. It was in the closet, but not on the outside wall. It was in the ceiling."

"Seriously? How did I miss that when we looked in the closet yesterday?"

"Because there was a false ceiling that was installed at the same height as the doorway. It was only a piece of board the same size as the shelves. Mike removed it for me. A flashlight confirmed it led to the attic."

"Did you go up there?"

"No. The six-foot stepladder I found in the garage is too short for me to reach. We have to pick up an extension ladder."

"Elliot, promise you'll wait until I get home. I want to go up there with you."

"I can pick you up from work again, and we can get one on the way home."

"Okay, that sounds good."

"So, how is your day going?"

"You know what it's like working in a lab environment. One day you make exceptionally good progress, then the next it's as slow as molasses going uphill in January. Needless to say, today is a slow day. That makes the day drag on, and now that we have something exciting to do after work, it will feel like an eternity until five o'clock."

"I could always pick the ladder up first, and you second. Then we could just head home."

"That sounds like a better plan, love. I'll see you around five, then."

"I'll be there. I hope the rest of your day goes by quicker than you think. I love you."

"Love you too, El. See you soon."

* * *

As promised, Elliot was waiting outside the lab at exactly five p.m. "Sorry, but you're going to have to share your space with the ladder," she said as Lia opened the passenger door. "I was barely able to fit it into the car."

"That's okay. We'll manage."

"I also picked up a black light. I was thinking we could use it in the apartment to look for hidden contamination that might be causing the stench. We'll take it into the attic as well. Mike said it smells pretty bad up there too."

"We use black lights in the lab for cancer cell analysis, and I know the forensics lab uses them all the time to detect blood."

"That's pretty much why I bought it. I'm curious as to whether blood is the cause of our odor problems."

"Interesting idea. By the way, what smells so good in here?"

"I hope you don't mind, but I picked up Chinese take-out for dinner."

"Why would I mind? I love Chinese take-out. Thank you for doing that, love."

"My pleasure. This way, we can either eat before we check out the attic, or just pop it into the microwave and eat afterwards."

"I vote we eat first. I'm starved."

"You, my dear, have a hearty appetite. Sometimes I wonder how you stay so beautifully svelte."

"It appears I'm eating for two these days, and Miss French Fry's appetite is bigger than mine. That's my story and I'm sticking to it."

Elliot laughed heartily. "I'm so glad your sense of humor is still intact through all of this."

"I'm trying, El. I'm really trying. I just hope there's an end to this madness. I can't imagine living the rest of our lives like this."

"I hope going into the attic will put us one step closer to resolving this, Lia."

"I'm right there with you. It certainly can't hurt."

"I hope not."

* * *

"Here's the last shelf." Elliot handed it down to Lia. "Now, let me move this stepladder out of the way and put the new ladder up."

Lia shone the flashlight into the hole in the closet ceiling as Elliot took care of exchanging the ladders. "Elliot, there's a light switch near the ceiling of the closet."

"It's probably for the attic. Scoot over and let me put the extension ladder in there." Once the ladder was in place, Elliot climbed up halfway. "Could you hand me the black light, please? Thanks, love. Let me turn the lights on, and then you can come up behind me, okay?"

Elliot climbed high enough to reach the light switch and flicked it on. Light flooded the attic. "Perfect. I'm going to step into the attic, then I'll hold the ladder for you to climb up."

Elliot was able to step directly from the ladder rung onto the attic floor. She took a quick look around, then stood behind the ladder to hold it in place. "Okay, come on up."

Lia stepped on the bottom rung and slowly made her way up the ladder, never breaking eye contact with Elliot as she climbed.

"Come on, Lia, slow and easy. Look here," Elliot said, pointing to her own eyes. "If you begin to feel anything odd, I want you to go back down."

Lia continued to look at Elliot as she climbed. "I'm okay."

When she reached the top, Elliot held her firmly by the arms and helped her step onto the attic floor. She took Lia's chin in her hand. "Are you okay?" she asked.

Lia's face was a mask of concentration except for her jaw muscles, which repeatedly contracted. She nodded in response to Elliot's question.

"Come away from the hole," Elliot said. She took Lia's hand and walked a few feet into the attic. "Wow. I can't believe all this stuff is still up here," she whispered.

As they looked down the length of the ninety-foot attic, they saw implements of torture everywhere. Dozens of chains and metal collars hung from the walls, cages were scattered about the room, and hard wooden tables with straps attached to them were plentiful. On the far wall was a shelf, upon which they could see paddles and whips as well as an array of knives, saws, thumb screws, tongue tearers, breast rippers, and other implements.

Elliot's throat closed with emotion as she imagined the horror the slaves lived through in this hellish place. She could feel Lia trembling beside her. She wrapped her arms around Lia and held her close. "I've got you, love. Are you okay? Do you want to go?"

Lia was shaking so violently, her teeth chattered as she spoke. "No. I need to do this. They lived through this hell. The least I can do is honor their memories."

Elliot held her closer. "You're shaking, my love. Breathe deeply. Try to calm down. You're going into shock. Maybe we should go."

"No!" Lia said loudly before closing her eyes and concentrating on controlling herself. "I'm sorry, Elliot. Please. I need to do this."

"Okay, but if this gets worse, you will no longer get a vote. Understood?"

Lia nodded.

"All right. Do you want to walk around a bit?"

"Yes, but please don't let go of me."

"Never—I promise. Let's start over here."

Elliot slowly led Lia down the length of the attic. On one wall alone, Elliot counted more than two dozen metal collars containing spikes along the inside rim, all attached to the walls by chains. There were hangman nooses extending from several rafters as well as an assortment of medieval torture devices at the far end of the room, including a crude chair lined with spikes, a limb-stretching rack and other evil-looking implements that Elliot could only imagine uses for.

"I can't believe how barbaric they were," Elliot whispered. "No wonder this house is haunted." She looked at Lia to see how she was handling the horrors before then, and realized she was crying. She stopped and took Lia's face between her palms. "I'm so sorry, love. I know how hard this is for you. Are you ready to go?"

Lia wiped the tears from her cheeks. "I'm okay. My heart's breaking, but I'm okay. Please, let's continue."

Slowly, they moved forward. It became apparent that the attic was divided into two parts, the far end where the torture took place, and the end near the opening where medical atrocities were performed.

"The master was a doctor, wasn't he?" Elliot asked as they moved slowly past the operating tables equipped with straps.

"Yes, he was. Most of the research blames the torture on the mistress, but I saw with my own eyes what he did to Celeste, and to the woman he murdered in front of her. I'm convinced he was as guilty as she was."

"You're most likely correct. Either way, they were both sick bastards. Okay, we're back at the beginning. I'm going to shut the lights off and use the black light, but I want you to go back downstairs first."

"I'm okay. I want to stay."

"Are you sure?"

"Yes. I'm fine."

Elliot turned on the black light. "Now to turn off the lights." She saw a light switch on a nearby pole. "I'm willing to bet this is hooked in a series with the light switch we found in the closet. Here goes nothing."

The attic was cast into sudden darkness, save for the glow of the black light. "Come here, love. Hold onto me." Elliot reached out her hand. Expecting immediate contact, yet feeling none, she called out, "Lia, take my hand. Lia?"

Elliot swung the black light around. A fast-moving object rushed toward her, clipped her shoulder, and knocked her to the floor. The black light flew from her hand and skidded across the floor ten feet from her.

"Lia, where are you?" Elliot called out. "Please answer me!" Elliot climbed to her feet and scrambled over to where her black light was. She picked it up held it high over her head. "Lia."

A sudden movement from behind her caused her to swing around, and once again, she saw something streak across the room. Knowing she and Lia were the only ones in the attic, she played a hunch and called out again. "Celeste."

"El-eee-ot," the voice responded.

"Celeste, where are you?"

"Isit la nan mitan mò yo k ap viv." (Here, among the living dead.)

"I don't know what you're saying. Please, give Lia back to me."

"Leya mwen se mouri. Leya ou ka delivre nou. Leya ou wè sa mwen wè. Wè mouri vivan an, Leya. Se k ap viv nan mouri." (My Lia is dead. Your Lia can save us. Your Lia sees what I see. See the living dead, Lia. See the living dead.)

"Damn it, Celeste. Give her to me." Elliot swung the black light around wildly and spotted the pole with the light switch on it. She lunged forward and turned the switch on, instantly flooding the attic with light.

"Elliot!"

"Lia! Sweetheart. Oh, my God," Elliot said as she spotted her wife.

"Elliot, help me."

Elliot ran across the width of the attic to where Lia was strapped to one of the operating tables. An array of scalpels and saws were on the table beside her. Elliot made quick work of the straps and helped her off the table. Lia wrapped herself around Elliot and held on for dear life.

"Come on. We need to get out of here." Elliot took Lia's hand and ran with her to the ladder extending from the hole in the floor. She held the ladder for Lia to climb down first, and scurried down the ladder behind her.

Once on the floor of the hallway, she collapsed the extension ladder and pushed it aside. She dragged the six-foot ladder back into the closet and collected the false ceiling board, hammer, and nails. After climbing the ladder, she turned off the attic lights, shoved the board into place, and nailed it securely. Satisfied that the entry to the attic was once again blocked, she climbed down the ladder, pulled it out of the closet, and closed the door. Her heart pounded violently as adrenaline coursed through her.

She expected to see Lia in the hall, but she was gone. "Lia?"

Elliot's instinct sent her first to their bedroom, where she found Lia naked, and asleep in the bed. "What the hell?" she whispered. She approached Lia and leaned down close to her face. She was sleeping soundly. Elliot kissed her on the cheek. "Wake up, sweetheart."

"It's late. Come to bed," Lia said without opening her eyes. Elliot stood erect and watched her for several moments. *It's not late. It's only eight p.m. At least it's her and not Celeste.* She kissed Lia on the cheek once more. *You're going to have one hell of a memory hangover in the morning, my love.*

Elliot walked to the window to close the drapes and immediately noticed Samuel standing on the street corner, watching the house. A sudden surge of anger filled her as she ran down both flights of stairs and out into the street. She dashed across the intersection and grabbed Samuel by the lapels. "I'm warning you. If Celeste takes her one more time, I won't be responsible for what happens. You got that?"

"We means Miss Lia no harm. She gots to find the way. Lia will show her the way."

"Enough with the goddamned riddles, Samuel," Elliot growled in the man's face. "Leave her alone. Do you hear me? Leave. Her. Alone."

Samuel remained silent. Elliot turned on her heel, returned to the house, and slammed the iron gate behind her.

CHAPTER 25

Wednesday

Elliot spent the next four hours sitting in a chair beside the bed, watching Lia sleep. Just as she was about to give up her vigil and go to bed, Lia began to stir. Elliot froze. Lia sat up and looked around the room. She looked right at Elliot, apparently without seeing her. In one swift movement, she threw the covers off and lowered her feet to the floor.

Elliot remained seated as Lia stood and walked toward the bedroom door, totally naked. As soon as Lia had cleared the doorway, Elliot got up and followed her, keeping a safe distance behind. Lia walked through the hallway toward the closet. She paused momentarily in front of the closet door and slowly moved on toward the small bedroom.

Where the hell is she going? Elliot peeked around the corner of the bedroom door just as Lia stepped onto the porch and walked to the edge of the balcony. She stood there for several long moments, looking out over the courtyard.

She raised her arms to the sides and lowered her head back. In the light of the full moon, Elliot could only see Lia's silhouette from her perch in the doorway. She imagined Lia's eyes were closed.

Lia rolled her head around in circles, and an eerie chant emerged from her throat. After a time, the chanting stopped and Lia lowered her chin. With her arms still held out to the sides, she looked down into the courtyard.

"Lanmò te fin sènen nou, ak doulè yo nan lanfè bagèt kenbe sou nou tout. Nan kote sa a nou te jwenn pwoblèm ak lapenn." (The sorrows of death encompass us, and the pains of hell got hold upon us all. In this place we found trouble and sorrow.)

What is she looking at? Elliot contemplated stepping onto the balcony, but she realized she could get a better view from the bedroom window that overlooked the courtyard. As she made her way across the bedroom toward the window, she heard Lia speak again.

"Kite sa fèt plezi ki apa pou ou, o Bondye mwen, nan trankil lespri sa yo anbarasman, ki se kounye a M'enerve; èske w'ap jounen jodi a mete lapè nan plas la nan enkyetid." (Let it be thy holy pleasure, oh, my God, to quiet these troublesome spirits, which are now restless; wilt thou presently send peace in the place of disquiet.)

Elliot reached the window and looked down. "Holy shit," she whispered. Gathered in the courtyard, illuminated by the eerie glow of the full moon, were dozens of people, all black, some in chains and many wearing blood-soaked clothes. In the middle of the pack, was Samuel.

"Seyè a Latè la! Se ou ki Bondye a sèlman, Seyè a, se ou menm pou kont li, libere sèvitè ou ki mete konfyans yo nan ou Non mwen nèt ale. Amèn." (Lord of the Earth! Thou art the only God, Jehovah, even thou alone, liberate thy servants who trusts in thy most holy name. Amen.)

"Lia!" Elliot screamed. She raced through the bedroom and threw the screen door open with a bang as it hit the opposite wall. "Lia," she called again and ran toward her.

Lia slumped forward. If not for Elliot's hold on her arm, she would have tumbled over the railing and into the courtyard three stories below.

"Lia, baby, I've got you," Elliot said as she lowered her to the porch floor. Elliot looked through the spindles of the railing. The courtyard was empty. "Damn you, Celeste," she mumbled as she turned her attention back to Lia.

"Elliot? What am I doing outside?"

"Let me get you inside, love, and I'll tell you all about it."

Elliot helped Lia to her feet and placed an arm around her waist.

"I'm naked. Why the hell am I outside and naked?"

Elliot led Lia back to their bedroom and sat her on the bed. She went into the closet and pulled an overnight bag from the shelf. She carried it to the bed and put it down beside Lia.

"What are you doing?" Lia asked.

"We're going to the hotel. Tonight."

"No. I don't want to leave."

"We're leaving, Lia. If I hadn't been on that balcony with you tonight, you would have fallen over the railing and died."

"Si ou pa t 'janm sou balkon la aswè a, li ta yo tou senpleman tounen san danje nan kabann ou."

Startled, then angry, Elliot put her hands on her hips. "What did you say?" she demanded.

"Celeste say, if you not be dere, she be returning safe to your bed."

"Why was she out there? Who were all those people?"

"Dey be tortured souls. Dey be tortured bodies. Dey be here because you let dem out."

"*I* let them out? From where? What the hell are you talking about?"

"You and my Lia. You let dem out of dey prison."

"We didn't ask for this, Celeste. We didn't ask for any of this. All we wanted was a nice home to live the rest of our lives in. You're quickly destroying all of that. You need to go. And you need to go, now."

"She be my Lia. Celeste not go until Lia find da way."

Elliot lunged forward, grabbed Celeste by the arms, and roughly shook her. "She is not your Lia. Now, get out of her. Do you hear me? Get out of her right now!"

"Elliot! You're hurting me. What's wrong with you?"

Elliot stopped and looked into Lia's eyes. "Lia?"

"Why were you shaking me?"

Elliot backed a few feet away until she encountered the wall. She slid down and sat on the floor with her face buried in her hands. She couldn't control herself as great sobs wracked her body.

Lia walked over to Elliot and knelt beside her. She placed her hand on Elliot's arm. "Elliot?"

Elliot turned her tortured gaze on Lia. "I'm sorry, love. I am so sorry."

"Talk to me. What happened here tonight?"

Elliot lowered her hands from her face and looked at Lia through tear-filled eyes. "Lia, we need to leave. The longer we stay, the more Celeste is taking control of you. In the beginning, the worst we had were bumps in the night, but now it's getting personal, and it's becoming dangerous— especially for you."

"I still don't know what happened. Why was I on the balcony? Why are you so upset?"

"Lia, what do you remember about the attic?"

"The attic?"

"Yes. Do you even remember going into the attic with me this afternoon?"

"Yes, I remember. I remember every horrible minute of it. I remember my heart breaking when I realized what those poor souls lived and died through. We need to get rid of that stuff in the attic. It gives me the creeps to know those instruments of torture are just a few feet above our heads at night."

"Do you remember what happened when I turned the lights off?"

"Not really. In fact, after being in the attic, the next thing I remember is being naked on the balcony."

Elliot climbed to her feet and began to pace. "Son of a bitch." she growled, her fists clenched by her sides. "She totally duped me. She made me believe she was you."

"Are you still talking about Celeste?" Lia asked.

Elliot approached Lia and reached her hand down to help her up. "Come on. Sit on the bed, and I'll get you some night clothes. Then we'll talk."

Elliot gathered a pair of panties and a T-shirt from Lia's dresser and helped her into the clothing. When Lia raised her arms for Elliot to pull the T-shirt over her head, bruising was already appearing on the undersides of both arms from Elliot's rough treatment of Celeste. When Elliot saw the marks, she fell to her knees in front of Lia and covered her face once more with her hands.

Lia leaned forward and grasped Elliot's wrists. "Talk to me, baby."

"I'm so ashamed of myself. Look what I've done to you."

"You didn't mean to do it, love. I know you. You would never intentionally hurt me. I trust you with my life."

"I'm sorry."

"I'm okay. Please tell me what happened in the attic."

Elliot got up and sat on the bed beside Lia. She reached for Lia's hand, brought it to her lips for a gentle kiss, and held it in her own lap. "When we shut the lights off to use the black light, somehow I lost track of you, which I know now was Celeste's doing. She toyed with me, Lia. She pushed me down in the dark and played a game of cat and mouse with me. Finally, I found the light switch. When I turned it on, you were strapped to one of those tables, and someone had moved some of the medical instruments to the table beside you."

"Are you serious? Oh, my God. If Celeste was in control of me, she was the one strapped to the table. Does that mean she died in the attic? Was she one of the master's medical experiments?"

Elliot shook her head. "I don't know. It's certainly possible. Anyway, you called my name and begged me to help you. I got us out of there as fast as I could. You went down the ladder first, and when I climbed down, I boarded the attic up again as fast as I could. When I was finished, I looked around and couldn't find you. In the few minutes it took me to board up the attic, you had come in here, taken off your clothes, and gone fast asleep in the bed."

"I don't remember any of that."

"Of course you don't, because it wasn't you. It was Celeste."

"Was it also Celeste on the balcony?"

"Yes. I was sitting in the chair watching you sleep, and when you got up, I followed you to the balcony." Elliot raised Lia's hand to her chest and held it close to her heart. "You were on the balcony talking to dozens of slave ghosts in the courtyard. I swear to you, I saw them with my own eyes, and Samuel was among them. They were all there, paying rapt attention to Celeste on the balcony. Almost as though she was their leader."

Lia pulled her hand away and stood up to face Elliot. "Slave ghosts? You saw them? Is it my imagination, or are things escalating these past few days?"

"Things have definitely escalated. I asked Celeste who they were, and she said they were the tortured souls and that we let them out."

"*We* let them out? As in you and I?"

"That's what she implied."

"Could they have been trapped in the attic?"

Elliot stood up and ran both hands through her hair. "I have no idea. I guess it's possible. Jesus, this is so overwhelming."

"What are we going to do?"

Elliot wrapped her arms around Lia and pulled her close. "I don't know, sweetheart. Maybe Julie can help us. Thank God they'll be here in two days. She says she still has connections in the town who know about these things."

"You've been speaking to Julie about this?"

"Yes. I was on the phone with her this morning, remember?" Elliot looked at the date displayed on her watch. "Or maybe I should say yesterday morning. It's two a.m. We need to get some sleep. I still think we should go to the hotel."

"I'm not going to let them chase us out of our home."

"Lia, you don't seem to have any control over Celeste's possessions. I'm worried about you."

"She has no reason to hurt me. From what you've said, she seems to be the one in charge here. She needs something from me."

CHAPTER 26

Lia appeared in the kitchen the next morning dressed like a gypsy, complete with a scarf on her head that was tied behind her neck, and wearing bright red lipstick. She went directly to the coffee machine.

Elliot looked up from where she was cooking at the stove. "Ah, you might want to change your clothes," she suggested.

Lia turned to Elliot while her coffee was brewing. "She didn't."

"She did. Go look in the mirror if you don't believe me."

Lia marched out of the kitchen, across the hall to the living room and into the parlor where there was a powder room.

Elliot continued to cook the scrambled eggs but paused when she heard loud curse coming from the other room.

"God damn it, Celeste. Would you please let me dress myself in the morning?" she heard Lia shout, followed by the sound of her wife stomping up the stairs.

Elliot grinned. "Someone's in trouble. Good enough for you, Celeste. It's time you were put in your place."

Lia returned ten minutes later dressed in black slacks, teal-colored blouse, a black tailored jacket and heels. The headscarf and red lipstick were gone.

"Now, there's my girl." Elliot put Lia's breakfast on the island in front of her. She kissed her on the cheek. "Eat up."

"What am I going to do about her, Elliot? She dresses me like a bar wench."

"Until we figure out how to get rid of her, you're going to have to compromise. Maybe you let her choose your outfits when you're home as long as you get to choose when you're leaving the house."

"She shouldn't get a choice at all."

"You're right—she shouldn't, but if I go to work before you do, there will be no one here to stop you from leaving the house wearing clothes circa 1834."

"I really hope Julie knows someone who can help. I'm so ready to put all of this behind us."

"I'm looking forward to seeing them and to spending an entire week with them. You've scheduled next week off, right?"

"Yes. I feel odd taking vacation so soon after starting a new job, but my employer understands the circumstances."

Elliot looked at the time and noted it was seven-thirty a.m. "It looks like you need a ride to work."

"Yes, I do, if you don't mind. After the night we put in, I just couldn't get out of bed at five a.m."

"Of course I don't mind. I'm ready when you are."

* * *

On her way home after dropping Lia off at work, Elliot stopped for a few groceries. She planned to surprise her with barbeque ribs slow-cooked on their new grill, corn on the cob, and a fresh garden salad for dinner. As she drove down Royal Street in the direction of her house, she spotted a car parked in front that looked familiar...very familiar. Two people stood at the iron gate at her front entrance, ringing the doorbell. She pulled up parallel to the car parked out front and rolled down the window. "I have it on good authority that they're not home," she called out the window.

The two people swung around, screamed, and ran toward her car.

"There you are," the blonde woman squealed.

"Out of the car, Walker, before I kick your ass," the brunette added.

Elliot threw the car in park and climbed out in time to take Marissa into her arms. "It's so good to see you, but you weren't supposed to be here until tomorrow."

"Julie told me what was happening around here, and I didn't want to waste another moment. So we put the pedal to the metal, and here we are."

Julie walked around the car. "My turn," she said as she hugged Elliot.

"Hey there, blondie," Elliot said. "I really missed you guys."

"Is this okay?" Marissa asked, pointing to the cars they had arrived in. "We didn't know where to park."

"Actually, I'll ask you to pull into the courtyard so we can take our time unloading over the next few days without worrying about the cars being broken into."

"Point the way." Julie climbed behind the wheel of the car she drove.

"Take the cars around the block one more time. That will give me time to park the rental and run through the house to open the courtyard gates from the inside. The entrance to the courtyard is just around the corner to the right."

As soon as Marissa and Julie drove their respective cars away from the curb, Elliot parked in their spot. She grabbed her groceries, locked the car and let herself in the front entrance. By the time she dropped the groceries off at the bottom of the spiral staircase and made her way to the courtyard, Marissa and Julie had returned from their trip around the block and were able to pull both cars into the courtyard side by side. Elliot closed and locked the courtyard gates as they climbed out of the cars.

"Wow," Marissa exclaimed as she looked around.

"Wow, indeed," Julie added. "This is a lot of house."

"Yeah. No fooling," Elliot replied. "Believe it or not, this is mostly one house. At least it is now. Over the past hundred years or so, it was broken into apartments and pieced back together a couple of times." Elliot pointed to the side of the building that shared a common wall with the Royal Street neighbor. "Do you see that wing over there? The first and second floors are still apartments. The only way to get to them is through the courtyard. The third floor of that wing is part of the master bedroom suite. There's also another apartment on the first floor and a fourth apartment above the library. Right now they're all pretty much empty."

"What possessed you to buy such a monstrosity?" Marissa asked.

Elliot frowned. "It's funny you used both the words 'possessed' and 'monstrosity' in that sentence Mar, considering it's both possessed and a monstrosity."

"But yet, you stay," Julie said.

"Lia won't leave. I've insisted several times that we move back to the hotel for a while, but she refuses."

"Are you sure it's her who is refusing?" Julie asked.

"What's that supposed to mean?" Marissa asked.

"El knows what I mean," Julie replied.

Marissa looked at Elliot with raised eyebrows.

"I have to admit, that thought has crossed my mind," Elliot said. "But still, Lia doesn't seem to be the least bit afraid of what's been going on here."

"Okay, stop right there," Marissa said. "Something tells me there's a lot more happening here than either of you has shared with me. I'd say cheesecake and wine are in order."

"Why don't we save that until Lia's home?" Elliot said. "Besides, it isn't even noon. I'd say that's just a bit early for wine."

"Fair enough. How about coffee?"

"Coffee, we can do. Follow me. I'll give you the grand tour first."

* * *

Elliot led the women through the doors into the first level and through each room, pointing out which ones originally housed menservants and stable hands.

"The servants were really slaves, weren't they?" Marissa asked. "I mean, it was the eighteen hundreds. If they could have slaves instead of paying for servants, one would think they'd choose that option."

"Unfortunately, yes. They were slaves. Lia had a real hard time coming to terms with that when we originally toured the house."

"When I was doing the property search for you, I remember how upset she was when she found out," Marissa said.

"How is she dealing with it now?" Julie asked.

Elliot grew solemn. "I'll let her tell you about that. Let's just say things began to get real weird around here yesterday. Not that it hasn't been somewhat odd right from the beginning. We can talk more about this over dinner. In the meantime, we have two more floors to tour."

Elliot led them into the foyer and picked up the groceries she had left at the bottom of the stairs.

"Holy Jesus," Marissa exclaimed. "This is an amazing stairway. I can see clear to the top floor."

"That's where we're headed—just as soon as I drop these off at the kitchen and we tour the second story," Elliot said.

Elliot smiled to herself at her friends' reactions to her new home. As they stepped onto the second-floor landing, Elliot said, "I guess the best place to start is in the kitchen. Follow me."

Like mice behind the Pied Piper, Marissa and Julie dutifully followed Elliot into the butler's pantry and then into the kitchen.

"I am so jealous," Julie said. "This is amazing."

"And much more modern that I would have thought," Marissa added.

"Give me a minute to put the groceries in the fridge. I bought ribs and corn on the cob for dinner. It's a good thing I bought extra."

"Sorry to drop in on you early, but we really were concerned about you two," Marissa said.

"No problem at all. I tend to over shop, so we have plenty. That's the main reason Lia usually does the grocery shopping. I guess it's a good thing I did it this time." Elliot walked to the back door. "This door leads to the second-story porch that wraps all around the courtyard. Come take a look."

Marissa and Julie followed Elliot onto the porch where they marveled once more about how big the house was. "This porch," Elliot said, "literally wraps around the side and front of the house as well. Follow me. I have something awesome to show you."

Elliot led them around the porch, stopped at the apartment wing—where they quickly looked around—and to the library on the opposite side of the courtyard from the kitchen. She stopped in front of the library door. "Go on in."

"Marissa opened the door and stepped into the library, with Julie right on her heels. "Oh, my freaking, God. How many books are there?"

"I have no idea," Elliot admitted. "We haven't spent enough time in here yet to count them. I'm really looking forward to a time when we can just relax and spend time here in the evenings."

Their tour of the library was interrupted by a loud crash above their heads.

Julie jumped. "Jesus Christ! What was that?"

"That's a good question," Elliot said. "There shouldn't be anyone up there. The workmen weren't supposed to come back until tomorrow."

"Workmen?" Marissa asked.

"The first time we opened that apartment, it smelled like something had died in there. In fact, it was in there that Lia fainted for the first time."

"From the smell?" Julie asked.

"I don't know. Like I said, that was the first time she fainted. She's fainted, or blacked out, several times since," Elliot explained.

"Maybe we should go check it out," Marissa suggested.

"Let's do that," Elliot said.

The trio left the library, closed the door, and took the corner stairway to the third floor. Elliot stood in front of the apartment door and looked nervously at her friends. "Here goes nothing," She swung the door open.

The cat came dashing out and jumped into Elliot's arms.

"Humph. Well, there, Miss Thing. Have you been locked in there all night? Serves you right for being so nosy." Elliot scratched behind the cat's ears.

"Miss Thing?" Julie asked.

"We have no idea what her name is, so we just call her Miss Thing. She's kind of adopted us."

Marissa looked into the apartment. "I see a wooden ladder on its side in there. I'm guessing Miss Thing jumped from the top of it to the floor and knocked it over."

"That would make sense," Elliot said. "Let's go take a look."

Elliot entered the apartment, followed by Marissa and Julie. "The aroma is certainly better in here, but I can still smell the decay. Did I tell you I found a dead rat in here the day we moved in?"

"That's gross," Julie said.

Still carrying the cat, Elliot walked around the perimeter of the room and inspected the job the cleaners had done. When she reached the far corner of the room, she opened the built-in wardrobe. As soon as she opened the door, the cat began to growl and hiss so badly that Elliot had to put her down. "Damn. What the hell is the matter with you?"

Julie inspected the open wardrobe while Elliot rubbed the sting out of the claw marks the cat had left on her arms.

"That's odd," Julie said. "There are scratch marks on the insides of these doors. I wonder how they got there."

"Beats the hell out of me," Elliot said. "This room was locked when we bought the house, so I doubt anyone has lived in here for a while."

"I'm guessing a kid was locked in there as punishment. Those marks are probably decades old," Marissa said.

"Did anyone see where Miss Spaz went? I don't want to lock her in here again," Elliot said as they walked back toward the entrance to the apartment.

"Yes, she ran onto the porch," Julie answered. "I think it's safe to close this door."

"All right then, let's take the porch back around to the kitchen and I'll show you the rest of the house. Then I need to get the ribs cooking really slow on the grill so they'll be ready for when Lia gets home. She's going to be so surprised to see you two."

Elliot escorted her friends through the dining room, living room, and parlor, then up the stairs to the third story.

The first place she took them was to the bedroom in the front corner of the house, facing Royal Street. "This is where you two will sleep," she said as she pushed the door open. She allowed Marissa and Julie to enter the room before her.

"Well, hello there, Miss Thing," Julie said.

"What? How did she get in here again?" Elliot entered the room behind Marissa and looked at the window near the corner of the room. "God damn it. The window's open again. I know I locked it."

"Great," Marissa teased. "You're putting us in a haunted room."

"I'm beginning to think there's no room in this house that isn't haunted," Elliot replied.

"It will be fine," Julie said. "We'll just close the window and lock it again. There. All set. See?"

"So this cat can scale walls too?" Marissa asked.

"Very funny, Mar. There's actually a ledge that runs below the windows all around the two street-sides of the house."

Julie lay on the bed. "I'm in heaven. This is very comfortable."

"I'll help you with your luggage after the tour's over." Elliot pointed to the far end of the bedroom. "You have your own bathroom over there."

"Sweet," Marissa said.

"Lia and I are just across the hall. Come with me and I'll show you."

Marissa and Julie followed Elliot through the entire length of the master suite and back, once again marveling at the size. They returned to the hall where Elliot pointed to the closet in the corner. "Lia swears she saw a woman dressed in eighteen-hundreds-period garb come out of the closet and disappear down the staircase two days ago."

"Are you serious?" Julie asked.

"There's more. If you look just to the right at the ceiling above the closet, you'll see a large rectangular indentation, almost like there used to be a hole there."

"I see it," Marissa said.

"There used to be another stairway right against the

bedroom wall that led to the attic. It opened onto the attic floor just above that closet. It has since been torn down and blocked off. I found the plans for it in an old blueprint."

"I wonder what's up there," Julie said.

"I found the entrance, and Lia and I went up there last night. It was the most horrid experience we've had since we moved in."

"Tell us what's up there," Marissa insisted.

"According to the stories and rumors about this house, that's where the slaves were tortured and killed, and where medical experiments were done on them. We confirmed last night that the stories were true. There are more torture implements up there than in a medieval dungeon. Lia was devastated."

"She must have really freaked out. I know I would have," Julie said.

"She didn't get a chance to freak out. Celeste took over when things really started to get weird, so she was unaware of what happened next."

"Jesus, Elliot. Why do you stay here?" Marissa asked.

"Lia doesn't want to leave."

"So what else has happened?"

"Let's go back to the kitchen so I can get the ribs started, and I'll tell you all about it. We'll cut through the courtyard bedroom, which you haven't seen yet, and take the porch steps down a level. They end up pretty near the kitchen."

***

"Get out of Dodge!" Julie said. "You actually *saw* them with your own eyes?"

"I did. There were dozens of them. Mind you, there wasn't much light, but I definitely saw distinct human forms. They were gathered in the courtyard like subjects straining to see a glimpse of their queen on the balcony. Lia was totally unaware of what was happening."

"Who the hell is this Celeste chick, anyway?" Marissa asked as she sipped her coffee.

"As far as I can tell, she was one of the slaves, but with certain benefits, if you know what I mean," Elliot said.

"Are you trying to tell us she was porking the master?" Marissa said.

"She was porking the master and the mistress."

"Damn," Marissa said.

"She must have gotten special treatment then," Julie surmised.

"I'm not so sure that's true. Apparently she bore the master's child and was repeatedly punished for it by the mistress. From what I can tell, she had sex with the mistress to keep her and her child safe from abuse. It appears she was tortured by the master as well. Lia and I think she died in the attic from one of the master's medical experiments."

"I would be out of this freaking house so fast your head would spin," Marissa said. "In fact, I'm not sure I want to stay here at all."

Julie slapped her on the arm. "Don't be a wuss," she said.

"So this Celeste chick—" Marissa began.

"Lia calls her Miss French Fry," Elliot interjected, chuckling.

"Ha, ha! That's funny. So, French Fry just takes over Lia's body whenever she wants?"

"More or less, although it tends to be more when Lia's guard is down...like when she's sleeping."

"Damn. This is really fucked up," Marissa said.

"That's putting it mildly, my friend," Elliot replied.

CHAPTER 27

Elliot glanced into the backseat of the car as they waited outside the Louisiana Cancer Institute. "Be sure to keep your heads down. I don't want her to see you until she gets into the car."

"You are evil, my friend," Marissa said.

"Shhh. Here she comes."

Lia walked around the car to the passenger side and opened the door. She slipped into the front seat, hooked her seatbelt, and leaned over to kiss Elliot.

"Surprise!" came the loud proclamation from the backseat.

"Ahhh!" Lia screamed, before she realized she'd been set up. "You scared the bejesus out of me. What are you two doing here? You weren't supposed to arrive until tomorrow. Come here and give me some love."

One by one, Julie, then Marissa stood and leaned over the front seat to hug and kiss their friend.

"You should have seen your face," Marissa teased.

Lia looked at Elliot and slugged her in the arm. "You, I will take care of later," she said.

"Promises, promises," Elliot said as a chorus of "Ooo's" came from the backseat.

Lia glanced at them. "You guys are incorrigible. Seriously, why are you here so early?"

"We heard you were looking for ghostbusters, and we thought we'd apply for the job," Marissa joked.

"That isn't funny, Mar," Lia said.

"No, really, we were concerned about you. From what we've heard, you have been dealing with some heavy stuff—especially you, Lia," Marissa explained.

"Sugar," Julie said. "I still have a lot of connections in this town. Over dinner, I want to throw out a few ideas about how to understand what's happening here. And maybe how to rid yourselves of these spirits."

"I don't think they're spirits, Jules. They're ghosts. For some reason, these poor souls haven't crossed over," Lia said.

"I stand corrected. You're absolutely right." Julie reached into the front seat and put her hand on Lia's shoulder. "We're worried about you. We want to help."

"I love you guys," Lia said.

"Love you too, toots," Marissa said before addressing Elliot. "Okay, El, time to hit the grocery store. We need some cheesecake and wine."

***

"El, sweetie," Lia said, "these ribs are to die for." She licked the barbeque sauce from her fingers.

"Glad you like them. There's plenty more on the grill if you're ready for seconds."

"Please." Lia handed her plate to Elliot.

Elliot looked around the kitchen island. "Anyone else?" she asked.

"I'd love some more," Julie said.

"I second that," Marissa added. "Let me give you a hand." Marissa took Julie's plate and followed Elliot onto the back porch.

Julie reached across the island and covered Lia's hand with her own. "How are you doin', darlin'?"

"Better, now that you guys are here. I'm hoping you can help us figure out what to do with this house. I know Elliot's pretty freaked out by what's been happening, not that I blame her."

"And you?"

"I don't exactly enjoy being possessed by a ghost, but to tell you the truth, Jules, I have this sense of serenity when I'm in this house. It's hard to explain."

"Is that why you don't want to leave?"

"I see no reason to leave. I'm not the least bit afraid of being here, even with all the odd events that have happened over the past few weeks."

"Elliot said you aren't aware of the possessions."

"She's right. I have no recollection of anything that happens when the little wench inhabits me."

Julie grinned. "The little wench?"

"You have no idea. It's a good thing Elliot has been home all this week. Otherwise I'd be going to work dressed for a Halloween party."

"She dresses you? Are you serious?"

"Dead serious. Oops, poor choice of words there, I guess, but yes, it's happened twice this week. Complete with bright red lipstick." Lia suddenly fell silent. "Holy shit."

"What?" Julie asked.

"The lipstick. That was her lipstick on the wineglass that night."

Elliot reentered the kitchen in time for Lia's declaration. "Whose lipstick?" she asked.

"The red lipstick on the wineglass that first night you were gone," Lia explained. "It was Celeste's."

Elliot placed the food on the table. "What I want to know is who was drinking from the other glass."

"What do you mean?" Marissa asked.

"Lia found two wine glasses and a plate of cheese and crackers on this island, but has no memory as to how they got there," Elliot explained.

"There were two glasses?" Julie asked.

"Yes," Lia replied.

"Then there was some other living person here with you," Julie said. "Ghosts cannot drink wine, or eat cheese."

"You're saying someone was in my house that night?"

"That's exactly what I'm saying. Was anything missing? Were you harmed in any way?"

"What are you implying, Julie?" Elliot interrupted.

"What I'm trying to determine, Elliot, is whether this person was a threat to her. They obviously knew how to get into the house and out again without leaving evidence they were here. Except for the wineglasses, of course."

"I honestly don't remember that evening," Lia said. "All I know is that I woke up in bed fully clothed and someone had put my groceries away and helped themselves to wine and cheese."

"You were fully clothed when you woke up?" Marissa asked.

"Yes, I was."

"Thank God for that," Julie said. "That basically means whoever was here with you means you no harm."

"Wait. Say that again," Elliot insisted.

"Say what?" Julie asked.

"That last sentence. Say it again."

"Whoever was here means Lia no harm."

"Son of a bitch." Elliot slammed her fork down and rose from her chair.

"Elliot, where are you going?" Lia asked.

"I'm getting to the bottom of this. Stay right here. I'll be back."

"I'm coming with you." Marissa went after Elliot.

"What just happened here?" Julie asked

"I don't know, but I plan to find out." Lia followed Marissa and Elliot. "Wait for me!"

Lia and Julie chased after the sounds of stomping footfalls down the spiral staircase to the first level, followed by the sound of the entry door hitting the wall as it was flung open. Lia could hear Elliot yelling.

"Samuel. You son of a bitch."

Elliot and Marissa were halfway across the intersection before Lia stepped onto the sidewalk, with Julie right behind her.

"Elliot, stop," Lia called as she ran across the street after her.

Despite Lia calling out her name, Elliot moved forward determinedly. When she reached Samuel, she once again grabbed him by the lapels and pushed him up against the nearest building.

"You were in my house, weren't you?" she growled.

"Elliot, maybe this isn't such a good idea," Marissa said nervously.

"Answer me, asshole," Elliot yelled.

"We means Miss Lia no harm," Samuel said.

By then, Lia had reached her side. "Elliot, let go of him."

Elliot ignored Lia and continued to stare into Samuel's face. "I asked you a question."

"We means Miss Lia no harm," Samuel said again.

"Elliot, let go of him, right now," Lia pried Elliot's fingers loose from Samuel's crumpled lapels.

Elliot finally released him and began to pace back and forth a few feet away.

Lia tried to straighten Samuel's jacket. "You must forgive her, Samuel. There have been a lot of odd things happening in the house, and she's concerned for me."

"Samuel would never hurt you, Miss Lia. We means you no harm."

"Why don't you come to the house and have some dinner with us?" Lia suggested.

Elliot exploded. "Are you out of your mind, Lia?" she shouted.

Marissa took Elliot's arm and dragged her away. "Who is this dude?" she asked.

"He's been stalking us. Specifically Lia, since we moved in here. He's apparently related to some of the slaves who lived here in the eighteen thirties. If you ask me, he's as creepy as all hell."

"There's not much he can do to her with the three of us standing here. This might be a chance to learn something about what's going on in the house," Marissa suggested.

"Samuel don't want to be no bother, Miss Lia."

"Nonsense. We'd be honored to have you for dinner. Wouldn't we, Elliot?" Lia looked pointedly at Elliot.

Marissa and Elliot stared back at her in silence, until Marissa elbowed Elliot in the ribs.

"Humph. Ah, yeah. Please come," Elliot said between her teeth.

Lia turned to Julie. "Julie, this is Samuel. Samuel, this is Julie and over there beside Elliot is Marissa. They're our dear friends from New York City."

"Nice to meet you, ma'am," Samuel said as he shook hands with both of them.

***

Lia pulled another stool up to the kitchen island and retrieved a clean plate from the cupboard. "Have a seat, Samuel. I'll be right back with the most wonderful ribs you'll ever want to eat," she called over her shoulder. "Jules, would you mind pouring Samuel some wine while he waits? Thanks, love."

Elliot followed Lia onto the porch. "Do you have any idea what you're doing?" she asked. "You're only encouraging him to stalk you more."

"I don't think he's stalking me. What has he actually done to deserve your mistrust?"

"He stands on that corner and watches our house every freaking night. Don't you think that's just a little odd?"

"Perhaps, but I'll ask again. What line has he crossed?"

"That's what I intend to find out," Elliot said and went back into the house.

Lia followed with Samuel's plate, to which she added corn on the cob and salad, and placed it in front of him. "Here you go, Samuel. I see you haven't touched your wine. Would you like a different kind?"

"Samuel don't drink wine, ma'am. I be obliged for a glass of water if it ain't too much trouble."

Elliot narrowed her eyes at Samuel. "You don't drink wine?" she asked.

"No, ma'am. Samuel come from a long line of drinkers, as far back as ancestors who slaved in this house. Drink done nothing but cause pain and sufferin' for folks."

"How about some lemonade?" Lia asked.

"Samuel appreciates that, ma'am."

Elliot put her hands on the island and leaned toward Samuel. "So you're telling me you weren't in this very kitchen over a week ago, drinking wine with Celeste?"

"Samuel don't drink wine, ma'am." Samuel voiced this response without looking at Elliot. "Mighty good ribs, ma'am," he said to Lia.

"Actually, Elliot made them," Lia replied.

Samuel nodded in Elliot's direction while he continued to eat.

Elliot looked at Marissa, who was leaning against the cabinet behind Samuel. Marissa shrugged her shoulders.

"You're telling me you weren't in this house with Celeste while I was out of town," Elliot stated.

"No, ma'am. I'm telling you Samuel doesn't drink wine."

Elliot slammed her hands down on the island. "Damn it, Samuel. I would appreciate a straight answer."

"Elliot. Samuel is our guest," Lia scolded.

"Li nan tout dwa, Metrès Leya. Li dwe konsène sou ou. Samyèl konprann." (It's all right, Miss Lia. She be concerned about you. Samuel understands.)

"I don't care if you understand, Samuel. It's still rude of her to treat you that way. You're our guest after all," Lia replied.

"Oh, my," Julie exclaimed.

"Ah...what just happened here?" Marissa asked.

Elliot took one of Lia's hands in her own. "He just spoke in Creole and you understood him."

Lia's eyes opened wide as she realized the significance of Elliot's statement.

"Lia, what is my mother's pet name for me?" Elliot asked.

"What's that got to do with the price of tea in China?" Marissa said.

Elliot ignored her friend and addressed Lia once more. "What is it, Lia?"

"Ellie-Belle."

Marissa snickered, soliciting a well-placed elbow to the ribs from Julie.

"Yes, Ellie-Belle. Celeste would not have known that. Lia, what just happened here?"

Samuel picked up his lemonade and drank the last swallow before standing. "The merge be starting," he said. "It almost be time."

Elliot grabbed Samuel's lapel once more. "Explain yourself, old man."

"Miss Lia be knowing soon. They be released. They be needin' they freedom."

"What the hell does that mean?" Elliot demanded.

"Lia know the way. Follow Lia. Samuel need to go now. Much obliged for the meal."

***

Elliot closed the gate behind Samuel, and reentered the house. Lia, Marissa and Julie were waiting for her in the foyer.

"What the hell happened tonight, Lia? How is it you understood what Samuel said in Creole?"

"I don't know, Elliot. I just did."

"He said something about the merging. Do you feel Celeste inside you? I mean, is it possible your self-awareness is merging with Celeste's?"

"Oh, God, don't even think that. It's bad enough when she takes over my consciousness. I can't imagine knowing when she's inside me."

Julie suddenly stepped between them. "Okay, this has got to stop before it gets out of hand. I'm going to make a few phone calls tonight."

"You mean it's not already out of hand? How much worse can it get?" Elliot asked.

CHAPTER 28

Julie carried a tray with four pieces of cheesecake and four glasses of wine into the living room, where she put it down on the coffee table. "Who wants dessert?" She handed the dessert and wine to her friends, took the last piece on the tray and sat in the wing-backed chair next to Marissa. Elliot and Lia sat on the couch opposite them. "I called Phoebe while I was in the kitchen. She can be here tomorrow around five p.m."

"Who is Phoebe?" Lia asked.

"Phoebe's a sensitive. She has the ability to contact spirits," Julie replied.

"If you'd said that to me a month ago, I would've given you some wise-assed comment," Elliot said, "but after what I've witnessed with my own eyes in this house, I'm ready to accept that just about anything's possible."

"She almost backed out when I told her where you guys live," Julie said.

"Does this house really have that bad a reputation?" Lia asked.

"You bet it does. As you know, some pretty heavy stuff went down here. There isn't a native in this town that doesn't know about it."

"But that was almost two hundred years ago," Elliot said.

"According to local lore, the haunting has never stopped, meaning the ghosts are still here."

"Tell me something we don't know. There's Celeste and the hordes I saw in the courtyard the other night. The question is, how do we get rid of them before they get rid of us?"

"That's what I'm hoping Phoebe can help us with," Julie said.

***

Lia slipped her blouse over her head and threw it in the laundry basket beside the bed. A loud yawn escaped before she could contain it.

"Tired, love?" Elliot asked.

"Exhausted. I'm hoping for a good night's sleep."

Elliot put her book on the bedside table and climbed to her knees. Like a cougar, she crept her way to the end of the bed where Lia was standing. "They say a good orgasm is great for inducing sleep," she purred.

"Do they?" Lia answered coyly as she turned around to face Elliot.

The height difference between her standing on the floor and Elliot kneeling on the bed put Lia's bare breasts at the exact level easily accessible to Elliot's eager mouth.

"Damn, you're beautiful," Elliot sat on the edge of the bed and pulled Lia close to stand between her legs. One by one, she suckled Lia's breasts, being careful of the bruised nipple, causing Lia to dip her head back and close her eyes. A moan escaped her throat.

"Hmm. If I had a dime for every time you...ah...every time you turned me to mush with your mouth, I'd be a very wealthy girl."

"That's what you get for teasing me."

"Teasing you?   And just how am I teasing you?" Lia asked, a hint of mirth in her voice.

"Every time you look at me, all I want to do is throw you on the bed and make love to you."

"So what are you waiting for?"

"You, my dear, are a vixen. Come here, woman," Elliot said as she invited Lia onto the bed.

Sometime later, Lia lay within the circle of Elliot's arms. "Your source appears to be correct," she mumbled.

"My source?" Elliot asked.

"Yes, whoever told you that orgasms induce sleep. I feel like a rag doll and even more exhausted than before."

"Mission accomplished," Elliot boasted.

"Indeed."

"Do you think we were loud enough for the girls to hear us?"

Lia raised her head to look at Elliot. "God, I hope not. That would be embarrassing."

"Well, you *are* sometimes loud enough to wake the dead," Elliot teased.

"El, that's not funny. Remember where you are. As it is, it creeps me out that Celeste is probably present on some level."

Elliot grinned. "I wonder if she climaxed right along with you?"

Lia slapped her on the stomach. "Stop that."

"I'd be the first lesbian in history to make two women come at the same time. Kind of a 'buy one, get one free' sale, don't you think?"

"Elliot Walker!"

"What?" Elliot said innocently.

Lia yawned again.

"Okay. I can see how tired you are. Come here."

Lia settled back down in Elliot's arms and wrapped her arm around Elliot's waist.

Elliot kissed her on the head. "Good night, sweetheart. Sweet dreams."

"You too, love."

***

"El-eee-ot."

Elliot moaned in her sleep.

"El-eee-ot."

Elliot opened her eyes and saw Lia leaning over her. Lia's hair was in wild disarray. "Are you okay, love?"

Lia nodded.

Elliot watched as the moonlight revealed a seductive mask on Lia's beautiful features.

Elliot grinned. "Are you ready for round two?"

"Hmmm," Lia moaned as she placed a light kiss on Elliot's lips then traced the outline of Elliot's mouth with her tongue.

Elliot took Lia's head between her hands and pulled her down to deepen the kiss, driving her tongue deep into Lia's mouth. Breathless, she broke the kiss and looked into Lia's eyes. "I can't get enough of you."

"I want you," Lia whispered into Elliot's ear. "Take me."

Elliot rolled Lia onto her back and covered her with her own body then spread Lia's legs to allow her to kneel between them. She reached under Lia's hips, lifted her bottom off the bed and pulled her forward so Lia's backside was resting on Elliot's knees while her shoulders and head remained on the bed. Elliot leaned forward and supported herself with her hands on either side of Lia's shoulders, while she ground her abdomen into Lia's core.

Lia moaned out her pleasure.

"You like that, huh?" Elliot asked.

"Fè m ' vini ankò, Elliot—jis tankou anvan." (Make me come again, Elliot—just like before.)

Elliot scrambled off the bed as fast as she could. "Whoa. What the fuck?" Elliot lunged forward and grabbed Celeste by the shoulders. "How dare you?" she screamed.

"You want Celeste should fuck you again, El-eee-ot?"

Elliot released her and stepped back. "That was you? I thought I was making love to my wife."

"She be here too."

"Why are you doing this?"

"Celeste need mistress's help to find dem. El-eee-ot can make mistress help Celeste."

"What the fuck are you talking about?" Elliot shouted.

"Celeste make El-eee-ot feel good. El-eee-ot help Celeste find dem."

Elliot ran her hands through her short blonde hair. "You have no right. Do you hear me? You have no right." Elliot grabbed her again. "Get out! Leave her alone."

Lia continued to stare directly into Elliot's eyes.

"Elliot. Let go of her." Marissa wrapped her arms around Elliot's waist from behind while Julie pried her hands loose from Lia's arms.

"Let go," Julie said. "Sweetie, let go of Lia."

"It isn't Lia," Elliot screamed.

"It *is* Lia," Julie insisted.

Elliot began to cry. "What do you want from us, Celeste?"

Suddenly, Lia's eyes closed and her head dropped back. She was unconscious.

"She's gone, Elliot. Celeste is gone. Let go of her," Julie said softly.

Elliot released Lia and she fell back into Julie's arms.

Marissa, who was still wrapped around Elliot from behind, held her close as Elliot rested the back of her head on Marissa's shoulder and cried.

"Come on, my friend. Come sit on the bed," Marissa said. "I'm going to find something for you and Lia to wear, okay?"

Elliot nodded but continued to cry. She looked at Lia lying unconscious on the bed beside her. Julie was stroking her hair. "Is she all right?"

Julie nodded. "She's fine. I assume this is one of her blackouts?"

"This is what happens when Celeste takes over." Elliot wiped the tears from her cheeks. "She'll have no memory of it when she wakes up."

"That's probably a good thing." Marissa retrieved nightclothes from the dresser and threw a set at Elliot. "She'd be pissed as hell with your treatment of her if she was aware of it."

Elliot looked at the clothing in her lap and began to cry again. "It wasn't Lia. It was Celeste."

"It was Celeste in Lia's body. Remember that the next time you decide to go all Conan the Barbarian on her," Marissa retorted.

"Mar, go easy on her. You don't know that you wouldn't do the same thing in her shoes," Julie said.

Marissa handed the second set of nightclothes to Julie. "I'd cut off my own hands before I'd hurt you, Jules."

"Yes, but these are special circumstances. Come here and give me some help with these clothes."

"Let me do it," Elliot said.

Marissa looked suspiciously at her.

"Don't worry, I won't hurt her. I promise. Why don't you two go back to bed and let me tend to my wife? I'm sorry I woke you."

Marissa held her hand out to Julie. "Come on, love."

Julie gave the clothes to Elliot then placed one palm on the side of Elliot's face and kissed her on the other cheek. "We'll be in the other room if you need us, okay?"

Elliot nodded and watched her friends leave the room.

***

Lia woke the next morning to find Elliot wrapped protectively around her. It was unusual for Elliot not to get up well before her. *Now, how to escape this glorious prison she has me trapped in.* Lia carefully lifted first Elliot's arm and then her leg from her person so she could get out of bed without waking her. Finally free, she slipped out of bed and went into the bathroom. She suddenly realized she had nightclothes on.

I don't remember putting these on. Lia opened the bathroom door a bit and looked at Elliot. *Humph, she's dressed, too. That's odd.*

Lia removed her underpants and lifted the T-shirt over her head so she could shower. As she pulled her head out of the collar of the shirt, she looked in the mirror over the sink and noticed bruises on the back of her arms. "What the hell happened here?" she said out loud.

"I'm sorry, love. I didn't mean to hurt you."

Lia swung around. Elliot stood in the open doorway between the bedroom and bathroom.

"Elliot?"

Elliot approached and knelt on the floor in front of her. She wrapped her arms around Lia's waist and sobbed. "I'm sorry. I'm so sorry."

Lia's hands held Elliot's head close to her abdomen. "Sweetheart, what happened last night?"

"Celeste. Celeste happened. She woke me up and started to make love to me. I thought it was you. I swear, I thought it was you. She gave herself away by speaking Creole to me."

Elliot rose and walked a few steps away. "I stopped as soon as I realized it was her and not you." Elliot clenched her fists. "I was so angry that she had the nerve to...to..."

Lia stepped forward and took Elliot into her arms. "It's okay, love. It's okay."

Elliot broke away again. "No. It's not okay." She grabbed one of Lia's arms and held it up. "Look at what I did to you again. If Mar and Jules hadn't interfered, I might have done worse."

"Marissa and Julie were there?"

"Yes. I was screaming at Celeste to leave you alone, and thank God, it woke them up. Lia, I don't know what comes over me when she's around. I feel a rage inside me that I didn't know I was capable of. It seems that each time Celeste appears, it's worse than the time before."

Elliot released Lia's arm "I think I should move into the courtyard bedroom until we get through this."

"No. If you move into that room, I'm moving with you."

"Look what I did to you. It's not safe for you to be with me. At least not when that bitch is inside you."

"I won't hear of it, Elliot. You're staying with me in our room, or I'll move to the other bedroom with you. End of discussion. Now I need to take a shower and get ready for work."

Lia turned the shower on and Elliot left the bathroom. Lia walked to the doorway between the bathroom and bedroom and saw Elliot sitting on the bed, sadly contemplating her hands. "Hey, chef," she said, grinning. "I'll take two eggs—scrambled with onion and cheese—wheat toast, black coffee, and a side of turkey bacon. I'll be down in fifteen minutes."

Lia leaned against the doorframe and watched a smile spread across Elliot's features.

Elliot looked up. "I really do love you, Lia."

"I know you do, sweetheart. I know you do."

CHAPTER 29

Elliot served Julie and Marissa breakfast and placed four pieces of wheat bread in the toaster while she scrambled more eggs with onion and cheese.

"This is great, Elliot. Do you always cook breakfast for the two of you?" Julie asked.

"Not always. When we're both working, we'll stop at the local coffee shop on the way to work for a beverage and pastry. When one of us is on vacation and the other's not, the one staying home gets to cook."

"What if you're both on vacation?" Marissa asked.

"Then whoever's out of bed first gets to cook, which is usually me."

"Doesn't that get old?" Marissa asked.

"Not really. Lia cooks most of the dinners, so the least I can do is breakfast."

"I think it's sweet," Julie said. "Someone, who shall remain nameless, should take a page out of your book."

"What?" Marissa objected. "I do my share of the cooking."

"If you say so." Julie rolled her eyes at Elliot.

"Ahhh!" A scream came from the hallway.

Marissa jumped up. "What the hell was that?"

"God damn it, Celeste. Stay out of my closet, and for God's sake, let me dress myself." Lia's voice came from the hallway, followed by the sound of feet stomping up the stairs.

Elliot continued to cook as if nothing had happened.

"Elliot. What the hell is wrong with you? Obviously something's happened to Lia," Marissa said.

"Yeah—Celeste happened to Lia," Elliot answered.

"Don't tell me. Lia didn't appreciate Celeste's choice of outfit for the day," Julie said.

"Bingo. She'll be back in a few minutes."

Marissa sat down again. "Did Lia say anything about last night?"

"She doesn't remember what happened last night, but she did find the evidence of it this morning."

"Evidence?" Julie asked.

"Yes. Both of her upper arms are bruised where I grabbed Celeste."

"It's so freaking weird to hear you talk about Lia like she's two different people," Marissa said.

"Is she upset with you?" Julie asked.

Elliot shook her head without looking up from cooking the eggs. "No, she isn't. I'm angrier with myself than she is with me. I offered to move into the other bedroom, but she wanted nothing to do with that idea."

"She must know its Celeste you're angry with, not her," Julie said.

"Yes, she does, but that doesn't excuse my actions. When Celeste is around, all I want to do is shake the hell out of her. I don't like that she's invading the body and soul of the one person I love with all my heart."

Marissa said, "You need to try to see beyond Celeste and to realize in the physical sense that it's Lia you're manhandling."

Elliot turned around and looked sternly at Marissa. "Tell me something I don't know, Mar. And, just so you know, I don't make a habit of manhandling my wife."

Julie took the spatula out of Elliot's hand. "Go pour yourself and your beautiful wife some coffee while I dish up your breakfast."

Lia entered the kitchen just as Julie set their breakfast plates on the island. "Just in time," Julie said.

Lia finished putting her earring in then placed her hands on her hips. "I'm sick to death of that Creole slut thinking she can butt in whenever she feels like it."

Elliot put two cups of coffee on the island. "Gypsy or bar wench?" she asked.

"Bar wench. It's a good thing we have that mirror hanging in the hallway. I would die if I was actually seen in public dressed like that."

"Well, you look beautiful as usual, love." Elliot kissed her on the cheek and sat down beside her.

"It really sucks that I have to work today. Some hostess *I* am."

"No worries, girlfriend," Marissa said. "It isn't your fault that we arrived a day early. And besides, we have Elliot to entertain us."

"Actually," Julie said, "I thought it would be nice for the three of us to visit the Garden District today. I haven't seen my family in a while, and I promised to stop by."

"That's a great idea, sweetie." Marissa shared a conspiratorial look with Elliot.

"No sense in using two cars. We can drop Lia off at work along the way, and pick her up on the way home after visiting your family," Elliot said.

Julie clapped her hands. "Sounds like a plan. Marissa, we should probably hop in the shower and get dressed so we won't make Lia late for work."

"Yes, ma'am." Marissa jumped to her feet.

"Leave the dishes. I'll take care of them," Elliot said.

She finished her eggs and collected the dirty dishes while Lia enjoyed her coffee. After loading the dishwasher, she kissed Lia on the cheek, walked to the opposite side of the island and leaned her elbows and forearms on the countertop.

Lia looked up at her and their gazes met. For several long moments, their eyes engaged in visual foreplay.

Elliot leaned farther across the island to place a kiss on Lia's lips. She was abruptly interrupted by the sound of scratching coming from the porch outside the kitchen.

"What the hell?" Elliot went to the door and opened it.

Miss Thing sat there on the porch.

Elliot scooped her up and scratched under her chin. "You little ragamuffin. I was about to collect a sweet kiss from the prettiest lady I know, and you come along and interrupt it."

She carried the cat into the kitchen and walked directly to Lia, who was putting her coffee cup in the dishwasher.

Miss Thing made a move like she was going to climb into Lia's arms.

"No, I don't think so, missy. I don't need to go to work with cat hair on my clothes."

Miss Thing became so agitated that Elliot put her down.

"What am I, chopped liver? When Miss Lia's in the room, I don't even exist. You'd think she was your mother or something. Sheesh!"

Miss Thing ran to the screen door and yowled to be let out.

"What is your problem? I just let you in." Elliot opened the door for the cat.

The cat ran out, jumped onto the railing, and began to pace back and forth on the narrow platform.

"She's the strangest cat I've ever seen," Elliot said.

Their attention was diverted by Marissa and Julie entering the kitchen.

"Here we are, showered and ready to go," Julie said. "I'm looking forward to seeing my family."

"Me too." Marissa's enthusiasm seemed forced.

Elliot grabbed the car keys from the hook beside the kitchen door. "Since we're all here, why don't we just head to the courtyard from the kitchen porch?"

They exited the kitchen and locked the door behind them. As soon as they stepped onto the porch, Miss Thing jumped to the floor and ran down the steps ahead of them.

"Weird cat." Elliot looked over the railing to see where the cat had gone. "Sweet Mother of God. I'm going to murder that cat," she exclaimed.

"What is it?" Lia asked.

"See for yourself." Elliot pointed to the courtyard.

Lia looked over the railing. "Damn it," she whispered.

By this time, Marissa and Julie had descended to the first level. Marissa stepped into the courtyard and looked up at Elliot and Lia on the second-level porch. "Ah, there's a huge hole in your courtyard."

"No shit, Sherlock." Elliot led Lia down the stairs. Upon reaching the courtyard, she walked around the edge of the hole. At least three feet in diameter, and nearly six inches deep, it lay directly beside the front tire of the car parked closest to the house.

Elliot looked around and saw the cat sitting in front of the shed door. She made a move toward the cat. "You little bastard," she shouted.

The cat hissed and ran away.

"If I get my hands on that little bitch…" Elliot stomped her feet in frustration then looked at her watch. "I'll need to fix this when we get back. If I do it now, Lia will be late for work."

"Let's take this car since we'll need to get it out of the way to repair the hole," Julie said.

Marissa approached Elliot as Julie and Lia climbed into the car. "Too bad we can't use this as an excuse to stay home and send Julie to the Garden District by herself," she joked.

Try as she might to remain angry, Elliot laughed at her friend's comment and threw an arm around Marissa's neck in a choke hold. "You are a nut. Why don't you go open the gate for me, okay?"

Marissa broke free of the hold and saluted. "Aye, aye, captain!"

***

"What time did you say Phoebe would be here?" Elliot guided the car into the parking space in front of the house.

"Five o'clock," Julie replied.

Lia looked at her watch. "Four-thirty. It's a good thing I was able to get out of work early."

Elliot unlocked the gate and let them all into the entryway.

Lia took over as they stepped into the foyer. "Okay, we need to divide and conquer. Elliot, how about you bury that hole in the courtyard, and I'll make some tea and put out some treats."

"I'll help with the hole," Marissa offered.

"I guess that leaves me to help with the tea," Julie said.

Elliot and Marissa cut through the first floor to the courtyard while Lia and Julie took the stairs to the second story. By the time they reached the kitchen, they could hear loud cursing coming from the courtyard.

Lia looked at Julie. "That doesn't sound good." They both headed toward the kitchen door. Lia opened the door and called out. "El, is everything okay?"

"No. Everything is definitely not okay," Elliot yelled back.

Lia pushed the porch door open and stepped out, followed by Julie. A second later, they stood by the railing and looked into the courtyard below. "Jesus Christ," Lia exclaimed.

"Wow," Julie said. "That's going to take more than a half hour to fill."

The hole, three-foot-wide, six-inch-deep was now at least six feet wide and one foot deep.

***

"Elliot, would you mind getting the door?" Lia said as the doorbell chimed loudly in the kitchen.

"I'll go with you," Julie said.

Marissa picked up a tray of finger sandwiches, sweetbreads, and petit fours and grabbed the teapot. Lia arranged five tea servings, sugar bowl, and creamer on another tray. "Okay," Lia said. "I think that should do it."

"We're taking these into the living room, right?" Marissa asked.

"Yes."

"After you," Marissa said.

Elliot opened the foyer door and stepped into the gated entryway, with Julie right on her heels. Standing on the sidewalk in front of the iron gate was the most-exotic, middle-aged woman Elliot had ever seen. Of medium height, she had graying black hair pulled loosely into a bun on top of her head and ringlets of hair hanging at her temples. She wore high-waisted, tailored slacks with low-heeled shoes, a white blouse, and a silk scarf around her neck. An assortment of bangle bracelets graced her right arm. The woman's makeup was extreme, with dark eye shadow from her lids to her eyebrows and very long false eyelashes. Perhaps the most striking feature was the crystal blue of her eyes, so light in color, they appeared nearly transparent. Elliot couldn't stop staring at the woman as she opened the gate.

"Phoebe!" Julie flew past the gate and into the woman's embrace.

Phoebe smiled broadly, hugged Julie, and held her an arm's length away. "Jules, you haven't changed a bit. You look amazing. How's that spitfire wife of yours?"

"Marissa's great. She's here with me."

"Wonderful. We'll have to have dinner together before you head back north."

"Absolutely, but right now, I'd like you to meet Elliot Walker. Elliot, this is Phoebe Frost."

Elliot stood dumbfounded by the woman.

"Elliot?" Julie said.

"Oh, ah, yes, Elliot Walker." Elliot stepped onto the sidewalk. She reached out to shake the woman's hand. "Forgive me, but you have the most incredible eyes."

Phoebe grinned. "I get that a lot."

Still holding Phoebe's hand, Elliot took a step toward the door and said, "Please come in."

Phoebe walked inside the gate immediately snatched her hand from Elliot's grasp, startling both Elliot and Julie.

"What's wrong? Did I offend you in some way?" Elliot asked.

Phoebe narrowed her eyes. "I don't know. I felt this very strong energy coming from you." Phoebe shook her head. "I'm sorry. It's probably nothing. Please, let's go inside."

Elliot pushed the door open and stood aside for Phoebe and Julie to enter.

As she stepped into the foyer, Phoebe placed a shaky hand on Julie's arm.

"Are you okay?" Julie asked.

"So much pain and suffering in this house," Phoebe replied.

"That was a long time ago," Elliot said as she closed the door behind them.

"For you, that was long ago. For them, it's everlasting," Phoebe said. "I feel more-intense energy above us."

"I suspect," Elliot explained, "that's because the living quarters are above. Two hundred years ago, this level was mostly storage, laundry, and quarters for the stable hands."

"You mean, slave quarters?" Phoebe asked.

"Yes. It's my understanding that most of the male slaves had quarters on this floor."

"Why don't we go upstairs?" Julie suggested.

Phoebe looked at Elliot. "Lead the way."

Elliot led her guest to the spiral staircase and stood aside to allow the women to ascend before her. Phoebe stopped halfway and looked around. She held on to the railing and closed her eyes. "The little one has been here recently," she said.

"Little one?" Elliot asked.

"Yes. A little girl. Her name is Lita, or Lena. No, wait, her name is Lia. The same as your wife's."

Elliot exchanged an uncomfortable look with Julie. "You said she's been here recently. What exactly do you mean?"

Phoebe opened her eyes and looked directly at Elliot. "You know exactly what I mean. You're the reason she's still here."

"What the hell does that mean?" A tinge of anger colored Elliot's voice.

Phoebe closed her eyes again and grabbed for the railing.

Julie took her other hand. "Phoebe, are you all right?"

"Yes. Just a little shaky. This house is so full of very powerful energy, it's a bit overwhelming."

"Do you want to leave?" Julie asked.

"No, I came to help. Let's move on."

Phoebe and Julie continued to move up the staircase while Elliot stood a few steps down. Julie looked over her shoulder at Elliot.

Elliot held her arms out to the sides, palms up, with an indignant look on her face.

Julie raised her eyebrows and jerked her head in a message for Elliot to follow them.

"Where the hell are they?" Marissa said. "The doorbell rang at least ten minutes ago. It doesn't take that long to climb one flight of stairs."

"Maybe we should go check on them," Lia suggested.

"Good idea. I'll be right back."

Marissa stepped into the hallway just as Phoebe, Elliot, and Julie reached the second-story landing.

"Marissa, it's so good to see you again," Phoebe said.

Marissa hugged Phoebe. "It's great to see you again as well. How's the ghostbusting business treating you?"

Phoebe gently slapped her arm. "You'll never change, will you? For your information, my work as a medium is doing just fine, thank you. Thanks to this town's less than pristine history, there's plenty of work to be found here. I just wish it wasn't so full of suffering."

"I understand, but at least you're able to bring comforting answers to the victims' survivors."

"Most of the time, yes, but occasionally, there's no answer to be had, and that's sad."

"Well, I'm hoping you'll be able to help our friends here. It would be a pity to have to give up this beautiful house."

Phoebe looked around. "It is beautiful indeed. On the surface, anyway."

Julie stepped forward and interrupted their conversation. "Why don't we go meet the lady of the house?" She took Phoebe's arm.

Marissa joined Elliot as Phoebe and Julie walked away.

"I don't like her, Mar," Elliot said.

Marissa frowned. "Why not?"

"On the way up the stairs, she blamed me for the bad vibes in this house."

"Are you serious?"

"Dead serious."

Marissa looked nervously toward Phoebe and Julie. "Come on, we'd better join them before I get the evil eye again from Julie."

Elliot and Marissa caught up to them just as they stepped into the living room.

Lia rose from her position on the couch.

Phoebe stopped short just inside the door and whispered one word. "Celeste."

CHAPTER 30

Lia stepped forward and extended her hand to Phoebe. "It's so nice to meet you. I'm Lia Purvis."

An awkward silence ensued as Phoebe remained frozen in place.

Julie placed a hand on Phoebe's arm. "Phoebe, are you all right?"

Phoebe snapped out of her trance-like state. "I'm sorry. I don't know what came over me." She placed her hand in Lia's. "Phoebe Frost. And the pleasure is all mine."

"Please sit. Would you like some tea?" Lia asked.

"Yes. That would be nice. Thank you," Phoebe replied, without breaking eye contact.

"Let me give you a hand with the tea." Elliot grabbed the teapot and filled all five cups.

Lia passed the tea out and stood aside as her guests helped themselves to cream and sugar as well as to the assortment of finger foods.

After a time, they settled into their seats.

It became apparent to Lia that Phoebe was covertly studying her with a degree of intensity that made her a little uncomfortable. She decided to break the ice by starting the conversation. "So, Phoebe, Julie tells us that you've been a medium for quite some time."

"Yes. Since I was a child. My mother first attributed my visions to 'imaginary friends,' but it soon became apparent that what I was seeing was definitely not in my imagination."

"What do you mean?" Lia asked.

"She sees dead people," Julie answered.

"You see dead people. Seriously?" Elliot seemed dubious.

"As a matter of fact, I do."

"Tell them about your aunt dying," Julie said.

"That was perhaps my first memory of paranormal contact. I think I was six years old. My elderly aunt was dying, and my mother made my siblings and me pay our last respects. While I was standing beside her bed, my grandma walked in and sat on the opposite side of the bed from me. She took my aunt's hand and nodded in my direction. I knew what I had to do. I told my Aunt Hildie that grandma said it was time to go. A few moments later, she took her last breath."

"How was that paranormal contact?" Elliot asked.

"My grandmother had been dead for five years by then."

"Do you see ghosts in this house?" Lia asked.

Phoebe put her teacup down on the coffee table. "I do."

Elliot scanned the room. "Where?"

"There are at least two in this room right now, but they're merging."

Elliot leaned forward. "That's the second time I've heard that term used. Just what does it mean?"

"It means they have hosts."

Elliot sat back down next to Lia and took her hand. "You see Celeste."

"I do." Phoebe's gaze moved to Lia. "You're a very beautiful woman. From what I can see, you look very much like her."

Lia touched her own cheek. "I do?"

"Yes. Of course, that makes sense, since you share her blood."

Elliot jumped to her feet. "Okay, this is beginning to creep me out. Just what do you mean, she shares Celeste's blood?"

"Are you sure, Phoebe?" Julie asked.

Just then, Miss Thing ran into the room, jumped into the space next to Lia and half-recline across Lia's lap.

Phoebe gasped audibly.

Lia looked alarmed. "Oh, I'm sorry. Are you allergic to cats? Elliot, could you put her outside, please?"

"No!" Phoebe nearly shouted. "No. I'm fine." She stared at the cat for several moments. Lia could see her struggle to regain control.

"Are you sure you're all right, Phoebe?" Marissa asked. "Can I get you a glass of water or something?"

"No, really, I'm fine. She just startled me." Phoebe looked from the cat to Lia. "She's a very pretty little girl."

Elliot's eyes narrowed.

"Yes, she is," Lia replied. "She's a bit of a troublemaker, though, and quite the Houdini. We've been here for about a month, and we have yet to figure out how she gets into the house. Sometimes she thinks she lives here."

"That's because she does. She has for a long time." Phoebe rose from her chair and approached Lia. She extended her hand to touch the cat.

As she neared, Lia could feel the cat's chest vibrate in a growl. Before Phoebe could touch her, Miss Thing hissed and ran off.

Phoebe turned quickly to follow her. "Don't run away, little one. I won't hurt you."

"What the hell?" Elliot exclaimed.

Elliot and Marissa followed Phoebe into the hall. When they got there, they found her looking around, confused.

"Where did she go?" Phoebe asked. "It's like she vanished into thin air."

Elliot chuckled. "Like Lia said, she's a little Houdini. She'll come back when she's good and ready."

"Is everything all right?" Lia asked from the doorway.

"Everything's fine. Miss Thing pulled her vanishing act again," Elliot explained.

"She'll come back when she's good and ready," Lia said.

"My words exactly," Elliot replied.

Julie appeared in the doorway beside Lia. "Is everything all right?"

"Do you hear an echo in here?" Marissa asked with a grin.

***

Lia touched Phoebe's arm. "Are you sure you're up for a tour?"

"Yes. Very much so, in fact," Phoebe replied.

"Okay, then. You've already seen the living room. The parlor is just beyond that, if you'd like to see it."

"Yes, please."

Lia led Phoebe back through the living room and into the parlor. Phoebe stepped into the room and slowly walked around. She stopped at the small secretary positioned beside the fireplace and ran her hand over the old wood. She closed her eyes and stood very still for a few moments. "This is where she did her correspondence. Invitations, thank-you notes, letters, bills of sales."

"Bills of sales? You mean, like receipts?" Marissa asked.

"Yes, for everything from groceries to slave purchases."

She walked next to the fireplace, where once again, she stood motionless.

Elliot chose that moment to enter the room.

Phoebe suddenly swung around to face Elliot, and pointed a finger at her. "You! You burned the child. You held her hand in the fire."

"What in God's name are you talking about?" Elliot replied angrily. "I did no such thing."

Phoebe grasped the mantel for support while Marissa led Elliot to the far end of the room.

"Don't take it personally, Elliot. You just happened to be standing there when she saw the vision," Marissa whispered.

"I don't like her, Mar. The sooner she's out of here..."

Lia touched Elliot's arm. "Are you okay, love?"

Elliot ran a hand through her hair. "You saw what happened, right? That's the second time she's said something derogatory about me."

Lia looked behind her to where Julie had led Phoebe to a chair. "Sweetie, just please let her do her job. It's important that we understand what's going on in this house. Please?"

"All right. All right. But I don't have to like it."

Lia kissed her tenderly. "Thank you."

"Grrr!" Elliot watched Lia return to their guest.

"How are you feeling, Phoebe?" Lia asked.

"You must forgive me. There's such a history of pain and suffering here. So much strong emotion and hatred. Please know that these outbursts are an artifact of that history, and not part of who I am."

"We understand. Do you wish to go on?"

"I do."

Lia led her entourage across the hall and into the dining room. As they entered, she turned on all the lights and flooded the room with brightness.

Phoebe looked around. "This is a room with the pain of hunger. It's rumored that the mistress allowed her slaves to eat the scraps left on her guests' plates and to drink leftover wine. I fear it was but an insignificant gesture of humanity on her part."

"The kitchen is this way," Lia said.

Marissa held the dining room door open for all to pass through and followed as they entered the kitchen.

Phoebe frowned and walked to the island. "Someone has been here recently. I see wine and I see cheese." She looked at Lia. "You were here with Samuel. You know he'll be beaten if he's caught imbibing the mistress's wine, Celeste."

Elliot stepped forward but was stopped by Lia's arm. "Why was Samuel here with me?" Lia asked.

"He's in love with you, but you belong to the mistress. You'd be wise to remember that, girl."

Phoebe moved farther into the room and stopped in front of the stove. She began to cry and fell to her knees.

Elliot was the first to reach her. "It's all right, Phoebe. Come on, on your feet. It's all right."

Phoebe grabbed Elliot's pant legs. "Please don't do dis, mistress. I needs to bury my baby girl. Gran comes right back to cook."

"Holy shit. What the hell is happening?" Marissa said.

"Gran is the older woman who was chained to the stove," Lia said. "I'm not sure putting Phoebe through this is a good idea."

Phoebe suddenly became still. "I'm all right. Just give me a minute, and we can continue."

"Are you sure?" Elliot helped Phoebe to her feet and sat her on a stool by the island. "Lia, would you mind getting her a glass of water?"

"I'm sure. This saps my energy, but it doesn't harm me in any way. If I can help you help these poor souls, it will be worth it." Phoebe thanked Lia for the water, drank thirstily and then put the glass down on the island. "I'm ready. Shall we continue?"

Lia looked over Phoebe's head at Elliot. "I guess the courtyard is next."

"Okay. Come on, I'll give you a hand." Elliot offered Phoebe her arm and they exited the kitchen onto the porch.

The first thing Phoebe did was walk to the railing and look down. She grabbed the railing with both hands and released a wail.

"Phoebe," Julie exclaimed. "Phoebe, what is it?"

"The souls must be freed. You must know their names. Their deaths must not be in vain. So many souls. So much death. So much pain."

Elliot wrapped her arms around Phoebe's waist and pulled her away from the railing. Phoebe instantly regained her awareness. "Are you okay?" Elliot asked.

Phoebe broke free of Elliot's embrace and walked to the railing once more. She pointed to the hole in the cobblestones. "Your little girl knows the way, but she won't find her salvation there."

All four ladies looked into the hole and saw Miss Thing digging in the deepest part of the hole.

"You little shit," Elliot yelled. She found an empty soda can on the porch and threw it toward the hole. The can hit the cobblestones a good distance from the hole, but it had the intended effect of scaring the cat away.

"Moving on..." Marissa said as she led the way around the porch toward the garage stairway in the corner.

The women stopped briefly in the two apartments on the inside wall of the courtyard, as well as in the library, and moved to the stairway in the corner. As they emerged onto the third-story porch, they found themselves directly in front of the apartment over the library.

Phoebe instinctively stopped in front of the door. "What's in here?" she asked.

"Nothing," Lia replied. "It's an empty apartment."

Phoebe turned the knob and pushed the door inward. The inner door to the living space was open. She suddenly grabbed the doorframe. "Great suffering. Suffocating heat. Too many bodies. There is death within. Free them. Release them from their earthly hell."

Lia put her arm around Phoebe's waist and guided her away from the door. "Phoebe, are you telling us slaves died in there?"

"Their souls are trapped in the ungodly conditions in which they lived."

Elliot pulled the door to the apartment closed, and took Lia aside before she could lead them into the back entrance to the master suite. "Do you think it's a good idea to take her into the third-floor hallway? We know what happened in the attic. We've been up there. If she's having this kind of reaction to the living conditions the slaves endured, can you imagine what would happen if she was close to the actual torture chamber?"

While they were discussing the merits of taking Phoebe into the third-floor interior, Marissa and Julie did just that. Lia and Elliot turned back toward the door, and they were gone.

"Shit," Elliot said as they both hurried toward the door. By the time they made it inside and down the hallway toward the bathroom, Marissa, Julie, and Phoebe were exiting the bedroom.

"Marissa, no," Elliot yelled as they stepped into the hall.

Marissa stopped and turned back while Julie and Phoebe walked on. "What?" she asked.

"I'll catch up with Julie and Phoebe," Lia said as she moved past them into the hall.

"We were thinking it might not be a good idea to let her near the old attic entry," Elliot said.

Just then, they heard an ear-shattering scream coming from the hallway, followed by pounding.

"Oh, no," Elliot said. She and Marissa ran into the hall and found Phoebe pounding on the closet door. Lia and Julie were lying on the floor behind her.

"Lia," Elliot screamed. She fell to her knees beside Lia, who was trying to get up. "Sweetheart, are you okay?"

"I'm fine. How's Julie?"

"I'm good," Julie said. "Man. She's stronger than she looks."

Phoebe continued to pound on the door as she chanted. "God of heaven, God of earth, we implore you to exorcize these demons. Free these spirits from the hell they endure. Blessed be God. Glory be to the Father. Blessed be the Goddess, holy Mother of us all."

Lia grabbed Elliot's arm. "Elliot, stop her before she hurts herself."

"I'll help," Marissa said. Together, they grabbed Phoebe's hands and wrestled her to the floor.

"Phoebe, listen to me," Elliot said. "You need to calm down."

"We have to get her out of here," Marissa suggested. "She seemed to be okay until we stepped into the hallway."

"Okay. Help me get her to my room."

The four of them half-carried, half-dragged Phoebe through the hall to the bedroom, where she almost immediately began to calm down. With her in a quieter state, they were able to lift her onto the bed and she visibly relaxed.

"She's bloodied her hands," Lia said. "Elliot, can you dampen a towel for me, please

"Coming right up. I'll grab the first-aid kit as well."

A short time later, Lia managed to wash the blood from Phoebe's hands and discovered the damage wasn't as bad as the blood had implied. She covered the cuts with a few Band-Aids. While she and Julie were busy tending to Phoebe, Marissa and Elliot cleaned the blood from the closet door.

"Did you see how crazy she got?" Marissa asked.

"I don't even want to think about it, Mar. A month ago, I didn't believe in any of this shit, and now, I'm living in the middle of spook central. I'm sincerely regretting ever buying this house."

"Maybe it wasn't a good idea to bring Phoebe here."

"I *am* concerned about what it's done to her. Like I said, we've been here for a month, and although Celeste's appearances are annoying, so far Lia hasn't been in any real danger because of it. Except maybe when she was strapped to the gurney in the attic."

"She was strapped to a gurney in the attic? When the hell did that happen?"

"Several days ago."

"Jesus, Elliot. I'm with you on this one. You need to convince Lia to leave this place."

"Yeah—well, good luck with that."

Lia stepped out of the bedroom. "She's awake and pretty much recovered. She's talking about going home. Julie said she would drive her there."

"We can't take her out through this hallway," Elliot said. "We'll have to go out the back exit and down the porch stairs to the kitchen level."

"Okay. Julie and I will get a head start."

"We're nearly finished here. We'll join you in a few minutes."

CHAPTER 31

Marissa and Elliot stood on the sidewalk and watched Julie drive away from the curb. "Man. That was exhausting," Marissa said.

"You're not kidding. That was one of the oddest afternoons I've ever lived through," Elliot replied.

"I found it strange that she attacked you for things you've never done."

"I know. Can you really see me holding a child's hand in the fire?"

Lia's voice above their heads drew their attention. She stood on the second-floor balcony. "Any chance I can talk you into going to the store? I thought I'd make a chicken curry salad to eat over greens for dinner, and I need a few ingredients."

"Sure," Elliot said. "Make a list. I'll be right in."

"Why don't you give Julie a call and ask her to pick stuff up on her way back?" Marissa suggested.

"I would, but knowing your wife, she'll stay and visit for an eternity. If you go for me, I'll have dinner ready by the time she gets back."

Marissa chuckled. "You're probably right. Okay. We'll be up in a second."

***

Julie glanced at Phoebe as she drove carefully through the narrow streets of the French Quarter. "Are you all right, Phoebe?"

"I'll be fine. It'll take a little time to recover from visiting that house, but I'll be fine."

"What is it about the house that's so disturbing?"

"There's a lot of negative energy there, which isn't surprising, considering the history it has. For someone as empathetic as I am, it's quite overwhelming, and even more so when a spirit commandeers my body. It's like running a marathon."

"Doesn't everyone have empathetic capability?"

"Yes. Some more than others. I sensed a great deal of sensitivity in Lia."

"That's probably why Celeste seems to have no problem controlling her at will."

"Partially, yes. But Celeste and Lia have a bloodline in common, which increases Lia's susceptibility significantly."

Julie stopped in front of Phoebe's house and shifted the car into park. "Here we are. I want to thank you for coming to the house."

"I'm glad I could help. Please extend my appreciation for the invitation to Lia and Elliot."

"Speaking of Elliot, what did you think of her?"

Phoebe fell silent for several long moments.

"Phoebe?"

Phoebe looked at her friend. "I hesitate to answer your question because I suspect I haven't met the real Elliot yet."

"What does that mean?"

"Elliot has an aura around her that's not healthy. I've never felt anything so sinister and evil as when she touched me. That's why I drew my hand away when she greeted me in the foyer of the house."

"Elliot isn't evil at all," Julie said. "In fact, she's a very loving and gentle soul."

"The Elliot you knew in New York may have been like that, but this house has had an effect on her. I recommend you keep an eye on her. I sensed a great deal of conflict brewing within her, relative to Lia, or perhaps more appropriately, Celeste."

***

Julie returned about ten minutes after Marissa and Elliot left for the store. She parked the car in front of the building, opened the iron gate with the spare key Elliot had given her, and let herself into the house. She climbed the stairs to the second level and made her way to the kitchen.

"Ah!" Lia screamed. "You scared me. I didn't expect you back so soon."

"Phoebe only lives two streets away."

"I know, but...but...oh, hell, I was sure you'd visit for a while before coming back."

"Well, I would have, darlin', but Phoebe wasn't in the mood to chitchat. In all the years I've known her, I've never seen her so rattled or exhausted. This house really spooked her."

"It does have a pretty horrid history."

"Where are the girls?"

"I sent them to the store for a few things."

"I could have picked them up for you."

"Yes, you could have, but I thought you would be away longer and I wanted to get dinner started."

"Sorry."

"No worries."

"That smells good. What are you making?"

"I thought I'd make curry chicken salad on greens, and it reminded me that I haven't made curry chicken soup in a while. So it looks like we're having a curry night."

"Is there something I can do to help?"

"Yes, ma'am. Grab that bag of carrots and celery in the refrigerator and cut them into bite-sized pieces, if you would."

For the next few minutes, the ladies worked side by side cutting vegetables in silence. Finally, Julie spoke.

"How did you like Phoebe?"

"She seemed really nice. I had a hard time not staring at her. She has the most amazing eyes I've ever seen."

"I know what you mean. I grew up with her, and as a child, I never gave it a thought, but now? Now, I'd kill to have those eyes. But seriously, what did you think of her."

"I've never met a psychic medium before, so I didn't know what to expect. I have to admit, I was a little concerned about her several times while touring the house. It was a little creepy when she channeled Gran and said I was related to Celeste by blood. How would she know that? Oh, and when Miss Thing came into the room, she talked about her as though she were a person instead of a cat."

"That kind of freaked me out as well."

"As a person, she was very nice, but when she slipped into a trance, or took on an entirely different personality, it was a bit disconcerting. Several times I thought Elliot was going to ask her to leave."

"I know. I can't believe she was so aggressive with El. I could see her becoming annoyed. Phoebe thinks the house might be affecting El."

"In what way?"

"She didn't say. Okay, the veggies are cut. Is there something else I can do?"

By the time Elliot and Marissa returned from the store, the soup was simmering and the individual bowls of salad greens prepared. Elliot and Marissa put their bags of groceries on the kitchen island and helped themselves to glasses of lemonade.

"It's hotter than hell out there," Marissa said. "I can't believe you lived in this kind of weather every day as a kid."

"You get used to it," Julie said.

Elliot finished her lemonade and put her glass in the sink. "How about giving me a hand with that hole in the courtyard while we wait for dinner, Mar?"

"Oh, no you don't," Lia said. "Dinner will be ready in about ten minutes. If you go out there now, you'll get all hot and sweaty in this humidity, and you'll have to shower before you eat. Besides, it's nearly eight o'clock, and it'll be dark in about an hour. I vote you put the hole off until tomorrow."

"She's got a point there, El," Marissa said. "I'd be happy to work on it tomorrow."

"Okay, then. Is there something I can do to help with dinner?" Elliot asked.

"Why don't you put plate settings on the island while I throw this chicken salad together?"

"That, I can do."

***

Lia lay nestled into Elliot's side, her head on Elliot's shoulder. "El, I think we should do my genealogy."

"Mmm?" Elliot didn't really answer.

"What if I am related to Celeste?"

"I can't imagine you are. Isn't your family from the Northeast?"

"Slaves were traded and sold all over the country. It's possible that some biological relative of Celeste was traded up North and eventually joined my family tree."

"I guess it's possible, but if you're going to do this, be sure to use a reputable genealogist. I don't want you to get burned by some Internet scam."

"I thought I might start with the New Orleans Hall of Records. Surely, they'll have a listing of all the slaves owned by the monsters who lived in this house at the time."

"Could be. You might also want to talk to Samuel. Didn't he say the elderly cook who started the fire all those years ago was his grandmother?"

"His great-great-great-great-grandmother," Lia said.

Elliot laughed. "I stand corrected."

"That actually might be significant, considering he's the seventh or eighth generation beyond that," Lia mused. "I wonder if Celeste was here at the same time his grandmother was."

"Maybe. If his grandmother was the one who started the fire, then she was the last generation of slaves to live in this house. That might make things a little harder to track down."

"What do you mean?"

"According to the newspaper clippings I found when I researched this house, the owners escaped when the torture room was found by the firemen. That means they would have abandoned their slaves, and unless family came forward to claim them, they were probably auctioned off and relocated elsewhere."

"So, the mistress and master never came back to reclaim the slaves?"

"They supposedly went to Paris or something and never returned. There were some rumors, however, that the mistress secretly came back and lived out her life in New Orleans with her friend Marie Laveau."

"Marie Laveau? As in the voodoo queen, Marie Laveau?" Lia asked.

"The very one. Nice to have friends in high places, huh?"

"Or low places, to be more precise."

"Rumor also has it that she's buried in Marie Laveau's tomb in Saint Louis Cemetery. It's about a mile and a half from here on Claiborne Street. Of course, none of that has been confirmed. Officially, they escaped and never came back, so the slaves would most likely have been auctioned off."

"I wonder where Celeste went," Lia said.

Elliot raised her head to look at Lia. "Sweetheart, if Celeste's ghost resides in this house, it most likely means she died here."

Lia sighed heavily. "You're probably right."

"If you're serious about this, maybe we can make a day of it tomorrow and visit the Historical Society as well. I'm sure Mar and Jules wouldn't mind helping with the search."

"Okay." Lia slipped her arm under Elliot's T-shirt and draped it across her bare stomach. "Thank you for indulging me, love."

"Anything for you."

Elliot placed a kiss on her forehead, just as the cat jumped onto the bed and tried to crawl in between them.

"Oh, no you don't, Miss Thing. Not tonight." Elliot climbed out of bed and grabbed the cat. She wrapped her hands around Miss Thing's middle and walked toward the bedroom door while holding the cat in front of her, blocking

Lia's view. "Why don't you go visit Mar and Julie? I bet they would just love to see you."

Lia sat up and watched Elliot walk across the room. When she reached the door, she draped the cat across one arm to free her other hand to open the door. When she did this, Lia gasped out loud. "Elliot, no!"

Elliot looked back at her. "It's just for the night. She'll be fine. Don't worry about her."

Elliot set the cat down in the hallway and turned away. A mocha-skinned little girl looked back and locked gazes with Lia as Elliot shut the door.

Lia was on her feet by the time Elliot reached the bed.

"Where are you going?" Elliot asked.

"It's Lia. The cat is Lia."

"The cat is Lia? What the hell are you talking about?"

"When you put her out of the room, she was no longer a cat. She was a little girl. I need to follow her, Elliot."

Elliot grabbed her shoulders. "Listen to yourself. This is insane."

"No. Samuel and Celeste have both told us that Lia knows the way. I need to follow her."

Apparently giving up, Elliot let go of Lia and stepped aside to let her pass.

Lia ran from the room and into the hallway just in time to see a few tendrils of long curly hair disappear around the bend in the spiral staircase. "Lia! Stop!"

Elliot entered the hall in time to see Lia run down the stairs while calling after the child.

"What's happening?" Marissa said from the bedroom door across the hall.

"Lia thinks the cat is the little girl that died in this house."

"A little girl died in this house?" Julie peeked out from behind Marissa.

"Yes. Story has it, the mistress chased her to the roof after she snagged her hair or something equally inane, and rather than face the mistress's wrath, she jumped off the roof to her death."

"That's horrible," Julie said as she and Marissa followed Elliot down the stairs after Lia.

They reached the second-story landing in time to hear the kitchen door open.

"She's going into the courtyard," Elliot said. She ran through the butler's pantry and into the kitchen.

She heard Lia's voice. "Leya, tounen isit la enstantane sa a. Koute manman ou," Lia shouted. (Lia, come back here this instant. Listen to your mother.)

Elliot pushed the porch screen door open and ran out, with Marissa and Julie right behind her. Lia was standing by the railing looking into the courtyard.

"Leya. Fanm deyò nan ap fwe ou nan nan yon pous nan lavi ou si w ap kenbe soti isit la lè li fè nwa." (Lia. The mistress will whip you to within an inch of your life if you're caught out here after dark.)

Elliot grabbed Lia by the shoulders and swung her around. "Celeste, get the fuck out of my wife's body."

Lia's head fell backwards onto her shoulders, and her legs became wobbly.

"I've got you, baby. I've got you." Elliot wrapped her arm around Lia's waist for support.

"Elliot?"

"It's all right. Celeste is gone for now."

"Where is Lia?"

"You mean, the cat?"

Lia nodded and stepped away from Elliot.

"I don't know."

"She's down there, digging in the hole again," Marissa said.

Lia rushed to the railing. "I have to help her."

Elliot grabbed Lia's arm. "Are you out of your mind? It's ten o'clock at night, and you're anything but dressed appropriately for digging holes."

Lia looked down at her T-shirt and panties. "Then I'll get dressed first. Don't you understand? She's been right under our noses the entire time and we didn't see her—until tonight. Lia knows the way, Elliot. She knows the way."

"Lia—" Elliot began to say.

"Maybe she's right, Elliot," Julie said. "The cat's been digging that hole for some reason. If Lia wants to help her dig, then I'll help too."

"Count me in," Marissa added.

Elliot looked at each member of the group. "You're serious, aren't you?"

"Yes. Are you in or not?" Lia asked.

Elliot put her hands on her hips. "I guess I'm outnumbered. Okay, I'm in, but we need to get some clothes and sturdy shoes on first. And I'll need to rig better lighting."

By midnight, the hole, six feet wide, one foot deep, had grown to ten feet wide by two feet deep. Lia stopped to wipe the sweat from her brow.

"Are you all right?" Elliot asked.

"I'm fine. Just hot. Does anyone want something to drink?"

A round of yes votes sent Lia on her way to the kitchen while the other three stepped out of the hole to take a break. In the kitchen, she poured four glasses of lemonade and placed them on a tray sturdy enough to carry the drinks. On her way back to the courtyard, she rested the tray on the railing and looked down, contemplating the progress they had made in two hours. As she lifted the tray again, she felt faint and rested it on the railing once more.

"Yo se prèske la, Mama," (They are almost there, Mama,) a small voice said beside her. She looked down and saw the little girl standing within a hair's breadth of her arm. She smiled. "Yes, sweetheart, they are almost there."

"What are you waiting for, Lia?" Elliot called from below. "We're thirsty down here."

Lia shook her head and carried the tray down the stairs to the courtyard where she passed out the refreshing drinks. "I think we're almost there," she said.

"How will we know when we've found what we're looking for?" Julie asked.

"Maybe we'll know when we see it," Marissa said.

Lia looked up and saw the cat sitting on the railing on the second-story porch, watching them. "Oh, we knows when we find da truth. We knows," she mumbled under her breath.

The ladies resumed digging as soon as they finished their drinks. Soon after, Elliot thrust her pointed shovel into the dirt in front of her and nearly fell on her face when the shovel slid sideways. "Whoa. Stop. I've hit something."

Lia, Julie, and Marissa climbed out of the hole and allowed Elliot to clear the dirt away from where her shovel slipped. "I think I've hit something metallic right here. Julie, let me have the flat shovel, if you would."

Elliot scraped the loose dirt to the side. A few minutes later, she had the whole center of the hole cleared out and had uncovered a large metal plate. "The plate extends beyond the hole. We need to make the hole wider until we find the edges."

An hour later, the metal plate was uncovered. It measured approximately twelve feet wide by sixteen feet long. The ladies stood around the hole and contemplated what to do next.

"I wonder what's under it," Julie said.

"Let's all get on one side and pry it up with our shovels," Elliot said.

Following Elliot's direction, they worked the tips of their shovels under one edge of the plate and levered the handles downward.

"Push," Elliot shouted, and they managed to lift the plate a full two inches before they ran out of steam. "Okay, let it down," Elliot said when she realized they were getting nowhere. She paced back and forth. "There's got to be another way to do this."

"We could hook onto the edge of it with a chain and pull it up with one of the cars," Marissa suggested.

"That's not a bad idea," Elliot said. "Let's hope there's a chain in the garage."

Fifteen minutes later, Elliot returned from the garage empty handed. "No luck. I hate to say it, but we're going to have to wait until tomorrow when the hardware store opens."

"That sucks," Marissa said.

"Yes, it does," Lia agreed. "But Elliot's right. I think I'd rather open it in the daylight anyway. I vote we get cleaned up and then sleep for a few hours."

"You'll get no argument from me," Julie said.

"You all go on ahead. I'll be right behind you as soon as I grab the lemonade glasses," Lia said.

One by one, Lia collected the glasses and put them on the tray as the girls went back into the house through the kitchen. She paused at the bottom of the stairs as a brief wave of dizziness overcame her, then she climbed the stairs to the second-level porch and stopped short at the top. There, on the railing, sat the little girl.

"Samuel be in da hole."

Lia narrowed her eyes. "What did you say?"

"Samuel be in da hole. He take Mama home soon. It be a shame Ethan not be wid dem. Gran send him 'way."

"I don't understand what you mean."

"Mama jump da broom wid Samuel. He take Mama home soon."

"Lia, are you coming in?" Elliot called from the screen door.

Lia's attention turned suddenly to Elliot. "Yes. Yes, I'll be right there."

She looked back in time to see the cat jump down from the railing and run down the stairs.

CHAPTER 32

Lia lay on her side, enveloped in Elliot's loving arms as she spooned against her wife. Try as she might, she struggled to find sleep. Her mind returned over and over to the words the little girl said to her on the back porch.

Samuel be in da hole. He take Mama home soon. It be a shame Ethan not be wid dem. Gran send him 'way.

What did the child mean? Who is Ethan? she asked herself.

She drifted off to sleep, only to be awakened again when she felt a hand on her arm. She opened her eyes, expecting to see Elliot. Instead, she saw a young black man with empty eye sockets and slash marks across his face. Her mind flew to what she had seen in the attic while being possessed the first time by Celeste.

She couldn't move, and couldn't scream. She stared wide-eyed into his mutilated face.

"Gots to take her wid me. Yous gots to find her," the young man said.

He shook her again. "Gots to take her wid me. Can't go wid out her. Yous gots to find her."

"I..." Lia managed to say.

"Samuel don't mean no harm, ma'am. Just gots to find her."

"Samuel?"

"Yes, ma'am. Gots to find her."

"Find who?"

Lia felt a movement behind her.

"Lia? Are you all right? Who are you talking to?" Elliot asked.

Lia turned her head to the side to look at Elliot and suddenly realized she was no longer immobilized. She quickly looked back to the side of the bed where her visitor had been. He was gone.

"Lia?" Elliot said.

"I'm okay, El. Go back to sleep."

"Who were you taking to?"

"I don't know. I thought..."

Elliot raised herself to rest on her elbow. "You thought what? Are you sure you're okay?"

"I'm fine. I thought someone was shaking me awake, but it must have been a dream. Please, go to back to sleep."

Elliot lay back down and gathered Lia into her arms once more.

Lia relaxed within Elliot's embrace and reveled at how safe she felt in her wife's arms. Twenty minutes later, she still lay there wide awake. She couldn't get the encounter out of her mind.

Did it really happen?

Was he really here?

Who was he?

Who was he trying to find?

And what does Samuel have to do with this?

A long time passed before she once again succumbed to sleep.

***

Lia woke before Elliot and slipped carefully out of bed so as to not disturb her. After taking care of bathroom chores, she dressed in shorts and a T-shirt as well as socks and running shoes, intent on starting her day with a brisk walk to think about the events of the previous evening. She descended to the second floor and grabbed a bottle of water from the refrigerator before exiting the house at street level through the front door. As soon as she stepped outside, she noticed Samuel standing on the corner diagonally across the street. *Hmmm. It's unusual for him to still be there in the morning.*

"Samuel," Lia called out as she waved and crossed the street in his direction.

Samuel shifted uneasily from foot to foot as she approached him.

"Good morning, Samuel," Lia said.

"'Morning, Miss Lia."

"Samuel, have you been out here all night?"

"Yes, ma'am."

"Could I ask why you're still here? You're usually gone by this time."

"Samuel mean no harm, Miss Lia."

"I had a visitor last night. A young black man."

"Yes, ma'am."

"You knew about this?" Lia asked incredulously.

"Yes, ma'am. Samuel mean no harm, ma'am."

Lia rubbed her forehead. "I really wish you wouldn't talk in riddles. I'm trying hard not to be alarmed by you watching our home every night, but you're not making this easy."

"I apologizes, Miss Lia, but Samuel mean no harm."

"Why was that young man in my bedroom last night?"

Samuel remained quiet.

"Samuel, I need an answer. Who was he? What does he expect of me?"

"Can't say, Miss Lia. It be over soon."

"What will be over soon?"

"Can't say."

Lia grabbed the sides of her head in frustration. "Ahhh. Could you please just give me a straight answer? I'm beginning to think Elliot is right about not trusting you."

"Samuel mean no harm, Miss Lia."

Lia crossed her arms. "Okay. I've had enough of this one-sided conversation." Lia turned her back on the man and walked away.

"It be over soon, ma'am," Samuel called behind her.

***

Lia returned from her walk an hour later and found Elliot, Marissa, and Julie drinking coffee around the kitchen island. Elliot poured a cup for her as she entered the kitchen.

"Thank you," Lia said.

"I assumed you went for a walk when I saw your running shoes were missing," Elliot said.

"Yes. I needed to clear my head. I put in a rough night."

"Any idea why?" Elliot asked.

"I had a visitor last night."

"What do you mean by a visitor?" Marissa asked.

"I assumed it was a ghost. A young black man."

"Oh, my," Julie exclaimed. "He didn't hurt you, did he?"

"No. In fact, after I got over the initial shock of seeing him there, I wasn't afraid at all, despite the fact that his face was disfigured and his eyes were gouged out."

"His eyes were gouged out? Why didn't you tell me about this last night?" Elliot asked.

"I wasn't sure I had even seen it. So much of it is a blur this morning, I'm still not sure it wasn't just a dream."

"Could it have been the ghost of one of the slaves murdered in the attic?" Marissa asked.

"I can only assume it was. It reminded me of what I had seen in the attic the first time I dreamed about this house. That was when you found me in the linen closet, Elliot. Do you remember that?"

"Do I remember? How could I forget? It was actually Celeste I pulled out of that closet, not you."

"Anyway, he kept pleading with me to find her...whoever 'her' is. He said he couldn't leave without her."

"Did he say anything else?" Elliot asked.

"He said, 'Samuel means no harm.'"

Elliot slammed her hands on the island. "Son of a bitch," she said. "I'm sick and tired of him interfering in our lives. I'm going to take care of this right now."

Lia grabbed Elliot's wrist. "No, you're not. I spoke with Samuel this morning before I went on my walk. It's no use talking to him. He isn't being very forthcoming with information, only that it will be over soon."

"What will be over soon?" Elliot demanded.

"I asked that very question of him this morning, but he refused to answer."

"We can't just ignore this," Elliot said sternly.

"I don't see that we have a choice. Besides, he's an old man and last night's visitor was relatively young, so it obviously wasn't him."

"I'd call the cops on him if I were you," Marissa said.

Elliot shook her head. "The problem is, he hasn't done anything wrong. He just stands out there and watches the house."

"Maybe it's time you move back into the hotel," Julie suggested.

"My point exactly," Elliot said.

"You know how I feel about that, Elliot," Lia said. "Running away won't solve anything. We need to understand what's going on here and figure out how to stop it."

"And how do you propose we do that?" Elliot asked.

"For starters, I think the hole in the backyard has something to do with what's been going on here. Otherwise, why would little Lia insist on digging it up?"

"Little Lia?" Elliot lifted her eyebrows.

"The cat. I know you think I'm crazy, Elliot, you carried the cat across the bedroom last night, and it was a little girl you put down in the hallway. It sounds bizarre, but I think the cat is a host for the little girl who died in this house nearly two hundred years ago. I don't think it's a coincidence that her mother is Celeste and that Celeste has been possessing me. Can't you see that it's all connected?"

"She may have a point there," Julie said.

"Then let's get our butts in gear and go buy a chain to remove that metal plate from the hole," Marissa said. "What have we got to lose except time?"

"That's a very good question, Mar," Elliot said.

***

Elliot slipped a heavy-duty chain with a hook on its end overtop the middle of the metal plate and connected the hook to the edge while Julie and Lia held it up slightly with their shovels. She hooked the other end of the chain to the trailer hitch of her SUV.

"Okay, Mar, move the car forward very slowly until the slack is out of the chain. I'll let you know when to stop. That's it…a little more. Okay, stop." Elliot looked to Lia and Julie. "I think it's safe to pull your shovels out now."

The metal plate lowered ever so slightly as the weight extended the chain to its limit.

"All right. Step back in case the chain breaks." Elliot waited for everyone to be outside the reach of the chain before she said, "Move forward slowly, Mar."

Marissa inched the car forward, pulling the edge of the metal plate upward as she moved. Elliot, Julie, and Lia stood aside, their gazes glued on what was under the plate.

Elliot shouted when the plate was at an angle of approximately forty-five degrees. "Whoa. Marissa, stop."

Marissa put the car in park and opened the door. "What's in the hole?" she asked as she walked toward the others.

"Hard to tell. Whatever's in there is covered with another layer of dirt," Lia said.

"You know," Marissa said, "it could just be a base layer for the cobblestones that are on top. There's a good chance there's nothing under that dirt."

"Then why the metal plate?" Julie asked. "Something doesn't feel right about this."

"There's one way to find out." Elliot jumped into the hole. "Somebody give me a shovel."

"Elliot, get out of that hole right now. What if the chain breaks, and the metal plate falls on you?" Lia said.

"Um, good point." Elliot climbed out of the hole and retrieved another hook and chain from their purchases that morning. "I bought a back-up chain in case the first one snapped. I'll hook it on the plate for reinforcement. That should do the trick. The chances of both chains breaking at the same time are pretty slim."

Once again, Elliot hooked one end of the chain to the metal plate and the other to the trailer hitch. "All right. Let's try this again." She jumped back into the hole and picked up her shovel.

While the others watched, Elliot stuck the pointed end of the shovel into the dirt, scooped out a mound of soil, and set it outside the hole near Lia's feet. On the third shovelful, an object came out of the hole along with the soil.

"Stop. I see something." Lia dropped to her knees and combed through the soil with her hands.

"What is it?" Julie asked.

Lia uncovered a thin white object approximately three inches long. "I don't know. It looks like a stick."

"Let me see it." Marissa took the object from Lia's hand. "Holy shit. It's a bone."

"A bone? Are you sure?" Elliot asked.

"Not totally, but it looks like one to me. You have medical training. See for yourself." Marissa handed it to Elliot, who was still standing in the hole.

Elliot examined the object carefully. "You're right. It looks like a bone to me, too. Probably a metacarpal or metatarsal bone."

"We need to call the police," Lia said.

"Not yet. For all we know, it's a chicken bone. I'm going to shovel a little bit more."

Elliot sank the tip of the shovel deep into the soil and immediately met with resistance. "What the hell? Whatever I hit is large. Probably a rock." She worked the point of the shovel around the object until it was loosened enough to get the shovel under it. "All right, here we go." Elliot lifted it from the hole and dumped it on the cobblestone.

It was a human skull.

CHAPTER 33

"Do you really need to leave the flashing lights on in front of the house, Officer Rocque?" Elliot asked.

"It is a crime scene, ma'am," Officer Rocque replied.

"Yes, a two-hundred-year-old crime scene. This place already has the reputation of being New Orleans' most haunted house. We really don't have to reinforce that notion by having flashing blue lights illuminating the whole street," Elliot said.

"We don't know that the bones are two hundred years old, ma'am."

"I can assure you they weren't put there by us. Do you have any clue what went on in this house one hundred and eighty years ago?" Elliot asked sarcastically.

"Yes, ma'am. I know the history of this house, but this is still a crime scene."

Just then, Lia entered the room. "Elliot, Detective Jameson would like to see you in the kitchen. Hello, Officer Rocque. So nice to see you again."

"You know him?" Elliot asked.

"Yes. This is the officer who came to investigate when I found the light on in the apartment over the library. Is Officer Nash with you?" she asked.

"No, ma'am. He's got the day off. Ah, Miss Purvis, do you have time for a few questions?"

Elliot interrupted. "Did you say I was needed in the kitchen?"

"Yes. Detective Jameson just finished interviewing me, Marissa, and Julie, and now he wants to talk to you."

"Okay. I'll be back soon."

Lia turned her attention to the police office after Elliot left the room. "What would you like to know?"

"How did you know to dig in that particular spot, Miss Purvis?"

"The cat led us there. She kept digging the same hole over and over each time we filled it. Finally, we decided to investigate what was so interesting to her and we found the metal plate under the cobblestone."

"The cat led you there?"

"Yes. I believe the cat is possessed with the spirit of the young girl who died here in the eighteen-thirties. I believe she led us to that hole on purpose."

Officer Rocque frowned. "Let me get this straight. The cat is possessed by a spirit?"

"Sometimes, yes. I've actually seen the little girl in the house and on the porch. She's even spoken directly to me."

"I see." Officer Rocque scribbled on his notepad and slipped it into his pocket. "I think I have all the information I need for now. Will you be available later if we have more questions?"

"Yes, of course. Elliot and I are on vacation this week. Marissa and Julie are our houseguests, so we'll all be around for the next several days."

***

The forensic pathologists spent most of the day monitoring and measuring the mass grave while Lia watched stoically from the balcony on the third floor. Julie periodically stood beside her, and Elliot and Marissa watched from the porch outside the kitchen.

"I'm worried about Lia," Elliot said. "She's been acting strangely since we uncovered the grave."

"Yeah, I'm worried too. Julie didn't want to alarm you, but she told me Lia has been mumbling unintelligible things all afternoon."

"I'm afraid that's not Lia standing up there. It's Celeste."

"You really need to get her out of this house before something serious happens."

"Marissa, I would like nothing better than to move into the hotel, but she won't agree to go, and I won't go without her."

"You might have to force her to go with you."

Elliot crossed her arms and frowned at her friend. "I have never used physical force against my wife, and I have no intention of starting now."

"I worry she's not in her right mind. In the few days we've been here, her behavior has been so off the wall, I barely recognize her."

"I know. I've been worried about the very same thing." Elliot looked at her watch. "It's nearly dinnertime. They've been at this all day. I wonder when they're going to remove the bodies."

"My guess would be sometime tomorrow."

"They'd better not suggest we leave the house during the exhumations, because I don't think Lia will agree to that."

Almost as if on cue, Officer Rocque stepped away from the agents congregated around the grave in the courtyard to address Elliot on the second-story porch. "Ms. Walker, we are nearly finished here for the day, but we'll be back early tomorrow morning to begin removing the remains. We'll allow you to stay in your home tonight if you'll agree not to enter the courtyard until the investigation is complete."

"Yes, of course," Elliot said.

Officer Rocque glanced at the third-floor balcony, back at Elliot. "She's been out there all day. You might want to look in on her."

"Thank you for your concern, officer. We're worried about her too."

"I'll see you in the morning, then. Good evening."

Elliot nodded. The crew of forensic investigators and detectives left through the Governor Nicholls Street gate. Elliot descended to the courtyard and closed the gate behind them.

***

"How is she?" Julie asked when Elliot returned to the living room.

"She's sleeping. Today has been pretty hard on her. I really think Celeste has been influencing her all day."

"What can we do about it? Should we hire an exorcist or something?" Marissa asked.

"Believe me when I say that thought has crossed my mind."

"I think we should ask Phoebe to come back," Julie said. "She's a medium, after all. Maybe she can talk to Celeste."

"Do you think she'd actually come back here? Her last visit was pretty rough," Elliot said.

"There's no harm in asking. The worse she can do is say no," Julie replied. "I'll call her in the morning."

"Speaking about morning, I suspect the law will descend quite early. I'm going to hit the sheets," Elliot said.

"Sweet dreams, El," Marissa said.

Elliot climbed the flight of stairs to the third story and entered her bedroom to find Lia sleeping soundly. She stripped off all but her panties, pulled a T-shirt over her head, and slipped into bed behind her. "Goodnight, my love," she whispered softly and placed a gentle kiss on her cheek.

Within moments, Elliot joined her wife in slumber.

***

"Fanm. Reveye." (Woman. Wake up.)

"Ale. Mwen fatige." (Go away. I am tired.)

"Reveye. Li se tan. Ou dwe gide yo." (Wake up. It is time. You must guide them.)

"Yo se toujou nan twou a." (They are still in the hole).

"Wi, men pòt la, se louvri. Yo bezwen yo dwe montre wout la. Ou se youn nan sèlman ki kapab gide yo lakay yo." (Yes, but the door is open. They need to be shown the way. You are the only one who can guide them home.)

Celeste rolled over and touched the side of her visitor's disfigured face. "Nou menm, Samyèl. Èske w ap ale lakay ou kòm byen?" (And you, Samuel. Will you go home as well?)

"Pa san yo pa ou." (Not without you.)

Elliot shifted in her sleep beside Celeste.

Celeste looked over her shoulder. "Nou dwe fè atansyon pa reveye fanm deyò la." (We must be careful not to wake the mistress.)

Samuel sneered. "Mwen rekonesan Mwen pa gen okenn je yo wè sa ki mal li, e pa gen vizyon gid men m' mete yon ponya gwo twou san fon nan kè nwasi li." (I wish I had eyes to see her and vision to guide my hand to thrust a dagger deep into her blackened heart.)

"Pèp nou an ap jwenn lapè lè yo kite kote sa a, epi li pral konnen sèlman dezespwa ak solitid." (Our people will know peace when they leave this place, and she will know only despair and loneliness.)

Samuel reached his hand forward. "Vini non. Li se tan." (Come. It is time.)

Elliot opened her eyes and watched as Celeste and Samuel walked hand in hand toward the bedroom door. *I will show you a blackened heart, you Negress whore. You will rue the day you invited my husband into your bed.*

Celeste and Samuel walked across the hall into the courtyard bedroom, with Elliot following a short distance behind. They passed through the bedroom and to the balcony. The screen door slammed behind them. Celeste stood close to the railing and held her arms out to the sides.

"What was that?" Marissa said as she bolted awake. She shook Julie. "Jules, wake up."

"What? What is it?" Julie replied sleepily.

"I heard a noise."

"What kind of noise?"

"Like a door slamming. I'm going to check it out."

"Sweetie, I'm sure it's nothing. Just go back to sleep."

"Jules, if it turns out to be more than nothing, I'd never be able to live with myself. With the way things have been going in this house, I don't want to assume odd bumps in the night are harmless."

"All right. I'll come with you."

Celeste looked into the courtyard. "Frè m ak sè m yo, ou te lage nan angaj yo pase isit sou latè sa yo ki te ki te fèt ou isit la pou lontan. Ou te jwenn, e kounye a, ou ka ale lakay ou." (Brothers and sisters, you have been released from the earthly bonds that have held you here for so long. You have been found, and now you may go home.)

Elliot slowly pushed the screen door open and quietly slipped onto the balcony with her back against the far wall to avoid being seen.

Celeste continued. "Se konsa, anpil doulè. Se konsa, anpil lapenn. Se konsa, gen anpil chagren soti nan kote sa a. Kòm ou travèse nan pi lwen pase a, ou yo pral gratis. Ou pral geri. Ou janm bliye doulè a, men konnen memwa ou pral pou tout tan ap viv nan twal nan kote sa a." (So much pain. So much sorrow. So much heartache has come from this place. As you cross into the beyond, you will be free. You will be healed. You will forget the pain, but know your memory will forever live in the fabric of this place.)

Elliot slowly stepped forward, unnoticed by both Celeste and Samuel, fueled by the anger raging in her chest. *I will see to it that you are trapped here forever, whore. I will not allow you to know peace after what you took from me.*

Marissa and Julie walked hand in hand through the upstairs hallway toward Elliot and Lia's bedroom. Marissa pushed the door open and looked in.

"They're not in bed."

"Maybe they heard the noise too," Julie replied.

"Come on. Something doesn't feel right. We need to find them."

Julie followed Marissa back into the hallway. "Mar, stop. Listen. Do you hear it?"

"I hear a voice," Marissa said. "It sounds like it's coming from the corner bedroom."

Marissa and Julie ran toward the courtyard bedroom and slowly entered the room. In the light of the moon, they could see movement on the balcony. They inched closer until they were near the screen door.

"Wait," Julie whispered as she strained to hear through the screen door. "Lia is on the balcony."

They watched as Lia raised her arms to the sides and tilted her head back. "Gen yon tan pou tout bagay ak tout bagay nan plas li. Se pou zanj lan nan Destiny gide ou pi lwen pase sa a enpas. Vwayaje nan lapè nan lòt bò a. benediksyon mwen sou nou tout. Pa volonte ki te pou papa nou an, konsa se pou li." (There is a time for everything and everything in its place. May the Angel of Destiny guide you beyond this impasse. Travel in peace to the other side. My blessings on all of you. By the will of our father, so be it.)

"What is she saying?" Julie asked.

"Beats the hell out of me. It's probably Creole," Marissa whispered. "That means it's Celeste out there, not Lia."

"Oh, my God, Mar. Look."

Julie pointed to the window beside the door that overlooked the courtyard. A focused shaft of light projected from the heavens into the courtyard. From their vantage point, they could see dozens of shadows rise from the mass grave and soar skyward into the light. As the shadows arose from the grave, they took on human form, but as they ascended, they dissolved into white mist.

"Holy fuck," Marissa whispered. "I can't believe I'm seeing this."

Julie shifted her gaze from the window back to Lia on the balcony. As more and more shadows rose, Lia appeared to become less and less stable on her feet.

"Mar, Lia needs us."

Marissa took a step toward the screen door. "I'm on it."

Marissa saw a sudden movement to her left just as she opened the screen door and stepped onto the balcony.

"Die, Negress whore!" Elliot lunged toward Lia and attempted to push her over the balcony.

"No." Marissa shouted. She grabbed a handful of T-shirt just in time to prevent her from toppling over the edge.

Julie was by her side in an instant and took control of Lia while Marissa confronted Elliot. She tackled Elliot to the floor and pinned her arms down.

"What the fuck are you thinking?" Marissa yelled into Elliot's face.

Elliot stared back at her, a blank expression on her face. "Marissa?" she said.

"Mar, we need to get Lia inside," Julie said.

Marissa climbed off Elliot and pointed directly at her. "I'll deal with you later, you piece of shit." She walked to where Julie had Lia cradled in her arms on the floor of the balcony.

"Why am I on the balcony?" Lia asked.

"All in good time, my friend," Julie said. "Let's get you to bed, and I'll tell you all about it."

CHAPTER 34

Marissa stood with her arm around Lia's waist and waited for Julie to pull down the covers on the bed. Elliot stood just inside the doorway at the far end of the bedroom.

"All right, in you go." Marissa helped her into the bed and pulled the blankets around her.

"What happened?" Lia asked.

"I'm thinking it might be better if we talk about it in the morning," Julie suggested.

"Julie, I feel like something significant happened here, and I want to know what it is," Lia said.

Elliot stepped forward. "I want to know as well."

Marissa blocked Elliot's path. "I think you need to leave."

Elliot narrowed her eyes. "Do you mind telling me what's got your panties in a wad tonight?"

"Don't tell me you can't remember," Marissa said incredulously.

"I can't. What the hell happened to make me public enemy number one all of a sudden?"

Marissa walked directly up to her and shoved her backward. "Do you want to know what happened? You tried to fucking kill her. That's what happened."

Lia sat up quickly. "Marissa. How can you say something so vile?"

Marissa's gaze turned sharply toward Lia. "Because it's true. She tried to push you off the balcony. If Jules and I hadn't been there, she would have succeeded."

Lia looked at Julie. "Is that true?"

Julie nodded. "I'm sorry, sweetie, but yes, it's true."

"No fucking way would I do anything to hurt Lia," Elliot shouted. She looked at Lia with desperation in her eyes. "You can't possibly believe I would do that to you."

Lia looked back and forth between her friends and her wife. "Of course I don't believe you would hurt me. Marissa, please tell me what happened tonight."

"Don't be too quick to trust her. Julie and I know what happened. Thank God we were there to stop it."

"Marissa, please," Lia said sternly.

Marissa looked at Julie, who simply nodded her head.

"All right," she began, but stopped abruptly when Elliot tried to sit on the side of the bed. "Oh, no, you don't. You need to put some distance between you and Lia. I don't trust you."

"For crying out loud, Mar," Lia said.

Elliot put her hands up in surrender. "No, it's all right. I'll just stand over here." She leaned against the wall and crossed her arms.

Julie sat on the bed beside Lia and took her hand.

"All right," Marissa said. "I heard a door slam so I woke Julie. God only knows what happened before that. We checked your room, but both of you were gone. We heard a sound from the corner bedroom and when we investigated, we saw you on the balcony."

"I don't remember going out there."

"Well, considering what we witnessed, I'm guessing it was Celeste who took you out there."

"What do you mean?" Lia asked.

"You were on the balcony, standing very close to the railing with your arms extended to the sides, and you were talking in a foreign language."

"That's exactly what happened the last time Celeste took her out there in the middle of the night," Elliot said from across the room.

"Your head was thrown back, and it sounded like you were chanting something. That's when we saw them," Marissa explained.

"Saw who?" Lia asked.

"The shadows," Julie replied. "We saw shadows rise from the grave and float into the sky."

270

"Seriously?" Lia asked.

"Yes," Marissa said. "We both saw it happen, and the longer you stood there, the shakier you became. Almost like it was sapping your energy. We were afraid you would collapse, so I stepped onto the porch to help. Just as I took a step toward you, Elliot came out of nowhere and rushed toward you, screaming obscenities."

"I did not," Elliot shouted.

"Yes, you did," Marissa insisted.

"What did I say?"

"It happened so fast, your exact words didn't register, but you were definitely angry. So angry that you tried to push Lia over the railing," Marissa said.

Tears filled Elliot's eyes as she shook her head. "No. I wouldn't do that. I couldn't do that. I love her."

Marissa ignored Elliot's comments as she addressed Lia once more. "Julie saw to your safety while I wrestled Elliot to the floor. When it was all over, you seemed dazed and confused." She looked at Elliot. "In fact, you both did."

"I don't remember any of this," Elliot said between choked sobs. "I would never intentionally hurt Lia. I would sooner die than hurt her."

Lia extended her hand toward Elliot. "Come," she said.

Elliot took a step toward the bed but stopped short when Marissa stood in her path once more.

"Mar, please let her by," Lia said.

Marissa stared directly at Elliot as she addressed Lia. "I don't trust her."

"You don't have to trust her. I do. Now, please let her pass."

Marissa lowered her face close to Elliot's. "If you do anything stupid, you'll have me to answer to. You got that?"

"If I do anything stupid, I will gladly submit to whatever punishment you wish to dole out," Elliot said.

Marissa stood aside and watched Elliot climb onto the bed and take Lia into her arms.

Julie walked around the bed and stood beside a very stoic Marissa. She slipped her arm around Marissa's waist. "Maybe it wasn't the Elliot we know out there on the balcony."

***

The next morning, Lia stood on the porch outside the kitchen and watched as the technicians from the coroner's office extracted the remains from the mass grave. Marissa joined her there with two cups of coffee.

"Here. I'm sure you can use this after last night," Marissa said.

Lia accepted the coffee. "Thank you. You know, you didn't need to sleep in the chair beside our bed all night."

"Yes I did, for my own peace of mind, if nothing else."

"Elliot would never intentionally hurt me. I'd bet my life on it."

"Well, you would have lost that bet last night."

Lia fell silent as she absorbed Marissa's words. She reached up to wipe a tear from the corner of her eye, a gesture not lost on Marissa.

Marissa sighed. "Look, Lia. I know Elliot loves you, and in her right mind, she would die to protect you, but last night, she was definitely not in her right mind. She was a crazy woman, like she was possessed or something."

Lia looked at her sharply. "Say that again."

"She was definitely not herself. It was like something, or someone else had control over her."

Lia covered her mouth with one hand. "Oh, my. I think I know what happened to her."

"Well, if you have thoughts about it, please share."

"Celeste possessed me for the first time just before Elliot went to New York to pack up the house. During that episode, Celeste became quite amorous with Elliot and apparently mistook her for the mistress of this house."

"The mistress?" Marissa asked. "You mean the sadistic, crazy bitch who tortured the slaves?"

"Yes. She thought Elliot was the mistress."

"Holy shit. Do you think it's possible this mistress's spirit is actually inside Elliot?"

"It would certainly explain why she tried to kill me last night."

"Elliot told me that she feels intense anger when Celeste is around," Marissa said. "She said all she wants to do is shake the shit out her. She said she has no control over it and that it scares her."

"Based on what I've learned through the visions and dreams, Celeste was forced to have relations with both the master and mistress. The little girl who jumped to her death from the roof to get away from the mistress was Celeste's daughter, and the master was the girl's father."

"Damn. If the mistress is possessing Elliot, it's no wonder she feels this sense of anger when Celeste is around." Marissa grabbed Lia's arm. "Lia, this is all the more reason we can't trust you to be alone with Elliot."

"Don't be foolish. Elliot is my wife."

"That hasn't stopped her from hurting you—or should I say hurting Celeste—or from trying to kill Celeste. Like it or not, I am not letting you out of my sight until we figure out what to do about this."

"Seriously, Mar? How are you going to do that when you and Julie go home in a few days?"

"Don't argue with me about this. We'll delay going home if we have to. By the way, where is Elliot this morning?"

"Just before you came outside, she was in the courtyard watching the activities." Lia scanned the group of people moving in and around the grave. "I don't see her now."

"Wait. Isn't that her over there?"

"Where?" Lia searched the area below.

"No. Not in the courtyard. Look over there, on the porch above the library."

Lia looked down the length of the third-story porch. "Okay. I see her now. I wonder what she's doing."

Elliot walked toward the corner of the porch, all the while, examining the area around her.

"That's odd," Marissa said. "She almost looks like she's trying not to be seen."

Lia waved her hand in an attempt to get Elliot's attention.

Marissa grabbed her arm and held it down. "What are you doing?"

"I'm trying to find out what she's up to."

"I say we wait until she leaves, then go check it out for ourselves."

"I'm not going in there. That apartment gives me the creeps."

"I thought it was empty."

"It is, but it has this horrible smell like something died in there."

Marissa narrowed her eyes. "Maybe something did."

"Hey, guys." Julie suddenly appeared in the kitchen doorway.

Marissa turned around. "Hey, love. Where've you been?"

"On the phone with Phoebe. She agreed to meet with us, but she's tied up for the next few hours. She's willing to come here tonight if we'd like her to, but I'm thinking we might want to wait until the grave diggers are gone."

"That's not a bad idea," Lia said. "If what you and Mar saw last night is the real deal, most of the bad juju should have left the premises along with the shadow spirits. That should make it easier for Phoebe to be here. The coroner indicated they should be finished with the excavation before dark."

"Did you tell Phoebe what we saw?" Marissa asked her wife.

"I did. She said it sounds like Celeste might have been some sort of Hoodoo priestess or something."

"It did seem like she was performing some type of ritual. The shadows began to rise out of the grave when she started that weird-ass chanting."

"I wish I could remember it," Lia said.

"Be grateful you don't remember. That whole scuffle with Elliot is something I hope we don't have to go through again anytime soon," Marissa said.

"Phoebe suggested we might want to have a ceremony honoring the dead who were buried in the mass grave," Julie said. "She thought it might help cleanse this place of the malevolent aura she felt when she was here."

"I'm willing to do anything that might give those poor souls some peace," Lia replied. "I'm sure Elliot would be happy to support that as well."

"Speaking of Elliot, she just came out of the apartment in the corner," Julie said. "I wonder what she was doing in there?"

Elliot made eye contact with Lia as she made her way toward them. "Hey, love," she said. "How are you feeling today?"

"I'm good. Tired—but fine. What were you doing in the apartment?" Lia asked.

"I had to use the bathroom. They've got most of the courtyard roped off, so it was the closest one without having to go outside the gates and walk around the house. I'm getting a little hungry. Can I interest anyone in going out for lunch?"

"Lunch is good. I could certainly eat," Lia said.

"Good." Elliot smiled at her. "I also thought we might stop at the Hall of Records and see if we can find out the names of the poor souls in the pit."

"And maybe begin my genealogy search as well," Lia added.

"It sounds like we have the rest of our day mapped out for us," Marissa said. "I vote for a good hearty meal before we begin our toils. How does Bubba Gump's sound to everyone?"

"Run, Forrest, Run!" Lia joked.

Elliot wrapped her arms around Lia. "If I remember right, you said those very words to me a few weeks ago, and it involved two bottles of wine and a soak in the tub."

"Yes. That was the night you cheated on me with Celeste."

"You cheated on her with Celeste?" Julie asked. "How could you?"

"No fair. I thought she was Lia."

"Except, I don't speak Creole," Lia reminded her.

"Yeah. She doesn't speak Creole," Marissa echoed.

"What is this? Gang-up-on-Elliot day?" Elliot teased. "Now move it or we'll get nothing done today."

Elliot stepped aside and allowed the other three to enter the kitchen first. Before following them, she turned to gaze at the apartment above the library. She felt her expression change to an evil sneer. "Soon, Celeste. Soon."

"Elliot, come on," Lia said from the kitchen doorway. "Last one to the car pays the bill."

"Come out here and say that to my face," Elliot challenged with a wide grin.

Lia stepped onto the porch and into Elliot's embrace. "I said, last one to the car pays the bill."

"That would be you." Elliot bolted ahead of her into the kitchen.

"You little shit," Lia yelled as she ran after her.

CHAPTER 35

The ladies returned to the house several hours later and found Phoebe waiting for them on the sidewalk in front of the gate.

"Phoebe," Julie said as she climbed out of the car, "you should have called. We would have picked you up."

"Nonsense. I'm only two streets away. The only reason I let you drive me home the other night was because it was nearly dark and I was wiped out."

The other three exited the car and greeted her as well.

Lia hugged her. "I'm glad you came back. I was worried this place had scared you away for good. Let me unlock the gate so we can go inside."

While Lia unlocked the gate, Elliot approached Phoebe and extended her hand. Phoebe maintained eye contact with her as she accepted the handshake. A smile immediately broke out on her face. "Finally, I meet the real Elliot," she said. "The malevolence has less hold on you outside of the house."

Finally, Marissa locked arms with her. "Let me escort you into the house," she said as Lia opened the doors.

Phoebe stepped inside the foyer and looked around. "I feel a calm that was not here before."

Elliot locked the gate and entered the house.

The moment Elliot stepped into the foyer, Phoebe turned sharply toward her. "The evil one has targeted your soul," she said. "Fight her, or those you love will suffer."

Elliot narrowed her eyes. "Care to explain yourself?"

Lia stepped between Phoebe and Elliot and took Phoebe's other arm. "I have a nice pitcher of lemonade in the refrigerator if you're interested, Phoebe."

"Actually, if you don't mind, I'd like to see the grave," Phoebe replied.

Lia raised her eyebrows in surprise. "Okay. I guess we can do that. Let's cut through this level to the courtyard." She led the group into the bowels of the house. Soon, they were standing in the courtyard, beside the open grave.

"Look, there's a note," Julie said. "It's from the coroner. It reads: 'Please be advised that all of the remains have been removed from the grave. However, we will return later in the week for additional forensic evidence. We ask that you do not disturb the site until we are finished with our investigation. Thank you.'"

Elliot walked to the side of the hole and stood there with her hands shoved deep into her pockets. A play of emotions crossed her face as her jaw clenched repeatedly.

"I feel your struggle, Elliot," Phoebe said.

"You know nothing of my struggle," Elliot said.

Lia walked over to Elliot and put her hand on Elliot's arm. "Sweetheart, are you okay?"

Elliot closed her eyes and reopened them. She shook her head as though to clear it. "I'm fine."

Lia looked across the open grave to Phoebe who stood on the opposite side. "Julie mentioned you wanted to have a ceremony to honor the slaves buried here. I think that's a wonderful idea."

Phoebe continued to stare at Elliot. "Yes. We will need to build an Ancestral Altar."

"How do we do that?" Marissa asked.

Phoebe finally broke her gaze with Elliot and turned to address Marissa. "It's quite simple. There's no special layout. A table will do, or even a board extended across two chairs. It's more symbolic than anything else. It's a place to venerate ancestors who have passed. Lia, you will be integral in the ceremony since you share blood with at least one of the victims."

"How would we know if Celeste is among them?" Lia asked.

"If she leaves you at peace once her spirit has been released."

"But," Julie said, "we saw Lia, or actually, Celeste, release the spirits of the other slaves, while she continued to possess Lia."

"That doesn't mean Celeste's spirit didn't join them." Phoebe turned to Lia. "Has Celeste taken control since the spirits were freed?"

"Not that I know of," Lia said. "But then, I'm almost never aware of her possessions."

"Has Celeste shown herself to any of you since the grave was uncovered?" Phoebe asked.

None of them could verify that Celeste was still present.

"We could confirm or deny her presence by trying to contact her," Phoebe suggested.

"You mean, like a séance?" Lia asked.

"Something like that," Phoebe replied.

"Oh, for crying out loud. You can't be serious," Elliot interrupted.

"I'm very serious," Phoebe said. "I've found it to be an especially effective way to communicate with the dead."

Lia took Elliot's hand in hers. "El, please keep an open mind. If we can get Celeste to talk to us, we'll know whether she's still here. And if she is, then maybe we can figure out how to free her too."

"I think we should do it," Julie said. "What do you think, Mar?"

"I'm game if you are, as long as it's safe," Marissa said.

"I wouldn't suggest it if it wasn't safe," Phoebe replied. "We can think about it while we do the ceremony."

"Is there anything in particular you need for the altar?" Lia asked.

"I need a white linen to serve as an altar cloth, a vial of holy water, two white candles, a lighter, white flowers, and either photographs, or belongings of the deceased to acknowledge their one-time existence on this earth."

"That last one will be a problem," Elliot said. "The bodies were interred almost two hundred years ago, and this house has changed hands countless times since. I'd venture to guess there's nothing left of any of them."

"We have the list of names we found at the Hall of Records," Marissa suggested. "There must be two dozen names or more on the list."

"I believe that will work," Phoebe said.

"About the holy water?" Lia added. "I'm afraid we gave up hope a long time ago that the Church would bless our union. Holy water is something we definitely don't have."

"That's all right. A vial of water and some salt will do nicely."

"All right. Altar cloth, candles, flowers, water, salt. Am I forgetting anything?" Lia asked.

"The list of names," Marissa said.

"Yes. The list of names. Give me a minute and I'll have everything you need," Lia said.

"I'll give you a hand," Julie offered. They left Phoebe, Marissa and Elliot standing around the grave.

While Lia and Julie were collecting the implements for the ceremony, Marissa enlisted Elliot's help in setting up an altar. They dragged two flower pedestals from beside the shed to the area next to the grave. On top of the pedestals, they placed a piece of lumber that was being used as a shelf inside the shed. They finished constructing the altar just as Lia and Julie returned.

"Wow, you two are resourceful," Lia said. "El, would you mind holding these so Julie and I can spread the altar cloth?" Lia handed the supplies to her. "Thanks, love."

Within moments, the altar was ready.

Phoebe stepped forward to begin.

"Wait," Lia said. "I think Samuel should be here for this. These are his kin as well."

"I'll go after him," Elliot offered. "I'll be back in a few minutes."

Elliot exited the courtyard through the gate on the Governor Nicholls Street side of the property.

"She is very conflicted about this," Phoebe said. "She's battling a very powerful demon within her. So far, the good in her is winning."

"It wasn't winning the other night," Marissa said.

"Yes, Julie told me about what happened." Phoebe looked at each of them. "She will need all of your help to survive this. In fact, you will all need each other."

A few moments later, the courtyard gate opened, admitting Elliot and Samuel.

Lia greeted Samuel with a hug. "Thank you for joining us, Samuel. I know this is hard, but we thought you should be here when the souls of your kin are released."

Samuel took off his hat and held it between his hands. "Samuel thanks you, Miss Lia."

Phoebe stepped up to the altar. "Before we arrange the implements, I'll need some dirt from the grave, placed in a line down the middle of the altar."

"Dirt from the grave?" Elliot said.

"Yes. It holds the essence of their souls," Phoebe explained.

"I'll get it." Marissa grabbed a shovel that stood against the shed and scooped a mound of dirt from the grave. Very carefully, she held it over the altar while Phoebe poured a few handfuls in a straight line, dividing the altar in two.

On the left side of the altar, Phoebe set the flowers, candles, water, and salt. She laid the list of names directly on top of the line of dirt. Next, she measured three pinches of salt into the vial of water and held it high.

In a clear voice, she called out. "The Lord is my shepherd. I shall not want. He maketh me to lie down in green pastures. He leadeth me beside the still waters. He restoreth my soul. He leadeth me in the paths of righteousness for his name's sake.

"Yea, though I walk through the valley of the shadow of death, I will fear no evil, for thou art with me. Thy rod and thy staff they comfort me.

"Thou preparest a table before me in the presence of mine enemies. Thou anointest my head with oil. My cup runneth over.

"Surely goodness and mercy shall follow me all the days of my life, and I will dwell in the house of the Lord forever."

Upon completing her recitation of the Twenty-third Psalm, Phoebe walked to the side of the grave, sprinkled the holy water into the pit, and returned to the altar.

She said to Lia. "I'll need you to move the candles and flowers to the right side of the altar as I recite the incantations."

Lia simply nodded in response.

Phoebe raised her arms to the sides. "White is the color of purity and represents the cleansing of your souls. Water is for renewal as your souls are released from the earthly bounds that have held you captive for so long. The first white candle is to light the path before you, so you can see your way to the promised land."

Lia moved the first candle to the far right side of the altar and lit it.

"The flowers represent rebirth as your love and hope take root with the Heavenly Father."

Lia moved the flowers to the right side of the altar.

"The second candle lights the path behind you, so you may return to guide us in our daily lives, interface with the Heavenly Father on our behalf, and protect us in times of need."

Lia moved the second candle to the right side and lit it.

Phoebe looked at Elliot, Marissa, Julie, and Samuel, all of whom stood with their heads bowed in reverence. "All who are here rejoice in the lives of our lost ones and pray that their souls will be redeemed in the image of the holy one. So shall it be."

Phoebe lowered her arms. "These candles will be allowed to burn until they are no more."

Lia opened her eyes and looked at the altar. "Oh, my God. Look."

Everyone approached the altar to see what startled Lia.

On the list of two-dozen names, only three remained: Samuel McGinty, Celeste Boudreau, and Lia Boudreau.

CHAPTER 36

"What does it mean?" Julie asked.

"It means all but three of the slaves who died in this house have crossed over," Phoebe explained.

"So Celeste is still here. Why is that?" Lia said.

"Either she has unfinished business, or her bones weren't in the grave," Phoebe replied.

"But what about Samuel? Lia told me he was in the hole," Lia said.

"Okay, this is getting weird. Samuel is right here," Elliot said. "And exactly when did you talk to the little girl?"

"The night we were digging the hole. She was on the porch when I brought the lemonade glasses upstairs. She told me Samuel was in the hole and he was taking Celeste home."

"Samuel be Celeste's husband," Samuel said. "He be livin' in da house when da she-devil be here."

"Wait. Wait a minute," Lia said. "Before buying this house, I came back for a second showing and I saw a vision in the kitchen. There was a slave named Samuel there. Is that the same Samuel we're talking about?"

"Yes, ma'am," Samuel said.

"Phoebe, you said something earlier about a séance," Marissa said.

"Yes. Is that something you're interested in doing?"

"I'm not so sure that's a good idea," Elliot said.

Phoebe looked directly at Elliot. "Are you afraid of what the others might learn?" she asked.

"What are you implying?" Elliot challenged.

"Elliot, we should do whatever we can to rid our home of all this unrest. I want to do this," Lia said.

"And what if it doesn't work? We could be putting ourselves through more emotional turmoil for nothing."

"We won't know unless we try. I love our home, Elliot. I don't want to leave, but I don't know how much longer either of us can live under this tension."

Elliot couldn't resist the anxiety in Lia's eyes. She took Lia's face between her palms. "Okay. Against my better judgment, I'll do this for you, but if it gets out of hand, I will stop it. Is that understood? I won't put you in danger."

"All right then. We should move this into the house," Phoebe said.

***

"We need a round or oval table that all of us can sit around, intimately," Phoebe said as they entered the kitchen.

"That kind of rules out the dining room table," Elliot replied. "It's big enough for an army."

"How about the coffee table in the parlor?" Lia said. "We could position chairs around it."

"That might work," Phoebe replied.

"Is there anything else we need?" Lia asked.

"The lights will need to be shut off," Phoebe said, "so candles would be good for dim lighting. Fortunately, it's later in the day, so sunlight shouldn't be a problem."

"Okay," Lia said. "I'll be back in a few minutes. There are some votive candles in the cabinet above the washing machine."

"We'll need at least three candles, Lia. The more the better," Phoebe said.

"I'll arrange the chairs around the coffee table while you fetch the candles," Julie said. She followed Lia out of the room, leaving Marissa, Elliot, and Phoebe in the kitchen.

Marissa looked around. "Where did Samuel go? I thought he would want to participate in this."

"Actually, since Samuel is a direct descendant of the slaves who lived in this house, it's important that he be here," Phoebe said.

"I'll go after him," Marissa said.

Elliot shook her head. "No, let me do it."

She ran down the spiral stairs to the first level and let herself out the front door. As usual, Samuel was standing on the corner diagonal to the house. Elliot stopped on the sidewalk and waved at him.

"Samuel, would you mind coming over here, please?" she called.

"Samuel be fine right here, Miss Walker," he said.

"Samuel, please. Apparently, you're important to this ceremony. Please join us."

"Don't believe I will, Miss Walker."

Elliot ran her hand through her short-cropped hair and crossed the road to meet Samuel on the corner. "Samuel, Lia is counting on your being there. It's important to her."

"There be evil in that house, Miss Walker. You should know that."

"Then help us chase the evil away."

"Or die tryin'?"

"Phoebe said it wasn't dangerous."

"It not be dangerous if Miss Phoebe control it. Samuel not sure she can."

"Samuel, you can leave at any time. I promise."

"Samuel know how the mistress's promises go. Promises she keep are ones that kill."

"The mistress has been gone from here for almost two hundred years, Samuel. She can't hurt you now."

Samuel narrowed his eyes at Elliot. "You don't know, do you?"

"Know what?"

"Samuel," Lia called from across the street. "Samuel, please join us. We need you to complete the circle of six."

Samuel and Elliot both looked at Lia standing on the opposite corner.

Elliot turned back to Samuel. "Samuel?"

"Never could resist that woman," Samuel said as he crossed the street.

***

"We're back," Lia announced as she, Elliot and Samuel entered the parlor.

The room was dark; lit only by a half-dozen candles strategically placed on the oval coffee table. Six chairs were positioned evenly around the table, with Phoebe sitting in one of the middle chairs.

"Please, sit," she said.

Samuel sat beside Phoebe followed by Lia, Elliot, Julie and Marissa. Elliot sat directly across the table from Phoebe. On the table in front of Phoebe was what remained of the list of slaves, used in the cross-over ceremony at the grave site. She picked up the list and put it in the center of the table.

"Please join hands to complete the circle and focus only on the task at hand," she said.

The group followed Phoebe's lead and raised their joined hands to chest level.

"We are here to celebrate the memories of Celeste, Samuel, and Lia. Commune with us and allow us to rejoice in your lives."

Several moments passed in silence as they waited for a response. After a time, Phoebe prompted again.

"Spirits of the past, I call on thee. Find favor with this summons and travel to greet us in our presence. Speak to us of things that need to be said. Be guided by the light of this world, and visit upon us for things that need to be done."

Samuel suddenly released Lia's hand and grabbed her arm. "Did yous find her yet? Can't goes wid out her."

Lia looked at Samuel's hand on her arm, then back to his face. "Find wh—?" In mid-sentence, Lia's head jerked back. "Ahh!" she exclaimed before regaining her composure. She smiled and reached forward to lay her palm gently on the side of Samuel's face. "Mwen te rate ou anpil," she said. (I have missed you so much.)

Samuel closed his eyes and smiled. "Celeste," he whispered.

Elliot, Marissa, and Julie sat wide-eyed as they watched Samuel and Celeste interact. Phoebe attempted to assure them with her gaze that everything was all right.

"Welcome," Phoebe said.

Samuel looked at Phoebe with trepidation. "Who you be?"

"My name is Phoebe. We are all here to greet you, Samuel. We have much to talk about."

"Don't knows you," Samuel said, a tinge of alarm in his voice. He looked at Celeste. "Don't knows her." His gaze scanned the others seated at the table. "Who dey be?"

Celeste took Samuel's hands in hers. "Dey be ones dat free you, Samuel."

Just then, the cat jumped into Celeste's lap. "Ah, baby girl. Mama be proud of you. You show dem da way. Dat be right, yes?"

"Samuel," Phoebe said, "your soul is free. The others have crossed over. Why are you still here?"

Samuel looked at Celeste. "Celeste be my heart. Can't goes wid out her."

"Were your bones in the pit?" Julie asked.

"Dey be dere. Samuel be happy you find dem, but Samuel can't goes wid out her."

"What happened to you, Samuel?" Marissa asked. "How did you die?"

Samuel looked around the table and locked eyes with Elliot. "Da mistress kilt me. She chain my Celeste to the wall and make her watch. She take my eyes. She cut my face. She stir my brains, and Celeste see. Celeste see it all."

Tears ran down Celeste's face. "Mwen se konsa regrèt, mwen renmen. Pa t 'gen mwen te kapab fè." (I am so sorry, my love. There was nothing I could do.) "Mwen te vle mouri nan plas ou." (I wanted to die in your place.)

Samuel clenched his fists and fought the tears running from his eyes. "No. She da reason Lia died. We lost Ethan on her account. I's glad for da torture if it save you from da same."

"You loved her," Julie said.

"Wid all my heart, ma'am. Samuel wish to save Celeste from da evil one's bed, but she kilt me afore I could. She leave her stench on my Celeste's skin. She make her share da bed to stop da beatings."

Elliot stared at the center of the table, totally immobile, save for the clenching of her jaw.

"Tell us about Ethan," Phoebe said.

Celeste blinked away her tears. "He be our boy. Mine and Samuel. Gran send him away afore he be kilt too. He be just a baby."

"What happened to him?" Julie asked.

"Gran found folks to take him North. Never seen him again."

Julie looked at Marissa. "My, God, Mar. My heart is in so much pain for them."

Marissa nodded and squeezed her hand. "Celeste, Samuel is still here because he can't bear to cross over without you. Why are you still here?"

"I not be found. Can't be leaving dis place. Mistress not let me leave."

"She won't let you leave? What do you mean?" Marissa asked.

"She be evil in her soul, dat one. She not be bound to dis place in body. She be bound by evil and heartache. She hide da bones. Dey be much sorrow. She be here as long as sorrow be here."

"And as long as you are here, there is sorrow," Julie said.

"Yes, ma'am."

Elliot jumped to her feet and pointed directly at Celeste. "You will never leave this place, whore. You thought you would trick me with your seductions. I will never tell you where your bones are." Elliot lunged forward and placed both her hands tightly around Lia's neck.

"Elliot!" Marissa grabbed Elliot's hands and pried them loose.

Phoebe blew out the candles and cast the room into darkness. The sound of thuds could be heard close by.

"Julie, please turn on the lights," Phoebe said.

Within seconds, the room was flooded with the warm glow of the table lamps. There on the floor, unconscious, lay Samuel, Lia, and Elliot.

CHAPTER 37

"What the fuck just happened here?" Marissa adjusted a pillow beneath Elliot's head. "Elliot was acting like a crazy woman."

"She's possessed by the spirit of the mistress," Phoebe explained. "It's apparent in the way she is with Celeste that she both loved her and hated her. And probably hated herself for the way she felt."

"You can't really believe the mistress loved Celeste!" Julie said. "Look at the way Elliot treats her. She tried to strangle her just now."

"Love and hate are very complicated emotions. Keep in mind that the mistress had to share Celeste with her husband, who impregnated her. She then had to share her with the baby. Finally, she had to share her with Samuel, and based on what he told us tonight, she tortured and killed Samuel as punishment for the love Celeste shared with him."

"How can someone be so sadistic? What drives a person to do something like this?" Marissa asked.

"Power, repressed anger, sexual sadism perhaps? Keep in mind that these events happened at a time when most power was in the hands of men. It's possible the mistress was repressed, or even abused, by her husband, and she, in turn, took it out on the slaves. My guess is that it started with minor discipline, such as slapping or punching. The sense of satisfaction she got from administering these punishments would have been like a drug, driving her to do more and more until she became psychopathic."

"Lia believes the husband was involved in some of the torture, or at the very least, the medical experiments done on some of the slaves," Julie said.

"That certainly is possible. He was a doctor, after all," Phoebe said. "Keep in mind that slaves were considered property, and subhuman. It's possible he valued their lives so little that he didn't give a second thought to using them for experimentation."

"What do we do now?" Marissa asked. "We can't possibly allow Elliot to be alone with Lia."

"We need to get them out of this house," Julie said. "The mistress doesn't seem to have any power over Elliot when she's away from the property."

"I'm not sure that will work," Phoebe said. "If you recall, Celeste said the mistress is not bound to this place in body. She's bound only by Celeste's sorrow. That means she has the ability to leave. She has less control over Elliot outside of the house, but she's still in her."

"Why Elliot?" Marissa asked. "I can understand why Celeste has possessed Lia, and why the two Samuels merged, both because of the common bloodlines, but Elliot isn't related to the psycho bitch. At least not that we're aware of."

"Possession doesn't require a bloodline to be accomplished," Phoebe explained. "Although it does make one more susceptible. Elliot is the most logical target— primarily because of her love for Lia, also known as, Celeste. By possessing Elliot, the mistress can have a relationship with Celeste through Lia. Bottom line is that Elliot is the only means she has right now of exerting power over Celeste."

"Has anyone else noticed that Elliot's behavior has become a lot more aggressive toward Lia since we uncovered the grave?" Julie asked.

"If what Celeste said was true and the mistress was drawing her power from sorrow, she would have lost a significant amount of that power when the poor souls in the grave were released," Phoebe said. "If that's the case, it makes sense that she would pour what's left of her energy into Elliot. I would think the more energy she pours into Elliot, the stronger the hold on her would be and the more malleable she'd be to doing the mistress's will."

"So Elliot is stuck with her?" Julie asked.

"At least until Celeste's sorrow is no longer in this house. And even then, there's a possibility that her spirit will refuse to release her hold on Elliot," Phoebe said.

"And if that happens, what are our options?" Marissa asked.

"Some form of exorcism," Phoebe replied.

"You mean like heads spinning around, and green vomit spewing all over the place?" Marissa asked.

Phoebe chuckled. "You, my dear, have been watching too many horror movies. No—there are other, less theatrical ways of conducting an exorcism, all of which carry some risk. Let's hope we won't have to go there."

"Then I guess we need to find Celeste's bones," Julie said.

"Oh, my God. What happened?" Lia said as she sat up. "Why am I on the floor?" She looked around and saw Elliot and Samuel beside her. She scrambled quickly to Elliot's side. "Elliot, sweetheart, wake up."

"She's okay." Marissa helped Lia to her feet. "They both are."

"What happened?" Lia asked.

"Things got a little out of control during the séance, so Phoebe had to end it abruptly. You, Elliot, and Samuel passed out when she did that," Marissa explained.

"Why didn't the rest of you pass out?"

"Because we weren't possessed. You three were."

"By whom?"

"You, by Celeste...but of course you already know that. Elliot, by the mistress, and Samuel was possessed by the slave Samuel who lived here at the same time as Celeste."

"Turns out Celeste and Samuel were lovers," Julie added.

"They were lovers?" Lia asked.

"Yes," Julie said. "Lia, it was so sad to hear Samuel talk about what happened to them. The mistress made Celeste watch as she tortured and killed him." Julie wiped the tears from her face.

"And apparently, they had a son together. His name was Ethan," Marissa said.

"Ethan? Little Lia told me about him. She said Gran sent him away," Lia said.

"Yes. That's what Celeste told us. Apparently, Gran found someone to take him North before the mistress could kill him as well," Julie added. "He was just a baby." Julie began to cry. "I am so angry and so heartbroken by what happened to these people."

Marissa took Julie into her arms. "It's okay, love. I've got you."

Phoebe joined the conversation after checking on Samuel and Elliot. "How are you feeling?" she asked Lia.

"I'm fine."

"Do you have any recollection of the séance?"

"No, but I'm anxious to know what we learned."

Phoebe inspected Lia's neck.

"What are you doing?" Lia asked.

"It will probably bruise," Phoebe said.

Lia's felt her neck. "It's a little sore. What happened?"

"Elliot tried to kill you again, this time by strangulation," Marissa said.

"Correction. The mistress tried to kill Celeste again," Phoebe said.

Lia's eyes grew wide. "Please don't say that."

"I'm sorry, but it's true," Phoebe said. "I fear the mistress is gaining more and more control over Elliot, out of self-preservation."

"What do you mean?" Lia asked.

"We learned through the séance that the mistress's hold on this house is based on the pain and suffering she put her slaves through here. When you found the grave, all the negative energy from their sorrow was released, which in turn, weakened the mistress's power. The only thing she has to cling to now, is the remaining sorrow from Celeste, Samuel and Lia. She appears to be focusing all her will on working through Elliot to keep them here, especially Celeste."

Marissa stepped forward and took Lia by the arms. "I know you won't want to hear this, but from this point forward, we're not going to allow you to be alone with Elliot. We just don't trust her around you."

"But she loves me. I know she does," Lia said.

"Yes, she does, but the mistress doesn't."

Lia cast a pleading glance at Julie.

"I agree with Marissa," Julie said. "We can't risk it."

A noise came from behind them.

"What the hell happened?" Elliot said as she sat up.

Lia ran to Elliot and dropped to her knees in front of her, while the others stood by. "Are you all right?"

Elliot looked directly at Lia. "I'm fine. A little concerned that I'm on the floor, but otherwise, I'm fine. What happened?"

"The mistress possessed you, and she attacked Lia again. Or more correctly, she attacked Celeste," Marissa explained.

"I don't remember doing that," Elliot said.

"If it makes you feel any better," Lia said, "I don't remember you doing it either."

"You were both under the influence of spiritual forces," Phoebe explained.

Elliot cupped the side of Lia's face with her palm. "Did I hurt you?"

Lia pressed her face into Elliot's hand and briefly closed her eyes. "Nothing that will cause any permanent damage."

Elliot narrowed her eyes as she noticed the bruises on Lia's neck. "Tell me I didn't do this." She looked at Marissa, who just nodded. "Damn it!" Elliot stood and walked a few feet away. "How did this happen?"

"What's the last thing you remember?" Phoebe asked.

"I remember Samuel telling us why he didn't cross over with the rest of the spirits."

"So you missed the discussion about how the mistress tortured and killed him while making Celeste watch," Marissa stated.

"I don't remember that."

"It seems like the mistress took control of you just as Celeste and Samuel were beginning to talk about her," Julie said. "You don't remember them telling us about how Gran sent Ethan away, and how the only thing holding the mistress in this house was Celeste's sorrow?"

Elliot shook her head. "I've got no memory of that. I have no idea who Ethan is." She looked directly at Marissa. "When did I attack Lia?"

"When Celeste told us we needed to find her remains in order to release her and eliminate the one thing holding the mistress here. When she said that, you lunged forward and grabbed her by the neck, vowing that she would never leave this place," Marissa grimaced. "Phoebe had to abruptly end the séance to stop you. That's why you woke up on the floor. All three of you who were possessed passed out when the séance ended."

Elliot turned to look at Lia, who was still kneeling on the floor. "I don't know what to say." Her voice was choked with emotion. "I am so sorry. I'll never forgive myself."

Lia stood and hurried toward Elliot, who backed away and put her hands out in front of her.

"No. Don't come near me. I don't trust what might happen."

"Elliot—" Lia began to say.

"No. Please." Elliot dashed from the room.

Julie suddenly interrupted them. "Look. Samuel is coming around."

Marissa and Julie rushed to Samuel and helped him to his feet. Phoebe brought a chair for him to sit on.

"What happened? Last thing Samuel remember is holding hands wid you all."

"The spirit of the slave Samuel came forth and spoke through you," Phoebe said. "We learned that he was in love with Celeste, and that they had a child together."

Samuel looked down at his hands and then turned his sorrow-filled gaze on Phoebe. "Yes, ma'am. Story be that he and Celeste jumped the broom. They had a son they named Ethan. The boy be born after Lia died."

Lia knelt at Samuel's feet and took his hand in hers. "Samuel, what happened to Ethan?" she asked.

"Story be told that Gran send the boy away, afore the mistress could kill him too. Send him North, she did."

"Does anyone know what happened to him?"

"He be raised by colored people that worked for fine white couple. He be the lucky one. He be treated kindly."

"Do you know his history, Samuel? What did he do when he grew up? Did he marry? Did he have children?" Lia asked.

"You ask a lot of questions, girl, but Samuel thinks you want to know if Ethan be your family."

"Do you know that, Samuel? Phoebe said that Celeste and I share a bloodline. Is that through Ethan?"

"That be Ethan."

Lia sat back on her heels and closed her eyes as a visible convulsion coursed through her. When she reopened her eyes, she smiled through her tears.

Julie placed her hand on Lia's shoulder. "Are you all right?" she asked.

Lia smiled at Julie. "Ethan lived. He not die. He lived and he be happy." She looked at Samuel. "Samuel, da boy lived."

Samuel smiled. "The boy lived, Celeste. Gran done right to send him North."

CHAPTER 38

Lia closed and locked the gate behind Samuel and reentered the foyer. "Man, that was an exhausting evening," she said to Marissa who was waiting there for her.

"I'll say. It was startling to see Celeste possess you like that," Marissa said. "Do you remember any of it?"

"For the most part, no. There have been times when Celeste has shown me her memories—generally bad ones— but I don't have any awareness when she takes over."

"I'm amazed at how calm you are about it. If it were me, I'd be freaking out."

"That's the odd part, Mar. Celeste has given me no reason to fear her. My heart hurts more from knowing what she and the other slaves lived through than from any actual harm she's done to me during the possessions."

"I can only imagine how it feels to be the host of a possession," Marissa said. "It's exhausting to watch. I can't wait for Julie to come back from taking Phoebe home so we can just relax and maybe hit the sheets early."

Lia glanced over her shoulder as Marissa followed her up the stairs to the main living area. "You didn't happen to see where Elliot went, did you?"

"I saw her leave the room just before Samuel woke up, but I haven't seen her since."

"I'm really worried about her. I know she feels horrible about her behavior toward me, but I don't blame her for it one bit. Under normal circumstances, she would never do anything to intentionally hurt me."

"We all know that, Lia, but things haven't exactly been normal around here."

"I'm going to search the house for her."

"I'm going with you. I need to talk to her about where she's going to sleep tonight, because it won't be with you," Marissa said.

"Really, Mar?"

"Yes, really. Look, none of us has any control over when that bitch decides to possess her, least of all, Elliot. I realize she isn't responsible for her actions when the mistress is in control, but I don't think you should be inviting danger by being around her unsupervised."

"Short of locking her up, what do you propose?"

"Actually, I *was* going to propose locking her up."

"Absolutely not. That's out of the question."

"We'll see about that. First, we need to find her," Marissa said.

"Why don't you look around down here and I'll search upstairs."

Marissa took Lia by the shoulders. "What part of 'I don't want you to be alone with her' do you not understand? We'll search together."

"All right. All right."

Ten minutes later, they returned to the stairway without having found Elliot.

"Up or down?" Lia said as they stood in the hallway.

"Up."

When they reached the top of the stairs, they went directly toward the bedroom, where they found Elliot packing a suitcase.

Lia rushed across the room and yanked the garment Elliot was holding out of her hand. "What do you think you're doing?"

"I'm leaving."

"No. I won't allow it."

"Well, you don't have a say in the matter," Elliot said. "It's the best thing for all of us. I don't trust myself around you, love." Elliot reached forward and moved Lia's hair away from her shoulder. "Look at what I've done to you this time."

"That wasn't you," Lia said.

"No, it wasn't, but I don't seem to have control over the one who's really behind this abuse, so in my mind, the best course of action is to remove myself—and her—from the situation."

"I have to agree with Elliot," Marissa said.

Lia looked angrily at Marissa and then back at Elliot. "Well, I don't. I don't want you to leave, Elliot."

"Putting some distance between us is the safest thing to do," Elliot said.

Lia dropped the garment she was holding on to the bed and stepped close to Elliot. She held Elliot's face between her hands. "Sweetheart, please don't go. Maybe there's someplace in this house you can stay until this mess is sorted out. It's certainly big enough."

Elliot stepped outside of Lia's embrace and walked to the window where she stared out over Royal Street. Without turning around, she said, "I'll agree to that only if you make it impossible for me to get to you."

"Do you mean, lock you up?" Lia asked.

"That's exactly what I mean." Elliot faced Lia, revealing the tears that dampened her cheeks. "I can't bear the thought of hurting you again. You don't deserve that."

"Exactly where would we do that?" Lia asked.

"In the one place I know you won't venture—the apartment over the library. You can lock me inside. There's already a padlock on the door."

"No, Elliot. That place gives me the creeps."

"It's there, or I move into the hotel. Your choice."

"But there's no furniture in there."

"Elliot and I can move a bed and a chair into the apartment," Marissa said. "And we can fill the cabinets and refrigerator with food as well. I agree with El on this one, Lia. We all know she isn't responsible for what she does when the mistress takes over. This is a good alternative until we find Celeste's remains."

***

Over the next hour, Elliot and Marissa moved the bed, a lamp, and a dresser, from the small bedroom at the end of the master suite, into the apartment, as well as several days' worth of clothing, toiletries, towels, and washcloths, while Lia collected food items and beverages from the kitchen. Elliot chose a half-dozen books from the library and made a trip to their bedroom for her cell phone charger. Finally, it was time to lock her in.

On the porch outside the apartment, Lia stood in the circle of Elliot's arms, crying uncontrollably. "Elliot, I'm so sorry for all of this. I love you so much. My heart's breaking for you."

"Shhh. It's okay, love. It won't be forever. I have my phone. I'll call you. We can talk. I'll miss holding you in my arms while we sleep, but this is for your safety. I'm willing to do anything I can to protect you, sweetheart. Even this."

"I love you, El."

"I love you too. Now please stop crying. It'll be okay. The sooner you find Celeste, the sooner this will be over."

"I won't stop looking until we find her. I need you with me, not locked up like some wild animal."

Elliot smiled a crooked grin. "I'll show you wild when this is all over." She raised her eyebrows up and down seductively.

Her efforts paid off as Lia smiled. "You are incorrigible, my love. I'll hold you to that promise."

Elliot kissed her once more then took a step backward into the apartment. "Take care of my girl, Mar," she said to her friend.

"You can count on it, El."

Elliot closed the door and listened from the inside to the padlock being snapped into place.

***

Julie sat on the couch in the living room, stroking Lia's hair as she lay beside her with her head in Julie's lap. She was crying softly. Marissa paced the floor in front of them.

"I'm so sorry we bought this house," Lia said between sobs.

"From the sounds of it, you really didn't have a choice," Julie said. "I don't believe everything that has happened is a coincidence. What are the chances that you would randomly purchase the house in which your ancestor was murdered?"

"I feel so bad for Elliot." Lia wiped at her tears.

"I do too," Marissa said, "but she's doing the right thing. She's doing what's necessary to protect you."

Marissa stopped pacing. "Look, it's getting late. I vote we get some sleep and begin our search for Celeste's remains early tomorrow morning."

"I think that's a great idea," Julie replied.

Marissa and Julie walked Lia to her room. They hugged her goodnight, and retired to their own room.

Lia sat on the bed and listened to the silence. When it became unbearable, she walked through the bathroom and down the hallway to the newly empty bedroom at the end of the master suite. She stood in front of the window by the door that exited onto the porch and noticed the light on under the door of the apartment over the library. While in the past, this sight alarmed her, this night it made her sad, knowing the one who owned her heart was trapped inside.

Unable to resist, she opened the door and walked across the porch to the apartment, where she sat on the deck and leaned her back against the door. She pulled her cell phone from her pocket and called Elliot.

"Hey, baby," Elliot answered.

"I miss you," Lia said softly.

"I miss you too. Where are you?"

"Outside your door."

"Then you're but a heartbeat away. I'm on the other side of the door. I've been sitting here for nearly an hour waiting for you to come."

"Are you all right?"

"I ache with the desire to hold you in my arms. Other than that, I'm fine. How are you holding up?"

"I don't believe I'll sleep tonight. My heart's breaking knowing you're locked up in there."

"It won't be for long, love."

"Tell me a story, El. Tell me a love story."

"All right. Once upon a time, there was this girl named Elliot. She was on her way to work one morning when she decided to stop at Starbucks for a latte. That day would change her life forever..."

***

"Lia, wake up. It's nearly eight o'clock. We wanted to get an early start this morning, remember?" Marissa called through the bedroom door. "Lia?"

Marissa turned the doorknob and pushed the door open. To her surprise, Lia's bed hadn't been slept in. *What the hell?* "Lia, where are you?"

Marissa charged through the master suite to the back door. She threw the door open, stepped onto the porch, and stopped short when she saw Lia lying on her side in front of the apartment door. "Oh, no." She ran to Lia's side and knelt down beside her. She gently placed her hand on Lia's arm.

Lia moaned and rolled onto her back.

Marissa shook her. "Lia. Wake up."

"Wha...what?" Lia threw her arm over her eyes, shading them from the light. "What time is it?"

"Nearly eight o'clock. What possessed you to sleep out here all night?"

"Elliot. We were talking on the phone. I guess I fell asleep."

"Jesus Christ. I'm sure your back really appreciates the hard bed you gave it last night. Come on. Julie's making breakfast."

"Marissa, is that you?" Elliot's voice came through the door.

"Yes. It's me. Do you realize your wife spent the night sleeping on the deck in front of this door?"

"I know. I tried to get her to go to bed, but she wouldn't listen to me."

"Jesus. I don't know which of you is more stubborn."

"That would be Lia," Elliot said. "Do me a favor and get her inside."

"Will do. Are you all right?" Marissa asked.

"Missing Lia like crazy, but I'd rather be in here than out there putting her in danger."

"I agree. Do you need anything?"

"No, I'm good. Good luck on your search today. And let me know the minute you find something."

"I will, my friend. I will."

***

"Where's Lia?" Julie asked as Marissa entered the kitchen alone.

"She's in the shower. Believe it or not, she spent the night sleeping on the porch in front of the apartment door."

"I can't say that I'm surprised. I'd probably have done the same thing."

Marissa put her hands on her hips. "Seriously?"

"Yes. If it were you locked in there, you'd better believe it."

Marissa smiled and took Julie into her arms. "Thank you, love."

"You're welcome. Where do we start our search this morning?"

Marissa released Julie and helped herself to a piece of bacon. "I thought we could start from the top and work down."

"Are you suggesting we go into the attic?"

Marissa stopped short. "I hadn't thought about that. Maybe we should."

"Lia and Elliot said the attic's still full of torture devices. It makes me ill just to think about what happened up there."

"Yeah. Me too. Maybe we should save that for last. We should only go up there if we absolutely have to."

"Good idea."

Just then, Lia entered the kitchen. "Good morning," she said. She walked directly to the coffeepot and poured herself a cup. "Breakfast smells great, Jules."

"Thanks. Have a seat. It'll be ready in two minutes."

A mewing sound drew their attention to the porch door.

"Well, look who's here." Marissa opened the door for the cat.

"Ah, baby girl. Come see your mama," Lia said.

Julie exchanged a questioning look with Marissa.

"Where you be little one? Lia be a good girl, eh?"

"Celeste?" Julie said.

Lia's gaze turned sharply toward Julie. "What did you say? I could have sworn you called me Celeste."

"Ah, no. Are you ready for breakfast?" Julie asked.

"Just as soon as I put Miss Thing down and wash my hands."

The cat wandered over and lay down in a corner.

Julie mouthed the words "what the hell?" to Marissa behind Lia's back as she washed her hands.

"How are you feeling after your shower?" Marissa asked.

"Much better. Where do we begin searching this morning?" Lia asked.

"I was telling Julie we should start from the top and work our way down, except I think we should go into the attic only as a last resort."

"Dey be no bones in da attic. Never bones in da attic. Death and pain, but no bones."

"Okay," Marissa said slowly. Once again, she exchanged a questioning glance with Marissa.

"Working from the top down sounds like a good idea, but there aren't a lot of places to hide bones," Lia said. "I suppose we should empty all the closets to begin with. Nearly all of them still contain things from the previous owners. Imagine leaving everything behind like that."

"That is kind of odd," Marissa agreed, trying very hard to act casual in front of her friend.

"Okay. Have a seat. Breakfast is ready," Julie said.

CHAPTER 39

Elliot paced back and forth across the room and tried to quell the anxiety she felt deep within her chest. She was exhausted. She'd stayed awake the previous night, silently watching over Lia as she slept on the other side of the door. She discovered that, if she lay on the floor, she could reach far enough under the door to touch Lia's arm with her fingertips. Having even that small measure of physical contact brought her comfort.

Now, she resisted sleep in the event a discovery was made. But the physical fatigue and diminishing mental capacity were getting the best of her as she half-walked, half-stumbled across the room. Finally, she gave in and sat on the edge of the bed. Within minutes, her head fell forward, abruptly waking her up.

Get a grip, Walker. Despite her best efforts, her chin once again met her chest and her head snapped upward again. Just a few minutes, she convinced herself as she lay down.

Elliot was asleep for a brief time when she felt someone slip into bed with her. In her dream state, she immediately recognized the gentle curves and soft touch of the woman beside her.

Try as she might, Elliot couldn't open her eyes. She savored the feel of the caresses as familiar fingertips danced around her nipples. Her chest involuntarily arched as she felt her nipple inhaled into the moist mouth of her lover. A small cry of pain escaped her lips when was caught between her teeth.

"I need you, Lia," Elliot whispered hoarsely.

"I am here," the woman's voice whispered.

Elliot felt the woman's hand slide into the front of her panties and slip into her folds.

"Oh, my God," Elliot exclaimed.

"You like?" the woman asked as she massaged Elliot's tender parts.

"I'm so close," Elliot said.

"You are so wet. I can feel your need."

"Lia?" Elliot asked.

"Where be da bones?"

On the brink of climax, Elliot's eyes flew open and she sat upright in bed. "No!"

She was alone.

***

"There's nothing here," Lia said. Marissa and Julie helped her reorganize the last closet in the guest room bordering the courtyard. "We've emptied every closet, checked for loose boards on every floor, checked for hidden cubbies and fake ceilings, and we've come up with nothing. I think it's safe to say Celeste is not on this level."

"Okay, then," Julie said. "I guess we start on the second floor. I recommend we divide and conquer. We've all got a pretty good idea of what to look for after working together on this floor."

"I'll take the living room and parlor," Marissa said. "Julie, you can do the kitchen and dining room, and Lia, you've got the apartment behind the parlor. We can meet up in the library and search that one together."

"Don't forget to look up the chimneys and check for loose stones in the fireplaces," Lia reminded them.

"Got it." Julie headed toward the stairs.

"Also look for odd indentations in the walls—kind of like the ceiling in the upstairs hallway where the attic stairs used to be," Marissa added. "It's possible her body was plastered into the wall."

Lia started down the stairs. "Do you realize how insane all of this sounds? I never, in a million years, would have thought I would be looking for a corpse in my own home. I'm a scientist, for Christ's sake. I'm not supposed to believe in things that go bump in the night."

"None of us expected this," Marissa said. "The fact is, it's happening. I don't think any of us can dispute that."

"It actually doesn't surprise me much," Julie admitted. "I grew up hearing ghost stories, but I never expected to live through one myself."

They reached the landing in the second-story hallway. "Okay," Lia said, "let's meet in the library in about an hour. Does that sound like enough time?"

All three women arrived in the library an hour later, defeated.

"I'm beginning to think that the body would not have been hidden in the main living quarters," Marissa said. "After a while it probably would have begun to smell pretty bad. From what we know of the mistress, she had elaborate dinner parties, so I doubt she would risk the stench of death in rooms her guests might be in. We should search the library, but I'm guessing we won't find anything here either."

"I'm not so sure about that, Mar. The research I did on this house says they found human remains buried under the floorboards of the kitchen, so I don't think any room is off limits," Lia said. "We need to search everywhere."

"We should also look in the garage and in the courtyard," Julie said.

"The garage would have been stables at the time, so that's an even greater possibility," Lia pointed out.

Lia walked to the middle of the courtyard and looked up at all the porches. "What time is it?" she asked.

"Almost three o'clock," Marissa replied.

"We've been searching this damned house for five hours, and we've found nothing," Lia complained.

"It has to be here someplace," Julie said. "Celeste's ghost wouldn't be here if her remains weren't."

"Okay. Let's look around," Lia said. "There are a lot of nooks and crannies. There are sheds and storage boxes and areas under the stairs. If we find nothing there, we look in the garage. Be careful not to disturb the grave site. It'll be great when the coroner's office is finished so we can repair this gigantic hole in the yard."

The three friends worked side by side and systematically searched every inch of the porches, to no avail. When they descended the stairs into the courtyard, they were met by the cat, who walked in figure eights in and around their legs.

Lia bent over and picked her up. She scratched under the cat's chin as she spoke. "Hey there, fur-ball. How about using your cat-sense and help us find the bones?"

The cat suddenly stopped purring and insisted on being put down.

"Well, aren't we becoming antisocial all of a sudden," Lia said as the cat ran away. "Oh, well. I guess the garage is next."

The ladies walked toward the garage and opened the door. Just as they did, the cat ran in ahead of them.

Lia frowned and looked at Marissa. "That was strange. Almost as though she was waiting for us to come in here."

The cat ran to the corner of the room, stopped in front of the workbench, and began to growl.

"Something tells me we should take this as a sign," Julie said. "After all, it was she who found the grave."

Marissa climbed under the workbench and moved several crates out of the way. "There appears to be a cover in the cement."

"A cover?" Lia asked.

"Yeah. It kind of looks like a septic tank cover."

"Lovely. We found the cover to the shit hole," Lia said.

Marissa climbed out from under the bench. "Give me a minute." She ran out of the garage and returned a few moments later with the shovel. "I can wedge this shovel into the opening and pry it up. Okay, Julie, grab that crowbar on the bench and use it like a lever."

Julie levered the cement cover partially upward long enough for Marissa to pull the shovel out and grab it with her hands. "Help me roll this out of the hole," Marissa said.

The three of them maneuvered the cover out of the hole and laid it on the cement floor.

Marissa knelt beside the opening. "It doesn't smell like a shit hole. Do you have a flashlight?"

"I'll be right back." Lia ran toward the house and returned in a few minutes. She handed the flashlight to Marissa.

Marissa directed the beam into the hole. "Holy shit!"

"What is it?" Lia said.

"See for yourself."

Marissa held the light above the hole while Lia peered into its depth. Lia's eyes grew wide and filled with tears as she sat back on her heels.

"Let me see," Julie said. She moved to the side of the hole and looked in. "Oh, my God."

"It's Lia. We've found the little girl," Lia said.

***

"Elliot, come to the door," Lia yelled. She waited for a few moments and then pounded on the door. "Elliot!"

Still no response.

"Marissa, unlock the door," Lia said.

"I don't think that's a good idea," Marissa replied.

"Something's wrong. I can feel it. Why isn't she answering me?"

"Call her," Julie suggested.

Lia pulled her cell phone out of her pocket and dialed Elliot's number. It rang four times before it was answered.

"Hello?"

"Elliot, are you okay?"

"Um, I was sleeping. Give me a minute."

"We have some news. We found Lia. We found the little girl."

Silence.

"Elliot?" Lia covered the receiver. "Marissa, unlock the door."

"Not happening," Marissa replied.

"Elliot. Talk to me."

"I'm sorry. I'm a little groggy. Did you say you found the little girl?"

"Yes. We found her remains in a hole in the garage. It looks like it might have been a well," Lia said.

"Do the police know?"

"No. I haven't called them yet."

"Don't call them."

"What?"

"Don't call them. They have no right to interfere in our lives," Elliot said.

"What are you saying?"

"I knew you would be nothing but trouble."

Lia pulled her phone away from her ear and looked questioningly at it.

"What's she saying?" Marissa asked.

Lia pressed the speaker button on the phone.

"Elliot. Come to the door," she said.

"You must leave this place and never come back."

"That doesn't sound like Elliot," Julie whispered.

"Elliot. I'm worried about you," Lia said.

"I should have killed you when I had you in the attic."

Lia responded as though she had been physically slapped. "Oh, my God. It's her. The mistress."

Marissa took the phone from Lia. "Listen, bitch. You're the one who needs to leave this place. Do you understand? This is no longer your home."

"You can't have her. She's mine. She has always been mine."

"Damn it, Marissa. Unlock the door," Lia said.

"If I unlock the door, I'm going in there, not you. Agreed?"

"Mar!" Julie exclaimed.

"I'll be all right, Julie. She can control Lia because of Celeste. She doesn't have a hold on me." Marissa looked at Lia. "Agreed?"

"Yes, just please unlock the door."

Marissa unlocked the door, but before removing the padlock, she looked at Julie. "Do not allow her to go in there, Jules. Is that clear?"

Julie nodded vigorously. "Please be careful," she said.

"I will."

Marissa slipped the padlock off and pushed the door open. They could see Elliot pacing back and forth across the room beyond the kitchen. She was ranting to herself. Marissa walked into the kitchen and stepped into the main room. "Elliot," she said.

Elliot stopped in her tracks and immediately fainted. Marissa caught her just before she hit the floor. She gently dragged her to the bed where she laid her down and verified that she was breathing calmly. Afterward, she joined Julie and Lia on the porch and relocked the door.

"Mar?" Lia asked.

"She passed out as soon as she saw me."

Lia began to cry. "What are we going to do? My poor Elliot."

Marissa wrapped her arms around Lia. "We're going to find Celeste's remains. That's all we can do."

CHAPTER 40

Lia sat at the kitchen island and pushed the food around on her plate.

"You need to eat," Marissa said.

Lia put her fork down and sat back. "I'm sorry. I'm just not very hungry. I can't stop thinking about Elliot locked in that apartment."

"Based on what we saw this evening, that's not Elliot in there," Julie said.

Lia pushed her chair back and stood.

"Where are you going?" Marissa asked.

"I can't just sit here. I need to keep looking for Celeste's remains," Lia replied.

"Where are you going to look? We've turned this entire house upside down," Marissa said.

"We haven't looked in the attic."

"Darlin', Celeste said there were no bones in the attic," Julie pointed out.

"I'm going up there anyway. I have to get the ladder from the garage first."

Lia walked toward the kitchen door.

"Lia, wait," Marissa said. "I'll go with you. I'm not letting you go up there alone."

"Count me in as well," Julie added.

"You don't have to do that," Lia said.

Marissa wrapped her arms around Lia. "She's our friend, too, sweetie. We want her out of lockup as much as you do."

Julie wrapped her arms around both Lia and Marissa.

"I love you guys," Lia said.

"Ditto, girlfriend. Now let's go get that ladder."

"All right, I've taken the shelves out. Hand me the ladder, would you?" Marissa asked.

Lia shone the flashlight into the hole above the doorway while Marissa positioned the ladder against the back wall of the closet.

Marissa looked into the open ceiling of the closet. "It sure is dark up there."

"There's a switch inside, close to where the ceiling would be if there was one. Right there." Lia pointed the beam of light at the switch.

Marissa climbed the first three steps of the ladder until she could reach the light switch. "Okay, we have light," she said. "Let me get back down and extend the ladder so we'll have an easier time stepping off at floor level." Marissa climbed down and pulled the rope on the extension, effectively raising the top of the ladder another four feet above the attic floor.

"That looks good," Julie said as she watched the top of the ladder.

"Let me go up first," Marissa said.

Lia and Julie watched as Marissa neared the top of the ladder.

"Really?" Marissa said. "I can't believe it."

"I know. I had the same reaction when I first saw it," Lia said.

"No. I mean, it's empty. Other than the horrible smell, there's nothing up here."

"What? That's impossible. I'm coming up," Lia said.

Marissa extended her hand to Lia as she stepped into the attic, closely followed by Julie.

"Eww, it does stink up here," Julie said.

Lia looked around in wide-eyed wonder. "No way. This can't be. There were chains and spiked collars along that wall and gurneys over there."

"Well, there's nothing here now," Marissa said.

Lia hurried to the far end of the attic, followed by her friends. "Where did it all go? I swear to you, it was here. This end of the attic had the torture devices and hangman nooses over those rafters."

"Lia, honey, all there is up here is dust," Julie said.

"Julie, I'm not crazy. I was sickened by the horror Elliot and I saw up here. It was here. I know it was."

"Maybe it's what you were intended to see," Julie said. "Maybe it was all an illusion."

"But I was strapped to the table. I was physically strapped to the table," Lia said.

"And Elliot was here with you, right?" Marissa asked.

"Yes, of course she was."

"And where is Elliot now?" Marissa asked.

"You know damned well where Elliot is right now. She's locked in that goddamned apartment, possessed by the mistress."

"My point exactly," Marissa replied.

Lia narrowed her eyes. "Are you implying Elliot was responsible for strapping me to that table?"

"What I'm saying is that she is possessed by the mistress, and because of that, anything is possible, including making you see the implements of horror that I totally believe were in this room one hundred and eighty years ago, but are obviously not here anymore."

"It was so real," Lia said.

Marissa rubbed her back. "I'm sure it was, but look around. Like Julie said, there's nothing here but dust."

"I guess while we're up here, we should look for Celeste," Julie suggested. "The sooner we find her, the sooner we can get Elliot out of that room."

Lia nodded. "Yes. Let's do that."

"This is just one large, open room," Marissa said. "There's obviously nothing in the middle, so let's look around the knee-walls, and remember to check for loose boards. I see a door at the far end. I'll check that out as well."

Ninety minutes later, Marissa closed the door of the closet after replacing the shelves. She turned to address Julie and Lia who were waiting in the hall. "It sucks that we didn't find anything."

Lia could only nod while trying not to cry.

Julie wrapped her arms around her.

Marissa put her hand on the ladder. "I don't know about you, but I could use a glass of wine. What do you say I take this ladder back to the garage, and meet you in the kitchen?"

"I need to check on Elliot first," Lia said.

"Okay," Marissa replied. "I'll meet you on the porch outside the apartment after I put the ladder away."

"Elliot, sweetheart, please come to the door." Lia waited patiently while listening for movement on the other side. She turned her fearful gaze on Julie. "I don't hear anything."

"Maybe she's sleeping."

"She hasn't answered her phone or text messages all day. What if something's wrong?"

Just then, Marissa appeared on the stairway leading to the garage. "How's Elliot?"

Lia stood with her forehead against the door. "Mar, please open the door."

"Lia—" Marissa began to say.

Lia turned sharply toward her friend. "Damn it, Mar. Open the door."

Julie touched Marissa's arm. "Elliot hasn't responded to communication at all today. Lia has reason to be worried."

Marissa sighed. "Okay, but let me check it out first." She fished the key to the padlock out of her pocket and removed the lock from the door. She pushed the door inward. The inner door was closed. "Damn, it stinks to high heaven in there. I don't know how Elliot can stand it. It smells like rotting flesh."

"It reminds me of how the attic smelled," Julie added.

Lia's eyes grew wide as she backed up against the far wall opposite the door. "Oh, my God. Mar. The smell of death. Elliot chose this place on purpose. She knew I wouldn't go in there."

Marissa took her by the arms. "What are you saying?"

"Celeste is in there. This is the only place we haven't looked. The smell of decay, the claw marks inside the wardrobe." Lia's eyes filled with tears.

"And the mistress is in there with her," Julie said.

"We need to get Elliot out of there." Marissa charged into the room and shoved against the inner door. It wouldn't move. "What the fuck? There's something blocking it."

"Let me help," Julie said.

Between them, they were able to push the door, and the dresser blocking it, aside.

Marissa stepped several feet into the room. "It's dark in here. I can't see anything."

"I've found the light switch." Julie turned on the lights.

Suddenly someone punched Marissa hard in the stomach. She flew into the wall behind her.

A screeching growl came from across the room. "You cannot have her. She's mine. Leave this place."

"Mar," Julie screamed and ran to Marissa.

Marissa lay on the floor holding her stomach. "I'm okay." She looked across the room. "Oh, my God. Elliot."

Elliot stood by the bed, covered in blood. The flesh on her arms and hands was covered in deep scratches from elbows to fingertips.

Marissa's gaze darted around the room. Blood splattered the walls and bedding and the open wardrobe in the corner. Inside the wardrobe, the plaster and lathe wall was broken to expose a large gaping hole. The ragged edges were also red with blood.

"Mar, look at the bed," Julie screamed.

There, on the bed behind Elliot, was a crudely assembled skeleton.

Elliot ran to the bed and threw the covers over the skeleton. "I won't let you take her."

"Lia, don't come in here," Marissa yelled.

The sound of Marissa's voice broke through the veil of fear that had paralyzed Lia. She dashed through the small kitchen and into the main room. Elliot held a blood-covered knife and was advancing on Marissa and Julie.

"Oh, my God, Elliot! You're hurt." Lia rushed to Elliot's side.

"Lia, no," Marissa screamed as Elliot sunk the knife deep into Lia's abdomen.

"Give her to me, bitch," Elliot growled. "She's mine."

Lia slowly sank to the floor in front of Elliot, her clothing covered in the blood of both of them.

Elliot's eyes grew wide as she appeared to regain her senses. She sunk to her knees in front of Lia and cried, "Lia! My God. What have I done?" She fell to the floor, unconscious.

"Mar, call nine-one-one," Julie shouted as she scurried to Lia's side. "Lia, sweetie. Hold on, love."

Lia grasped Julie's hand. "Celeste be free. It be over. Tell Lia, Celeste love her and tank her to give Celeste freedom."

Julie laid her head on Lia's chest. "Lia, no. Please don't go."

Suddenly, Lia's chest thrust upward, throwing Julie backward. A shadow rose from Lia and floated across the room. It hovered over the skeleton on the bed for the slightest of moments before it disappeared.

Sirens could be heard in the distance. Lia lay motionless on the floor.

CHAPTER 41

Marissa sat on a bench in the waiting room, bent at the waist, elbows on her knees and head buried between her hands. Julie paced the floor in front of her; teeth worrying her bottom lip as tears coursed down her cheeks. Not a word passed between them while they waited.

After what seemed like an eternity, the door opened and the doctor walked in. "I'm looking for the family of Lia Purvis."

Marissa was immediately on her feet. "That would be us." She took Julie's hand. "How is she?"

"She's in recovery and will be moved to the ICU soon."

"The ICU? Will she be all right?" Julie asked.

"It's too early to tell. We had a difficult time with exsanguination."

"What does that mean?" Marissa asked.

"Exsanguination is the loss of the majority of circulating blood volume...intensive blood loss, most of which was within the abdominal cavity. The knife also penetrated her bowel and punctured her kidney. The bowel injury could develop into peritonitis. The ambulance crew indicated this was an accidental stabbing."

"Yes," Marissa said. "The person holding the knife was bleeding from a injury and Lia ran to help...directly into the knife."

"Generally this type of stabbing doesn't penetrate as deep as this one. It did a significant amount of damage."

Julie turned into Marissa's side and began to cry. Marissa held her close and kissed her head before addressing the doctor once more. "How long until we know if she's going to survive?"

"It's hard to tell. I wish I had better news for you, but the extreme blood loss has put her at greater risk. She experienced class three hemorrhaging, losing about thirty percent of her blood volume. At this point, it's a waiting game. It may be days, or even weeks before we know. It could go either way."

"Can we see her?" Marissa asked.

"Like I said, she in recovery right now. I suspect she'll be moved to the ICU in the next few hours. You'll be able to visit her there for short periods of time. I recommend you stay right here, and I'll ask the nursing staff to let you know when she comes out of recovery."

Marissa extended her hand. "Thank you, Doctor."

After the doctor left the room, Marissa sat back down and resumed her previous pose.

"We have a couple of hours to wait. I suppose we should check on Elliot," Julie said.

Marissa looked up. "I don't trust myself around her right now, Jules."

Julie knelt on one knee in front of Marissa. "Mar, she isn't responsible for what happened. Do you think for one minute that she would intentionally stab Lia? You were there. You saw what happened. Aren't you at all concerned about her mental state after all this?"

Marissa rose to her feet and walked a few feet away, keeping her back to Julie. She shoved her hands deep into her pockets and turned around. "What I need is someone to blame for all this, Jules. One friend is possibly dying, and if that happens, the other friend will wish she was dead. I don't see a winner in this scenario."

"Regardless of what happens, Mar, Elliot needs us."

Marissa sighed and lowered her chin to her chest. "I know."

Julie approached Marissa and stopped directly in front of her. She cupped the side of Marissa's face with her palm. "It breaks my heart to see you so sad. Don't lose hope, Mar. We'll get through this."

Marissa nodded. "The question is, how many of us will come out the other end?"

Julie and Marissa approached the receptionist's desk in the emergency room.

"Could you tell us if Elliot Walker has been admitted?" Julie asked.

The receptionist typed Elliot's name into her computer. "Yes. Mr. Walker has been moved to the psych ward, room eleven."

"Ah, that's *Ms.* Walker, and what the hell is she doing in the psych ward?" Marissa asked.

"I'm sorry, you'll have to ask her attending physician that question, ma'am."

Marissa took Julie's hand. "Come on. We need to get to the bottom of this."

Marissa and Julie walked determinedly down the hall and to the bank of elevators. Marissa's jaw clenched repeatedly as she waited for the car to arrive.

"There's got to be a good reason for this," Julie said. "Maybe she's just distraught after what happened."

"Or maybe the bitch is in charge, and Elliot's out of control."

A few minutes later, they stepped out of the elevator in front of the nurse's desk on the psych ward.

"Let me handle this." Julie walked up to the desk. "Hello. We're here to see Elliot Walker."

"Friends or family?" the nurse asked.

"Family," Marissa said. "This is Elliot's sister and I'm her wife."

Julie looked at Marissa, then quickly back at the nurse. "Yes. I'm Elliot's sister."

"Ms. Walker is in room eleven. Turn right at the corner. She's four doors down on the left."

Marissa and Julie rounded the corner and walked toward Elliot's room. The first thing they noticed was a guard at the door.

"Oh, no." Julie increased her pace.

The guard stopped them from directly entering the room. "She's been somewhat volatile. That's why I'm here."

Marissa nodded. "I understand. Thanks for letting us know."

The guard stepped aside and allowed them to pass.

The person in the bed hardly bore any resemblance to Elliot. Both hands and arms were swathed in gauze bandages, all the way to her shoulders. Her hair was greasy and quite directionally challenged as it stuck out at odd angles all over her head. There were dark, sunken circles under her eyes.

Elliot turned her face toward them. Her eyes immediately filled with tears.

Julie went directly to her bedside and sat down on the edge of the bed. She laid her palm on Elliot's chest, leaned in and kissed her on the cheek. "Hey love. How are you feeling?"

Elliot looked at the ceiling and fought back her tears.

Marissa put her hand on Elliot's shoulder. "Hey, tough guy. It's okay to cry, you know."

Elliot turned her head and looked at Marissa. "I killed her. I killed Lia," she choked out.

Marissa clenched her teeth to keep herself from saying something in anger.

"Sweetie, Lia just came out of surgery," Julie said. "She's still alive, but she needs our prayers."

"I can't live without her. My God, what did I do?"

"It wasn't you, El. It wasn't you. We all know that," Julie said.

"That doesn't improve Lia's chances, does it?" Elliot said angrily.

Marissa squeezed Elliot's shoulder. "Take it easy. Julie doesn't deserve your wrath. Save it for the bitch that made you do this."

"I can feel her inside me, Mar. It's a struggle to keep her at bay."

"When you get out of here, we need to take care of that," Julie said.

"If Lia dies, I won't care what happens to me."

"Don't say that, Elliot. She can't die. We all need her," Julie said.

"What happened? The only thing I remember is that Lia fell to the floor at my feet, and I suddenly realized I had stabbed her."

"We searched the whole house for Celeste's remains," Marissa said, "and couldn't find them. We even went into the attic again."

"You went into the attic?" Elliot asked.

"Yes, and oddly, it was empty," Julie added. "All the torture devices you described to us were gone."

"Anyway," Marissa continued, "we went to check on you before turning in for the night. You didn't answer us, and Lia demanded I unlock the door. When I opened the outside door, the odor of decay hit me right in the face. It was then we realized the apartment was the only place we hadn't searched for Celeste's remains.

"I tried to open the inside door, but it was blocked. Julie helped me, and together, we pushed it open. You had moved the dresser in front of it."

"I don't remember doing that," Elliot said.

"I'm sure you don't," Julie said. "My guess is that the mistress has pretty much had control over you almost from the moment you walked into that apartment."

Marissa continued. "We pushed the dresser aside and opened the door. When we turned the light on, all hell broke loose. Something hit me square in the solar plexus and threw me into the wall. You were standing in the middle of the room covered with blood. The skin on your hands and arms was in shreds, probably from tearing the plaster and lathe off the wall inside the wardrobe. There was blood everywhere. You were terrifying, El. Even your voice changed to this evil octave when you told us we couldn't have Celeste, that she was all yours."

"Why would I tear the wall down?" Elliot asked.

"El, there was a skeleton on the bed," Julie explained. "We assumed it was Celeste. She was apparently plastered into the space behind the wall, inside the wardrobe."

Elliot closed her eyes as she absorbed what her friends told her. Streaks of tears fell down the sides of her face and into her ears. "How did I hurt Lia?"

"She came into the room," Julie said, "and when she saw you were bleeding, she ran to you, or more precisely, she ran to the mistress. That's when it happened."

Elliot looked through tear-filled eyes at her friends. "She was afraid of that room. She refused to go in there. Why did she go in? It makes no sense."

"Her love for you overruled her fear," Marissa said. "When she realized you were hurt, all fear of that place flew out the window."

Elliot sobbed and rolled her head side to side. "Lia, I'm so sorry." She attempted to wipe the tears from her face, but her movement was limited by the bandages on her arms.

Julie reached for a tissue on her bedside table and wiped the tears for her. "Calm down, love. You didn't do this to her. The mistress did. Please don't beat yourself up over it."

"One other thing," Marissa said. "After Lia collapsed on the floor, Jules and I saw Celeste's shadow leave Lia's body. That means the primary source of the mistress's power should be gone."

Elliot looked at Marissa. "I can still feel her inside me, Mar. I feel such rage and darkness."

"Phoebe said that might happen," Julie said. "We need to see her when you get out of here. She might be able to help."

Marissa looked at her watch. "They'll be moving Lia into the ICU soon. We should probably get back to the waiting room so we're there when they come to let us know."

"Yes, maybe we should." Julie stood and then bent over Elliot. "Don't give up on Lia. Pray. Pray for her with everything you are. We'll check in on you again before we leave for the day, okay?"

Elliot nodded. "Tell her I'm sorry, and I love her with all my heart."

"If I have anything to say about it, you'll get the chance to tell her that yourself, but yes, I'll pass that along to her." Julie kissed her on the cheek then stood aside to allow Marissa to move in.

"I'm going to go one further and tell you not to give up on yourself either, my friend. Lia's going to need you when she gets out of this place. We'll be back in a while." Marissa kissed her on the forehead and they left.

***

Marissa and Julie sat beside Lia's still form and listened to the monitors beeping and hissing in rhythm with each other. For several hours they watched and hoped for some response or movement from Lia. But none came.

At some point, Marissa sat in the visitor chair while Julie curled up on her lap. Soon, they fell asleep.

"Wake up. Come on, wake up."

Marissa snapped awake. The night nurse was gently shaking her.

"Visiting hours have been over for a while now. You'll need to go," the nurse said.

Julie awoke. "Mar, what time is it?"

"Time for us to go home. Visiting hours are over," Marissa replied. "Has there been any change?" she asked the nurse.

"Unfortunately, no. She's one sick lady. Hopefully there'll be some sign of improvement tomorrow after a few more blood transfusions."

Julie walked to Lia's side and kissed her lightly on the cheek. "Fight! Do you hear me? Fight like a girl. You can beat this, love, and we'll be right beside you all the way."

Marissa squeezed her hand. "What she said. We expect you to open those beautiful brown eyes for us tomorrow, okay? We love you, chica."

Julie dabbed at the corners of her eyes as they left Lia's room. "Is it too late to check in on Elliot?" she asked.

Marissa looked at her watch. "Damn, it's almost midnight. I'm guessing we've missed our opportunity."

"Let's head home then. We'll check in with Elliot first thing in the morning."

"Okay. I'm ready to hit the sheets anyway. This ghostbusting gig is tiring!"

CHAPTER 42

An intense wave of sadness and regret washed over Elliot as she watched Marissa and Julie leave her hospital room.

What have I done? Lia's near death, and it's my fault. I'll never forgive myself. She thought about what might occur if Lia survived and they went back to living in the Royal Street house. *I can't allow that to happen. As long as this monster's inside of me, I can never be alone with her. I need to get rid of the bitch...or leave Lia.*

After two more hours of lying in the hospital bed contemplating everything from exorcism to suicide, she made a decision. Feigning sleep, she waited until the ten p.m. shift change to make her move. She listened for the guard outside her door to say his goodnights, and she waited until the night nurse had taken headcount and read her chart from earlier in the day. Luckily, the nurse pulled the door closed behind her when she left the room. Soon, all was quiet.

Elliot painfully threw her covers off and maneuvered into a seated position. Her arms throbbed like a toothache, and she saw signs of blood oozing through her bandages. But she couldn't afford the time or the inconvenience of asking for new dressings. The last thing she needed was to put off her decision.

She searched the drawers and closets in her room to find her clothing, to no avail. Considering the condition her arms were in, she assumed they were covered with blood and probably thrown away.

As she stood in the middle of her hospital room, contemplating what to do next, the lights in the hallway suddenly dimmed. She thanked the heavens above for the added cover. She stepped out of her room and quietly moved through the hall until she came upon the nurse's lounge. Luckily for her, it was empty. On the far end of the room was a row of lockers in which she found a set of scrubs, clogs and a lab coat. Just as she closed the locker, she heard voices in the hall. *Shit. Please don't come in here.*

Elliot darted into the adjoining bathroom and closed the door just before the owners of the voices entered the room. She slipped the lock on the door and leaned against it to calm her nerves. Silently cursing the pain in her arms, she struggled to dress herself in the clothing she had found, and slipped her feet into the clogs.

When it became apparent that her visitors were in no hurry to leave, she flushed the toilet, turned on the tap as if washing her hands, and activated the hand dryer for a full minute. She took a deep breath and threw the door open. Without greeting her unwanted roommates, she walked directly out the door and down the hall, all the way to the exit.

She had made it. She was free.

***

Samuel stood on the corner opposite 1140 Royal Street and watched curiously as a taxi pulled up in front of the house. He saw Elliot exit the cab and feel around the ground just inside the gated entry before unlocking the gate and rushing inside while the cab waited. A few minutes later, Elliot reemerged and leaned inside the passenger window of the cab, after which the cab drove away.

"Miss Walker, what you be up to?" Samuel mumbled to himself.

***

After paying the taxi driver, Elliot went back into the house and directly to her bedroom. She replaced her stolen clothing with some of her own. She stood in front of the bathroom vanity and rummaged through the medicine cabinet, looking for bandages. All she found was a box of Band-Aids. Knowing her injuries were more extensive than could be covered with simple strip bandages, she elected to leave the soiled ones in place.

While she stood in front of the sink, she looked out the small window beside it and noticed at light was on in the apartment over the library. She grabbed the edge of the sink as a wave of nausea swept over her. A sudden rage threatened to overwhelm her, and she fought to stay in control.

"No. I won't let you do it. I won't let you control me," she growled.

The nausea passed and Elliot pulled herself together. She strode down the hall through the master suite and onto the porch across from the apartment. She pushed the door open and stepped inside. Gone was the odor of decay. She walked through the kitchen and into the main room, totally unprepared for the amount of blood that covered nearly everything. A pool of blood marked the spot on the floor where Lia had lain.

Elliot grasped the doorframe and once again felt the sudden rage rise up in her chest. "Leave me alone," she shouted. Fighting to suppress the anger, she looked around the room once more...noting the blood...noting the large hole in the wall inside the wardrobe...noting the bloody, rumpled bedspread where Celeste bones had been carelessly arranged by the mistress. Those remains were no longer there.

Elliot reached inside the room and extinguished the light. She pulled the doors closed, in the main room and in the kitchen. With long, determined strides, she walked back through the master suite, through the bedroom and hallway, down two flights of stairs, and let herself out of the gated entry onto the sidewalk.

Elliot strode purposefully down Royal Street toward Ursuline and continued to Rampart, Basin and Iberville, until finally turning right onto North Claiborne Avenue. In the lateness of the night, she was able to traverse her route without drawing attention to herself. A short time later, she reached her destination—the Saint Louis Cemetery.

While standing in front of the cemetery gates, she pulled her cell phone out of her pocket and opened a search engine. In the address field, she typed the words, *location of Marie*

Laveau's tomb in Saint Louis Cemetery. In seconds, a map appeared. After orienting herself, she entered the cemetery and began her search.

***

Phoebe made herself a cup of tea and sat to enjoy a new book she had just ordered. A short while later, her reading was interrupted by a pounding on her door.

Who could that be? She put her book on the table beside her and rose to answer the door. She looked into the peephole to identify her caller and frowned when she saw who it was.

"Samuel," she said as she opened the door.

Samuel held his cap between his hands. "Evenin,' ma'am."

"Please, come in." Phoebe could feel the man's anxious awkwardness. "Is everything all right?" she asked.

"No, ma'am. Ain't all right at all. Miss Walker be in trouble."

"Elliot?"

"Yes, ma'am. There be lots of blood. Look like someone die in there. Ambulance be taking them away."

"Whoa, slow down. The ambulance took who away?"

"Miss Lia and Miss Walker. Samuel went in after they be gone. Lots of blood. Celeste be there too."

Phoebe reached for her phone on the table beside her chair. "Samuel, when did all of this happen?"

"Around dinnertime, ma'am."

"So Elliot and Lia are in the hospital?" she asked.

"No ma'am. Miss Lia, maybe, but Samuel seen Miss Walker come home in a taxi and leave again on foot. She be at the Saint Louis Cemetery now. Samuel follow her there."

"Jesus Christ. Elliot, what are you up to?" she said out loud as she dialed her phone.

"One more thing, Miss Frost, Miss Walker had bandages all up her arms. Bloody bandages."

"Marissa, this is Phoebe," Phoebe said into her phone.

"Phoebe? Do you know how late it is?" Marissa replied.

"Yes, but this is important. Look, Samuel's here. He told me about Elliot and Lia going to the hospital today."

"Yes, they did. Elliot tried to kill Lia. She stabbed her in the stomach with a knife she found in the kitchen of the apartment."

Phoebe's eyes grew wide. "Are you serious? Holy Jesus. Surely it was the mistress. Will Lia be okay?"

"It's touch and go. She lost a lot of blood. We're hoping she improves overnight."

Phoebe's eyes filled with tears. "I'll pray for her. How are you and Julie holding up?"

"Julie's a mess, and quite frankly, I'm struggling to hold it together as well."

"Marissa, I'm calling because Samuel told me Elliot is at the Saint Louis Cemetery."

"No way. She's in the hospital. Her arms are torn to shreds from tearing down a plaster and lathe wall with her bare hands. Turns out Celeste's remains were plastered into the wall in the apartment."

"Samuel said she arrived home in a taxi...what, an hour ago, Samuel?" she asked her guest, who nodded in response. "Yes, Samuel said she got home about an hour ago and left again on foot. He followed her to the cemetery."

"What the hell is in that cemetery that Elliot would want?" Marissa asked.

"It's one of the oldest cemeteries in New Orleans. The most infamous resident is Marie Laveau." Phoebe abruptly stopped talking. "Oh, my God. Marissa, there are those who believe the mistress came back secretly from Paris and lived the rest of her life in New Orleans, specifically under the protection of Marie Laveau. They even believe she's buried in Marie's crypt."

"Son of a bitch. Elliot won't need to worry about the mistress when I get my hands on her," Marissa said.

"I'm going to collect a few of my tools and head over there. I suspect she intends to find the mistress's bones. There's no way she can stand up to both the mistress and

Marie Laveau. She's as good as dead if she desecrates that tomb."

"Where is this cemetery?" Marissa asked.

"Julie knows where it is. We used to play there as children."

"Okay. We're on our way."

***

St. Louis Cemetery was filled with hundreds of above-ground tombs, most of which were very old and constructed with bricks. Many of them were crumbling, and several bore signs of damage from Katrina years earlier.

Elliot entered the cemetery on the Claiborne Avenue side and walked slowly through the narrow alleys, while referring to the map she had found on the Internet. For a short time, she managed to follow the path outlined on the map, but she soon lost her bearings and struggled to locate her touchstones.

She stumbled around the graveyard, using the flashlight app on her cell phone to light the way. "Where the hell is it? This place is like a huge maze," she said out loud as she passed the same grave marker for the third time. She stopped and ran a hand through her hair. "This is bull shit. I'm just running around in circles. There's no way I'm going to find it in the dark."

Discouraged, she sat on the ground and leaned against the nearest tomb. Her arms throbbed, and she felt heat radiating through the bandages. She rested the back of her head against the tomb. Tears coursed down her cheeks as she thought about Lia lying in the hospital, fighting for her life.

Elliot's mind was filled with anguish. *Why is this happening to us? All we wanted was a fresh start and a chance to renew our love. And now? Now, Lia might die and I'll live with that guilt for the rest of my life.*

Elliot wiped her tears with the back of her bandaged hand, unknowingly smearing blood on her face. *Why did we have to buy that damned house? Lia, sweetheart, I'll never forgive myself. I'm so sorry. If I lose you, life won't be worth living.*

Great sobs escaped Elliot's throat as an uncontrollable rage began to build in her chest. She found it difficult to breathe. An animalistic growl erupted from deep within her, rising to a pitch that could surely be heard from a great distance.

Marissa and Julie followed closely behind Phoebe as they made their way through the cemetery gates.

"I sure hope you know where you're going," Marissa said.

"Trust me, I do. This way," Phoebe replied.

"Wait. Stop. Did you hear that?" Julie asked.

All three paused to listen to the anguished scream coming from deep within the cemetery.

Elliot suddenly lost control over her traitorous body as she rose to her feet and walked purposefully through the maze of crypts, toward the center of the cemetery. *Leave me alone!* her mind shouted as she battled valiantly against the intense hatred that threatened to consume her.

Finally, some unseen force threw her to the ground in front of a brick tomb. Waves of pain coursed through her arms as they contacted the cement walkway. She rolled onto her back and stared at the crumbling structure that was eerily illuminated by the moonlight. She instinctively knew this was what she was looking for—the tomb of Marie Laveau.

Elliot couldn't look away. Despite the pain in her arms, she pushed herself into a kneeling position and reached out to touch the bricks. She felt drawn to the structure and placed both hands on the heavily mortared door, which was covered with an array of markings. On the ground in front of the tomb were apparent offerings, left by individuals who hoped to benefit from voodoo magic.

A sudden sound drew her gaze sharply away from the tomb.

CHAPTER 43

"There she is," Phoebe said as they approached the tomb of Marie Laveau.

"Elliot," Julie called out.

Marissa grabbed Julie's arm and stopped her from advancing toward Elliot. "Stop. Look at her. Something's wrong."

Elliot's appearance startled them. Her hair was in wild disarray. Her clothing was covered with dirt and her face smeared with blood. The bandages on her arms were so saturated they appeared crimson. Perhaps the most disturbing of all was the look of hatred in her eyes.

"Elliot, we're here to help you," Phoebe said.

Elliot rose to her feet and faced her friends. "No." She raised her hands and extended them, palms outward.

An unseen force threw Marissa, Julie, and Phoebe backward into the tombs several yards behind them. Their bodies hit the brick-and-mortar structures with sickening thuds, and they fell to the cement walkway.

Elliot turned her back on them and refocused her attention on the tomb.

"Oh, my God." Marissa climbed to her knees. "Julie, Phoebe, are you okay?"

Julie struggled to catch her breath. "What happened?"

"There are some powerful forces in control here. I fear we may already be too late." Phoebe also climbed to her knees and sat back on her heels.

"Don't say that." Julie's voice choked with tears. "We have to help her."

"I understand what Elliot intended to do," Phoebe continued. "With Celeste and the other slaves, once their remains were found, their spirits were released. I'm sure

Elliot intended to reunite the mistress's spirit with her bones, thereby freeing herself from the mistress's control."

"That makes sense to me," Marissa said.

"Normally, yes, but in this case, the mistress doesn't *want* to be free. She's looking for a permanent host."

"We can't allow her to control Elliot for the rest of her life. We need to do something," Marissa replied.

Phoebe removed her satchel from around her neck. "It will be dangerous for all of us, but especially for Elliot. She might not survive it."

"I don't see that we have a choice," Marissa said. "Tell me what to do, and I'll do it."

Phoebe looked at her companions. "You love her, don't you?"

"She and Lia are our sisters," Marissa replied. "Yes, we love them both very much."

Phoebe nodded. "Keep that love at the forefront of your minds. Love is a powerful force. It will help us as we try to defeat this monster."

"Tell us what we need to do," Julie said.

Phoebe began removing implements from her bag. "We need to immobilize her. Obviously, the dark force that controls her will make it difficult to get close to her. It had no problem picking all three of us up and tossing us away like rag dolls."

"So how are we going to do that?" Julie asked.

Phoebe pulled a plastic bag out of her satchel. "Open your hands."

"What is that?" Marissa asked.

"A mixture of cinnamon, five-finger grass, ague weed, garlic, and sage. It's widely known in Wiccan and hoodoo circles to protect one from evil spirits. Put it in your pockets."

"This is supposed to protect us from psycho-bitch?" Marissa asked.

"She won't be able to physically touch you if this herb mixture is on your person."

Marissa raised her eyebrows. "But she'll still be able to throw her power shit at us, right?"

"Unfortunately, yes. She'll have to be distracted from doing so while I neutralize her power."

"You aren't going to hurt Elliot, are you?" Julie asked.

"If she becomes injured during this ritual, it will be the mistress inflicting the harm, not me. Like I said earlier, this will be dangerous for her, and maybe even for us."

Julie looked at Elliot who still stood in front of the tomb. Her hands were raised to the sides, and her head was tilted back. Even from yards away, Julie could see Elliot's eyes rolled back so that only the whites could be seen. A low keening sound was coming from deep within her throat.

"Something's happening, Phoebe," Julie said.

Phoebe pulled the remaining items from her bag, holy water, a candle, paper and pen, a sage bundle, lighter, and finally, a bag of salt. "The mistress is merging with her soul. We need to do this quickly or there will be no hope for her."

"Tell us what to do," Marissa said.

Phoebe handed the holy water to Marissa and the sage bundle to Julie. "We need to confine her to a small area so I can carry out the banishing ceremony. Marissa, you need to get in close enough to splash the holy water on her. Julie, light the sage and walk in a semicircle around the tomb to prevent the spirit from escaping should she choose to leave Elliot's body. While you distract her, I'll lay a salt barrier. Any questions?"

"Don't we want the spirit to escape Elliot's body? Isn't that why we're doing this in the first place?" Marissa asked incredulously.

"Yes, and no. We want the spirit out of Elliot, but we don't want it to escape. If we don't do this right, one of us could easily become her next host."

Marissa held her hands up. "Okay. You're the boss. Let's do this!"

Julie lit the sage and waited until the tips were glowing and a thick plume of smoke emitted from the bundle. "Okay. It's ready," She and Marissa stealthily advanced on Elliot.

When they were within a few feet of Elliot, she suddenly turned around. "Away with you," she shouted. Once again, she raised her hands toward them.

Before she slammed them with the power thrust, Marissa shook the bottle of holy water in her direction, saturated the front of her shirt. Elliot dropped to her knees, wailing and pulling at the garment. A sizzling sound could be heard as steam rose from the water on the garment.

"You will die for this," Elliot screamed.

Julie hurried to carry the burning sage in a semicircle around Elliot with the tomb providing the diameter of the circle.

While Elliot was distracted, Phoebe moved in and poured a semicircle of salt along the same path Julie had traversed.

Elliot surged to her feet and backed up against the tomb, as far away from the salt as she could be. In a deep menacing timbre, she shouted, "What are you doing? You are ruining everything."

Marissa and Julie stepped back. Phoebe approached Elliot, stopped a few feet short, and placed the lit candle on the ground in front of her. She wrote the mistress's name on the paper and held it before her.

"Marissa, I need a brick from this tomb. You should be able to find a loose one on the other side," Phoebe said.

"You can't do this." Elliot yelled. "I will not allow it!"

Phoebe ignored Elliot's ranting. She accepted the brick from Marissa and put it on the ground beside the candle. She raised her arms out to the sides and began to chant.

"We cast you out, unclean spirit. We release you from the land of the living. We remove your satanic power."

Elliot began to writhe and growl deeply from within her chest.

"You are the murderer of innocents and torturer of the helpless. You abused your position and power to wreak pain and suffering on those around you. We cast out your diabolical and sadistic heart."

"Stop," Elliot hissed. "You will not get away with this. I am the mistress. You cannot control me."

"You are the infernal adversary of all that is good. We cast you out in the name and by the power of our Lord."

Elliot fell to her knees and cried out in pain. "No. You can't do this. I am the mistress. You must obey me."

"We command you, be gone far from this place, far from the Church of God, and far from all souls made in His image."

Elliot rolled onto her side, pulled her knees into her chest, and wrapped her bloody, bandaged arms around them. Her eyes rolled back and her body began to convulse. Dark shadows emerged from the ground around them and engulfed Elliot's body as she writhed. "No." she shouted. "Stop. You have no right to do this. Stop!"

Phoebe ignored Elliot's rants and continued to pray. "We exorcise you in the name of the Father and of the Goddess, Mother Earth. As we will it, so shall it be."

A strong gust of wind arose as the dark shadows continued to encircle Elliot. Suddenly, her chest arched high into the air and a guttural moan escaped her throat. Marissa and Julie stood by horrified as a ghostly mass burst from her chest. The dark shadows immediately surrounded it and pulled it downward into the ground.

Slowly, the convulsions subsided. One by one, the shadows disappeared. Elliot lay motionless inside the semicircle of salt. The last shadow faded, and the wind stilled. A deathly silence descended over the cemetery.

Marissa wrapped her arms around Julie and they watched Phoebe. She lowered the paper containing the mistress's name into the flame of the candle, and placed the burning paper on top of the brick beside it. Before long, the paper transformed into ash. Phoebe picked up the candle and tipped it over the ash long enough for melted wax to completely cover the top of the brick. While she carried out this task, she chanted, "I symbolically confine your spirit to this prison for all eternity. In the name of all that is good and holy, your evil will never again roam free."

She picked up the brick and placed it directly on top of the tomb, then crossed the line of salt and knelt beside Elliot's still form. A few moments later, she looked up at her friends.

Her chest heaved and she said, "She's gone."

EPILOGUE

Three months later...

Marissa wrapped her arms around her wife. "You're beautiful, my love, even dressed in black."

Julie rested her head against Marissa's shoulder. "It's so sad. Such a waste of life."

Marissa nodded. "I know. They were much too young to die. When I think of how much they still had left to do…" Marissa's voice trailed off.

"Phoebe and Samuel should be here soon."

"Yeah, we should probably meet them out front."

Marissa and Julie walked toward the spiral staircase. Before descending, Marissa looked up toward the third floor.

Julie put her hand on Marissa's arm. "They're gone, love."

Marissa nodded. "For a moment, I forgot."

"Come on." Julie took Marissa's hand. They descended to the first level and let themselves out the gated entry. Samuel was waiting on the sidewalk.

"You look very handsome, Samuel," Julie said.

Samuel tugged on the hem of his suit coat and looked down shyly. "Only time the suit come out, be for weddings and funerals," he said.

Marissa looked at her watch. "I expect Phoebe will be here soon."

No sooner had the words left Marissa's mouth, than Phoebe pulled her car to a stop in front of the house. Samuel sat in the front seat with Phoebe while Marissa and Julie climbed into the back.

"Where's the ceremony?" Marissa asked.

Phoebe looked into the rearview mirror. "It begins at the Saint Louis Cathedral."

"Begins?" Marissa said.

"Yes. There will be a mass, then a procession through the French Quarter on the way to the cemetery—complete with jazz music and dancing."

"Music and dancing? Seriously?" Marissa asked.

"Yes. The music and dancing are intended to help the dead find their way to heaven. There will be dancing, music, chants, drums, tambourines, and singing. Funerals like the one you're about to witness were especially popular when a slave died. It was considered a release from the binds inflicted upon them by their masters. Considering where they lived, I think a jazz funeral is appropriate in this case."

"Normally, a New Orleans funeral march is a sight to see, but being so close to this one, it just makes me sad," Julie said.

"I suspect the turnout will be relatively small. I'm sure there aren't a lot of people around here who knew them," Marissa said.

No reply was warranted as they rode the rest of the way to the church in silence.

The group of friends sat in the front pew as the Catholic mass was presided over by an elderly priest. Two caskets sat side by side in front of the altar. Each was adorned with a white lace veil and topped with a large bouquet of flowers.

At the end of the ceremony, the priest stood at the podium and addressed the gathering.

"Friends, we are here to celebrate the spiritual ascension into heaven of our two sisters, and all of those who went before them. As I look around, it warms this old heart to see so many parishioners joining in this celebration of life. Even though they were unknown in the community, their lives were nonetheless valuable and worthy of our honor. Their lives were cut short by evil, and as such, we pray for their souls in the hopes they walk with the Heavenly Father, even as we celebrate their lives here on Earth.

"Please join us as we entomb their remains in the Saint Louis Cemetery, followed by a community reception at their home at 1140 Royal Street in the French Quarter. Please bow your heads as we recite one last benediction in their honor."

The priest raised his arms to the sides and closed his eyes. "Holy Father, look upon the souls of our sisters and bless them with entrance into your heavenly realm. May we always remember them with love and reverence and vow to never again allow the reason for their demise to darken the life of this city. I say this in the name of the Father, the Son, and the Holy Spirit."

Julie wiped a tear from the corner of her eye as Marissa squeezed her hand.

"Are you all right?" Marissa asked.

Julie nodded. "It's just so heartbreaking," she said.

"I know. I've been fighting back tears all morning. There was so much promise lost in that house. In a way, I'm glad it's over. Now it's time for the healing to begin," Marissa said.

The procession to the cemetery was lively as the mourners sang, danced, and played loud jazz music through the streets of the French Quarter. When they reached the cemetery, as many of the mourners as possible gathered around the above-ground crypt as the two caskets were interred. All heads were bowed as the priest said a final prayer. Marissa, Julie, Samuel, and Phoebe stood in the front of the crowd, all holding hands to support each other.

"Brothers and sisters, pray with me that our Heavenly Father will accept our sisters into his arms. Can I get an Amen?"

A chorus of "Amens" rang out.

"Lord, forgive the sins of our sisters and protect their souls from eternal damnation."

"Amen," the crowd cried out again.

"With the power invested in me by the Catholic diocese of New Orleans, I commend their spirits to your care. Hallelujah, Lord!"

"Hallelujah!"

"Let our sisters rise from their grave on Judgment Day and sing praises to the Lord."

"Amen."

The jazz music began anew and the mourners danced and sang their way out of the cemetery and back to the church where most of them had left their cars.

Intense emotion filled the car on the drive home.

"Three months ago, I would have never believed we'd be here right now," Julie said sorrowfully.

"I know. I thought it would never be over, but Lia wasn't ready to go. It was the right thing to do to wait for her and to entomb them together," Marissa said.

"They belong together. Always have. Always will. We done right by them to wait," Samuel added.

Phoebe stopped in front of the Royal Street house and shut off the ignition. She turned around in her seat. "A year from now, this will all seem like a dream, but we can never forget what happened here, or risk history repeating itself. No one should ever have to go through what they did, ever again."

Marissa nodded. She threw the door open and climbed out of the car. She looked down the street and saw a crowd of people walking their way. Several of them still carried jazz instruments. She reached into the car and helped Julie out. "Here they come. We'll need to get inside and help take care of our guests."

The mourners flooded the entryway as soon as Marissa opened the iron gate. She was nearly crushed against the door as she struggled to get the keys to it out of her pocket. Before she was able to slip the key into the lock, the door suddenly swung open.

"Welcome." Elliot and Lia said. They stepped aside and allowed their guests to enter.

"The living room is up one level," Lia shouted above the din. "There are refreshments on the kitchen island."

Once all the guests were inside, Lia closed the door and embraced Julie and Marissa. "Thank you so much for representing us at the funeral. There is no way we could've been ready for this reception if we had gone."

"How did it go?" Elliot asked.

"It was crazy. I've never been to a New Orleans jazz funeral before," Marissa said.

Elliot walked to Samuel and embraced him. "So our girls are finally laid to rest," she said.

"Yes, Miss Walker. It was the right thing to wait for little Lia to be buried with Celeste. Celeste was her mama. They belongs together," he said.

"Samuel, don't you think it's time to drop the Miss Walker thing? After all, I'm married to your distant cousin. We're family, Samuel."

"Yes, Miss Walker." He wore a hint of a grin on his face as he baited her.

"What do you say we take care of our guests," Lia said, "and then after they leave, you can tell us all about the funeral."

***

Elliot dropped down onto the couch beside Lia in the living room. "Phew! I'm glad that's over." She placed her hand on Lia's thigh. "The last one just left. I can't believe what a turnout we had, considering no one who attended actually knew Celeste and Lia."

Lia covered Elliot's hand with her own. "They knew *of* them. I don't think there's a soul in this town that doesn't know about what happened here. It warms my heart to see so many turn out to celebrate their lives."

Elliot picked up Lia's hand and kissed it. "Never again will I take life for granted, especially my life with you."

"It was touch and go there for a while," Lia said.

"More than once during those first two weeks, I thought I was going to lose you. If you had died, I would have lain right down beside you. I'm not sure if you were aware of it, but I spent day and night by your bedside until they upgraded you from critical to stable status and moved you out of the ICU."

"At one point, I thought we were going to lose both of you," Marissa said.

"It all seems like such a blur now," Julie said, "but it was one of the most horrific things I ever witnessed. Walking into that apartment and finding Elliot covered in blood, and then the stabbing. It all happened so fast, yet it felt like we were stuck in a slow-motion picture. I don't know how else to describe it."

"Thank God," Marissa said, "that Samuel was at his usual post when you came home from the hospital, Elliot. Otherwise, we wouldn't have known you went to the cemetery. Heaven knows what might have happened to you if psycho-bitch had been able to permanently set her hooks in you. You certainly wouldn't be here right now celebrating Celeste's and little Lia's lives."

"Celeste," Lia said. "Oddly, I miss her in some ways. I was pretty much unaware when she took over, but somehow I still knew she was there. I don't think it's a coincidence that we bought this house. I mean, what are the odds that I would be related to someone who lived and died here?"

"I'm glad Samuel took her bones," Elliot said, "and I'm glad the forensics lab didn't take forever to return Lia's remains to us. It was good to be able to bury them together. It felt like the right thing to do."

Julie leaned forward in her chair. "You two have the rest of your lives to spend together in this beautiful home, knowing you have set history right and freed the souls of those wretched slaves who suffered and died here." She sat back and wiped her eyes.

"Are you crying?" Marissa teased.

"I can't help it. I'm a sucker for a happy ending. "

Lia wiped her own tears and covered her mouth with her hand.

"What's wrong?" Marissa asked. "Are you okay?"

"I was just thinking about how much I'm going to miss you two when you go back to New York again. I about died of a broken heart when you left three months ago. Thank you so much for coming back to help with the funeral."

Marissa and Julie exchanged covert grins, a fact not lost on Elliot.

"Okay. What are you two grinning about?" Elliot asked.

"Actually," Julie said, "we went back to New York three months ago to close up the house. Marissa asked for a transfer to the New Orleans office, and it was accepted. Now I'll have a chance to reconnect with my family."

Lia stood and screamed. "Oh, my God. Are you serious?"

"Dead serious," Marissa said. "In fact, we want to ask if we could camp out here until we find a house. We're here to stay."

"Sweetheart, you can stay here for as long as you like. Come here and give me some love." Lia met Julie in the middle of the room for warm hugs.

Elliot and Marissa embraced each other in bear hugs.

"Way cool," Elliot said. "Way cool."

"So what do you say we give you a hand cleaning up this mess and then hit the hay? It's been a long and tiring day," Marissa suggested.

"It's Saturday. How about we leave this mess until tomorrow?" Elliot replied. "I have definite plans about how I want to spend my Saturday night, and it sure as hell isn't doing housework."

"A little frisky, are we?" Marissa teased.

"You're damned right I am. After what we've been through since we moved into this house, I'm ready to begin enjoying life, and that includes making mad passionate love to my wife every chance I get."

"All right then. I guess we'll say our goodnights," Julie said. She hugged both her friends, wished them sweet dreams, and walked hand in hand with Marissa toward the spiral stairs.

When they were out of sight, Lia turned to Elliot. "This has been one of the best days I've had since we moved here. Finally, the drama is behind us. I am so looking forward to building a life with you here."

Elliot took Lia's face between her palms and kissed her tenderly. "Are you ready for bed, love?"

"I will be, right after I make the rounds of locking the doors and windows."

"I'll check the downstairs doors and meet you in the kitchen," Elliot said.

Lia walked slowly around the kitchen, imagining Gran cooking by the great wood stove. She paused and closed her eyes as once again the aroma of hot apple pie invaded her senses.

"You done good, girl," Gran said.

Lia smiled. "None of this would have happened if not for you setting that fire all those years ago."

"Tank ye for giving my babies a proper burial. Dey done nothing to deserve what dey got from dat she-devil."

"You're welcome. They deserved nothing less, Gran."

"Dis old body can rest now. I be smilin' on ye, girl. I be watchin' over you. Miss Elliot be good people. Hold her close to yer heart. She love you to de moon and back."

Tears coursed down Lia's cheeks. "I will, Gran. Hug Celeste and Lia for me when you see them. Tell them I love them and I'm honored to be their kin."

"Dey's already know dat, girlie. We loves you too. For all you done, and for all you are."

"Goodbye, Gran."

Lia opened her eyes and found herself standing alone in the kitchen. She wiped the tears from her cheeks. When she went to the door to close and lock it, she could hear her name being called from outside the house.

Elliot entered the kitchen just as Lia was about to push the screen door open. "Everything's secure downstairs," she said. "Where are you going?" she added when she realized Lia was about to open the door.

"Someone was calling my name."

"Hold on. I'm going with you."

Lia and Elliot stepped onto the porch and walked to the edge of the railing. They could see a ray of light coming from the area where the slaves had been buried in the courtyard. They stood mesmerized as two figures appeared in the center of the beam, one decidedly male and the other female.

"Lia, where are you, child?" the female said.

Lia made a move as though to reply, but Elliot stopped her. "Wait. It's Celeste. Celeste and Samuel."

"Lia come. It time to go home."

Lia and Elliot watched as a shadow moved from the garage door toward the beam of light. As it entered the light, they could see it was a little girl.

"I here, Mama," the girl said.

Celeste tucked a strand of hair behind the child's ear. "It time to go home, Lia," she said again.

"Yes, Mama."

As the child stood beside her mother, she looked directly at Lia. She waved, blew a kiss, and took her mother's hand. All three raised their faces to the sky and closed their eyes. The intensity of the light increased as they rose skyward, dissolving into a white mist before slowly fading away. All that remained where they stood, was the cat.

Lia looked at Elliot and unabashedly allowed the tears to run down her face. "They're going home, El. They're finally going home."

Elliot traced the side of Lia's face with her fingertip, ending at Lia's chin. "Yes, they are, and it's all because of you. I love you, Lia."

Lia suddenly jumped as she felt something touch her leg. "Jesus, you scared me," she exclaimed as she bent and picked up the cat. "I knew it was you who made it possible for Lia to visit us, you little scamp."

Elliot scratched the cat under its chin and listened to it purr. "She's quite the attention ho."

Lia cocked her head to one side and grinned. "Speaking of attention, I thought you had definite plans for this Saturday night."

Elliot smiled. "Yes, I do, and for every Saturday night for the rest of our lives. And for your information, Miss Thing, those plans definitely do not include you in the middle of things."

"Do those plans involve a soak in the tub and a bottle or two of wine?"

"If you wish."

"I have just one thing to say about that."

"And that is?"

"Run, Forrest! Run!"

THE END

POSTSCRIPT

This book is loosely based on allegedly true events that took place at 1140 Royal Street in New Orleans, Louisiana. In the early 1830's the house was owned by Delphine LaLaurie, a wealthy aristocrat, and her surgeon husband, Dr. Louis LaLaurie. Delphine LaLaurie was highly regarded in New Orleans society, and was known for hosting lavish dinner parties.

Behind closed doors, the sinister side of the LaLauries emerged. In particular, Madame LaLaurie was rumored to be a cruel and sadistic woman who was responsible for brutally torturing dozens of slaves. The attic at 1140 Royal Street was a virtual torture chamber where medical experiments were performed on slaves and torture of every kind imaginable was administered.

In 1834, a fire broke out in the kitchen of the mansion, reportedly set by an elderly black cook who was chained to the stove. When the firemen arrived the old cook alerted them to the goings-on in the attic. Their investigation revealed rotting corpses, slaves chained to the walls, slaves with holes in their heads from which sticks protruded, half-dead slaves in cages, slaves with sex-change operations performed on them, slaves with no limbs, and yet another with no skin, and slaves with their abdomens cut open and their intestines tied around them. Most were dead, but some were still alive, begging to be put out of their misery.

The LaLaurie's escaped while the authorities tended the fire and were never heard from again, although rumors have it that Madame LaLaurie returned to New Orleans to live out the rest of her life under the protection of Marie Laveau.

Today, the house at 1140 Royal Street is reported to be the most haunted property in New Orleans.

This is a part of history that must never repeat itself.

To learn more about the LaLauries, type "1140 Royal Street, New Orleans" into any search engine.

Photo Credit: Song of Myself Photography

See Karen's author page at

www.karendbadger.com

Karen D. Badger

About the Author

Karen D. Badger is the author of *On A Wing And A Prayer, Yesterday Once More* (a 2009 Golden Crown Literary Award winner for Speculative Fiction), *In A Family Way, Unchained Memories, Happy Campers, Collective Identity, Sweet Angel, and Relative-ly Speaking* (Books I, II, III, IV, V and VI of the Commitment Series), *The Blue Feather, All My Tomorrows* (sequel to the 2009 award winning *Yesterday Once More*), and this, her current novel, *1140 Rue Royale*...all of which have been released by Badger Bliss Books, which Karen co-owns with her wife Barbara Sawyer (aka "Bliss').

Born and raised in Vermont, Karen is the second of five children raised by a fiercely independent mother, who remains one of her best friends. Karen earned her B.A. in 1978 in Theater and in Elementary Education, and in 1994, earned a B.S. in mathematics. In addition to her novels, Karen is the author of many technical papers on photomask manufacturing, which she has presented at numerous semiconductor industry conferences, and is the holder if several technical patents. Karen is currently in her 39th year as a Principal Member of the Technical Staff with a prominent semiconductor manufacturer in Vermont.

Karen and her wife, Barb (a retired Lt. Col., US Air Force) live in the beautiful state of Vermont—home of Ben and Jerry's. They spend their spare time with family as well as doing home improvement projects on both their homes in Vermont and New Mexico. They also enjoy camping, kayaking, motorcycling and singing Karaoke.

Please take a moment to visit Karen's author website at www.karendbadger.com, or the Badger Bliss Books website at www.badgerblissbooks.com. Also like us on Facebook!

TITLES BY KAREN D. BADGER

www.badgerblissbooks.com

On A Wing and A Prayer
First edition published by Blue Feather Books, Sept, 2005
Second edition published by Badger Bliss Books, Sept, 2014
Third edition published by Badger Bliss Books, August, 2016
ISBN 13: 978-1-945761-01-0, ISBN 10: 1-945761-01-6

Yesterday Once More
First edition published by Blue Feather Books, July, 2008
Second edition published by Badger Bliss Books ,Sept, 2014
Third edition published by Badger Bliss Books, August, 2016
ISBN 13: 978-1-945761-02-7, ISBN 10: 1-945761-02-4
2009 Golden Crown Literary Society Award - Speculative Fiction

In A Family Way – Book One of the Commitment Series
First edition published by Blue Feather Books, March, 2010
Second edition published by Badger Bliss Books, Sept, 2014
Third edition published by Badger Bliss Books, August, 2016
ISBN 13: 978-1-945761-05-8, ISBN 10: 1-945761-05-9

Unchained Memories – Book Two of the Commitment Series
First edition published by Blue Feather Books, Oct, 2011
Second edition published by Badger Bliss Books, Sept, 2014
Third edition published by Badger Bliss Books, August, 2016
ISBN 13: 978-1-945761-06-5, ISBN 10: 1-945761-06-7

Happy Campers - Book Three of the Commitment Series
First edition published by Blue Feather Books, Sept, 2013
Second edition published by Badger Bliss Books, Sept, 2014
Third edition published by Badger Bliss Books, August, 2016
ISBN 13: 978-1-945761-07-2, ISBN 10: 1-945761-07-5

The Blue Feather
First edition published by Blue Feather Books, July, 2014
Second edition published by Badger Bliss Books, Sept, 2014
Third edition published by Badger Bliss Books, August, 2016
ISBN 13: 978-1-945761-04-1, ISBN 10: 1-945761-04-0

Collective Identity – Book Four of the Commitment Series
First edition published by Badger Bliss Books, January, 2015
Second edition published by Badger Bliss Books, August, 2016
ISBN 13: 978-1-945761-08-9, ISBN 10: 1-945761-08-3

All My Tomorrows – Sequel to Yesterday Once More
First edition published by Badger Bliss Books, May, 2015
Second edition published by Badger Bliss Books, August, 2016
ISBN 13: 978-1-945761-03-4, ISBN 10: 1-945761-03-2

Sweet Angel – Book Five of the Commitment Series
First edition published by Badger Bliss Books, June, 2015
Second edition published by Badger Bliss Books, August, 2016
ISBN 13: 978-1-945761-09-6, ISBN 10: 1-945-761-09-1

Relative-ly Speaking – Book Six of the Commitment Series
First edition published by Badger Bliss Books, March, 2016
Second edition published by Badger Bliss Books, August, 2016
ISBN 13: 978-1-945761-10-2, ISBN 10: 1-945-761-10-5

1140 Rue Royale
First edition published by Badger Bliss Books, Sept, 2016
ISBN 13: 978-1-945761-00-3, ISBN 10: 1-945761-00-8

COMING SOON FROM KAREN D. BADGER AND BADGER BLISS BOOKS

www.badgerblissbooks.com

Tailspin – Book Seven of the Commitment Series
Expected release: Spring, 2017

Teenagers!

Have you ever thought your kids are trying to drive you crazy? Real life hits Billie and Cat square in the face, sending them into their own tailspin as they deal with the growing pains of their children and the insurmountable heartbreak of their friends' loss. As new friends enter their lives, old friendships are challenged.

In the midst of it all, Cat is faced with one of the most sobering experiences of her life, making her realize what really is important...friends, family and love.

Tailspin

Book Seven
of
The Commitment Series

B

A BADGER BLISS BOOK

By

Karen D. Badger

CHAPTER 1

"Do you see them?" Cat strained to see over the heads of the crowd at the airpor. As usual, her short stature put her at a definite disadvantage.

Billie scanned the area until she caught sight of corn silk yellow hair atop the head of a tall, slender young man. "There they are." She reached for Cat's hand and drew her through the crowd waiting at the gate.

"Seth! Kids! Over here," Billie waived excitedly.

A broad grin broke out across boy-man features as Seth noticed his mother. He took his little sister's hand and shuffled her along in front of him while keeping a watchful eye on the other young lady who walked by his side. "Come on, Tara, keep up. I don't want to lose you in this crowd." Tara clamped down on his arm to avoid being separated from her siblings.

Sixteen-year-old Seth, fourteen-year-old Tara, and nine-year-old Skylar were just returning from their yearly month-long summer vacation with their great grandmothers, Josephine Wyclyffe and Alexandria Spirakas in Charleston, South Carolina. The family tradition had started three years earlier during an emotional family reunion.

Finally, the distance between the mothers and children closed as warm embraces quelled feelings of yearning and homesickness.

"God, I missed you so much," Cat embraced each child lovingly. Her voice was choked with emotion.

Seth endured the wet kissed Cat placed on his cheeks. "Sheesh, Ma. You'd think we were gone for a year instead of a month."

Billie grinned at the humorous sight before her. Seth, six book and bristly-chinned bent nearly in half at the waist, submit himself to the attentions of his very excited, and very vertically challenged mother. As for herself, she was accosted by Skylar, who had thrown herself into her Mommy's arms the moment she was within arms' reach.

"Mommy, I missed you," Skylar burrowed her face into Billie's neck.

Billie wrapped her arms around the child and held her close. "I missed you too, kitten."

"Well, it feels like a year! Come here, you," Cat turned her attentions to Tara. At fourteen, Tara Charland was already promising to be a stunning beauty. As tall as Cat, her slim figure was developing shapely curves that she tried very hard to camouflage under baggy jeans and oversized T-shirts. Short, spiked, red-gold hair provided stark relief against a peaches and cream complexion.

After several death-grip hugs, Cat held her daughter at arm's length and exclaimed. "Tara, what have you done to your hair?!"

Tara grinned ear to ear. "Grandma Jo took me to get it done. Cool, huh?"

"Very cool, Tare," Billie said. She gave Tara girl a high-five, and leaned in close to a fuming Cat. "She's *your* grandmother." Billie winked at Tara, and acknowledged the silent "thank you" her daughter sent her way. She then turned her attention to Seth as Skylar went willingly into her other mother's arms.

"Oomph! Goodness, Sky-baby, you're such a big girl. Pretty soon you'll be bigger than Mama," Cat struggled to hold her daughter.

"Ma, you don't have to be very tall to be bigger than you," Seth teased.

"Why you little rugrat," Cat replied. "I ought to—"

"Ought to *what?*" Seth said, towering over Cat and glaring down at her, trying desperately to keep a straight face.

Cat put Skylar down and started tickling her son mercilessly, knowing exactly where the sensitive spots were around his middle.

"Okay. Stop. I give." Seth conceded defeat to the much smaller woman.

"Smart man," Billie said. "Now why don't you and your sisters go fetch the luggage before round two begins."

The kids headed to the luggage carousel while Billie and Cat waited.

"Billie, did you see her hair? How could you tell her it was cool?" Cat said.

Billie placed her hands on Cat's shoulders. "Look, love," she explained. "If our daughter wants to look like a punk rocker, then fine. She's just expressing herself. She could be doing a lot worse than spiking her hair and wearing baggy clothes."

Cat looked into Billie's expressive face and remembered the marijuana incident with Tara and her cousin Crystal in the park two years earlier. Silently chiding her wife of eight years, Cat thought, *God, Billie, I hate it when you're right.*

Outwardly, she shrugged. "Yeah, I guess you're right, but if she keeps this up, I'm buying stock in Miss Clairol," she said, referring to the child-induced gray hairs that were beginning to peek through her red-gold mane.

Billie laughed. "Count me in!"

Cat rested her head on Billie's arm and looked across the terminal at their children approaching them, laden with luggage. All three wore golden tans, their hair lightened by the South Carolina sun.

"She looks healthy, doesn't she?" Cat remarked, referring to their youngest daughter who had spent two of the last three years on a low maintenance dose of chemotherapy to completely rid her body of leukemia.

"She looks *very* healthy, Cat. She's been cancer-free for nearly a year now. I'd say she's won that battle," Billie replied as she rested her head atop Cat's.

"I can't believe how tall she's grown in the past month."

"Cat, everyone looks tall to you." Billie grinned unashamedly down at her wife.

Cat flashed a crooked smile Billie. "Now I know where your son gets it. You will pay for that later."

"I'm counting on it," Billie replied.

Cat hip-checked Billie then quickly scooted away before revenge could be administered. She took Skylar's duffel bag from her and threw it over her shoulder, took her daughter's hand and led the troops to the parking garage.

On the trip home, the kids were full of questions about Steve, Karissa and Missy. Having been gone for a month, they were anxious to get home to spend the rest of their summer vacation with friends.

Cat and Billie sat side by side in the front seat of the family station wagon, sending nostalgic glances toward each other as they listened to the children talk. If felt good to be together again.

***

"Do you think dinner will be edible?" Cat asked Jen as they set paper dinner plates around the picnic table.

Jen glanced over at Billie and Fred who were diligently tending the burgers and hot dogs on the grill. "Well, unless they charcoal them black there's not much else they can do to kill them," Jen replied. "At least there'll be salads and chips if we *do* end up calling the morgue," she added, chuckling.

Cat joined her friend in laughter as they put their heads together to enjoy their private joke.

"I know you guys are talking about us," Billie shouted from across the yard. She turned to Fred. "They think we can't cook. If they only knew we pretend to be lousy at it so we don't have to do it very often." She chuckled at her own secret joke, but soon stopped when she realized he wasn't laughing. "You can cook, can't you Fred?" she asked.

Fred's eyebrows arched upward. "Nope," he replied, grinning ear to ear. "And from what I hear, neither can you."

"Can too," Billie countered.

"Can not," Fred replied.

"Can too," she said again adamantly, shaking the spatula at him.

"Not," he insisted.

"Kids," Billie yelled to the five heads bobbing up and down in the pool. "Tell Fred I can cook."

"Oh, sure you can, Mom," Tara said sarcastically, rolling her eyes at Karissa.

"Well, you can heat up a pretty mean can of soup," Seth added. Stevie nodding his agreement.

"Mommy makes good microwave popcorn," Skylar offered helpfully.

"Madame Microwave! It takes a lot of skill to operate such a complicated piece of equipment. And to produce mouth-watering dishes at the same time – well, I'm impressed," Fred said teasingly.

Billie was steaming. Not only had her kids betrayed her (the ungrateful wretches), but she had to endure culinary jokes from someone who couldn't even boil water. "Oh yeah?

Impress *this*," she exclaimed as she shoved Fred into the pool, chef's hat and all.

Everyone in the yard collectively held their breaths as the spray of water from Fred's belly flop settled around them.

Fred rose to his feet in the shallow end of the pool, soaked to the bone. Struggling to wade to the edge of the pool, he approached Billie, a wide grin on his face. "Okay, you got me," he said. "I guess I deserved that."

"Yes you did," Billie added as she reached down to pull him onto the deck.

"And you deserve this," Fred exclaimed as he planted his feet and yanked backward, sending Billie over his head into the pool behind him.

Billie broke through the surface of the water, spitting and sputtering. She took one look at Fred standing there in the shallow end of the pool, the limp chef's hat sitting crookedly on his head, water running in rivulets down his face, and burst out laughing.

The two friends fell into each other's arms and laughed heartily as the children splashed them. Their wives stood by, shaking their heads at the childish antics of their spouses.

Suddenly Skylar shouted, "Fire!"

All heads turned to the grill where black smoke could be seen billowing out of every crack. Jen reached it first and threw the cover open as she turned off the gas.

Cat approached her friend and looked at the black lumps that neatly lined the rack. "Call the morgue?" Cat asked.

"Call the morgue," Jen agreed.

Billie and Fred looked at each and once more fell into peals of laughter.

***

Cat sat at her vanity, carefully applying a thin layer of night cream to her face. Billie approached her from behind, placed her chin on Cat's shoulder and wrapped her arms around her. She grinned at her in the mirror. "You really don't need to wear that stuff; your skin is soft and beautiful all by itself." She planted a kiss on her neck.

"It's soft because I do this each night, Billie," she replied. "You ought to try it. " Cat dropped a dab of cream on Billie's nose.

Billie snapped her head back. "Hey!" she exclaimed. Billie wiped the cream off and sniffed at it. "Hmm. Smells nice."

Cat looked at Billie in the mirror. "I had a good time at Jen and Fred's this afternoon. It was really nice of them to host a picnic to welcome the kids home."

Billie grinned. "Yeah, it was fun, wasn't it?"

"They're good friends, Billie. We're lucky to have them."

"The best," Billie agreed.

"They'd have to be. Not everyone would put up with your cooking."

Billie clutched at her heart. "Ouch! I'm wounded."

"C'mere and let me kiss the booboo," Cat said.

Billie eagerly approached her still sitting wife and dropped to her knees.

Cat grabbed the sides of Billie's robe and pulled them open, exposing generous, creamy white breasts. Eyes wide, Cat visually feasted on the sight before her. "Now where did you say you were wounded?"

Billie pointed to hr right nipple. "Right here."

"Oh, really?" Cat leaned in and took the erect nipple into her mouth, causing Billie to gasp. "Oh, I can see by your reaction that it really does hurt. Maybe I should kiss it some more?"

"Yeah, that's it. More kisses," Billie replied, short of breath.

Cat feasted hungrily for several more minutes, then stopped to look at Billie once more. "Are you hurt anywhere else, my love?"

"Let me see. Oh, yeah, right here. I'm hurt over here too!" Billie pointed to her left nipple.

Cat was more than happy to administer additional first aid as Billie moaned in mock agony. Several moments later,

Cat stopped and rose to her feet. She took Billie's hand, led her to the bed and pushed her down onto in the middle of it.

"Billie, I think I need to do a thorough examination—you know—just to be safe. Is that all right with you?"

"You're the doctor, Cat, but before you start, tell me, will this be a very expensive house call?"

"Oh, yes, very expensive I'm afraid. I'm not sure you can afford it."

"Well, maybe we can work out some alternative method of payment."

Cat rubbed her chin and walked back and forth at the foot of the bed. "Hmm, let me think." After a little more pacing, she stopped and faced Billie. "Well, I'll tell you what, I'll take partial payment tonight, and then we can barter for the rest of the bill. You know—you do something for me—I do something for you. Get the idea?"

Billie rose to her elbows. "You mean, like taking it out in trade?" Her eyebrows danced wickedly on her forehead.

"Exactly!"

"You're on, Doc," Billie threw herself flat on the bed, her arms and legs spread wide. "Go for it!"

Cat dropped all pretense, dove on top of Billie and began the most thorough and lengthy examination in the history of medicine.

Karen D. Badger

Made in the USA
Las Vegas, NV
11 December 2023

82631724R00207